Robert G. Barrett was raised in Bondi where he worked mainly as a butcher. After thirty years he moved to Terrigal on the Central Coast of New South Wales. Robert appeared in a number of films and TV commercials but preferred to concentrate on a career as a writer. He is the author of 24 books which includes the bestselling Les Norton series.

ROBERT G BARRETT

LES NORTON IN

THE
REAL THING

PAN

Pan Macmillan Australia

First published 1986 in in Pan by Pan Books (Australia) Pty Ltd
This edition published 2019 in Pan by Pan Macmillan Australia Pty Ltd
1 Market Street, Sydney, New South Wales, Australia, 2000

Copyright © Robert G. Barrett 1986

A catalogue record for this
book is available from the
National Library of Australia

Typeset by Post Pre-press Group
Printed by IVE

The author and the publisher have made every effort to contact copyright
holders for material used in this book. Any person or organisation that may
have been overlooked should contact the publisher.

MIX
Paper | Supporting
responsible forestry
FSC® C018183

The paper in this book is FSC® certified.
FSC® promotes environmentally responsible,
socially beneficial and economically viable
management of the world's forests.

This book is dedicated to Thomas Barrett,
the first man hanged in Australia
— February 1788.

The Publisher would like to acknowledge that the author is giving 10% of his royalty earnings to Greenpeace, an organisation which he deeply respects.

CONTENTS

CONTENTS

Steve's Birthday

Detective Joe Warren loosened his tie a little more and took another quiet sip on his Scotch and dry. Seated next to him Detective Alan Redman did pretty much the same thing. Across from the two tough vice-squad detectives Price Galese and George Brennan were seated at Price's desk, their drinks standing idly on the oak top. To their left, Eddie Salita sat quietly in the corner absently picking at his watch. Les Norton and Billy Dunne had entered the office about five minutes earlier and were parked comfortably in two leather chairs to Price's right holding their drinks in their laps. No one was talking. No one was laughing.

Thursday night at the Kelly Club had finished almost an hour ago. The money was counted and in the safe, the club was locked up and the staff and punters had drifted off into the night. Outside, Kings Cross was still pumping along in its own gawdy, happy sort of way, but at 4 a.m. on Friday morning the atmosphere in Price Galese's office was deadly serious. You didn't have to be Einstein to figure out there was a bit of trouble in the air.

Price Galese took a light sip on his drink and looked over at Detective Joe Warren. 'All right Joe,' he said easily, 'now what's this business you were talking to me about on the phone earlier? There's trouble coming up from Melbourne. Is that right?'

Detective Warren ran his finger round the rim of his glass and stole a quick glance at his partner. 'That's right Price. There's going to be a hit on you this Saturday night. Right here in the club.'

'And it's Vince Rossiter.'

Detective Warren nodded his head solemnly.

9

'It's not a load of shit either Price,' said his partner. 'We've got it straight from the armed hold-up boys in Collins Street.'

'Mm.' Price drummed his fingers lightly on the top of the desk. It was so tense and electrifyingly quiet in the plush, roomy office you could distinctly hear the ice-cubes cracking in George Brennan's still untouched drink. 'And this mug Rossiter says he's going to do it this Saturday night. In here.'

'We know he's a mug Price,' replied Detective Warren. 'There's no two ways about that. But he's also mad as a meat axe.'

'He's gotta be,' grunted Les Norton.

There'd been a bungled attempt on Price's life by two mixed-up hit-men from Melbourne about twelve months earlier. Luckily it had been thwarted by Les. As soon as Price found out who it was he sent Eddie Salita down to deal with them. Eddie, with the help of an old mate from Vietnam who was living in Brunswick, shot both of them and dumped their weighted bodies in Port Phillip Bay. One of the bodies belonged to Steve Rossiter — Vince Rossiter's brother.

The Rossiters were a close knit, not very intelligent, but highly feared family from around the South Melbourne markets. The two brothers, Vince and Steve, besides being extremely violent and totally unpredictable, were just about inseparable. Vince was reputed to be almost bordering on insanity. The painters' and dockers' union used them for bagmen and they'd been involved in a number of unsolved shootings. They also specialised in armed hold-ups on the side — Vince was a master of disguise.

By sheer intimidation they'd managed to stay one step ahead of the law — though at the time of Steve's disappearance the police had finally managed to lag Vince with a three-with-a-one for assault and malicious wounding. A publican in Footscray, had asked him to leave his hotel, so Vince put a glass in the man's face and beat up his wife.

When he got news of his brother's disappearance Vince went almost insane with grief. When he found out who was responsible he vowed instant revenge as soon as he was released. It didn't matter that his dim-witted brother had tried to kill one of the most popular and heaviest men in Sydney — to Vince's twisted way of thinking that didn't count. He would have his revenge, and now that his beloved brother was gone it didn't matter if he lost his own life in the process. He had confided all this to one of his cronies in Pentridge, the crony told the screws, the screws told the right Melbourne police and it wasn't long before it went on the old mates network to Sydney where it finally got to Price.

'And how long has this Rossiter clown been out of the nick?' asked Price.

'Just on a week,' replied Detective Warren.

'What makes you so convinced he'll have a go this Saturday night?' asked George Brennan.

'He was heard bragging how he was going to celebrate his brother's birthday right under the so-called Sydney heavies' noses,' said Detective Redman. 'We've run Steve's record through the computer and it turns out this Saturday would have been his birthday. Vince hasn't been sighted since Wednesday, so you can bet your bottom dollar that's what he was on about and he doesn't care if he dies doing it. We're not dealing with a rational human being here Price. Vince Rossiter is a mad dog.'

'He's certainly got some front, I'll give him that,' said Price, adding a contemptuous laugh.

'The thing is, Price, we can only do so much,' said Detective Warren. 'There was nothing the boys in Melbourne could hold him on and it would have looked too obvious if something had happened to him as soon as he got out of the can. By the same token, if there's a gun fight in here or out the front the papers'll get hold of it, shit'll come flying back on us, we'll have to do something and there'll be trouble for everyone.'

'You can say that again,' replied Price grimly.

'What you do is your business,' said Detective Redman, flashing a quick glance at Eddie Salita sitting impassively in the corner. 'To be fair dinkum, if Vince Rossiter disappears you'll be doing everyone a favour. But you're going to have to be extremely careful and very, very discreet.'

'Mm,' mused Price. He paused quietly for a few moments, then smiled. 'All right Joe, Alan,' he said, taking two manilla envelopes from a drawer in the large oak desk. 'You've been a great help. I really appreciate what you've just done.' He slid the two fat envelopes across the desk. 'There's a nice drink there and there'll be another one up here for you next Thursday night when all this is settled.'

The two detectives rose from their seats and picked up the envelopes. 'Just make sure you're here next Thursday Price,' said Detective Warren sincerely, slipping the envelope into the inside pocket of his jacket.

'That goes for me too Price,' said Detective Redman.

Price Galese smiled, stood up and shook the two detectives'

11

hands. 'I'll be here next Thursday,' he winked. 'I don't know about your mate Rossiter though. I'll see you then. Good night lads and thanks again.' He turned to Norton. 'Les, will you let the boys out?'

'Sure.' Norton got up and ushered them to the front door. No one said a word while Les was gone; they were still sitting there silently waiting for him when he returned about five minutes later.

Price waited till Les was seated before he spoke. 'Well, there it is boys,' he said, slapping his hands together and rubbing them lightly. 'This prick from Melbourne's going to get in here on Saturday night and try and neck me. I know it's a pain in the arse but we're going to have to knock him.' He glanced quizzingly around the sombre faces in the office. 'Any suggestions?'

There was silence for a few seconds, then George Brennan spoke. 'Why don't you just not be here Saturday night,' he said, with a light shrug of his shoulders.

Price shook his head. 'I can't be doing that George,' he said adamantly. 'If I start running away from every shit-pot bloody hood that threatens me, I'll be doing it all the time.' He took another sip on his drink. 'Besides,' he added, 'I'd rather get it over and done with. One way or the other.'

'If you can tell me what he looks like,' said Norton, 'I'll let him in then get him on the stairs and break his neck. Then we can just dump him or bury him somewhere.' He took a look around the room at the others. 'That's one way of doin' it, ain't it?'

Price smiled. 'It's certainly a thought Les,' he said with a light laugh at Norton's casual but serious idea of how to kill Vince Rossiter. 'But I'm not sure what he looks like and you could make a blue. And I lose one of my lovely customers. It is one way of doing it though.'

Finally he turned to Eddie Salita still sitting quietly in the corner. 'Well Eddie, what do you reckon? You're in charge of the killing department. Have you got any SP on this Rossiter imbecile?'

Eddie picked at his watch for a second or two before he spoke. 'Yeah I know him all right,' he said softly.

'You do?' said Price as every eye in the office riveted on Eddie.

'Yeah. I met him a couple of years ago, just before he went in the nick.' Eddie looked up at Price. 'Remember when we had that rort going through Melbourne customs with those Mercedes Benz cars, and I had to go down and sort out those two dealers?'

'Yeah,' Price nodded slowly.

'Well, I met him in a pub in Fitzroy — him and his brother, and he's a ratbag all right, you needn't worry about that.'

'What's he look like?' asked Billy Dunne.

'Oh he's about five foot, ten, pretty solid, black hair. He looks a bit like that Johnny Sattler the footballer — same square jaw and piercing eyes, only Vince's are a bright green.'

'You reckon you'd be able to tell him if he came in here though?' asked Billy. 'Remember what that copper said. He's an expert in getting done up in disguise. That's why they can't pin those bank jobs on him. And you can bet your life he'll be just about unrecognisable when he lobs here on Saturday night.'

'I'll know him all right,' replied Eddie. 'He's got a certain way he moves around with one shoulder sort of dipped below the other. Evidently he got his collarbone broken with a baseball bat a long time ago, and it never set properly. I got a habit of checking out people's mannerisms and I found out about it.'

'And you're certain that will enable you to recognise him on Saturday night?' Price sounded just a little sceptical.

'That, plus his eyes. Plus he doesn't know that we know he's coming, and he doesn't know I'll be here and I know what he looks like.'

'So what do you intend to do?' asked Price.

'Nothing. Just let him inside like anyone else you want to let in.'

'Let him inside?' chorused the others.

Eddie smiled to himself. 'That's right,' he said easily. 'All I want is for you to put another bloke on the door with Billy and leave Les inside with me all night.'

'That's no problem,' said Price. 'Are you sure one bloke will be enough? I'll get a dozen if you like.'

'No, one'll do. Get Danny McCormack, he's pretty reliable and just leave the big Queenslander with me for the night.' Eddie gave Les a sinister smile. 'Might show you a little trick I learnt during my second tour of Vietnam, when I was with the Yanks. It's a good'n mate.'

'Yeah?' Norton's eyes lit up and he rubbed his hands together vigorously. 'Bit of CIA stuff Eddie? Poison blow guns, death rays, what about an exploding toilet seat in the brascoe? Or are you gonna get done up like a Ninja and come down from the ceiling on a rope?'

'Something like that,' replied Eddie. His eyes flashed murderously, the smile on his face turned into an evil grin. 'But you'll like it Les. It's a beauty.'

'Yeah? It sure sounds all right,' said Norton. 'I can't wait for Saturday night. I'm looking forward to this.'

Suddenly Price stood up and glared at Norton. 'You're looking forward to this aren't you,' he bellowed. 'I've got some psychopath coming in here to try and kill me on Saturday night, and you're looking forward to it. You fuckin' Queensland hillbilly, I only wish one of my suits fitted you; I'd stick you in it with a grey wig on your big boofhead and put you in charge for the night. This Rossiter might think you're me and shoot you instead, you wombat.'

'Hold on Price,' said Norton, holding his hands out in front of him. 'I didn't mean it like that.'

'In fact,' said Price, 'I might even do it myself. Right now.' He started rummaging through the drawers in his desk. 'George. where's that bloody .45? Eddie, just give me one of yours for a sec. And make sure there's plenty of bullets in it.'

Despite Price's outburst, a ripple of laughter and relief ran round the office. Eddie's calm, reassuring, businesslike approach to the harrowing matter of what to do on Saturday night had eased the tension in the room and soothed everybody's fears noticeably. When it came to organising a hit or securing Price's safety there was no one better in Australia than the steely-eyed ex-Vietnam veteran.

While he was up, Price got everyone a fresh drink and handed them around. 'All jokes aside Eddie,' he said, as he eased himself comfortably back into his Swedish, padded-leather chair. 'Just what do you reckon this Rossiter will try and pull on Saturday night?'

Eddie took a sip on his drink and started crunching a piece of ice up in his mouth. 'Deep inside, I'd say he's on a death wish because of losing his brother. Being a nut that's how it's affected him. He'll probably come in here, see you and open up with what ever he's got. Probably a couple of automatics, possibly he'll try and get a small machine gun in — like a Mac 10 or a Skorpion. He'll indiscriminately kill as many people as possible before he gets shot himself, figuring that if he makes a big enough scene in here it'll be end of the Kelly Club. The publicity in the papers will finish it.'

'Jesus, you can say that again,' shuddered George Brennan.

'But not to worry,' continued Eddie, 'as soon as I spot him he'll be dead three seconds later.'

'Three seconds?' asked Les.

Eddie nodded his head slowly and winked. He didn't elaborate any further on what would happen on Saturday night, just that he'd organise the disposal of Rossiter's body, and he'd give them a few more details on Friday night. In the meantime they could all relax a little and stay cool — there was nothing to worry about, he assured them. They finished their drinks, then decided to lock up and call it a night.

The stars had just begun to disappear. In the east a faint glimmer of dawn was just starting to blush shyly in the inky blue of the night sky when they stepped out of the Kelly Club and paused for a moment on the footpath. Without much to-do Les and Billy walked Price to his car; George got in the back and Eddie drove them home.

'I'll give you a ring about two,' yawned Les, as he and Billy watched the big brown Rolls draw out of sight.

'Righto mate. See you then,' replied Billy. They headed for their cars and went home to bed.

Friday was a typical summer's day in Sydney. Warm and clear with hardly a cloud in the sky. A brisk nor'easter whipped across the city scattering any smog and keeping the temperature down to a pleasant eighty degrees. Norton was up at about midday. After a late breakfast he rang Billy at about 1.30. They decided not to do any training together as Billy had to give his wife a hand with some shopping that afternoon. They also agreed it was pretty pointless their worrying about anything happening to Price as Eddie would soon be sorting that business out the following night. However they decided they both might get to work a bit early that night and keep an extra sharp look out just in case. Les told Billy he'd see him at the club at about 8, then hung up.

For exercise Norton opted to run a few lengths of Bondi with Tom the beach inspector, then have a work out in North Bondi Surf Club. After that he sat around North Bondi on his banana-chair and had a mag to some of the wharfies, a few of the East's footballers — and a few other 'shifties' who always seem to find plenty of time to hang around the north corner enjoying the sun and the good life.

While Norton was enjoying the afternoon bludge in the sun at North Bondi, in a spacious, white brick house settled into a quiet cul-de-sac in Edgecliff, just up from Cooper Park, Eddie

Salita was happily running the lawn mower over his well-kept back yard. He switched the motor off, began to rake up the leaves and grass clippings then called out to his wife who was working inside the house.

'Hey Lindy! Bring us out a can of mineral water, will you?'

Lindy, an attractive blonde in her mid-twenties, came to Eddie's side with his drink.

'Garden's looking good Ed,' she said, admiring the rows of neatly trimmed edges and flowers. Eddie took a lengthy pull on the can. 'Especially those roses. That new fertiliser's working a treat.'

'Yeah,' Eddie belched. 'That's that chicken shit I was telling you about. It's the go all right.' He walked over, took one of the roses in his hand and took a deep sniff, then had another swig from the can of mineral water. 'Listen, when the kids get home from school, you want to get them and Fritz and we might go down Centennial Park for a while? I wouldn't mind going for a bit of a jog.'

'Yeah righto, that'd be good Ed,' replied Lindy enthusiastically. 'The boys'll be rapt. They love it down there.'

'I'll get cleaned up when we get back,' said Eddie, running his dirt-caked hands over his jeans. 'Then we might just have a bit of chops and salad for tea eh? It's too hot for anything else.'

'Righto.' Eddie drained the last of his mineral water and Lindy took the empty can and went back inside the house.

About an hour later Brenndan and Martin arrived home noisily from school on their BMX bikes. They were still making plenty of noise when Eddie bundled them and Lindy, plus their pet schnausser Fritz and a soccer ball into the Mercedes and headed for Centennial Park. He drove into the Birrel Street, entrance and parked underneath the spreading shade of an old Moreton Bay fig tree, just up from one of the ponds. After playing with Fritz and watching the boys kick the soccer ball to each other for a while, Eddie told Lindy he was going for a jog and he'd be back in about thirty minutes. He wrapped a sweat band round his head and trotted off.

With his wiry frame and easy running style Eddie looked just like any other fit person in his thirties running round the park; the type that seems to thrive on training and looks like he can run all day. However, when he reached the Randwick Racecourse side of the park near the kiosk, he stopped, walked down to the edge of one of the ponds where some people were throwing pieces of bread to some ducks and swans and started looking among the flowers and plants at the water's edge. The people sitting there glanced idly at him at first, then continued feeding the birds. After searching for a while he found what he was looking for — a small, brown, vine-like plant with a purple flower growing right at edge of the pond. He reached into the water and carefully dug it out with his hands taking extra care not to damage the small bulbous root at the bottom. When he had it out he snipped the vine off with his thumbnail, then, taking a small plastic bag from his running shorts, he put the bulb (about same size and shape as a radish) inside and tucked it into the crutch of his underpants. Then, after an instinctive glance at the people around him, he made sure the package was secure and jogged back to his family on the other side of the park.

Eddie did a few exercises then sat around with his wife playing with the kids and the dog, just like any other normal man enjoying an afternoon in the cool, green seclusion of Centennial Park. After an hour or so he bundled them all into the car, kids laughing, dog barking and headed home.

'What time will tea be ready?' Eddie asked his wife, as he came from the shower and into the kitchen.

'About half an hour,' replied Lindy. 'Why? Are you in a hurry? I remember you said you have to go to the club tonight.'

'Yeah. But there's no rush. If you want me, I'll be in the garage.'

'Okay.'

Eddie clicked on the fluorescent light above his work bench and removed the small, white plant-bulb from the plastic bag placing it on a flat piece of board. After checking his fingers thoroughly for any cuts or scratches he dissected the bulb with a small, sharp knife, scooped out the greenish middle which he placed in an old cup and started to crush into a creamy green paste with the heel of an old sheath knife. When that was done, he put it to one side and, taking another flat piece of board, cut out a section roughly the same size as a fifty-cent coin, only thicker. Cutting a small piece from one of the kid's old bike tyre-tubes he carefully tacked a small strip of rubber across the circular piece of board and slipped his middle finger throught it. Satisfied it held securely against his fingers he removed it then, using a small plastic-handled screwdriver, worked a thin, four-centimetre screw through the centre. He lay it back down on the workbench and by working downwards with a small three-sided file sharpened the end of the screw almost as finely as a needlepoint. After gingerly pricking the point against his left thumb he put the file down and with a paddle-pop stick started smearing the acidic-smelling green paste in the old cup into the thread of the screw, making sure none went near the pinprick on his left thumb. It didn't take much and when the thread was full of paste he covered the screw with cotton wool and placed it in a small thick, cardboard box which he then placed inside another small plastic bag. Whistling softly to himself Eddie put the cup, the paddle-pop stick and anything else that had come in contact with the green paste into a plastic bag which he dropped inside the garbage bin. Then, after cleaning up any remaining mess, he switched off the light and went into the kitchen where he placed the plastic bag containing the cardboard box at the back of the deep freeze on top of the fridge.

'That was good timing,' said Lindy. 'I was just about to call you. This'll be ready in a few minutes.'

Eddie slipped his arms round his wife's waist and nuzzled her neck. 'Sure smells all right,' he said. 'Watch out when I finish dinner, I don't have you for dessert. I'm feeling pretty frisky after that run.'

'Watch out I don't switch the stove off and have you for an entree,' replied Lindy, patting her hand lightly against Eddie's fly. Eddie slapped his wife on the backside, got a twist-top from the fridge and went into the lounge where the kids were watching TV.

'Righto Martin,' he growled, 'who said you could sit in your father's seat.'

'Sorry dad.'

'What are you watching anyway?'

'Would you believe — Maxwell Smart, chief?' replied Brenndan.

'That'll do me 99,' laughed Eddie, and eased himself into his favourite lounge chair to wait for dinner.

Back at North Bondi Norton packed up at about five o'clock, went home, had a nap for an hour or so, then got cleaned up. After two schooners at the Royal in Bondi Road and a gigantic steak at the Boka across the street he got to the Kelly Club just on eight. Price and Eddie were already there — Billy arrived about five minutes later.

'Now there's nothing to worry about,' said Eddie reassuringly, as they stood in Price's office drinking coffee before the punters started to arrive. 'Just hang out the front like a normal Friday night or any other night. I'll be standing at the top of the stairs all night though, just in case. But I can't see any trouble tonight. Tomorrow night's the night.' Eddie put his cup down, grinned and stood back in front of the boys with his hands out by his sides. 'Anyway,' he said 'what about my grouse new suit? How do I look? Tops or what?' Eddie was wearing an immaculately cut, char-grey, three-piece suit with a thin, matching check tie and highly polished Italian casual shoes.

Norton stood back and smiled. It was the first time he could ever remember seeing Eddie out of a T-shirt and jeans. 'You look different Eddie, I'll give you that,' he said. 'What did you do? Cover yourself in super-glue and walk through your wardrobe?'

'Dark colours don't suit you either Eddie,' chimed in Billy Dunne. 'You're too thin. You look like a rolled-up umbrella.'

Eddie smiled icily. 'I've got a little something rolled up here for mugs,' he said, letting his coat fall open far enough to just reveal the shiny black butt of a nine-millimetre Ruger automatic. 'Now get down the front where you belong,' he added, with a jerk of his thumb, 'and bash up a few cripples, before I give you both a third ear hole.'

'That sounds like a good idea to me,' said Billy, draining his cup of coffee. 'What do you say Lester?'

'I couldn't agree more William,' replied Norton.

Behind them Price Galese shook his head and smiled at George Brennan. Despite the veiled threats, the roasting and the tension in the air he felt safer than a mouse in a malt heap.

Eddie was right in his prediction about Friday night and it went along as smoothly as silk. There was only one bit of trouble all night. A couple of young, off-duty coppers who should have known better came up wanting to get in. They were both drunk so Billy barred them. The biggest one started to get a bit stroppy and tried to push Les out of the way. With all the tension in the air the boy's nerves were a bit on edge. They weren't in the mood for being stuffed around, so Norton gave the copper a quick back-hander that loosened all his fillings, split his bottom lip open and flipped him backwards over the bonnet of Eddie's Mercedes parked out the front. When the young copper got to his feet he flashed his badge and threatened to do all sorts of things. Billy noted the policeman's name and number.

'Do you know what I am and what I can do?' he screamed, as he stood mopping the blood from his mouth with a hanky.

'Yeah, I know exactly what you can do smart arse,' said

19

Billy. 'You can get yourself a nice big road map of New South Wales, cause when I tell Price about your little performance you're gonna need it.'

Billy gave Price the young copper's name and badge number and a week later, Probationary Constable Kevin Dengate found out just how much pull Price Galese had when he was getting the stitches taken out of his mouth in a doctor's surgery in Tipooburra.

'So apart from that, it was a fairly quiet night for you lads,' said Price, as they were having a quiet drink in his office after they'd shut the club up and got the money in the safe.

'Yeah, it was good,' said Billy. 'And no sign of Rossiter either, or anyone that looked like him.'

'He was out there all right,' said Eddie quietly.

'What?'

'I spotted him out the window, on the other side of the road. Twice.'

'Jesus,' exclaimed Norton. 'What was he doing?'

'Nothing. Just walking past, casing the joint for tomorrow night. He had on an old pair of overalls and a beanie. Like a street cleaner.' Eddie gave a bit of laugh. 'He's a cunning cunt all right.'

'Bloody hell,' said George Brennan, taking a hefty pull on his Scotch and dry.

'No worries George,' said Eddie, giving the casino manager a light pat on the shoulder. Price watched from his desk slightly amazed at Eddie's statement. 'I don't think Vince is going to like the cake I got for him though. Anyone want another drink?' he asked. A ripple of laughter ran round the office.

After getting everyone a fresh drink Eddie gave Les and Billy a few brief instructions about what he wanted them to do on Saturday night — which wasn't a great deal — then they decided to go home. The only difference from the night before was that this time, Price went home in Eddie's Mercedes.

The following Saturday afternoon — just after the first race at Rosehill — Les and Billy were going hell for leather across Bondi on a couple of surf skis they'd borrowed from some clubbies Les knew in North Bondi Surf Club. Their paddling style wasn't the best but what they lacked in finesse they more than made up for with sheer strength, fitness and determination. They were just finishing their sixth and final lap and (as the boys were full of 'ag' at the time) they were giving heaps to that final lap coming back from the baths.

The aggravation was understandably brought on by Vince

Rossiter. It wasn't so much that their job was to look after the security of the Kelly Club and some nutcase from Melbourne was making things hard for them, but what had the boys absolutely filthy was to think that some prick — who was completely in the wrong anyway — was going to try and kill the one person, apart from those in their immediate families, who the boys genuinely loved. So they were trying to release as much of the 'ag' as they could with a good hard paddle.

The summer nor'easter had begun to increase noticeably when they churned up to the boat sheds. It was starting to form countless 'white horses' and whipped across Bondi Bay steadily forcing the murk, from the sewerage treatment works underneath the golf club, up against the rocks.

A couple of skindivers were oblivious to the increased cloudiness of the water as they searched for any drummer or morwong among the green shallows of Ben Buckler. They surfaced near by with a great 'whoosh' of water from their snorkels. The boys bobbed gently up and down in the sheltered waters near the big rock on the point getting their breath back while the solitary mermaid on the big rock seemed to be staring forlornly over the top of them. One of the blokes in the boat sheds recognised Les and gave him a wave. Les waved back, scooped up a huge handful of water and splashed it over his sweating face.

'No wonder they call them fuckin' iron men,' he said, his ample chest heaving up and down while the paddle lay loosely across his thighs. 'This is bloody hard work.'

'You can say that again,' puffed Billy.

They sat in silence for another minute or two, taking in huge gulps of air, their legs dangling over the sides of the surf skis, and enjoying the warm summer sun. It should have been a carefree, pleasant afternoon at the beach except that one thing was burning on their minds.

'Eddie seems pretty confident about tonight,' said Les. 'I mean there's not a real lot he wants us to do. Remember what he said last night?'

'Yeah. It's a funny one all right,' replied Billy, blowing his nose into his hand and flicking the contents into the water. 'You start out the front with me at eight. Danny lobs at nine and you go upstairs with Eddie. We keep Price's Rolls parked out the front with the doors unlocked. Eddie hits Rossiter in the club somehow, you bring him downstairs, put him in the Rolls then you and Eddie drive off.' Billy shrugged his shoulders. 'Eddie said he'd tell you what to do after that.'

'Sure sounds easy don't it?' said Les, shaking his head slowly. 'Too easy if you ask me.' He screwed his face up slightly. 'I mean how's he gonna get Rossiter out of the club without a great commotion? Shoot him, stab him, what? It's got me fucked.'

'I wouldn't worry too much,' smiled Billy. 'If Eddie says he's gonna do it in the club, he'll do it in the club. He's the best in the business.'

'Oh I'm not disputin' that. It's just that ... I dunno. It's a funny one, that's all. Still, I s'pose everything'll be sweet.'

'Anyway,' said Billy, looking at his watch, 'that race is on in a couple of minutes. We goin' in to listen to it?'

'Yeah, righto.'

'Did you back Eskimo Joker?'

'Yeah. I had $200 each way with Billy Harris.'

'You got on with The Brute, did you? Jesus he'll scream if it gets up. Come on, I'll race you in to the beach.'

'You're on.'

With the help of a flying start and a bit more paddling experience, Billy beat Les to the beach by about the width of TAB ticket, where they arrived just in time to hear Price's horse win by two lengths — at thirteen to two. The Brute certainly screamed all right.

Despite the understandable air of tension in the air that night, Price and the boys were in reasonably good spirits as they stood around the office sipping coffee just before they opened the club.

'Bad luck all this trouble's about, Price,' said Les. 'It'd be a good day otherwise, with your horse winning and all that. I had a few bob on it, too. Thanks for the tip.'

Price shrugged his shoulders and smiled. In view of what could happen to him if anything went wrong he was surprisingly cool and relaxed.

'Don't worry Les,' he said quietly. 'It'll still be a good night. A ripper in fact. Won't it Eddie?'

Eddie winked and smiled, but behind the wink there was a hardness and a steely glint in his dark eyes. 'It'll be a beauty Les, and why shouldn't it? It's someone's birthday, isn't it?'

A murmur of nervous laughter rippled quietly round the room. They finished their coffee, and it was time to take up their positions. Les and Billy out the front, Eddie at the top of the stairs. At bang on nine o'clock Danny McCormack arrived.

Danny's hands were in his trouser pockets and he had his

usual cheeky grin plastered across his craggy face as he walked up Kelly Street.

'So, what's the story boys?' were the first words he said, as he walked up to Les and Billy standing at the door. 'Gettin' a bit too much for you two big sheilas is it? Got to put a real man on for a change?'

'Yeah, you're right again Danny,' smiled Billy. 'As soon as Price said get a good man for the night you were the first bloke we thought of.'

'Fair enough too,' replied Danny, with a nod of his head.

'Les is feeling a bit crook to tell you the truth,' said Billy. 'He might be going home a bit early.'

'Bit crook are you, love?' said Danny, turning to Les. 'Oh, that's no good. Might be just a bit of PMT coming on.'

'Dunno what it is,' said Norton. 'I've been like it ever since I changed me pill. I'm going upstairs anyway.' Les threw a straight left at Danny which stopped about a centimetre from the big wharfie's already badly broken nose. 'I'll tell Price you're here,' he winked.

'Is Les fair dinkum crook?' enquired Danny, as Norton disappeared up the stairway into the club.

Billy looked at Danny for a moment. 'Come here Danny,' he said. 'I'll tell you exactly what's going on.'

Eddie was standing quietly at the top of the stairs. He pulled Norton aside as soon as he got to him.

'Danny here?'

'Yeah. Just arrived.'

'Good. Now you know what to do. Just stick around me, not too close, make out you're not really with me. I'll give you the nod, and as soon as you see me walk towards Price follow straight behind. Okay?'

'Good as gold.'

'Righto then.' Eddie clapped his hands together lightly. 'Let's just wait for Rossiter and see what happens.'

With about six or eight feet separating them they stood sentry-like at the top of the stairs giving everyone who entered a thorough perusal: Norton in his tuxedo, Eddie in a light brown sports coat and matching trousers. Eddie, being hardly known to most of the patrons was able to keep his ominous presence fairly unobtrusive. Norton, on the other hand being almost part of the furniture at the club, had to put on a bit of a casual front so as not to alarm any of the regulars who might get a bit worried if they were to see him scowling at the top of the stairs all night instead of out the front greeting them and having a joke with Billy. Around them the beautiful Kelly Club hostesses in their slinky, black evening gowns would glide effortlessly among the well-heeled, well-dressed gamblers taking orders for the drinks the club supplied or getting change or plastic chips. Every now and again one of the croupiers or dealers would look up from the rattle of the dice, the clicking of the roulette wheel or the flicking of the cards on the blackjack tables and glance curiously, through the blue cigarette haze which swirled in the lights above the green felt tables, at Les and Eddie standing grim-faced, menacing and unmoving at the top of the stairs. They were all certain something was going on, but a lot of things went on in the Kelly Club that didn't really concern them so they did their job and minded their own business; if it had been anything worth worrying about, they were sure Price would have told them.

If Price himself was worried he didn't show it. He was his usual urbane, pleasant self moving easily among the patrons, sharing a bit of a joke with the men, sometimes going for his kick to lend a punter a stake, but mostly chatting with the small crowds of adoring women who seemed to follow him everywhere. Occasionally, if he was going to the office to cram some more money into the safe, he'd look up and catch Eddie's eye; Eddie would shake his head almost imperceptibly and they'd carry on as normal. To anyone who didn't know, it looked like a typical, possibly a little busier than usual, Saturday night at the Kelly Club.

By around midnight the place was just about packed. Billy and Danny on guard out the front were letting in a few more than usual to make sure they didn't inadvertently knock Vince Rossiter back, and ruin Eddie's plan to kill him. The extra crowd didn't make it any easier for Les either. Having to carefully scan all the additional faces was difficult enough, but while he was doing this some of the punters and a few others who just liked to dag heavies, would see him inside on his own for a change and would come over and try to get a mag on with him. Norton would be as pleasant as he could under the circumstances for a few seconds but by his aloof manner and politely ignoring them they all soon got the message that he preferred to be left alone and drifted off to rejoin their friends; all except Pattie Franks.

Pattie was a good-looking, gay divorceé in her early thirties; she'd been married twice. Her first husband owned a big trucking business but was accidently killed at work leaving Pattie a motza. Her second husband was a rich SP bookmaker who also sprayed Pattie with plenty of money before he gave her the elbow and left her with a new BMW, a wardrobe full of jewels and furs, and a three-bedroom penthouse overlooking Tamarama Beach. A pixie-faced, well-stacked, slightly auburn-ish blonde, Pattie, in her modelling days, used to be one of the best sorts in Sydney. Even now, thanks to liberal injections of silicone, aerobic dancing and the odd face-lift once in a while, she was still a bit of a stunner. Pattie's main pleasures in life were spending money, hanging around the Kelly Club and throwing as many good-looking young men up in the air as she could get her well-manicured hands on. One bloke she was red-hot keen to get her hands on for some strange reason was Norton — possibly because, being a big fit bloke, she imagined he'd be all right in the cot but mainly because he always seemed to avoid her. Pattie, in a subtle sort of way, must have put the word on Norton almost a hundred times in and out of the club but Norton would always politely find some excuse not to go back to her place for a drink or a smoke or a whatever.

This both mystified and frustrated Pattie. With her money and looks she had hordes of good-looking young men literally clawing over each other to get to her, yet here was a bloke, nothing more than a bouncer in an illegal gambling casino and in Pattie's eyes a half-baked Queensland hillbilly as well who wouldn't wear her if she was a mink coat.

However it wasn't as if Pattie didn't turn Norton on; Les would have loved to get into Pattie's pants and gone for a spin in the nice new BMW. It was just that Norton wasn't too keen to screw any of the women who worked at or hung around the Kelly Club. It could lead to complications. Les was a firm believer in Billy Dunne's advice: 'never shit in your own nest'. Besides, there were that many women living in Bondi he didn't have to bother anyway. But Pattie had noticed Les standing inside on his own instead of out the front and tonight, of all nights, she was determined to get the big red-headed Queenslander one way or the other.

The minute she spotted Les, walking up the stairs of the club around eleven p.m., her baby-blue eyes lit up like a Christmas tree and she tried to get him for a bit of a con-versation. Norton in his usual polite manner, maybe a little more aloof than normal, spoke to her for a short while eventually managing to move her along; but she kept coming back — five times in the next hour. Norton was always affable enough but would continually find some excuse to get rid of her. This only got under Pattie's skin all the more; Norton was inside the club, on his own and she was determined to get through to him no matter what. Finally, at about 12.30, and with about ten brandy alexanders under her belt, she stormed back up to Les and put it straight on him.

'Les Norton, why have you been avoiding me?' she said defiantly. 'You've been positively rude to me all night. Aren't I young enough or good-looking enough for you?' she sniffed.

Les smiled wearily at her. 'I haven't been avoiding you Pattie,' he replied slowly. 'I'm just busy that's all. I mean, I do work here you know.'

Standing there in front of him, her eyes swimming from the brandy alexanders, Norton took a good look at her and for the first time noticed what she had on. Pattie was wearing the skimpiest pink-knitted top you could ever imagine and no bra — which made absolutely no difference at all to her ample silicone-reinforced boobs. The rest of her was tucked tightly into a pair of black leather pants which looked as if they'd been sprayed on and fitted her so snugly round the crumpet she must have poked the edges in with a sharpened pencil.

'And as for your looks Pattie,' he added, 'in that outfit you look hornier than a longboat full of Viking's helmets. It's just that I'm busy tonight. That's all.' He turned away and tried to ignore her continuing to check out the people coming up the stairs. But Pattie was persistent.

She took a deep breath and moved up closer to Les poking her massive boobs in his chest. 'Les,' she cooed 'what's the matter with me? Don't you find me exciting?' She moved in closer again. 'Have you ever been excited Les? When was the last time you were excited?'

Norton looked at her quizzingly. He didn't quite know what to do. Maybe if he said something stupid to her she might go away. 'The last time I was excited Pattie?' he said. 'Let me think. That would have been when I was playing second row for Dirranbandi against Cobar. We were down sixteen to fourteen with two minutes to go, and I ran the length of the field to score a try. That was exciting.'

Pattie Franks let out a little sigh of frustration. 'That's not what I meant,' she said, gritting her teeth slightly. She moved in closer to Norton and pushed her self up against him rubbing her boobs across the lapels of his tuxedo. 'I mean really excited Les. When was the last time you were really excited?'

Norton looked at her again for a moment. More people were

starting to come up the stairs and he was beginning to get a bit annoyed. 'Really excited eh? All right. I was playing front row for Dirranbandi against Goondiwindi in the grand final. We were behind ten-to-six with a minute to go, and I managed to crash over from dummy-half and score a try right under the posts, making it ten-to-nine. That was really exciting.'

Pattie gave another sigh of frustration. She couldn't believe Norton's stoicism and the answers he was giving her. 'That's not what I meant,' she said angrily. 'Come here.' She took Norton's hand and placed it fair on her prominent crutch, pushing it hard into the fork. 'There' she said 'that's what I mean Les. Can you remember the last time you felt a nice cunt?'

Norton looked at her and slowly nodded his head. 'Yeah. When I missed the conversion . . . Now look Pattie, will you piss off and leave me alone? I've got work to do.' He turned away from her. She spun on her heel and disappeared in the crowd. She was almost in tears.

With Pattie finally out of the road Norton was now able to concentrate his attention on the people coming up the stairs. So far he hadn't noticed anyone who aroused his, or Eddie's suspicions. Around them the place was still quite crowded and although Les had been intently scanning everybody who came up the stairs, gazing into the well-dressed assemblage milling about the club he began to notice just who was there. There were at least a dozen well-known TV and media personalities. They seemed to be mingling among a heavy concentration of wealthy racehorse owners — trainers and jockeys. Scores of bejewelled socialites were rubbing elbows with some notorious villains and over near a blackjack table, Price was standing with his arms folded one hand cupped round his chin having a joke with two bishops. *Christ,* thought Norton, *if Rossiter does go off in here before we can get to him it'll make headlines for the next six months.* He glanced over at Eddie with raised eyebrows. Eddie caught his eye, grimaced slightly and shook his head almost imperceptibly from side to side.

A tall, leggy, blonde model, playing roulette with the editor of a leading men's magazine caught his attention momentarily when, out of the corner of his eye, Norton thought he saw Eddie stiffening at the top of the stairway; he quickly switched his attention to what Eddie was staring at. As he got to the top of the stairs Les could see it was an old bloke, possibly somewhere in his sixties, wearing a conservatively cut, blue, pinstriped suit and tinted horn-rimmed glasses. On his arm was a sexy-looking redhead old enough to be his daughter. From his experiences around the Cross, Les tipped her to be a high-class hooker.

They stood at the top of the stairs for a moment then the old bloke said something to the redhead and she moved off towards the ladies'; the old bloke remained, either getting his bearings or waiting for her. He didn't look like an old bloke thought Les, watching him as he stood there; he was ramrod straight; there was no stoop at all and no sign of paunch. He looked across and noticed Eddie was staring intently at the old bloke, too.

On the other side of the room Price was still talking to the two bishops. The old bloke seemed to notice Price, slipped his hand under his coat and moved towards him. As he moved out into the crowd, Les wasn't sure but he thought he noticed a slight dip in the old bloke's shoulder. He was about to draw Eddie's attention to this when like a phantom Eddie zoomed in behind the old bloke. He was about a third of the way towards Price when Eddie reached him, he whispered something in the old bloke's ear, the old bloke froze, turned his head slightly then Eddie seemed to pat the old bloke in the small of his back with his right hand and gripped him under the armpit with his left. Eddie had scarcely touched the old bloke when Norton appeared on the other side, took the old bloke under the right arm and they started moving him towards the door.

As they eased him through the crowd Les was surprised at the way the old bloke, whoever it was, put up absolutely no struggle at all. His legs seemed to be moving but the rest of him felt uncannily limp. His eyes stared straight ahead and he just had a slightly surprised look on his face, almost mild shock. Apart from that his face was expressionless. He never said a word or uttered a sound — it was almost as if he was in a trance.

Effortlessly, and without anyone in the club noticing a thing out of the ordinary, they walked the old bloke to the top of the stairs where Eddie stopped, turned towards Price and nodded his head briefly. Under his tight grip Norton could feel the muscled hardness in the old bloke's arms; a quick glance close up revealed a pair of very surprised, bright green eyes behind the tinted horn-rimmed glasses.

'Is this Rossiter?' he asked, as they started moving him down the stairs.

'It's him alright,' replied Eddie tightly, then called out to Billy to open the car door.

They didn't rush; they just moved the still trance-like Rossiter down the stairs, through the door and out onto the footpath. Big Danny, standing grim-faced in doorway, gave Les a knowing wink as he went past to let him know he knew exactly what was going on. They shuffled Rossiter across the footpath to where Billy was standing, holding the rear door of the Rolls open. They sat Rossiter on the back seat. Billy closed the door and Les walked round and got in the other side. As he did he noticed Eddie say something to Billy and point towards the club then jump in behind the wheel. From the time they spotted Rossiter in the club, to Eddie hitting him and them getting him into the Rolls wouldn't have taken more than two minutes.

'That was pretty smooth mate', said Les, his adrenalin still pumping slightly.

'Yeah,' replied Eddie, as he started the motor. 'I just told Billy to grab that sheila Rossiter came in with, give her a hundred bucks and tell her her gentleman friend took sick suddenly, had to go home and left her the money for a cab.'

'Who do you reckon she was?'

'No one. Just some escort he's grabbed for the night to make sure he could get into the club.' Eddie snatched a quick glance in the rear-vision mirror, slipped the Rolls into drive and made a U-turn back up Kelly Street. 'Righto,' he said, 'let's go and get rid of the cunt.'

With Rossiter propped up next to the window on the back seat, still staring straight ahead and Les alongside watching him out of the corner of his eye, Eddie turned the gleaming, brown Rolls right into Bayswater Road, up Victoria, past the fire station and headed for South Dowling Street. He didn't speed; he just cruised along at a nice leisurely pace almost as if they were all going for a pleasant Sunday afternoon drive in the country.

'Where we goin' anyway?' asked Les, as they stopped for the lights on the corner of South Dowling and Oxford.

'Out the airport,' replied Eddie.

'Kingsford-Smith?'

'Yeah.'

As they waited at the lights Norton noticed the people in the cars alongside staring at them. At first it unnerved him slightly, then he realised they were only admiring the shiny new Rolls Royce and probably wondering who the toffs were inside. *This is the style,* he thought, winking at a young girl sitting in the front seat of a battered old Kingswood propped alongside; she giggled and said something to her pimply-faced boyfriend who scowled back jealously at Norton. Rossiter was still propped up next to him staring straight ahead, looking calm and relaxed and appearing for all the world as if he knew exactly what was going on around him. A few tiny bubbles had formed around one corner of his mouth and even though he was completely motionless, his face still had plenty of colour. At one stage Norton thought he saw him blink.

'Hey Eddie,' he said, a little trepidatiously as they pulled away from the lights. 'Is he dead, or what?'

Eddie laughed quietly to himself. 'Yeah, he's dead all right.'

'Are you sure?'

Eddie smiled at Les in the rear-vision mirror. 'Course I'm sure. I'm fuckin positive.'

They cruised further along South Dowling till they stopped for the lights at the start of Moore Park Road. Rossiter was still gently rocking from side to side but as they pulled up at the lights his neck gave a twitch, and in the reflection of the passing cars Norton thought he saw Rossiter blink again.

'Hey Eddie,' he called out. 'I don't think he's dead y'know.'

'Les, he's deader than Sunday in fuckin' Melbourne I'm tellin' you. Stop worrying.'

'Yeah, I dunno,' said Norton, still staring at the motionless Rossiter. 'I don't like the way he keeps lookin' at me. I reckon we ought to have a meetin' about this.

'Ah, you fuckin' old sheila Les. All right, I'll pull over down the road and show you. I want to check him out anyway.'

They crossed Cleveland Street and a bit further on past Moore Park golf links Eddie found a spot by the side of the road and pulled over. He turned the motor off and left the parking lights on.

'Righto,' said Eddie, swivelling around in his seat to face Rossiter. 'Vince, are you dead or what?' Rossiter just sat motionless, still staring straight ahead.

'I doubt if he's gonna tell you whether he's dead or not Eddie,' said Norton. 'Not even Houdini could tell you that. I just don't reckon he is meself. That's all. Look at the colour in his face. He don't look dead to me.'

Eddie laughed and shook his head. 'Have I got to prove it to you, have I? All right.'

He reached down to his sock and pulled out a small switch-blade knife. As he brought it up he thumbed a catch on the

30

side and a glistening silver blade, about ten centimetres long shot straight out of the handle. He reached over and rested the point of the blade against Rossiter's chest, just where his heart was. 'Now watch this Les,' he said, and plunged the blade up to the hilt in Rossiter's heart. Norton expected a great torrent of blood to start bubbling out but not a drop came through as Rossiter still sat staring vacantly into space. The bubbles on the side of his mouth started to solidify and turned into a trickle of saliva that glistened as it ran down his chin, but that was hardly a sign of life.

'There you are Les,' said Eddie, pulling out the knife and showing Norton the dark red, almost black blood still clinging to the blade. 'Dead as a doornail. Aren't you Vince? Just like your silly fuckin' brother.' Eddie wiped the blood off on Rossiter's coat, reset the blade and put the knife back in his sock.

'Well, I'll be fucked,' said Norton. 'He's dead all right.'

'They don't come any deader Les,' smiled Eddie.

'What did you do to him in the first place?'

'I'll tell you in a minute,' said Eddie. 'I just want to check something out first.'

He reached over and removed Rossiter's horn-rimmed glasses, folded them and put them in the top pocket of his coat. A tug at Rossiter's grey hair proved it to be a very expensive, well-fitting wig. Eddie left it sitting loosely on his head. He undid the buttons on Rossiter's coat to reveal a gun in a shoulder holster tucked neatly under his left arm, and pinned with large safety pins to the inside of his coat were four hand grenades.

'Phew.' Norton let out a long, low whistle. 'Have a go at that.'

'Yeah,' Eddie carefully unpinned one of the grenades and held it in his hand. 'M203 fragmentation grenades. US issue. Christ, I wonder where he got these.'

'Jesus. Imagine what would have happened if he'd dropped one of them in the club tonight.'

'You and I wouldn't be here to worry about it, I'll guarantee you that.' Eddie unclipped the rest of the grenades, placed them gently on the floor of the car and covered them with a large beach towel he had on the front seat.

'Will they be all right there?' asked Norton, a little nervously.

'As long as you don't pull the pins out.'

'Not much chance of that.'

Eddie removed Rossiter's gun which turned out to be a Walther PPK.32 automatic. 'Well, well, well,' chuckled Eddie, as he looked at the shiny, blue-black pistol for a moment then slipped it into his coat pocket. 'Vince must've been watching some old James Bond movies on TV. Like a drink Mr Bond?' said Eddie, slapping Rossiter lightly on the jaw. 'Vodka martini? Twist of lemon, shaken not stirred?' Rossiter sat staring obliquely into eternity. The only movement was his jaw, which had begun to drop slightly. Eddie slipped his hand into Rossiter's inside coat pocket and came out with a rather fat wallet. 'Hello, what have we got here? Some chops?' He counted the money quickly. 'Two grand. There you go Les. One each.'

'Something,' replied Norton, slipping the wad of notes into his back pocket.

'Better than a poke in the eye with a broken coat hanger. Well that ought to just about do Vince,' said Eddie, putting the empty wallet back in his pocket. 'Shove him down on the floor and hop in the front, and we'll get going.'

Norton pushed Rossiter's body, which had started to stiffen just a little, onto the floor then walked round and got in the front. As soon as he closed the door Eddie started the motor and the big Rolls cruised off majestically towards Mascot Airport.

'Well Eddie,' said Les, 'I've got to give it to you. That was pretty neat whatever you did to him in the club. You gonna tell me what it was?'

'Sure.' Eddie loosened his tie and settled back into the plush driver's seat of the Rolls. 'I hit him with this.' He reached down between the two front seats and showed Norton the circle of wood with the sharpened screw sticking through it wrapped in a hanky. Les went to take hold of it. 'Hey, don't go grabbing it,' said Eddie quickly. 'Just hold it by the wooden part. Don't touch that sharpened bit or you'll finish up like your mate in the back.'

Norton held the strange little object delicately between his forefinger and thumb, examined it carefully then handed it back to Eddie who flicked the hanky back over it and replaced it between the seats.

'What is it anyway?' asked Les.

'A punji stick.'

'A what?'

'A punji stick; or at least a Western version of it. It's a little trick I learnt in Vietnam. The VC used to dig these little holes in the bush and they'd put sharpened bamboo stakes on the bottom which they'd smear with human shit then cover

32

the holes over. Some poor mug'd come walking along, step into one of the holes and bingo, he gets a stake through his foot. The shit makes your foot blow up like a balloon and if "evac" unit doesn't get to you, you can lose your foot, sometimes your leg.'

'Sounds lovely.'

'Yeah. Anyway, the second time I went back to 'Nam, working with the CIA and the US 101st Airborne, I was up in a place called Cheo Reo. It's an old Montagnard tribe district. I ended up pretty good mates with the Monts and they showed me another variation of it. They've got this little plant they call "the cobra's heart". It grows near ponds in the jungle and funnily enough it grows over here too — if you know where to look. Anyway the root contains one of the most deadly poisons on earth. It causes instant paralysis. Just like you were a car and someone switched the motor off. We used to use it if we had to waste someone on the sly, like an ARVN informer or a VC sympathiser. You just crush the root up, smear it on a punji stick and jab 'em with it. The trick is, though, to get them right in the spinal chord. It stops them dead but you can generally walk them along a few metres then put them down somewhere and they just sit there, all nice and quiet, just staring into space. But dead as a doornail.'

'And that's what you used on Rossiter?'

'Yep.'

Norton looked at Eddie for a moment, with the lights from the dashboard reflecting on his face, and couldn't help shuddering slightly at the matter-of-fact manner in which the deadly little assassin discussed one of his sinister killing methods — like he was talking about a new way of changing an oil filter on a car.

'But how did you know for sure it was Rossiter?' he asked. 'I thought I saw you say something to him when you stepped up behind him.'

Eddie laughted softly. 'Well, when I saw him coming up the stairs, I thought this bloke's in pretty good shape for an old fella.'

'Yeah. I thought that myself,' said Norton.

'I couldn't quite see his eyes but as he started walking towards Price I sprung that dip in his shoulder. So I walked up behind him and said, "Hello Vince, wish your brother a happy birthday for me." He gave himself away then, and that's when I hit him.'

Norton shook his head slowly. 'Well fuck me.'

Eddie looked at Norton and smiled. 'Not particularly thanks Les.'

By now they were about halfway along General Holmes Drive, going past the airport heading towards Brighton-le-Sands. It was getting on for 1.30 and there weren't a great deal of cars on the road as Eddie slowed down the Rolls and had a look in the rear-vision mirror. 'I hope there's no cops around,' he said, as he spun the big car up over the median-strip and did a quick U-turn to bring them over on the side of the freeway facing back to the city. He cruised along a few hundred metres, driving slowly and looking out Norton's window. 'Here it is,' he said. He pulled the car up off the road and switched off the motor.

Norton put his head up against the window and peered out into the darkness; all he could see was mangrove brush and other scrub growing up against a corroded, cyclone-wire fence which ran off in the shadows on either side of the car. Just in front of his face the brush cleared away to reveal a cyclone-wire gate with a chain and padlock holding it.

'Righto Les,' said Eddie, pointing out the car window. 'You see that gate there? I'm going to go and open it — I've got the key. You get Rossiter out and drag him over, then we'll both drag him off into the bush. You right? Let's go.'

Eddie got out and trotted over to the gate. By the time he'd got the lock open Norton had Rossiter out of the Rolls and, after a quick check for passing cars, took Rossiter firmly by the collar and dragged him across to where Eddie was waiting with the gate open. He whipped the body straight through as Eddie closed the gate and draped the chain loosely round the bolt.

'Righto Les,' said Eddie, taking a grip on Rossiter's collar alongside Norton, 'up this way — there's a bit of a path. I've got a torch.'

Eddie switched on a small torch and, with Rossiter between them, they started dragging him toes-up along a narrow, sandy trail which led off into the bush.

After about a hundred metres of half-stumbling, half-jogging in the darkness, lit faintly by the bouncing beam of Eddie's tiny torch, the bush started to clear. About the same distance in front of them Norton could make out a group of construction workers pouring concrete underneath a bank of arc lights; their voices and the sounds of cement mixers and other heavy machinery were quite audible in the still of the night. They proceeded about another fifty metres and Eddie called a halt. 'Okay. Just wait here a minute,' he said quietly.

Norton let go of Rossiter and got down on his haunches noticing they'd stopped up against one of four wooden piers, formed up with scaffolding, ready for pouring. They were a little wider than a phone booth and a couple of metres higher, but went down another six metres into the sand and were to be part of a row of concrete piers supporting a new air-strip running out over Botany Bay.

As they squatted there Eddie produced a small beeper from one of his pockets. He pressed a button and Norton heard a voice boom out from among the workers barely fifty metres in front of them. 'I'm just gonna duck over for a piss. I'll be back in a minute,' said one of the construction workers who detached himself from the others and started walking towards them. Crouching low, Eddie moved to the furthest pier and waited for him, hiding in the shadow from the others.

As he approached Les could see he was a big, bull-necked construction worker wearing a pair of blue overalls and a red safety-helmet. He stood next to the pier Eddie was hiding behind, unzipped his fly and started to let out a great torrent of urine which splashed and bubbled in the sand at his feet. In the distant gleam of the arc lights Norton could just make out JW. Foreman, on the front of his safety helmet. Still hidden from the others, Eddie stood up and whispered something to the man who banged the pier next to him with his fist. A wad of money changed hands then the man zipped up his fly and without saying a word turned and walked back to the others.

'Okay, everything's sweet,' said Eddie, returning to Norton. 'We've got to dump him in that pier I was sitting next to. You right?'

They took Rossiter by the collar once more and dragged him over to the pier where they stood him up against the scaffolding, keeping it between them and the workers. Rossiter's body had stiffened a little more by now and in the moonlight his face had turned a ghostly, chalky white.

'I'll climb up on the scaffolding,' said Eddie, 'and you pass him up to me.' Eddie clambered up the metal pipes a few metres, reached down and took Rossiter by the collar. 'Okay. Pass him up Les.' Norton bent down, got a firm grip on Rossiter's ankles and lifted him up to shoulder height. 'Okay, now give him one good shove.' Les switched his grip to beneath Rossiter's feet, got his chest under him and heaved him straight up. Eddie tilted Rossiter's head back over the side of the empty scaffolding and gravity did the rest. Vince Rossiter's body tumbled down the shaft to land with a dull splash in a couple of metres of muddy rainwater.

Eddie jumped down and they ran back and hid in the darkness at the edge of the last pier. 'Just wait here a minute,' he said, spitting out a few grains of sand.

They crouched in the shadows, silently wiping sand and picking twigs from their clothes. Before long a huge, rumbling cement truck, its load spinning slowly round on the back, led by the man with JW. Foreman on his hat, started backing up to the pier containing Rossiter's body. When it got close enough, the foreman blew his whistle, the truck stopped and two men came round and unshackled a short metal chute from the back of the truck which they swung over the empty shaft. A third man wet the chute with a hose then at a signal from one of the other men, the foreman blew his whistle again, the truckdriver waved his arm out the window, hit the tilt button and fifty tonnes of wet, blue-metal-thickened cement splattered down on top of Vince Rossiter entombing him there forever.

Eddie slapped Norton on the shoulder. 'Come on. Let's piss off.' He picked up the trail with his torch and they headed back for the car.

'I might give Price a call,' said Eddie, picking up the radio-telephone from between the two front seats of the Rolls. 'Better let him know everything's sweet.'

'Yeah righto,' replied Norton gruffly, his door still open. 'I'll get some of this bloody sand out of my shoes. You'd think I just come through the Simpson fuckin' Desert.'

While Les removed his shoes and socks, Eddie hit the buttons and got through to the Kelly Club. 'Hello George. It's Eddie. Is Price there?'

'Hold on a sec mate. I'll get him,' replied George Brennan. In a few moments Price was on the phone.

'Hello Eddie. How did it go? Everything sweet?' His voice was quiet but it was obvious he was in a state of great excitement.

'Good as gold,' replied Eddie. 'Your friend is resting well and I don't think he'll be bothering anyone for quite some time.'

'Good on you. By Jesus that was smooth work son,' Price chuckled into the phone.

Eddie glanced at Norton hunched in the car door, banging

his shoes on the ground. 'I couldn't have asked for a better back-up.'

'He's a good, staunch man Les.'

'One of the best Price.'

'I know. So listen, there's a briefcase in the boot with twenty-five grand in it. Give him that when you drop him off home. In fact, why don't you both take the rest of the night off, get a couple of sheilas and go and have a blow out somewhere? Take the Rolls and bridge up a bit. Charge it all to me.'

'Righto. We might just do that. You sure you can afford it?'

Price burst out laughing. 'Can I afford it? Eddie you're not going to believe this. You know Jilly Mantella who runs the Touch of Style?'

'Yeah.'

'Well, her and one of her best girls walked in here just after you left with two Arab oil sheiks. Prince Waddi someone or other and his cousin.'

'Yeah, go on.'

'They haven't been here an hour and they've just dropped about half a million.'

'Fair dinkum?'

'Oh mate, you've got no idea. And they're laughing their silly bloody heads off. I'll end up taking these two glorified bowser-boys for a million before the night's out.' Price burst out laughing again. 'Steve Rossiter's birthday and I get all the presents. Happy birthday to you — happy birthday to you.'

Eddie laughed and shook his head. 'You're not bad Price.'

'I know. Listen, I've got to go. I've got to keep at these two camel drivers while they're on the boil. Say hello to Les for me, and tell him I'll give him a call tomorrow. In fact I'll probably call round. And I'll see you when you bring the car round. Okay?'

'Righto, see you then. Goodbye Price.'

'Goodbye Eddie. Thanks mate.' They both hung up.

'How was Price?' asked Norton, closing the car door.

'Good as gold. He said to take the rest of the night off and have a drink on him and there's a nice bonus for you when I drop you off — and he'll see you tomorrow.'

'Oh beauty.'

'Well, where do you fancy going?' said Eddie, starting the car.

'Well, I wouldn't mind goin' home and getting changed first.'

'All right.' The big Rolls rejoined the traffic on General Holmes Drive and they headed towards Bondi.

They cruised along silently for a while each man immersed in his own thoughts as they absently listened to some music on the car radio. Norton was still slightly bewildered by the speed and deadly efficiency of the night's events. After all, it isn't every day, or night, you help to murder someone with poison in an illegal gambling casino, whisk his body halfway across town in a Rolls Royce, then, after robbing him, bury his body in tonnes of concrete underneath an international airport — all more or less with the cooperation of two detectives. Even now Norton still found it a little hard to believe it had all happened.

Finally Eddie reached over and slapped Les on the thigh. 'Listen mate,' he said 'I want to thank you, too, for tonight. You were terrific all the way.'

Norton shrugged his shoulders. 'That's all right Eddie. It's part of my job anyway.'

'Yeah, there's a bit more to it than that though,' smiled Eddie.

'Maybe. These Rolls Royces are all right, aren't they,' said Norton, changing the subject and easing himself a bit more luxuriously back into the seat.

'You like toffing up Les?'

'Oh yeah. Why not?'

'Well here you are, grab one of these.' Eddie produced two large, expensive Havana cigars out of a compartment from somewhere under the radio-casette player. He put one in his mouth and handed one to Les then pressed the lighter on the dash. Within a few seconds they were puffing away ostentatiously. 'Well, what do you reckon?' said Eddie, grinning as he let out a great cloud of blue smoke.

'Not bad. Be better if I smoked,' laughed Norton, coughing slightly.

They went along a bit further, quietly, comfortably, up Darley Road past Queens Park, puffing away at the two huge cigars when suddenly the headlights picked up two young girls hitch-hiking along the side of the road.

'Hello,' said Eddie, slowing down. 'Two young spunks lookin' for a lift. We throw 'em in?'

'My oath,' replied Norton, 'they might be all right.'

Eddie stopped the car and the two girls ran up alongside.

'Where are you going to girls?' asked Norton, as the window swished down.

'Bondi.' The two young girls couldn't quite believe their eyes when they saw the gleaming, brown Rolls Royce.

'So are we. Jump in.' Les leaned over and opened the door as the two girls excitedly bundled in. While he was closing the door Norton checked the two girls out under the interior light.

They weren't bad little sorts, blondes, both about eighteen wearing tight fitting jeans, sneakers and denim shirts with little coloured plastic nicnacs pinned on the front. From their sun-tanned, pimple-free faces, Norton tipped them to be girls who, if they didn't actually surf, spent a fair bit of time on the beach.

'Where have you been anyway?' said Eddie, as they moved off.

'A party at Randwick,' said the blonde behind Les.

'Any good?' he enquired.

'No, it was up to shit.'

It turned out that the girl sitting behind Les was Ricky and the other one was Lea: both had just turned nineteen. They both came from Newcastle but had been living in Bondi for six months — most of the time out of work, like now. They'd been invited to this party but in the girl's words, it was a real drag. The guys they went with were creeps and kept hassling them. There was a fight so they decided to split and, not having much money, they either had to walk or thumb it to Bondi. They certainly weren't expecting a lift in a brand spanking new Rolls Royce.

'So where are you off to now girls?' asked Norton, turning around to Ricky sitting behind him. 'Going straight home, are you?'

'S'pose so,' said Ricky, smiling back at Les. 'I don't really want to but there's nothing else to do, is there?'

'Well, we've just been to a party ourselves,' continued Norton. 'A send-off for a friend of ours, but it was a bit formal and I'm just on my way home to get changed, then we're going up the Cross for a feed.' He gave the cigar a bit of a puff and smiled at both girls. 'Would you like to join us? Have a nice steak and a couple of bottles of wine? What do you reckon Eddie?'

Eddie looked at the two spunky young blondes in the rear-vision mirror and grinned at Norton. 'I think it would only

39

be the gentlemanly thing to do Les. Want to come with us girls? There's a place we go's got the biggest steaks and the best veal scallopini in Sydney.'

Ricky and Lea both nearly fainted. 'Reckon we would,' they chorused. Since a week after they'd got their last dole cheque they'd been living on cheap fruit and whatever they could thieve out of supermarkets. The whole time they'd been living in Bondi no one had ever shouted them so much as a meat pie. They were just about ready to jump all over Eddie and Les.

'Do you think we should book ahead?' said Les, picking up the radio-telephone and winking at Eddie.

'Oh there's no real need,' replied Eddie. 'Maxim's has generally always got a table waiting for us.'

'Yeah, you're right. If he hasn't, I'll buy the place and have him dismissed.'

Ricky spread her cute little bum a bit more comfortably on the back seat and had a good look at the opulent luxury surrounding her in the Rolls Royce. 'Wow, this is a really great car,' she said. 'What do you guys do for a living?'

'Do for a living,' replied Norton. 'We own a film company.'

'Oh wow!' The two girl's hearts started to soar again; this was the icing on the cake for them. Not only were they being taken out to dinner in a Rolls Royce by two rich, nice, mature men — now they could see themselves in showbusiness.

'Yes, I'm a director,' said Les, 'and Edward here is a producer.'

'Really? Oh wow! What sort of movies do you make?' asked Lea.

'Oh telemovies, documentaries, commercials,' replied Eddie. 'All sorts of things. In fact we're starting production on a new movie next week.'

'Fair dinkum?' cried Ricky. 'Wow! what's it called?'

'Ah — "Goodbye Vince",' said Les. 'It's about a guy who likes standing around watching aeroplanes.'

'Wow! Any beach scenes in it?' asked Lea.

'Yeah sure,' replied Norton. 'The main guy in it is a surfie.'

'Far out. Oh look, we surf. What about giving us a part in your movie?' Lea was almost squealing with delight.

'Yeah go on, why don't you?' said Ricky. 'And we got terrific bodies, too. Look.'

As they slowed up for the lights at Charing Cross, Ricky and Lea undid the fronts of their faded, denim shirts and thrust their chests up at Norton, who nearly fainted. Right before his eyes burst four of the firmest, brownest, most beautiful boobs he'd ever seen in his life. They looked like four huge grapefruits, with a tiny, delicate, pink strawberry sitting on each.

'Jesus Christ,' he said, nearly biting the end off his cigar, as Eddie, looking on goggle-eyed in the rear-vision mirror, almost ran up the arse of the old Ford station-wagon in front of them. Ricky and Lea started undoing their jeans and sliding them down over their hips.

'Just hold on there a sec girls,' said Norton quickly. 'I think we might be better off discussing this back at my place.'

'You sure?' said Ricky.

'Oh yeah. We'll sort it out over a nice bottle of French champagne.'

Ricky shrugged her beautiful, brown shoulders. 'All right, she said, back at your place.' The girls started putting their clothes back on.

'Well? What do you reckon Edward?' said Norton, turning to Eddie. 'We going to give the girls a part in our movie or what?'

Eddie was wild-eyed and gripping the steering wheel like he was going to rip it out of the dash. 'Give them anything they want,' he said.

'Yeah, go on Les. Give us a part in your movie,' said Ricky.

'Yeah, give us a contract. Go on,' said Lea.

'Oh, I don't know about a contract,' said Norton.

'Oh, go on,' said Ricky. 'Give us a contract.

'If they want a contract, give'em a bloody contract,' said Eddie.

'Well, we'll see what happens back at my place,' said Norton. He pulled the thousand dollars out of his pocket and gave the girls a hundred each. They both sat back slack-jawed. 'I suppose we could give the girls some sort of work on the movie,' he said. 'But there's just one thing.' Norton turned to Eddie, took a puff on his cigar and blew a large smoke ring towards the roof of the car. 'At this stage of production, I don't think we should offer the girls anything concrete.'

First Day in the D's.

Although it wasn't the best of days Detective Constable Fred Mooney was feeling pretty good inside. He and Detective Sergeant Len Simmiti were cruising along Bronte Road in the squad car heading from Charing Cross to Waverley police station. With his styled, rather lengthy blonde hair, pudgy, almost baby face and a bit of a twinkle in his pale blue eyes, Fred looked more like a young advertising executive than a detective on the tough Waverley beat. The only thing that added any obvious hardness to his twenty-five years, apart from his solid build, was a slightly broken nose and a faint scar under his chin, a legacy from his rugby-league days with South Sydney, and later Easts. Behind the wheel, Detective Simmiti's thinning, dark brown hair, piercing hazel eyes and permanent five o'clock shadow on his craggy, slightly jowled face gave him the appearance of someone who had definitely been a detective for twelve years; twelve years and a day more than his partner.

The main reason for Detective Frederick Mooney's increasing feeling of self-satisfaction was that today was officially his first day as a detective. Certainly he'd put in some time on the A-list and the ungraded list but now he could put his blue uniform in mothballs. From now on he was a detective and just quietly, there was no one else in the force he'd rather be assigned to as a partner than Len Simmiti. Although Len was a bit of a hard-nose and liked to keep to himself he was one extra smart cop and a tough one, and the majority of villains in the Eastern suburbs were a wake-up to the fact that if you knew what was good for you, you didn't try putting any shit on 'Simmo'. And he was Simmo's partner. He glanced out the window of the Ford Falcon at cold, windy Bronte Road and smiled to himself once more. Detective Fred Mooney. Yes, he thought, nodding his head slightly, *it's definitely got a nice ring to it.*

Les Norton, on the other hand, wasn't in the best of moods. He pulled the collar of his leather jacket up against the wind and strode moodily along Bronte Road also in the direction of Waverley police station. The look on Norton's face was a cross between a dingo with its foot caught in a trap and someone who had just started to eat a packet of Lifesavers and discovered they were a roll of corn pads. He'd just put his old Ford in at Ronnie Phillip's garage for a quick tune-up and what should have been a cheap thirty-dollar job was now going to be closer to $250. 'Chicka' had told him his generator was stuffed, so was the coil, there was a crack in the distributor cap, the petrol pump was on the way out and he needed a new set of plugs. And don't worry about picking it up at lunchtime, try four o'clock that afternoon. Great. And if that wasn't enough to give you the shits, tucked in the back pocket of Norton's jeans were two parking tickets for another eighty dollars. *What a bloody ripper,* thought the big red-headed Queenslander spitting bitterly into the gutter. *Three hundred straight down the drain.* He gazed up at the cloudy, bleak, July sky and gave a mirthless smile. *You sure like to kick a bloke when he's down don't you boss,* he said to himself, and slowly shook his craggy red head.

It wasn't as if Les couldn't afford the $300. It's just that there were better things to do with it than give it to Chicka and the coppers, like put it in the building society at eleven-and-a-half percent and hope you live to be 200. Still, he thought, with a bit of a wry smile, apart from the lost $300 it wasn't as if Tuesday was going to be a complete disaster. That night he'd arranged to take a girl out to dinner, a good-looking, well-stacked blonde from Coogee he'd met at a party in Edgecliff on Sunday. She'd been all over Norton like ants at a picnic so he knew he was on a fairly good thing that night. Though ostensibly what was going to be a nice dinner in a decent restaurant over a couple of bottles of good wine, would now be a Chinese feed somewhere in Bondi Junction — probably the Sun Kuong — and a few drinks at the Woolahra and listen to the band afterwards.

He checked his watch — it was just after ten — then jammed his hands back inside the pockets of his jacket and quickened his pace because of the chilly south-west wind. But there was plenty of time to slip into Waverley police station and pay the fines, then catch the train into town and take in an eleven o'clock movie. He'd been up since seven for a run and a training session with Billy Dunne and had only had a very light breakfast of fruit, so he decided he'd slip into the Athenia and have a nice feed of Greek lamb and vegetables after the movie to stop the rumbling that was just starting in the pit of his stomach. After that, a bit of a perv on the office girls in town for a while, then his car should be ready. *I s'pose there's worse ways of spending a winter's day, he thought, even if it does mean having to go to the bank and make a withdrawal. That eggplant and okra's gonna taste good by 1.30.* A little saliva started to form in his mouth.

Travelling along in the squad car, Detective Mooney was feeling pretty much the same way. He'd been up a little late playing cards and having a few drinks with some mates the night before, and apart from a bit of coffee and toast, he'd missed breakfast as well. Although today was a bit of a big day for him and he didn't have to start till 8.30 on the day-shift he'd still been slightly hung-over and too cold and lazy to get out of bed.

'Hey Len', he said, turning to his partner. 'How about we duck up the Jungo and get some toasted sandwiches? I'm starving. We can eat them back at the station while we type up those B and Es.'

Detective Simmiti nodded his head impassively. 'Yeah righto', he said. The boring task of typing up what lately seemed to be a never ending list of break and enters at no time enthused him, and some coffee and sandwiches would help make it a little less tedious. He put his foot down slightly on the accelerator when Detective Mooney, recognising the broad shoulders and red hair of a certain person striding along the footpath adjacent to the car, tapped Simmiti on the shoulder. 'Hey hold on Len, just pull up alongside that bloke in the black leather jacket', he said with a bit of a smile. 'I think it's an old football mate of mine.'

All that was on Norton's mind as he hurried past the bus stop outside Waverley public school was how good the fetta cheese salad was going to taste at the Athenia, when the sudden squealing of tyres stopping alongside him made him spin round with a bit of a start.

'Good morning Mr Norton. Mind if we ask you a few questions?'

Norton looked at Fred Mooney's face smiling up at him from the car window for a second or two, then a derisive grin

45

spread across his own craggy face.

'Well, well, well,' he laughed. 'If it isn't one of New South Wales's finest. What's doing Moon?'

'Not a great deal. Just cruising around looking for villains. I don't think we'll go any further.' Detective Mooney gave a bit of a laugh. Norton stepped up to the car window. 'Anyway how's things Les?' he said extending his hand. 'I haven't seen you for a while.'

'Oh, I can't complain I s'pose' replied Norton, giving Fred's hand a quick shake. 'Just pluggin' along, gettin' a quid the best way I can. How's it goin' with you?'

'Pretty good mate. I can't whinge either.'

Suddenly Norton noticed Fred's smartly cut Harris-tweed sports coat and matching trousers. 'Hey what's with the grouse clobber Moon?' he said, giving the sleeve a pluck between his forefinger and thumb. 'Don't tell me they've made you a D.'

Fred grinned up at Norton. 'Yep. I finally got there, and this is my first day more or less.'

'Your first day in the D's eh?'

'Yeah. Detective Fred Mooney.' He pointed his finger at Norton. 'So watch out.'

Les threw back his head and laughed. 'Jesus Moon. It won't be long now and you'll have a couple of blocks of flats at Surfers, a Swiss bank account, probably a diamond mine in South Africa.' He gave Fred a knowing wink. 'I always said you were more than just a pretty face Fred.'

Detective Mooney smiled and shook his head. 'Don't give me a hard time Les. Not on my first day.'

'Just don't come up the Kelly Club annoying me and poor old Price,' continued Norton. 'Things are tough enough as it is.'

'What Kelly Club?' replied Detective Mooney indignantly. 'I've never heard of it.'

'Oh yeah, that's right I forgot Fred. The commisioner said there's no such place, didn't he?' They both had a bit of a laugh.

'Anyway Les. You met my partner Len? Len Simmiti: Les Norton.'

'No. I've seen you around before though.' Norton reached across and took Detective Simmiti's firm handshake. 'Pleased to meet you Len.'

'Les. How are you? I've heard a bit about you.'

46

'All good I hope,' replied Norton. Detective Simmiti smiled back evenly.

Norton jammed his hands back into the pockets of his leather jacket and leant up against the car to have a bit of a mag to Fred for a while; not about anything in particular, mainly football and a few funny incidents when they played together for Easts and how the team was going that year, which wasn't too bad for a change. They talked and laughed about several other things, although, naturally enough being on completely opposite sides of the social spectrum, there were a lot of things Les couldn't mention to Fred and vice-versa. Nevertheless Norton did say how he was going down to Waverley police station to pay two parking fines, and he hoped the rotten bloody building would fall down once he was back outside. Finally, Detective Simmiti's fingers drumming on the steering wheel told Fred, in a subtle sort of way, that there were sandwiches to be bought and reports to be typed up and it was time they got going. Norton saw it, too.

'Anyway Moon,' he said, 'I s'pose I'd better let you go.'

'Yeah righto Les. Why don't you call over one day and have a drink? You know where I live.' Fred shared a flat with another young cop about two streets from Norton.

'Yeah I'll do that for sure. Anyway, I'll see you Moon. See you again Len.'

Detective Simmiti nodded and smiled back as Fred wound up the window. They started to edge back out into the fairly heavy traffic inching along Bronte Road. Norton gave them a bit of a wave and continued on his way.

He was completely lost in thought as he strode along the gusty street laughing to himself about a funny incident that happened at the Sports Ground one Sunday when he and Fred were playing against Wests. Fred had only had a few games in first grade and one of the Wests forwards, knowing Fred was a young cop, was giving him a hard time. Norton shortened the big Wests forward up, but the referee thought it was Fred and sent him off and Fred got a month's suspension, mainly because of the horrendous injuries sustained by the Wests forward. Norton was chuckling away to himself when he realised he'd walked right past Waverley police station and was almost outside a small grocer's shop not far from the council garbage depot.

'Ah, shit,' he said, as he propped and slapped at the two parking tickets in the back pocket of his jeans.

Not completely watching what he was doing, he almost collided with an old foreign lady coming the other way and carrying two string shopping bags full of groceries and vegetables. With her dumpy build and a huge red scarf wrapped round her rosy, wizened face, she looked like she'd just walked out of a TV commercial inviting you to ring mum in the old country ISD.

'Oh, sorry love,' apologised Norton, taking the old girl gently by the arm to steady her.

She was about to say something when unexpectedly a dark haired, vicious-faced youth wearing scruffy jeans and one of those cheap, khaki army jackets burst out of the grocer's shop, and bumped into Les causing him to cannon into the old foreign lady. She let out a wail and screamed something in either Hungarian or Serbo-Croat as she went up in the air in a shower of eggs, potatoes, onions, celery, almost all the contents of her two string shopping bags.

'Hey, watch where you're goin', you fuckin' idiot,' Norton remonstrated to the youth. As he turned from the old lady to face him, the youth brought up a huge revolver and levelled it about a metre from Norton's face.

In that horrifying instant time seemed to stand still for Les. He stared into the young hood's pimply, unshaven face and crazy, smacked-up eyes. Though the face didn't register on him Norton couldn't help being fascinated by the young junkie's left ear: half of it was missing and through the stump glittered a large gold earing. Norton stared at it as if in some sort of a trance because, as he looked from that to the barrel of the gun in front of his face, Norton was convinced they were the last two things he was ever going to see in this world.

Like he was taking part in a slow-motion movie and his arms were made of lead Norton made a desperate, clumsy lunge at the gun. As he did his foot slipped on a broken egg from the old lady's upturned shopping bag causing him to slip slightly to one side which was just as well, because at the same instant, the junkie pulled the trigger and the revolver went off with a thunderous roar. Norton felt the shock waves on his face and smelt the cordite as the bullet hummed past his ear. What should have been almost certain death for the big Queenslander was averted by about one centimetre and a broken egg.

In an instant everything returned to normal. Norton let out a blistering oath of shock and anger and in an unthinking, clumsy rage made another lunge for the junkie. However not only was he slightly over-balanced, he slipped on another broken egg causing him to trip over the old foreign lady, who was still screaming and flopping around in her groceries scattered all over the footpath. Norton pitched forward onto the asphalt alongside her. The junkie aimed the gun at Norton's chest, paused for a second, then unexpectedly turned on his heel and sped off down the street. By the time Norton had regained his feet the kid had turned down Birrel Street, and was heading for Centennial Park quicker than a tomcat which had just been hit in the arse with a slug gun.

Idling impatiently in the traffic because a woman had stalled her Celica at the Birrel Street lights, the two detectives turned to each other quizzically at the sound of the revolver going off.

'Did you hear that?' said Detective Simmiti.

'Yeah. Sounded like a gun,' replied Detective Mooney. He swivelled round in his seat to see Norton who was bending over the still wildly yelling, old lady and trying to help her to her feet. The shopkeeper had run out by this time and was hopping around next to them gesticulating frantically with his hands.

'Hey, pull in' Mooney said, pointing to the kerb. 'There's something going on back there.'

They pulled up abruptly and walked swiftly but cautiously back to the trio standing among the groceries scattered on the footpath outside the shop.

'What the bloody hell happened here?' asked Fred, looking at the mess, then at Les.

'What happened,' roared Norton. 'Some greasy little turd just tried to fuckin' well shoot me. I'm lucky I'm a-fuckin'-live.'

The two detectives stared at the wild-eyed, florid-faced Norton for a moment or two. They were about to say something when the other two opened up.

'You are police?' shouted the shopkeeper. An ancient but still solid Lebanese with a completely bald head and a huge droopy moustache, he turned out to be a Mr Ahmed Malouf.

'Detective Simmiti, Waverley,' replied Len, giving his badge a quick flick.

'Robber bastard, robber bastard,' screamed Mr Malouf, pointing in every direction at once.

Then it was the old girl's turn.

'This man knock me down' she shrieked, jabbing a fat finger full of gold rings at Les. 'My eggs. My tomatoes. Eberytink,' she wailed, pointing to her groceries scattered all over the footpath. At that they both opened up in broken English and their native tongues gesticulating madly with their hands. Detective Simmiti rolled his eyes and held up his own hands in exasperation.

'Fred,' he said, turning to the other detective, 'take Les over to the car, get a statement off him and ring the base. I'll try and sort this rattle out here.'

'Righto,' replied Detective Mooney. 'Come on Les.'

They trotted over to the Ford Falcon. Fred climbed in the passenger seat and picked up the receiver. 'I'll just call in and then you can tell us what happened.' Norton grunted something and nodded his head.

'Twenty-nine-twenty-one. Over.'

'Twenty-nine-twenty-one. Go ahead' came the crackling, abrupt voice over the VKG.

'We have a signal one. Shots fired at ...' Detective Mooney had a quick look at the flats opposite the car, then back at the shop. '332 Bronte Road. A small grocer's shop. Over.'

'Acknowledge 29-21. Over.'

'No one has been hurt. We have three witnesses. We will be at the station in ten minutes. Over and out.'

'Twenty-nine-twenty-one. Over and out.'

Detective Mooney replaced the receiver and climbed back out of the car. 'Right. Now, what happened back there Les?' he asked taking a note pad and biro from his coat's inside pocket.

Norton took a deep breath and paused for a moment or two before he replied. Although extremely angry, he was still visibly shaken at suddenly being almost killed for absolutely nothing. He told Detective Mooney everything he could concluding with him getting a quick glance at the kid as he escaped along Bronte Road.

'And you honestly couldn't describe him? Even though you were only a few metres away?' Detective Mooney sounded a little sceptical as he looked up from his note pad. He was thinking Norton might be telling a bit of a lie there, and preparing to go looking for the kid himself for a personal square-up.

However, try as he might, Norton couldn't recollect the kid's features; the shock of almost being killed had made his mind a blank for those few moments.

'Fair dinkum, Fred I... I just can't remember. I can remember the gun and what he was wearing, and that he had something wrong with one of his ears. But...that's it. Honest.'

50

'Mm...all right,' replied Detective Mooney, closing his note pad. 'That's understandable, I suppose. But you'll have to come back to the station and make a statement.'

'Oh, fair dinkum. Do I have to?' protested Norton. 'I hate goin' in there.'

'Yeah, you'll have to Les. We've got to find this cunt. We can't have some ratbag running around firing guns at people. Anyway it'll only take a few minutes. Come on, let's go and see how Len's getting on.'

When they got back to Detective Simmiti he just about had everything under control except the old lady who turned out to be Yugoslavian — Mrs Kolodzeij. As soon as she spotted Norton's big, red head she erupted again.

'This man! This man,' she shrieked. 'He is the one. I'm doesn't doing anything but walking along footpath and he attacking me. Bastard.' She raised herself up to a full, dumpy metre and a half, and thumped Norton in the stomach.

Norton tensed then glared down at the fuming old lady. 'Listen, you stupid old bag,' he hissed. 'I didn't lay a friggin' hand on you. It was that bloody kid.' But as he cursed at the old Yugoslavian lady, he realised that if it hadn't been for her broken eggs he'd probably be lying down next to them dead on the footpath. 'Look, you horrible old shit,' he said, taking some money out of his back pocket. 'Here's twenty bucks for your rotten bloody groceries. Now leave me alone will you, for Christ's sake.'

The old lady snatched the twenty out of Les's hand. The two detectives had a quick confab.

'We'll get nothing out of the old girl,' said Detective Simmiti, 'so we'll let her go. I'll take Mr Malouf back to the station in the car. How about you walk up with Les and I'll see you back there in about ten minutes?'

'Righto' replied Detective Mooney. As he spoke a paddy-wagon pulled up alongside and a young, worried-looking constable climbed out.

'Everything all right here?' he asked.

'Yeah, sweet,' replied Detective Simmiti. 'We're all going back to the station now. Mr Malouf — would you mind coming with me please?'

The old shopkeeper yelled something in Lebanese to his equally old wife standing nervously in the doorway tugging at her apron, then followed Detective Simmiti up to the Ford Falcon with the young constable. The old Yugoslavian lady had by this time retrieved what she could of her groceries and being more than appeased at Norton's twenty dollars had left the scene of the crime, completely oblivious to the fact that one man, possibly two, had almost been killed next to her.

'Come on Les. You right?' Detective Mooney gave Les a pat on the shoulder and they started walking towards Waverley police station barely a few hundred metres away.

'Jesus they're gettin fuckin' game these days,' said Detective Mooney, shaking his head. 'Fancy holding up the joint almost next door. Fuckin' smack freaks.' He spat contemptuously into the gutter. 'Next thing they'll be holding up the bloody station.'

'I reckon if they got into your and Simmo's lockers they'd get plenty,' replied Norton sarcastically.

Fred turned to Norton and winked. 'Just think Les,' he smiled. 'My first day in the D's and it was almost your last day in Bondi.' He laughed out loud at the filthy look Norton gave him then gave him another slap on the back. They walked the remaining fifty metres in silence except for Fred chuckling to himself every now and again.

There was the usual throng of police, lawyers and defendants milling around out the front of Waverley court; all in small separate groups talking quietly and earnestly trying to take advantage of the few warm rays of sunshine which occasionally broke through the cloud-thick July sky and reflected off the courthouse walls, offering some relief from the bitter sou'-wester whipping the papers and dust along Bronte Road. Fred nodded briefly to a couple of people he recognised. Mooney and Norton stepped past the neatly landscaped entrance and through the shiny plate-glass doors that make Waverley police station one of the nicer looking stations in Sydney.

'Jesus, that bloody wind's freezing, isn't it?' said Detective Mooney giving his hands a quick rub as they walked past the large, modern reception desk to the concrete stairs leading up to the detectives' rooms.

'Up this way mate.' Fred turned round and smiled at Norton. 'Though I think you know your way around here by now, don't you Les?'

'I hope your lousy, walloper's coffee's improved since last time I was here,' replied Norton flatly. Detective Mooney returned the remark with a grin and a wink.

In the course of his duties at the Kelly Club and knocking around the Eastern suburbs, Norton had, on more than one occasion, been up on various assault charges. They had all been fairly smartly dropped due to the influence and wealth of one Price Galese. As they climbed the stairs Norton recognised two senior detectives. They weren't exactly on Price's payroll, but Norton knew they were getting the odd 'drink' now and again. As they drew level the first one stopped.

'Hello Les,' he said quietly. He had a quick glance at Detective Mooney and his face turned serious. 'Are you in any sort of trouble?'

'No,' replied Norton with a quick shake of his head. 'Everything's sweet.'

'Okay. But if you need us, we're just out the back.' The hard-faced detective nodded his head at the top of the stairs. 'All right?'

'Yeah righto. Thanks anyway.'

'You know everyone, don't you Les?' said Detective Mooney, as they got to the top of the stairs.

'We've got a saying in Queensland Moon,' replied Norton. 'Strangers are only friends you've never met. Even with coppers.'

Fred gave Norton a condescending smile and led him along a well-lit but drafty corridor to a room running off to the left. 'In here mate,' he said, stopping to let Norton enter. 'Grab a seat, I'll be back in a minute.'

Norton plonked himself down on a padded, vinyl seat facing a large pine-veneer desk with a bulky looking, manual typewriter sitting on it, and glanced around the fairly spartan room. A single, uncovered window let the daylight in on several chipped, grey metal filing cabinets pushed up against two of the walls; most of which were covered in dog-eared 'wanted' and 'missing persons' posters. One wall had markings painted on it for measuring height. In front of it stood a spindly, metal tripod with a flash camera on top. A single pot plant and a couple of waste-paper baskets sat on the blue carpeted floor, and that was about it. Before long Detective Mooney returned with several voluminous files of mug shots. He dumped these on the desk in front of Norton then eased himself into the swivel chair in front of the typewriter and fed a sheet of paper into it.

'Righto Les,' he said, loosening his tie and taking out his note pad. 'Have a look through those and see if you can spot your junkie mate, while I type this up.'

As Detective Mooney thumped away at the typewriter Norton started leafing idly through the pages of black and white photos. After he'd gone through the first folder he hadn't come across anyone who resembled the kid who tried to shoot him, but he had noticed, apart from them all being a rather villainous looking lot, that several faces were quite familiar. Every now and again Detective Mooney would look up from his typing to see Norton chuckling softly and talking light-heartedly to himself.

'Jesus, Porky Fletcher. What's he done? Car stealing and assault. Hah! Hello. Here's Davo Hakes. Shit, I never knew he'd been in the nick. Ronnie Gordon? What's he done? Assault, resisting arrest, and malicious wounding. Christ — Garfish Gordon? You wouldn't think he'd break an egg. Hello, here's one; Freddie fuckin'-Legs. Fraud, uttering, conspiracy, conspiracy to import cocaine. Yeah that'd be Fred all right. Wouldn't work in an iron lung.'

'Recognise a few friends, do you Les?' smiled Detective Mooney.

'Yeah, they're all here. It's like a regular who's-who of the Kelly Club and down the beach. How come I'm not in here?'

'Because you're an honest man Les. Plus you've got a guardian angel who drives a Rolls Royce and owns about five million dollars worth of racehorses as well as half of Sydney, and it's very hard to make anything stick to you.'

'Ah, I'm just a good bloke. Why don't you admit it you cunt? Anyway I haven't come across the kid yet.'

'Yeah. Well just keep looking. I should have this finished soon.'

'Hey how come it's taking you so long Moon?'

'Quadruplicate Les. Everything has to be in fours.'

'Yeah?'

'Yep. Everything. Even when we have a shit it has to be done four turds at a time.' Detective Mooney laughed at his own joke and continued typing. Norton went through the rest of the mug shots, finishing the last book about the same time as Fred stopped typing.

'Well, he ain't in none of these,' said Norton, closing the last file.

'Can't see him?'

'No.'

'Mm. Oh well, he might be from interstate. He might even be a clean-skin. Anyway, here's this statement. Have a read. You don't have to sign it if you don't want to.'

Norton took the statement and gave it a quick but thorough read. 'Yeah, that looks all right Moon. Give us a biro. I may as well sign the bloody thing — save you having to get up in court and verbal me anyway.'

54

Detective Mooney handed Les a pen. As he did, Detective Simmiti walked into the room, a slightly bemused look on his usually impassive face.

'How did you go Fred? Get a description?' he asked.

'No. No luck at all,' replied Detective Mooney, retrieving the signed statement from Norton.'

'I did all right. I got several to tell you the truth.'

'Yeah?'

'Yeah. The grocer-shop owner was most helpful. According to Mr Malouf, the suspect is somewhere between one and two metres with either long, blonde or short, dark hair, slightly built but then again he could have been a footballer. He's not sure whether he was wearing a red, roll-neck pullover or a dark blue suit, but he had a definite foreign accent. Chinese, possibly Irish or Scots.'

The two detectives shook their heads as Norton started to laugh. 'So this is life in the D's, eh Fred? You can stick it in your arse for mine.'

'Now you've got an idea of what we've got to go through. It's not quite Hawaii Five-0, is it?' Detective Mooney looked up at Detective Simmiti. 'We may as well let Les go Len.' Detective Simmiti nodded his head in agreement. In an instant Norton was on his feet heading for the door.

'All right then, I'll get crackin'. Sorry I couldn't have been more help.'

'Ah, that's okay,' sighed Dectective Mooney. 'Just one thing before you go though Les.'

Norton paused at the door. 'Yeah what?'

'If you do happen to spot this young prick, don't do anything silly. Come and get us — all right?'

Norton looked from one detective to the other. 'Sure,' he replied, with a shrug of his huge shoulders. 'That's what you're getting paid for, isn't it? And admirably, too, I might add.' He gave them a last wink. 'See youse,' he added, and disappeared down the corridor.

Don't do anything silly eh? he said to himself, as he stood outside the police station and zipped up his jacket against the bitter sou'-wester still whipping along Bronte Road. *No I won't do anything silly if I find that junkie. I'll just throw him in the boot of my car, drive him out to Frenchs Forest and break both his arms and legs, then bury him — alive.* He took a glance at his watch. *Look at the bloody time: twelve o'clock. There goes the eleven o'clock movie — and my feed at the Greeks.* With one last look at Waverley police station he turned the collar up on his jacket, jammed his hands in the pockets and proceeded along Bronte Road towards Bondi Junction, his original destination.

He was lost in all sorts of confused thoughts as he strode morosely along the windy street. On one hand he was absolutely ropeable to think that some little creep had almost killed him and looked like getting away with it. On the other hand he was grateful that he was alive. He looked up at the banks of grey clouds scudding across the sky and although he wasn't a fully religious man winked a quick thanks to whoever was out there looking after him.

The little grocer's shop was closed when he reached it, but he noticed a few pieces of eggshell and dried yolk were still stuck to the footpath out the front. He stopped for a moment and idly kicked at it with the toe of his sneaker. *Jesus, that was close,* he said to himself, as a few butterflies gave a quick flutter in the pit of his stomach. *I know what I am gonna do though. I'm gonna have a couple of beers when I get to the Junction and possibly a nice double brandy.* He proceeded to the Tea-Gardens hotel in Bronte Road.

Outside the pub he stopped and changed his mind about going in. There were a couple of half-pie mates of Billy Dunne's — thieves — whom he didn't particularly go much on sitting just inside the door, and he knew if he went in he'd probably have to talk to them. *No I won't go in there. I'll duck over to Billy the Pig's and barbecue myself a nice slice of rump. Besides, they don't have a bad drop of Toohey's New in the public bar and I know one of the barmaids. I can have a bit of a mag to her.* He turned and started walking towards Grace Bros.

Just outside the main entrance he noticed a police paddy-wagon parked up on the footpath. The sight of it suddenly jogged his memory. *Oh shit,* he groaned, stopping to slap his back pocket again. *I still haven't paid those friggin' parking fines.* He stood there for a moment and heaved a great sigh of exasperation. *Christ, I just left the bloody police station too. Bugger it!* As he started walking again he could see two uniformed policemen escorting a young girl out of the side entrance to Grace Bros. next to the travel-agency. She was young, with blonde hair, stockily built, wearing jeans and a leather jacket not unlike Les's, only brown. A thick, red woollen scarf was wrapped round her neck, and slung over her shoulder was a large leather bag, the same colour as her jacket. *Hello,* thought Norton, *looks like Grace Bros. has caught another hoister.* As he drew closer to the young girl, dwarfed between the two policemen, he got a good look at her face and, although she was wearing a bit of a defiant smirk, he recognised the small nose, china-blue eyes and freckles. It was Margaret, the seventeen-year-old daughter of one of the croupiers at the Kelly Club — Bob McKenna. Norton was only a few metres away as the big sergeant, a grizzled old cop in his fifties, started to unlock the back of the cage.

'Hey Margo,' he called out. 'What's happening?'

Margaret looked up, a little embarrassed, to see who was calling her name: when she saw it was Norton her eyes immediately lit up.

'Oh Les,' she cried. 'Les, can you do us a favour? I'm in trouble. Can you come up and bail me out? Me old man'll kill if he finds out.'

The two cops ignored Les. He watched the younger one help her up into the cage. 'Yeah righto Margo,' said Norton. 'I'll sort it out. Don't worry.'

'Thanks Les,' was the muffled reply as the old sergeant closed the door on her and locked it. He handed the keys to the young constable who walked up to the driver's seat. Norton followed the slower moving sergeant round to the other side.

'Hey sarge,' he said as politely as he could, 'what's the young girl done?'

The old sergeant half turned to Norton stoney-faced, almost ignoring him. He looked at Norton for a moment before opening the door. 'She got caught shoplifting. We're taking her up to Waverley to book her.'

'All right if I come up and bail her out?'

'You can do what you like when we're finished booking her.' With an audible grunt and a great effort the old, grizzle faced sergeant heaved himself up into the front of the paddy-wagon.

'You couldn't give us a lift up there could you?' asked Les.

The sergeant closed the door and glared down at Norton. 'What do you think this is — a bloody taxi?'

'No,' replied Les, 'but I've just bloody walked down from up there.'

The old sergeant turned and ignored Norton muttering something like 'piss-off you prick,' under his breath. Norton was about to turn away when the young constable — an up-and-coming footballer with Easts — recognised Norton from his days with the club.

'Hey,' he called out, with a bit of a smile, 'are you Les Norton?'

'Yeah.'

'Did you nearly get shot in a hold-up this morning?'

'Yeah. Just down from the station.'

'I thought it was you. We've been out looking for the kid. They still haven't found him.' Norton nodded his head as the young constable turned to the sergeant. 'I know this bloke sarge. He's all right. You want to give him a lift up?'

The old sergeant looked at Norton and at the young constable. He took off his hat and placed it above the dashboard. 'Yeah, all right,' he mumbled reluctantly and opened the door.

'Good on you fellas — thanks a lot.' Norton climbed up next to the old sergeant and closed the door after him.

The young constable driving put his hat on the dash also, backed the paddy-wagon a little further onto the footpath, did a half U-turn, then headed up Oxford Street to turn left into Bronte Road. Sitting in the front of the wagon, Norton could see why the old sergeant was reluctant to let him in; he made Jackie Gleason look like he'd just got out of Changi. Every time they turned in the traffic he almost crushed Les to death up against the door. When he wasn't getting squashed Norton started up a bit of conversation mainly about the shooting earlier, thinking that if he sweetened things up with the sergeant he might go a bit easy on Margo's bail. The old sergeant, like most New South Wales cops when they get to know you, dropped the horrible mask they're forced to wear in public and started to warm up a bit to Norton, thinking it was quite funny him nearly getting shot and Detective Simmiti's story back at the station about the description of the suspect Mr Malouf the grocer had given them.

'They're not very nice things those guns, are they? Especially when they're being fired at you,' said the old sergeant, as a great surge of laughter rumbled up from his huge stomach and rippled through the mass of double-chins under his face.

'You can say that again,' replied Norton earnestly. 'I bloody near shit myself I can tell you.'

The old sergeant started laughing again. 'Even the thought of it upsets my stomach,' he rumbled, giving his vast expanse of stomach a pat. 'Oh shit,' he chuckled, 'now you've done it.'

The old sergeant broke wind in the loudest, most reprehensible manner Norton had ever heard. It sounded like somebody ripping a double-bed sheet in half.

'Oh, not a-fuckin'-gain,' groaned the young constable, as he hurried to wind down his window. 'Jesus, you stink, you rotten fat bludger.'

'Hey, don't talk to your superior officer like that,' chortled the sergeant, but he was laughing so much he had to wheeze the words out. Then, right on top of Norton's empty stomach, the obnoxious odour of the old sergeant's previous night's schooners and curried lamb chops, hit Les in the face like a punch, making him gag and frantically wind down the window in a panic.

'Oh Jesus, that's off,' he spluttered, quickly shoving his head out into the cold air. 'What have you been eatin'? Tinned rat?'

'Get out,' laughed the old sergeant. 'It's not that bad.'

'Not bad?' protested Norton. 'You're kiddin'. It'd scorch the husk of a coconut.'

'You're not wrong,' said the young constable, his whitened face still stuck outside the window.

'Christ, why didn't I walk? Open the back door I'll get inside with the girl.'

The old sergeant chuckled to himself thinking it was a great joke, broke wind again and laughed like a drain all the way to the station.

'I've been framed Les. Fair dinkum,' said Margo, a bit of a smirk on her face as the two, now serious, policemen took her out of the back of the paddy-wagon.

'Margo, shut up,' said Norton, holding his hands out in front of him. 'Just go in with the police, get your fingerprints taken, and when they're finished with you I'll be waiting at the desk.'

'Fingerprints?' Margo's jaw dropped and the smirk disappeared from her face.

Norton nodded. 'Yeah, that's right Margo, fingerprints. This isn't a game you know.'

Margo was dumbfounded and blinking as they led her into the station and out the back to the cells to be processed. She emerged about twenty-five minutes later still trying to wipe the ink off her fingers and looking like she'd just swallowed cyanide.

'Jesus Les,' she said walking up to Norton waiting for her at the counter. 'They photographed me and everything, like I was some sort of criminal.'

'Well what do you think you are?' replied Norton. 'Shoplifting's not a game Margo. It's thieving.'

'Yeah, but it was only a lousy pair of jeans. I mean that's not a real crime — is it?'

'It is if you get caught Margo.'

The old sergeant who'd driven them up to the station read Margo her bail conditions but there was no laughing and joking now. Margo signed the blue transcripts binding her over to appear at Waverley court in a fortnight and Norton paid the bail — $150. Margo nervously put the receipt in her purse. Les thanked the old sergeant and they went outside.

Margo was still ashen-faced as they stood outside the courthouse trying to find a bit of shelter from the biting sou'-wester. 'Jesus what do you think will happen now Les?' she asked.

'Well, you'll front court when it says, then it's up to the beak,' replied Norton. 'Is it your first offence?'

'Yeah.'

'Well you won't go to jail but you'll probably get a fine and a bond. Being your first time up you could get off on a 556A but you'll still have a record of it against you.'

'Mm.' Margo stared at the ground for a moment. 'Do you reckon I might be able to talk the judge out of it Les? I could tell him I had the flu and I'd been taking antihistamines and I didn't know what I was doing. I know what,' Margo's eyes lit up, 'I'll tell him I had PMT and I was all upset and I was on my menstrual cycle. That oughta work.'

Norton shook his head and gave Margo a tired smile. 'Margo the beak won't care if you were on a Yamaha 250. They've heard it all before. You're just gonna have to take your lumps and cop it sweet. But just make sure when you front you take a good lawyer.'

The smile faded from Margo's face. 'Do you know a good one Les?'

'Yeah my bloke. Graham Cameron just up in Charing Cross. He's about the best there is. Ring him up and tell him you know me. He'll look after you.'

'I'll do that. Thanks Les.'

'That's all right.' Norton paused for a moment and looked at Bob McKenna's usually cheeky young daughter: standing in the cold with all the cheek taken out of her he couldn't but feel a little sorry. 'Margo, I got to get going mate. I'd give you a lift home but my car's in the garage. Have you got enough for a cab?'

'Yeah I'm right thanks Les. It's only just down Bronte.'

'Okay. Well I'll get goin' mate. Are you sure you're all right now?'

'Yeah. Thanks for everything Les.' She reached up and gave Norton a kiss on the cheek. 'Just don't say nothin' to dad, will you?'

'No Margo. Not a word.'

'Okay, I'll see you later Les. Thanks again.'

'That's all right. See you Margo.'

Norton watched her walk towards Charing Cross, then with a slow shake of his head turned and started back towards Bondi Junction for the third time that day. *Jesus, have a go at the time* he said to himself as he took a look at his watch. *Quarter past bloody one — and I still ain't had nothing to eat.*

Norton's stomach was growling like a pack of pine-wolves as he strode along Bronte Road past the still-closed grocer's shop. As he crossed Birrel Street the bitter sou'-wester whipping up the hill felt like it was going to go straight through him. The cold was making him hungrier adding to his increasing disgruntlement.

Christ, hasn't it been a lovely day, he thought. *I've almost been killed, I've had nothing to eat, I'm half frozen and now, thanks to Margo and that old reffo sheila I'm 200 dollars lighter. Plus Chicka's going to relieve me of another 250 and another 80 dollars for those parking fines.*

'Oh shit,' he groaned out loud as he stopped abruptly and slapped the back pocket of his jeans again. *I still haven't paid those bloody things and I've been past the cop-shop three bloody times. Right, well that's it.*

He punched his open hand, turned on his heel and headed back towards Waverley police station, grimly determined *I'm gonna pay these bastards of things once and for all before they drive me fuckin' mad.*

Norton's face was a mixture of hunger, cold and sheer annoyance, gritting his teeth and retracing his steps along Bronte Road. The fines, even apart from having to fork over the eighty dollars, were now getting to be a pain in the arse: this time he was going to get them out of the road once and for all and nothing was going to stop him.

He'd almost broken into a jog as he approached an old, badly neglected block of flats just past Mr Malouf's still-closed grocer's shop. Suddenly he slowed down. There was something oddly familiar about a figure, the hands stuffed in the pockets of an old, grey, op-shop gaberdine overcoat, walking towards him. Something — but what? It was like just waking up from an extremely vivid dream and, for the hell of it, you can't remember what you've just been dreaming about. As the youth drew near Norton had a peg out of the side of his eye. The youth had his head bowed slightly staring straight ahead at the footpath and although he had the collar of the old overcoat turned up against the cold, the side closest to Les had fallen down — and that's when the alarm bells started clanging inside Norton's head. He only got a quick glimpse as they passed but he was certain half the youth's ear was missing and he could have sworn he saw the twinkle from a gold earring.

With the butterflies just starting to take off in his stomach Norton slowed right down as the youth went by, then slowly turned round to see him disappear into the old block of flats they'd just passed.

Norton waited for a moment, a hotbed of emotions, uncertain what to do. Almost positive that he had found the kid who tried to kill him he wanted to race straight up, grab him and sort it out his own way — fuck waiting for the cops. He stared at the run-down block of flats for a moment then ran inside, stopping quietly in the foyer.

It was quite cloudy outside so he had no trouble adjusting to the light. There appeared to be four flats on each floor, with a threadbare brown carpet running up to a flight of stairs flanked by a row of wooden bannisters. The varnish was chipped and fading on those that weren't missing. With the tempo of his heart increasing as he nervously stood in the quiet, dim light, he could still hear the youth walking up the stairs. He quickly and silently ran over and climbed halfway up the first flight. From the sound of the youth's footsteps it seemed like he'd only gone as far as the first floor. Crouching low, Norton climbed to the top of the stairs just in time to see the figure in the gaberdine overcoat disappear into one of the flats furthest from the stairs. He stepped up onto the landing where a quick check of the numbers around him told him it was number eight. He didn't bother walking any farther but carefully retraced his steps, almost knocking over a sickly looking potted palm sitting in a cheap plastic pot and barely visible in the dim light at the top of the stairs. Outside in the street he stood looking up at the block of flats trying to figure out the junkie's way of thinking, and what would be the best thing to do.

It was fairly obvious why the junkie had held up the shop next to where he lived and barely a stone's throw from the police station. To his heroin-crazed way of thinking he'd probably figured the last place the cops would look would be next door, and he was half-right. The police were scattered all over the Eastern suburbs looking for him — anywhere but a couple of hundred metres down from the station. But what should Norton do? Get Eddie Salita and take the kid out? He liked the idea of revenge. Wait till the kid came outside and do it himself? That sounded all right but he had no bloody car. Or should he just leave it to the cops? While he was standing in the chilly wind, deep in thought, he didn't immediately notice the light blue Ford Falcon coming along the opposite side of the road.

'Hey, isn't that your mate Les over there?' said Detective Simmiti, slowing down.

'Yeah. Yeah it is,' replied Fred. 'I wonder what he's doing back up here? Pull up and I'll find out what's going on.'

As they drew into the kerb Norton spotted them and came running over.

'What are you doing?' asked Detective Mooney as he wound down the window.

'I think I just saw that kid from this morning,' replied Les. 'Let us in the back out of this wind, and I'll tell you what's going on.'

Inside the car Norton told the two detectives how he came to be up there and how he just happened to come across the kid.

'Are you sure it's him though?' said Detective Simmiti.

'Well I think it is,' replied Les. 'I couldn't be certain, but there's just something tells me it's him.'

'Something tells you it's him, eh?' said Detective Mooney, a sceptical smile on his face. 'You couldn't give us any description at all earlier. Now you reckon it's him.' He turned to his partner. 'What do you reckon Len?'

Detective Simmiti shrugged his shoulders and screwed his face up a little. 'I dunno. It just seems funny some bloke'd rob the place next door to where he lives and less that 500 metres from a police station. I mean even the most desperate junkies aren't that stupid.'

'That's probably why the little prick thought he'd get away with it,' said Norton.

'Mm.' Detective Simmiti began to sound more sceptical than his partner.

'It does seem a bit unlikely Les,' said Detective Mooney. 'If you ask me, the bloke that tried to shoot you is probably half way to Brisbane by now.'

'Well you might be right Moon. But I still reckon that's him up there in number eight,' said Les.

Detective Mooney looked at his partner for a moment. 'What do you reckon Len? We go and have a look just in case?'

Detective Simmiti glanced over at the old block of flats, then back at his partner giving his shoulders a slight shrug. 'I suppose we could go over and have a quick gander — it'll only take us five minutes. I still reckon it's a waste of time though.'

'Righto, we'll go and have a look,' said Detective Mooney. 'I'll just radio the base.'

'Are you gonna get some back-ups?' asked Norton.

'What? For one skinny junkie?' winked Detective Mooney. 'We can't anyway. Some other team's just held up the State Bank at Clovelly and a teller got shot in the hand. Every available car's over there. We were just going over ourselves when we saw you — and, of course, you get top priority Les.' Detective Mooney radioed in, then they all got out of the car and slowly crossed the street to the block of flats.

'You want to take the front or the back?' Detective Mooney asked his partner.

'I don't care,' replied Detective Simmiti. 'But I may as well go round the back just in case it is him and he tries to make a bolt for it.'

'Righto. Let's get it over with then.'

'What do you want me to do?' asked Norton.

'Nothing,' said Detective Simmiti. 'Just stay down the front. I know you're willing and all that Les but this is our department, okay?'

'Fair enough,' shrugged Norton.

While Norton stood in the dusty gloom of the foyer, Detective Mooney began to climb the stairs, his footsteps scarcely making a sound on the frayed carpet. Detective Simmiti went round the back to cover the fire-escape.

Jesus, I just hope nothing goes wrong, thought Norton, as he nervously moved in from the foyer a little closer to the stairs. He gazed up through the bannisters towards the sound of Detective Mooney's footsteps creaking softly across the landing above his head. *There's something about this I just don't like.* He stood grim-faced, apprehensively opening and closing his hands. The hairs on his neck bristled slightly as he heard Fred's staccato knock on the door. There appeared to be no answer. About ten or fifteen seconds later Detective Mooney knocked again — a little louder this time.

'Open the door! Police here.'

There was still no answer, and, in the electrifying silence,

Norton swore he could hear the steady beating of his heart and the ticking of his wristwatch.

Norton was about to call out to Detective Mooney when suddenly, like a thunderclap, the gloomy silence was shattered by two muffled explosions followed by a horrifying scream and the sound of someone falling.

'Shit!'

Norton grabbed the bottom bannister and flung himself up the stairs, his adrenalin racing. The sound of the two shots, apparently coming from inside the flat, still seemed to echo throughout the old building.

When he reached the top of the stairs Norton propped. Detective Mooney was slumped against the wall, coughing and gagging hideously, clawing at his chest in shocked disbelief. Unexpectedly the door of number eight opened and, like he was watching a slow-motion movie again, Norton saw the kid in the khaki army jacket step out holding a still-smoking revolver in his hand — the same huge gun that had almost claimed Norton's life earlier. The junkie raised the gun slowly. Norton could distinctly see him smile sardonically and hear the click, as the junkie thumbed back the hammer. Holding the gun with both hands, he placed the muzzle about five centimetres away from Detective Mooney's forehead.

'Oh Jesus don't kid,' pleaded Detective Mooney. But he could hardly get the words out. He coughed with agony and jammed his eyes shut ready for the bullet that was going to blast him into eternity and his brains all over the place.

Just then Norton roared out at the top of his voice. 'HEY!' Wild-eyed the junkie spun round. Norton picked up the flower pot on the landing near his feet and flung it at the smack-freak's head. He instinctively ducked and it smashed into the wall behind him in a shower of stringy brown leaves and clammy soil. He let out a curse and fired a quick shot off in Norton's direction which hummed past Norton's face and slammed into the wall sending plaster and mortar everywhere and ricochetting down the stairs with an angry whine.

Norton flung himself on the stairs as another deafening explosion sent part of the staircase above him erupting around his head in a blur of ripped-up carpet and great splinters of wood. *Christ almighty*, he thought, *what's this kid got up there? The Hyde Park bloody cannon?* Then there was silence, quickly followed by a flurry of footsteps as the junkie ran back inside the flat and slammed the door behind him. Norton waited a few seconds then picked himself up and in a half crouch moved cautiously across the landing towards Detective Mooney still lying crumpled up with pain against the wall. Above him, the sweet, blue gunpowder smoke swirled around the corridor, caught in the dim light from a small, dirt-caked window over their heads.

'Moon? You okay?' whispered Norton.

'Oh ... Jesus Les. I don't know,' was Fred's painful, strangled reply. Detective Mooney's face was ashen. He feebly clutched at his chest, the blood bubbling up through his fingers. Although the first shot had missed him, the second had torn through his chest, shattering his shoulder blade and ricochetting off the wall into the back of his thigh.

Norton looked down with both sorrow and anger at his old football mate, and placed Fred's hands a little more firmly on the hole in his chest. 'Hang on Moon,' he said, as softly as he could. 'You're gonna be all right mate.' Then blinding rage overtook Norton.

He stood up and, with one tremendous kick, smashed the door in determined to get his hands on the callous, gun-crazy animal inside. As the door burst off its hinges he heard a voice call out, then one loud explosion followed by two smaller ones and a short, gasping scream.

Detective Simmiti was standing in the courtyard at the rear of the flats trying to figure out which fire-escape was connected to which flat. He wasn't taking it all too seriously, still convinced Norton was imagining things, even having a slight chuckle to himself as the thought of Mr Malouf's description of the youth crossed his mind. Nevertheless, he gave his service revolver, sitting snugly in its holster at his waist, a quick check.

He was glancing up at the fire-escapes rusty iron steps littered with garbage tins and flower boxes when the sound of two gunshots sent every nerve in his body jangling. 'Jesus Christ!' he said out aloud, whipping the .38 out of its holster and thumbing off the 'safety'. He had run towards the stairs leading up to where he thought number eight was, and started to climb them when he heard the sound of a door crash open and a garbage tin going over. He stepped back for a better view and saw the youth in the khaki jacket standing on the landing about ten metres above him. In his hand was the unmistakable shape of a gun.

Detective Simmiti dropped to a half crouch and centred his own weapon on the youth's chest. 'Police here!' he shouted. 'Drop your weapon!'

The crazed junkie glared down defiantly then fired a shot

66

which hummed over Detective Simmiti's head and smashed into the concrete yard behind him. The junkie was about to pull the trigger again when the detective fired two quick shots. The first bullet tore through the side of the junkie's neck, the second slammed into the middle of his chest, angled off bone and tore into his heart. He had time to let out a strangled scream, then crashed down among the pot plants and garbage tins. He was dead before he hit the landing.

Norton burst through the doorway and stood momentarily in the gloom of the dingy flat. The light steered him towards the open kitchen door. He got to the landing just in time to see the junkie's nerves give a last twitch. One look at the dark red, almost black, blood bubbling out from deep inside him told Les it was all over. Below him he could see Detective Simmiti with the smoking revolver still aimed up in his direction. 'Don't shoot Len, it's me—Les.'

Detective Simmiti lowered his gun and came running up the stairs. He took one, quick, pitiless look at the dead junkie then back at Les.

'Fred's been shot,' said Norton. 'He's out in the hallway.'

Detective Simmiti let out an oath, gritted his teeth and followed Norton through the dimly lit flat to where Detective Mooney was propped up against the wall. His eyes were clenched tightly and the grimaces of pain spread across his face every time he tried to breathe. Strangely enough, despite all the noise and the gunshots no one had come out of any of the other flats to investigate.

At the sound of footsteps Detective Mooney looked up. 'Sorry ... Len,' he said apologetically, almost in a whisper. 'I should have been ... more careful.'

'Don't try to talk Fred,' replied Detective Simmiti, kneeling by his side and placing his hand softly on his good shoulder. 'You're going to be all right mate. I promise you.'

'It's not his fault,' said Norton. 'He never had a chance. The rotten little cunt fired straight through the door.'

Norton gave Detective Simmiti a brief rundown on what had happened, at the same time removing Detective Mooney's hand from the hole in his chest and replacing it with his own. Fred winced as Norton was forced to increase the pressure to stem the flow of blood.

'Len, you'd better get the paramedics as quick as you can. I'll keep an eye on Fred.'

'Good on you Les.' Detective Simmiti rose to his feet and stared down grimly at Detective Mooney. 'You're going to be all right Fred,' he repeated. 'I promise you.' Then he turned and sped off down the stairs.

Norton looked at Detective Mooney and noticed the flickering in his eyes. *Christ*, he thought to himself, *he's starting to go into a coma I've got to try and keep him awake.*

'Come on Moon,' he said gruffly, raising his voice. 'Don't start going to sleep on me. I'm holding you together, the least you can do is talk to me, you ignorant prick.'

'Oh Jesus Les,' replied Detective Mooney feebly. 'I don't ... feel real ... good.'

'Yeah? Well if you don't feel real good, there's a bloke out on the landing ain't feeling anything at all. Not now anyway.' Norton told Detective Mooney what had happened to the gunman, which made Fred feel a tiny bit better.

'Anyway I don't know what you're whingeing about Moon. There's hardly anything wrong with you. The kid only had a little .22 pistol.' He didn't tell Detective Mooney there was an ex-army .44 revolver lying next to the junkie's body out on the landing.

'A .22? Shit. I ... feel like I've been ... hit with an anti-tank rocket.' Detective Mooney gave a couple of coughs and small rivulet of blood appeared in one corner of his mouth. 'I ... think I've been ... hit in the leg ... too Les.'

'Where? Give us a look.' Norton ran his hand up the blood-sodden left leg of Detective Mooney's trousers till he found the hole. Blood was still seeping through and he could feel the torn flesh underneath. 'Well I'll be buggered, you have, too,' he said forcing a laugh. 'I felt the warmth and I thought you'd just pissed yourself. Anyway, give us your hand Moon you can hold this one yourself. I can't do every bloody thing.'

Norton took Fred's hand and placed it over the leg wound, then bent Fred's knee up against his chest and, with the weight of his own body, pinned Fred's hand against the wound, effectively stopping most of the bleeding. With his free hand he undid Detective Mooney's tie and shirt to examine the wound in his chest. It was a dreadful, jagged hole but due to the constant, although painful, pressure from Norton's hand the bleeding had slowed considerably. He took a clean handkerchief from Fred's top pocket, folded it and placed it over the wound.

'I owe you one Les,' said Detective Mooney. 'A big one. You ... know ... that, don't you?'

'What are you going on about now Moon, you fuckin' idiot.'

'You ... saved my life Les. That kid was just about to pull the trigger ... when you threw that flower pot.'

'Ah I dunno. Maybe. But if I did Moon, do us a favour, will you?'

'Sure ... Les. What?'

'Just don't tell anybody. I've hardly got any friends around Bondi as it is now.'

Detective Mooney gave another painful little cough as he tried not to laugh. 'You're all ... tact ... aren't you Les?'

'Yeah yeah. What ever you say Moon.' Norton started to laugh. 'What were you saying earlier, something about your first day in the D's nearly being my last day in Bondi? Well have a look at you now you dope. You didn't even have a chance to get a bribe. Who's going to pick up all your slings now? Simmo I suppose. That's if you make it. You know what I might get them to put on your gravestone Moon? Not a bad bloke Detective Fred Mooney, but that bent he coudn't hang his picture straight on a wall.'

Norton kept up an incessant line of patter — mostly insults about Fred being a shonky copper and his past performances on the football field — while he waited for the ambulance to arrive. Every now and again he'd lightly slap Fred's face if he looked like closing his eyes for any length of time. Then suddenly he stopped talking, screwed up his face and turned an ear towards the open door behind him.

'Hey Moon,' he said curiously. 'Can you hear what I hear?'

Detective Mooney blinked for a second or two then looked at Les. 'Is ... that a ... baby?'

From inside the dead junkie's flat came the unmistakable, gurgling, happy squeals of a baby at play.

'Hold on to this for a sec Moon, while I just see what's going on in there.' Norton took Detective Mooney's hand and place it on the hanky covering the wound in his chest, then got up and entered the flat.

It was dark, dingy and heavily curtained inside. Norton found a light switch on the wall and turned it on. When he did the horrifying sight that unfolded before his eyes sent a shiver up his spine and almost made him sick.

The faint light shining from a fly-specked paper lamp shade hanging from the flaking ceiling revealed a sparsely furnished room with the same sort of threadbare carpet as in the hallway and foyer. A cheap, sliding-glass cabinet covered in empty bottles, magazines and other odds and ends was pushed up against one wall where several faded rock posters compensated for the patches of missing wallpaper. A second-hand stereo and an old black and white TV were against the opposite wall faced by a tattered, cloth lounge, the rips being covered by a dirty, red, cotton batik. It was what was on the lounge that made Norton's skin crawl.

A young woman, no more than twenty, her lank, dark hair pinned loosely behind her head with a rubber-band was sprawled along the lounge; a grimy T-shirt covered her torso and her cheap cotton skirt had risen up over her knees to show she was wearing no underwear. One arm was resting across her breasts the other dangled loosely over the edge of the lounge. A length of thin rubber tube was wrapped round her arm just above the elbow, and a thin rivulet of blood ran towards her fingertips which, even in death, seemed to be groping towards the bent spoon and matchbox lying on the floor.

Just in front of the dead mother, a little baby, its blonde hair as fine as a peach's, wearing a nappy and a 'Life-Be-In-It' singlet was playing and gurgling happily, completely oblivious to the death and degradation around it. It was clapping its tiny hands together. In one hand was the filthy hypodermic syringe, the mother's blood still stained on the needle. The baby laughed and clapped its little hands together again; the spike missed its chubby, pink fingers by a centimetre.

Norton's face paled slightly in horror and apprehension. He let out an oath, reached down and tore the needle from the baby's hand, flinging it against the far wall in disgust. The baby, its tiny face a picture of mystified innocence, looked up at Norton and blinked. Norton reached down again and scooped the baby up in his huge arms.

Norton took another look at the mother sprawled dead on the lounge and looked across at the kitchen where what he imagined was the father lay dead in a pool of blood on the landing. 'Come on mate,' he said softly to the baby. 'Let's get you out of here.'

Detective Mooney had his eyes closed and his head resting back against the wall when Norton sat back down beside him.

'Hey Moon, have a look at this,' he said, replacing Detective Mooney's hand on the blood-soaked hanky with his own. 'I've brought you a present.'

The young detective looked at the baby gurgling contentedly away in Norton's arms and smiled tiredly. 'Jesus ... what've you got ... there Les?'

'It's a baby,' replied Norton. 'What'd you think it was, you goose? A bowl of bloody goldfish?' The smile on his face faded. 'The poor little bugger's an orphan now though.' He told

Detective Mooney about the sickening sight he'd uncovered in the flat.

Detective Mooney closed his eyes and shook his head slowly. 'Good stuff ... that ... heroin. Isn't it, Les?'

'Yeah. Just great,' replied the big redheaded Queenslander, spitting contemptuously through the open door of the flat.

They made quite an unusual sight, Norton with a baby in one arm and blood all over both of them when Detective Simmiti came thundering up the stairs followed by the two paramedics, another detective and two concerned young policewomen.

The paramedics gave Detective Mooney a quick 100 milligrams of pethidine, applied two pressure bandages, stuck an IV infusion in his arm then eased him on to a stretcher. Norton handed the baby to one of the policewomen making them both go a bit clucky. Their cluckiness soon disappeared when Norton showed them the scene in the lounge-room.

'Les,' said Detective Simmiti, 'this is Detective Ray Mattes from Waverley.' Norton nodded to a tall, grim young cop, dressed pretty casually like himself. 'Will you give him a statement while I ride up to the hospital with Fred? I'll see you back at the station in about half an hour.'

'Yeah righto,' replied Norton. Two more uniformed cops came running up the stairs to give the paramedics a hand followed by the forensic team with their aluminium cases and cameras. 'You reckon we can get this over with pretty smartly Ray?' he said as he followed the rangy detective back into flat. 'I'd like to get to the shithouse out of here.'

'Yeah sure Les,' replied Detective Mattes. 'I understand.'

The tall, young detective produced a small notebook and began taking down Norton's version of what happened in the hallway; how he arrived on the landing just as Detective Simmiti shot the youth and how he'd found the baby and the dead mother. Norton watched the two young policewomen change the baby's dirty nappy with a packet of clean disposable nappies they'd found in one of the bedrooms; it was then that the him turned out to be a her.

'What happens to her now?' Les asked one of the policewomen as she searched the flat for something that would identify the two bodies.

'She'll be processed and if no relatives of the deceased come forward to claim her, she'll become a ward of the state.'

'Processed, eh? Just like a couple of kilos of sausages.'

'It sounds worse than it is Les, I know,' replied the young policewoman. 'But she'll be all right.'

'I sure hope so.' Norton looked softly at the tiny infant now sound asleep in the other policewoman's arms and gently squeezed one of its tiny pink fingers. 'She's a pretty little thing.'

They stood looking at the baby while Detective Mattes went over Norton's statement. The two morgue attendants in their white uniforms arrived with their stretchers and bodybags. One was eating an apple, the other a mandarin. They looked as though they'd just arrived at a friend's place for a few drinks.

'Two stiffs to take away — is that right?' said the fair-haired one eating the apple dumping a body bag next to the dead girl on the lounge. 'Will there be any french fries with that?' he added, looking around the room.

By now Norton's sense of humour had vanished, along with his appetite — he looked at the morgue attendant in disgust. 'We gonna be much longer?' he said, turning to Detective Mattes.

'No. That should do it. But we're going to have to go back to the station and type it up. That shouldn't take long though.' Norton nodded his head uninterestedly. 'Okay Les,' said Detective Mattes, pocketing his notebook. 'Let's get going then.'

As they started to walk out Norton stopped and had one last look at the baby snoring softly in the policewoman's arms. He raised his hand to touch it, then let it drop — without saying a word he followed Detective Mattes down the stairs.

The Channel Ten Eyewitness News team had pulled up across the street and were forcing their way through the crowd out the front of the flats, followed by news teams from the other channels. One of the journalists spotted the blood on Norton's jeans and started moving in their direction.

'I'm not talking to no reporters,' growled Norton to Detective Mattes.

'Neither am I. Come on.' They sprinted the short distance to Waverley police station.

'You know it's funny,' said Norton, 'that's the same seat Fred was sitting in before he got shot.' He had another quick glance around the room he'd been in earlier with Detective Mooney.

Detective Mattes smiled across at Les as he fed a sheet of paper into the typewriter. 'I just got word back from the hospital. Fred's going to be all right. He's a bit shook up and he's lost a bit of blood but he's going to be as good as gold — thanks to you Les.'

Norton shrugged his shoulders. 'That's good,' he said shortly. He'd been sitting for about fifteen minutes, quietly watching while Detective Mattes thumped steadily away at the old type-writer, when Detective Simmiti walked in the door holding a brown paper bag, a big smile on his usually serious face.

'I suppose you heard the news,' he said. 'Fred's okay.'

'Yeah, we did,' replied Norton. 'Unreal.'

Detective Simmiti placed the paper bag on the desk and looked at Norton for a second or two. 'Thank's Les,' he said sincerely, reaching down and warmly shaking the big redhead's hand. 'Fred told me what happened when he was going up in the ambulance.'

'You don't have to thank me,' shrugged Norton. 'Fred's an old mate.'

'Thanks anyway Les.'

'Yeah and that goes for me, too.' Detective Mattes stood up from behind the typewriter and did the same thing.

'Jesus what is this?' said Norton, starting to feel a little embarrassed. 'The next thing you'll be wanting to give me a VC.'

'Listen Les,' said Detective Simmiti. 'That could have been me at that door instead of Fred. And if Fred hadn't made it — I'd have felt responsible.'

'Yeah fair enough, I s'pose,' replied Norton.

'Anyway — I can't give you a VC, but I don't suppose you'd say no to a cool one.' Detective Simmiti opened the brown paper bag and handed Norton a bottle of Reschs' Premier Lager, then gave one to Detective Mattes.

'Are you kidding. I've been fanging for a beer since bloody ten o'clock this morning.' Norton tore the bottle out of Detective Simmiti's hand and ripped off the ring-pull top. 'Cheers boys,' he said, and downed almost half of it in one go, followed by a huge, contented belch.

'Where did you take Moon anyway?' he asked, taking another swig on his bottle.

'Up the War Memorial in Birrell Street,' replied Detective Simmiti.

'Oh yeah, up near Waverley College. Nothin' but the best for Fred, eh?'

'He asked if you'd go up and see him when you get a chance.' Detective Simmiti screwed up his face. 'He said something about hanging a picture up on a wall for him or something. I couldn't quite follow him.'

Norton threw back his head and laughed. 'I know what he means.'

While Detective Mattes finished typing up the statement

the three of them knocked over the half-dozen beers, in a jubilant mood that everything had turned out for the best — especially with Fred. Detective Simmiti gave Norton the impression that he showed no remorse at all for the junkie he'd just shot — in fact he seemed almost glad he'd put him away. There was some feeling from the two detectives about the dead mother — about as much feeling as you can have for a junkie who's OD'd — but they all agreed it was a crying bloody shame about the unfortunate little baby who'd been left behind. Eventually Norton got to his feet to leave.

'Well fellas, I might get crackin'. I've seen enough of Waverley police station today to last me the rest of my life.'

'Fair enough,' said Detective Mattes, getting up; as he did Detective Simmiti reached across and closed the door behind them.

'Listen Les,' he said, the serious look back. 'If ever you're in any sort of strife — doesn't matter what it is — you come and see me or Ray. All right?'

'Yeah righto,' nodded Norton.

'Anything. Anything at all.' Detective Simmiti emphasised the last words with a slashing motion of his hand. 'You come and see me or Ray.'

'Thanks. I'll remember that.' Norton shook hands with the two detectives once more and moved towards the door.

'Can we give you a lift anywhere?' asked Detective Mattes.

'No it's all right. I feel like going for a bit of a walk to tell you the truth.' Norton said his last goodbyes and left the station. On the way out all the uniform cops gave him a big smile and most of them waved.

Outside in Birrell Street it still wasn't only cold, the sun had started to go down and now it was cold, bleak and dark. *Have a look at the time*, thought Norton, checking his watch. *Bloody near five o'clock. And Chicka closes at 4.30 sharp. That means no bloody car — and I'd have more chance of moving Ayers Rock than getting Chicka out of the Robin Hood to open the garage for me. Ah well, I can borrow Warren's Celica for tonight I s'pose.* He turned the collar of his leather jacket up, jammed his hands in the pockets and headed towards Bondi Junction to have a couple more beers then catch a cab home.

The news teams had gone but there were still a few people standing outside the block of flats shuffling against the cold as they tried to get a look at what, they probably didn't know themselves. A paddy wagon parked half up on the footpath indicated a police guard was still inside. Norton shook his head thoughtfully, stood for a moment and continued on his way.

At the Birrell Street corner he had to wait for the lights to change: as he stood in the cold wind a big smile spread across his face. *Fuck it,* he thought. *I'll duck up and see Moon, it's only just up the road.* He turned right and headed up Birrel Street towards the Waverley War Memorial hospital.

A sign at the entrance (in the same blue and gold colours as Waverley College) stood in front of what looked like a small cottage with 'Winston O'Reilly Building' written above the door. Behind a small reception desk Norton could see a sister, somewhere in her thirties, wearing an immaculate starched, white uniform and cap, shuffling some papers around. He walked up to her, and politely introduced himself. He told her exactly what had happened and would it be all right if he went and saw Detective Mooney for a few minutes? The sister was a little hesitant at first, then said it would be all right provided he wasn't too long and he checked with the doctor if he happened to be outside the rooms. She then told him Detective Mooney was in room nineteen and how to get there.

Norton thanked her and followed a path through some beautifully landscaped gardens, past a small coffee shop and kiosk till he came to a white concrete courtyard surrounded by marble statues. Two more statues holding lights above their heads flanked a set of concrete steps that led up to the E. Vickery Memorial Building where Fred was. As he was about to climb the steps Norton noticed another blue and gold sign above the door of a large white building opposite saying briefly: 'And He Healed Them'. He stopped at the bottom of the steps and looked up at the darkening sky. *You didn't bother to heal those two up in Birrell Street did you?* he thought. *Then again, I don't s'pose they were really worth healin', were they?* He trotted up the stairs and went inside.

Jesus, this is all right, thought Norton, as he gazed around the red carpeted foyer surrounded by more smaller marble statues holding lamps, glass cabinets and carefully and tastefully hung antique oil paintings. *This joint looks more like a palace than a hospital,* he thought. *If anything ever happens to me I hope I finish up in here.* A massive crystal chandelier hung majestically above a red carpeted, oak staircase. There appeared to be no one around so he went straight up.

Room nineteen was like something you'd see in old, first-class English or European hotels: spacious, comfortable and centrally-heated. Detective Mooney was propped up in an enormous brass bed surrounded by huge, fluffy pillows and crisp, white sheets. His left leg was raised slightly in a sling and above his head a bottle led to an intravaneous drip in his arm. A smaller plastic tube was taped into his nose. He wasn't asleep but was sedated and resting after his operation. He didn't notice Norton enter the room until he was standing next to the bed.

'Hello Moon. How's things?'

Detective Mooney opened his eyes and blinked up at Norton's smiling face several times before he spoke. 'Les. Hey ... How are you mate?' His voice was understandably weak and he sounded tired and drowsy from the post-op sedation.

'Good. How's y'self. I just thought I'd call in and see if you felt like a game of squash.'

Detective Mooney smiled tiredly up at Norton. 'I ... didn't bring a pair of white shorts with me ... mate. Sorry.'

'Oh well, don't worry about it. Listen, I got a couple of young sheilas out in the car. You feel like a root? I'll bring 'em in if you like. They've both got big tits.'

Fred tried to laugh but it finished up a series of weak coughs. 'It'll have to be ... a quickie. I'll tell you that.'

Norton sat down on a chair next to the bed and tapped Fred lightly on his good arm. 'The head nurse says you're okay and you should be up and about in a week or two.'

'Yeah. I was ... lucky. The bullet missed my heart by about two centimetres.'

'I heard it was deflected off your wallet.'

'I know one thing ... Les. If it ... hadn't been for you I wouldn't be here now.'

'Oh bullshit.'

'No Les. I owe you ... my life.'

'Get out. You owe me nothin'.'

There were a few seconds of awkward silence. Norton smiled across at his young detective mate. Fred held up his hand and shook Norton's. The strength wasn't there but the feeling was. Finally Les spoke.

'So Moon, you're first day, in the D's eh? You were nearly like that pub down the Quay — the First And Last.'

'I'm not real keen to get back ... I'll tell you. Fuck the heroics. I'll settle for a ... nice desk job when I do.'

Norton laughed and gave Fred an encouraging pat on the

76

arm. He talked for a few more minutes till he could see Fred closing his eyes for longer periods of time.

'Well Moon,' he finally said, getting up from the chair, 'I'd better get going and you've got to get some rest. I'll duck up and see you through the week.'

'Okay. Thanks for calling in.'

'That's all right.'

Detective Mooney looked up at Norton for a second or two before he spoke. 'Listen Les,' he said slowly. 'If ever there's anything I can do ... anything at all ... you come and see me. Okay? Any time at all.'

Norton started to laugh again. 'Moon, I just got all this bullshit off Simmiti and Mattes back at Waverley,' he said. 'You don't owe me nothin' Moon. Forget it.'

'Yeah. Well anyway ... Les. If ever I can do anything ... you let me know ... all right? I owe you mate.'

'Oh arseholes.'

Norton stood smiling at Fred for a moment or two longer. Although he'd been liberally dosed with morphine Fred was still obviously in a lot of pain yet was still doing his best to smile back. Norton shifted his gaze to a gap in the curtains covering a large sliding-glass door next to the bed, where he could see it was completely dark outside and hear the bitter sou'-wester as it whined through the power-lines and whipped around the statues with their soft lights illuminating the court-yard below. He could imagine how cold and miserable it would be walking back to Bondi Junction and he was a little reluctant to have to leave the soporific warmth of Fred's centrally-heated room. But it would only be a matter of time before a nurse or a doctor came along and asked him to leave. He zipped up his leather jacket and clapped his hands together.

'Anyway I'm going. I'll see you through the week Moon.'

'Righto Les. See you mate.'

'See you Moon. Take it easy.'

Norton walked across to the door and opened it. As he did he stopped suddenly, slapped the back pocket of his jeans and slowly turned around, a strange grin on his face. He walked back over to the bed.

'Hey Moon,' he said thoughtfully. 'Did you say, if ever I wanted anything, to see you? Anything at all?'

Detective Mooney looked up quizzingly at Norton. 'Yeah... sure.'

'Well here you are.' Norton pulled the two summonses, still

smeared with Fred's blood, out of his back pocket and dropped them on the bed.

Detective Mooney looked at them, then back at Norton.

'Parking tickets?'

'Well you said anything didn't you?'

Wheels

Standing in the milky shadows, cast by the pale, blue light of the Kelly Club, the faces on the two consorting squad detectives showed mild concern. They were speaking quietly to two solid doormen who were leaning casually against the wall on either side of the entrance. Les Norton and Billy Dunne's faces, on the other hand, did show some concern but it was just as much curious amusement as anything else.

Detectives Henderson and Teague had been scouring the traps around the Cross and the eastern suburbs looking for a certain Barry Chester Black. 'Big Barry', as he was nicknamed, was involved with some other gentlemen in massage parlours around the Cross and Double Bay; he also helped run a health studio in Coogee with an ex-prostitute Thelma Cowley. Big Barry had belted Thelma over some money and he'd also been shooting his mouth off a bit too much to the wrong people about the massage parlour rort and the word was out that Big Barry wasn't going to be in this world a great deal longer. There wasn't a great deal the two detectives could do about that, but they were rather keen to have a word with Big Barry before he went to meet his maker in the big massage parlour in the sky. The two doormen had assured the two detectives that Big Barry wasn't on the premises nor had they seen him around for well over a week. Not that the two doormen would have concealed the fact if they had seen Big Barry. At times the consorting squad can be a doorman's and a club's best friend when it comes to getting rid of an undesirable. As Black, a hulking, brooding bully, was by no means the most popular man going around Sydney it was no skin of their noses what happened to him. But the boys genuinely hadn't seen him and that was that.

However, the non-appearance of Barry Chester Black wasn't what really concerned the two hard-faced detectives. The thing that concerned them the most was why Price Galese would want to close the Kelly Club at 11.30 — especially on a busy Saturday night — and this concern was well and truly registered on their faces as they stood on the footpath talking to Price Galese's two best doormen.

'What did Price say to you again?' asked tall, fair-haired Detective Henderson, scratching his chin thoughtfully.

'He didn't say much at all,' replied Billy Dunne, with a smile and a shrug of his shoulders. 'We got here about nine and he rang up just before we arrived to tell us to close at 11.30 and make sure they're all out by twelve.' He nodded up towards the stairs leading into the club. 'There wouldn't be fifty people up there, just the regulars. And they'll be gone in an hour,' he added, glancing at his watch.

Detective Henderson's shorter, darker, almost bald offsider screwed up his face and shook his head. 'It's got me stuffed,' he said. 'I had a drink with the gaming squad blokes yesterday afternoon and they didn't say anything about a raid. Especially not here. They put their heads in the 44 the other week and took away a couple of dozen stooges but that was only for an hour or so.' The nuggety detective shook his head again. 'Buggered if I know,' he said.

'You know Price,' smiled Les Norton. 'He could be up to any-bloody-thing.'

'Yeah, you're not wrong. Oh well.' Detective Teague glanced up at his taller mate. 'Anyway, I s'pose we'd better get going, and see if we can find Mr Black before his business associates do.' He turned back to the two doormen. 'Are you guys playing touch down Centennial Park tomorrow 'arvo?'

'No,' replied Billy. 'We're having a game against the armed hold-up squad at Dunningham Park on Monday morning. You gonna come down and have a look? We'll probably go over the Coogee Bay and have a beer after.'

'Yeah, if we're doing nothing we might come down,' replied Detective Henderson, as they both started to make a move. 'See you later anyway.'

'Yeah righto. See you,' chorused the two doormen.

They watched in silence as the two detectives climbed into their Holden and moved slowly off down Kelly Street; each slightly lost in thought trying to figure out what their enigmatic boss, Price Galese, was up to this time.

'I'd love to know what's going on,' said Les.

'Well, we'll know shortly,' repied Billy, 'here's Price now.' Norton looked up just as the casino owner's shiny, beige, Rolls Royce glided majestically to a halt a few metres down from the entrance to the club.

Eddie Salita got out first, quickly walked round and, after an instinctive glance up and down the street, opened the door for Price. As soon as the smiling casino owner stepped out and started walking towards them, Billy and Les were somewhat taken back by a rather unusual sight that immediately added more mystery to an already extraordinary night which had started by Price's strange phone call earlier. Instead of being his customary, superbly dressed self, Price was wearing a T-shirt tucked into a pair of faded Levis and an old pair of white sneakers: draped loosely across his shoulders was an expensive, pale-blue, cashmere cardigan opened at the front. However, with his neat, silvery hair and tanned urbane looks he was still the natural epitome of class and style.

'Hello boys, how's things?' he said, smiling broadly at the puzzled looks on Les and Billy's faces.

'Good. How's y'self Price? G'day Eddie,' chorused the two doormen.

'Did you get that message earlier?' asked Price.

'Yeah,' replied Norton slowly. 'What's going on?'

'Oh nothing much,' grinned Price, rubbing his carefully manicured hands together gleefully. 'But I'll leave Eddie to tell you. I want to duck upstairs and have a quick word with George. Don't forget. I want everyone, staff and all, out by twelve.' He gave Norton a friendly punch on the arm and disappeared up the stairway.

As soon as he was out of sight Billy turned to Eddie Salita.

'Well what's going on Eddie?'

'Yeah, what's the story?' echoed Norton.

'What's the story?' grinned Price's number one hit man. 'The story is, we're burning the place down tonight. Price done his arse at the punt today and he needs the insurance. I've got the petrol in the boot of the Rolls.'

'You're what?' the two astonished doormen almost shouted as one.

'You heard,' replied Eddie, with a casual movement of his hands.

'Jesus, that's a bit drastic, isn't it?' said Billy, staring wide-eyed at Eddie.

81

'Burning the joint down. Christ!' Norton took his hands out of his pockets and put them on his hips. 'Christ!' he exclaimed again.

'Sometimes a man's just gotta do what a man's just gotta do,' replied Eddie, glancing nonchalantly up at the open windows of the Kelly Club. The lazily drifting cigarette smoke and the faint sounds from inside floated out in their soft yellow light.

'Yeah, but burning the bloody place down,' said Billy. 'Shit.' Norton didn't say anything. He just stood staring incredulously at the po-faced hit man. He didn't quite know what to think but he wouldn't put anything past Price and Eddie once they got their heads together. Suddenly, Eddie threw back his head and roared laughing.

'Fair dinkum,' he chortled, 'you two have got to be the biggest pair of Botany Bay mullets I've ever seen. You come in with your big gobs open every time. Have a go at your bloody faces. Burning the place down,' he sniggered. 'We're not burning the fuckin' joint down. We're putting in a new roulette wheel.'

When Eddie stopped laughing at the looks on their faces and the two chagrined but happy doormen finished pushing him all over the footpath he explained to them what was going on.

The wheel inside was just about worn out, mainly from just being overworked. The green felt was starting to get a bit tatty and the bearings round the chrome spinner had worked so loose that at times it seemed to take forever for the little white ball to drop into one of the red or black slots. Actually, the whole thing hadn't been quite the same since the night Norton demolished Iron-Bar Muljak and his mate on it. So Price decided to buy a new one and claim it as a business deduction through someone he knew high up in the taxation department.

The one he'd ordered was made especially for him in St Nazaire, France by the finest craftsmen in Europe. It cost the best part of $150,000 and there were only two like it in the world; the other was in one of the big casinos in Monte Carlo. The problem was, that it wasn't supposed to arrive in Australia for another three weeks, but due to a mix-up in the shipping it had been landed in Sydney on Friday and was now being held in bond. So rather than have an expensive and just about irreplaceable object like that lying around in storage, where it could get damaged or brought to the public's attention if some crafty journalist with an eye for a good story got on to it, Price decided to put it straight into the Kelly Club.

The only other problem was the wheel and its huge felt table were much too big to go up the stairs, so the front windows of the club were being taken out and somehow or other they were going to get it in there. And that was why Price wanted the place empty by twelve because at five past the carpenters and bricklayers would arrive to dismantle the old table and knock out the windows for when the new one arrived at seven the next morning.

'So that's the story boys,' said Eddie. 'And Price said he wants you both up here at seven tomorrow in case he needs you to help get it in.'

Norton stepped out on to the footpath and tilted his head up towards the row of windows overlooking Kelly Street. The blue neon sign was at least three metres above their heads and the windows were a good four metres above that. 'How's he going to get the bloody thing up there?' he asked incredulously. 'Shit, if the new table's anything like the old one it'll weigh a bloody tonne.'

'It's bigger actually,' grinned Eddie. 'But we'll get it in there — easy. You wait and see.'

Billy stepped over and joined Les looking up at the windows. 'I'll tell you what,' he said seriously. 'You're gonna need more than a block and bloody tackle to get the fuckin' thing up there Eddie, that's for sure.'

'It's all sweet,' grinned Eddie, making excited little gestures with his hands. 'Don't worry about it. You'll see in the morning.'

'All right,' shrugged Billy, 'if you say so.'

'Anyway,' Eddie clapped his hands together and shaped up in front of Les as if he was going to fight him. 'I'm going upstairs. It's nearly eleven you may as well start getting them out in half an hour. I'll see you up there.' He flashed them a quick wink and vanished up the stairs.

'So that's what it was all about, eh? A new roulette wheel.'

'Yeah.' Billy smiled and gave his chin a bit of a thoughtful scratch. 'I should have jerried what was going on. George mentioned it to me a few weeks ago but it slipped my mind.'

'Knowing your mind Billy, that'd be about par for the course.'

Billy ignored Norton's remark and flashed him a devilish smile. 'You know who bought the thing for Price, don't you?'

'What do you mean, bought it for him?'

'Who went to France and ordered it, and took the money over.'

83

'Who?'

'Jack Atkins.'

Norton stared at Billy in slight disbelief. 'Sir Jack Atkins the ex-premier? Are you fair dinkum?'

Billy nodded his head and smiled tightly. Billy was about to elaborate on this when a party of four regulars approached and smiled their customary greetings to the two popular doormen before entering the club. Their smiles faded somewhat when the boys told them that they'd be closing in about half an hour; they were all welcome to go up and have a quick flutter if they wanted to but they'd have to be out by twelve. The slightly surprised punters discussed this among themselves for a minute or two then decided to give it a miss and try their luck up at the 44 Club in William Street. They thanked the boys then headed for Bayswater Road to get a taxi. As they drew out of sight Norton turned back to Billy, his eyes slightly narrowed and all ears.

'What were you going to say before, about Jack Atkins?' he asked.

By 11.55 they had everybody out of the club including the staff, who were all happy and laughing as they trooped down the stairs ready to celebrate their early mark with a night out on the tiles. They were laughing all the more after Price had given them $100 each to have a drink on him and celebrate the arrival of the new roulette wheel, and also celebrate the fact that Price's newest horse Tango Prince had got up that afternoon at fifteen to one and Price had given all the rails bookies at Canterbury a dreadful shellacking. Like Norton said earlier: he was an old villain all right, but you couldn't help liking him.

Seeing as Price had suggested it might be an idea if they didn't have any after-work drinks, as it might slow the builders down if they saw the boys hanging around sucking on cold tinnies or bourbons or whatever, they just stood round the old roulette table checking it out and talking quietly before Billy and Les went home.

'What are you going to do with the old one Price?' asked Billy.

The casino owner smiled to himself for a second or two before he answered. 'I'll dismantle it and keep it over my place for a while. Then I might put it in a new casino I might, just might, be opening.'

'A new one eh? Whereabouts?'

'Up on the Central Coast Billy,' replied Price, smiling as

he ran his hand fondly across the faded green baize of the old table like he was patting an old faithful dog. 'I've got the two top coppers on side up there and I might get one going in Gosford with a Greek who owns a pub up there.'

At the mention of the Central Coast a ripple of laughter ran through the small group standing next to the table. All eyes turned to Norton

'We might even give you a job up there,' laughed George the casino manager. 'You must be just about breaking your neck to get back up there and see your old girlfriend from Terrigal. What was her name. Sonia? Sarah?'

'Sophia,' growled Norton. He was about to tell George what he could do with the central coast when a raucous 'Hello you big red-headed goose' booming out from the top of the stairs heralded the arrival of the builders. Norton turned slowly round to see a big blonde head with a broken nose grinning at him from the other side of the room. It was one of his old football mates, Colin Jones.

'Jesus Christ,' chuckled Norton, 'don't tell me they've got you doing this Jonesy. It'll take a hundred years.'

'Turn it up son,' replied Colin. 'You know our motto. For service and quality don't make no bones: Just get on the blower and call Col Jones. And here I am. Any hour of the day or night.'

'You've probably just been thrown out of a brothel,' said Norton, shaking his head and laughing.

Colin Jones was a stocky, square-jawed, good style of a bloke roughly the same size as Norton only with a little, whispy moustache under his flattened nose and much neater hair. Like Les he was a pretty hard man on the football field and one of the best front-on tacklers in the game. But also like Les, he didn't get on too well with the Easts hierarchy, and seeing as he had a small building company making plenty of money Colin realised there were better things to do during winter than bash your head around on a football field and cop shit from club officials for your trouble — like drinking piss, smoking plenty of hot ones and chasing snow bunnies around Thredbo. So Colin brushed Easts not long after Les but they were still good mates and often had a drink together and a game of touch up at Waverley Oval or down Centennial Park.

With a big grin on his rugged face Jonesy ambled across the room towards Les and the others. Behind him came several stocky building workers of all shapes and sizes, wearing mainly shorts and flannelette shirts minus the sleeves and carrying two huge, paint-spattered canvas tarpaulins. After saying hello to Price and the others he quickly introduced his team around. Colin then set them to work stacking up the furniture and tables and spreading out the two tarpaulins. Les and Billy figured that this would be as good a time as any to get going before they started getting in the road, so they said goodnight and told Price they'd see him up there first thing in the morning.

Walking up to their cars at that hour of the night the boys naturally enough felt a bit strange. Usually when they finished work the Cross was starting to slow down a bit, instead there were cars and people everywhere running around like rats in a neon sewer.

'You feel like a cup of coffee or something on the way home?' suggested Norton, as they got to their cars.

'No, not really mate,' replied Billy. 'We got to get up first thing. Besides, seeing it's still early I might even give the missus a tap on the shoulder when I get into bed,' he added with a wink.

'Half you luck,' chuckled Les. 'Hey, you still want to go for a run when we finish?'

'Oh yeah, for sure. I'll see you in the morning.'

They got into their cars and headed for home.

The table lamp was still on and there was an empty bottle of Dom Perignon on the coffee table in the lounge-room, plus a handbag and a pair of women's shoes when Norton arrived home. Soft music was coming from Warren's slightly open, bedroom door accompanied by a lot of moaning and groaning and the odd muffled scream of ecstasy. Between that and what Billy had said earlier about tapping his wife on the shoulder Norton was almost tempted to make a late night phone call. Instead he had a mug of Ovaltine, listened to the kitchen radio for a while and went to bed.

Sunday morning was a typical, early autumn day that helps to make Sydney the peach of a town it is: sunny, mild, scarcely a cloud in the sky and the barest nor'-wester whispering across the city which would turn nor'-east in the late afternoon to welcome the few tufts of pinky, grey clouds that gather over the ocean as the sun goes down.

Norton was up about 6.15 and had a quick cup of coffee and a toasted cheese sandwich watching the sparrows bobbing around on the dewy grass in his backyard. The handbag and shoes were still in the lounge-room so Norton had a quick peek through Warren's still slightly open bedroom door to see if there was any early morning action: but it was all quiet on the Western front. With a bit of an envious chuckle he closed the front door quietly and went out to his car.

It might have been quiet in Cox Avenue, Bondi but when Les pulled up behind Billy's Holden station wagon in Bayswater Road, Kelly Street was a hive of activity.

A row of yellow, diagonal-striped council barricades, manned by several beefy council workers in overalls blocked off either end of Kelly Street, and next to these were positioned two police patrol wagons with several uniformed policemen leaning against them sipping coffee out of paper cups. A couple of street cleaners with their brooms and bins on wheels like little chariots had propped there too, and the local garbage-truck was parked up on the footpath outside the hotel on the corner with the garbos milling around in their beanies and football jumpers.

Norton locked his car and strode across the road and, after nodding his head to a couple of young local coppers he knew, walked up to where Colin Jones and his crew were sitting in the sun on the footpath outside the Kelly Club, sipping coffee and eating steak sandwiches from a stack in a cardboard carton. They were all covered in dust and plaster and above them was a huge gap where the windows of the casino had been.

'Hello Jonesy,' smiled Les. 'How's it goin' mate?'

'Good as gold,' replied Colin. 'We're nearly an hour in front. You want a steak sanger?' He nodded towards the cardboard carton.

'I might have one later,' said Les. 'Price upstairs?'

'Yeah.'

'I'll just duck up and see what's goin' on. I'll be back in a minute.'

Inside the casino there was surprisingly little mess. The old roulette table was nowhere to be seen and Billy was standing on the tarpaulin next to two large industrial vacuum cleaners inspecting where the row of bay windows had been. He turned round at the sound of Norton's footsteps.

'G'day Les.'

'Hello Billy. What's doin'?'

Through the open office door Norton could see the others sitting around a huge pot of tea eating toast and reading the Sunday papers. They were all laughing about something. Norton walked in and smiled hello, noticing Price and Eddie were as fresh as daisies whereas George's eyes were a little puffy and bloodshot.

'Have a look at this,' said Price, handing Norton the *Sunday Telegraph* open at the sporting section. There were two photos of a beaming Price. One leading Tango Prince into the winner's enclosure with Ron Quigley on top and another of him collecting an enormous stack of money from Sydney's biggest rails bookmaker Bill Waterman. Waterman was trying his best to smile for the camera but his face looked like a kilo of rotten tripe.

'Have a go at his miserable dial,' laughed Price. 'You'd think he'd just swallowed arsenic. $200,000 I got him for. And couldn't have done it to a nicer bloke.'

'Good on you.' Les handed Price back the paper. 'I might grab a cup of tea.'

'Go for your life.'

'Jesus you've got it well organised outside,' said Norton. 'There's council barricades and coppers blockin' off the street. How'd you work that?'

Price winked up at Norton as he idly thumbed through the Sunday paper. 'That's called corruption on a grand scale Les. You don't see that up in sunny Queensland, do you?'

'Well . . . not in Dirranbandi anyway.'

Norton sipped his cup of tea and glanced at a spare Sunday paper when Billy came to the door.

'Hey Price,' he said, 'they want you out the front. I think the new table's arrived.'

'Ho, here we go.' Price clapped his hands together and stood up. Norton took his cup of tea and joined them as they all walked over to the window.

'The truck's here Mr Galese,' a thick-set council worker in a pair of blue overalls and a Paddington Colts football jumper yelled up from the street below.

'Righto Alan. Thanks mate,' Price called back. 'Okay boys here she is. Let's go down and have a look.'

Norton quickly finished his cup of tea, and they all trooped down the stairs to arrive out the front just as the council workers moved away the barricades. While the police directed traffic around the barricades, a wide-backed, flat-deck truck reversed through the gap and started backing slowly down Kelly Street towards the club. On the back, secured firmly with ropes and padding, was the roulette wheel and table packed in an enormous wooden crate covered in stencilling. Next to it were several other small crates also secured with rope. The driver spotted Price and gave him a wave; he waved back as Colin Jones guided the truck till the rear wheels were resting up against the gutter outside the entrance to the club.

At almost the same moment the truck pulled up, a whistle blew at the other end of the street and through the barricades rumbled a monstrous mobile crane: the derrick, with the huge hook swaying beneath it on the front, had to be at least fifteen metres high. As it rolled noisily down the street towards them Norton noticed the four policemen standing next to the patrol wagons snap to a smart salute as a white commonwealth limousine with the 'Z' number plates followed the fork-lift through the barricades and eased to a halt alongside the foot path opposite them. Sitting in the back Norton was slightly shocked to see a familiar, corpulent figure with slicked back silvery hair puffing away on a large cigar.

'Hello,' smiled Price, taking a quick glance at his watch. 'Here's me old mate Sir Jack — right on time. I suppose I'd better go over and say hello. All right Colin,' he said turning to the big, fair-haired builder. 'I'll leave it all up to you. If you want me, I'll be in that white Fairlane across the road.'

'Righto Price. No worries,' replied Colin, moving towards the mobile-crane to have a word with the driver.

'What do you want me to do?' asked Norton.

'I dunno,' shrugged Price. 'See Colin. He's running the show.'

'All right.'

Price started walking across the street followed closely by Eddie Salita. He climbed in the back seat of the Fairlane and opened the window to let some of the cigar smoke out. Eddie stood round the front talking to Sir Jack's bodyguard and the driver.

'What do you want us to do?' asked Norton, as he and Billy followed Colin Jones over to the crane.

'Nothing yet. Me and my team should be able to handle this, but just stand over by the club and if we need you I'll give you a yell.'

Les and Billy nodded in agreement. They walked over and leant up against the wall of the Kelly Club alongside George Brennan. George, the overweight, 'bon vivant' casino manager didn't mind a bodysurf or a game of handball now and again, but manual labour was a Spanish guitar player as far as he was concerned and he had absolutely no intentions whatsoever of getting involved in any of the physical activity going on around him — so he was leaning up against the brickwork getting into one of the steak sandwiches. Norton saw there were several still left in the carton so giving Billy a tap on the shoulder, he reached down and took one out of the cardboard

89

box. Billy looked at the remaining steak sandwiches for a second or two then helped himself to one as well.

'Hey, there's nothing wrong with these steak sangers,' said Norton, taking a huge bite.

'Plenty of onions, too,' added Billy.

George finished his first one, wiped his mouth and fingers on the paper it was wrapped in, then screwed it up in a ball and dropped it in the cardboard carton. 'Bloody beautiful,' he mumbled, reaching down for another one.

And with the bright autumn sunshine, slowly warming up the bricks behind them, the three smiling men stood casually against the wall of the Kelly Club eating steak sandwiches in the sun. In an atmosphere of blatant corruption, unprecedented anywhere else in Australia, Colin Jones galvanised the fifteen or so workers around him into action.

The first thing they did was unload the five smaller crates sitting on the back of the truck and manhandle them as carefully as possible up the stairs. Billy and Les offered to help but were told they weren't needed so they continued eating. The crates didn't take very long. Then from somewhere on the back of the truck the driver produced two thick stainless-steel cables with heavy metal eyes on either end which were quickly but meticulously slung round the solid wooden crate containing the new roulette wheel. Colin gave a toot on a small whistle he had tied round his neck, the crane driver lowered the derrick and the two cables were attached to the huge metal hook swaying slightly underneath. Making doubly sure everything was secure, Jonesy raised one hand above his head, blew on the whistle and, in unison with the whistle and his hand movements, the crane driver raised the cumbersome wooden crate from the back of the truck.

'Hey, have a go what's written on the side,' laughed Norton, pointing at the huge crate as it swung side on to them.

Stencilled across the wooden panelling in bold black letters was an arrow and the words, 'This side up. Washing-machine parts. Handle with care.'

'Washing machine parts,' guffawed Billy. 'I wonder whose bloody idea that was.'

'Price's I suppose,' mused George. 'Then again it's appropriate, isn't it? I mean we're laundering that much black money up there what else would you put on it?'

With a toot of his whistle Colin stopped the crate just above his head and attached a length of rope to one of the stainless-steel cables just in case the crate should sway too much. With two of his crew standing on the footpath holding on to the rope Jonesy blew a few more toots on his whistle, and he and the crane driver slowly guided the wooden crate up till it was level, lengthwise, with the gap in the wall of the club where the windows had been. He stopped it there.

'Righto Les, Billy,' he called out, as he jumped down from the back of the truck. 'You want to come up and give us a hand to get it in?'

The two amused doormen followed Colin up the stairs two at a time into the casino where the rest of his crew were standing at the window watching the crated roulette wheel swaying gently in the breeze just outside.

'Righto fellas, easy now.' With Jonesy still directing things each man reached out and took a firm grip on the sides of the crate to gently edge it into the gap and with the crane driver slowly easing off the slack they slid the giant crate through the window space like somebody sliding a letter sideways into a letter box.

Everybody, except Billy, gave a bit of a cheer when it finally landed inside — he was too busy swearing while he pulled a large splinter out of his thumb. Colin removed the two cables and draped them over the hook while one of his men started prising open the crate with a crowbar.

'Well, what's doing Jonesy?' asked Les. 'Do you need us here any longer?'

'No, you may as well piss off,' replied the big blond-headed builder. 'Good thing you both came in though,' he added, with a derisive smile. 'We'd have been absolutely fucked without you. What did Price bring you in for anyway?'

'He just likes having us around,' smiled Billy, sucking a bit of blood from his thumb.

'He must.' Colin paused for a moment to watch the man with the crowbar then turned back to Norton. 'Where are youse off to now?'

'Down North Bondi to have a run and a swim.'

'Not a bad idea. It's a top day outside. I might even see you down there later. We should be out of here by lunchtime.'

'Yeah come down,' said Billy. 'We'll have a beer and a counter-lunch over the Diggers.'

'Righto.'

The boys said goodbye to Jonesy and his crew then trooped happily down the stairs. George was still standing in the sun up against the wall wiping his face with a handkerchief. Except for a few screwed-up balls of grease-stained, white paper, the cardboard carton next to him was completely empty.

'Have a go at this,' said Billy, giving the empty box a nudge with his foot. 'There's not a crumb, not a piece of gristle not even a sauce stain left. No wonder you get around looking like someone's had a bike-pump up your arse George.'

'Leave me alone, will you, you punch-drunk imbecile,' replied George. He gave Billy a tried smile and neatly folded his hanky and placed it in his inside, coat pocket.

Norton smiled and shook his head as he placed his hand on George's shoulder. 'Don't worry George, I understand how it is mate. Anyway, Jonesy don't need us anymore so we're gonna piss off. Where's Price?'

'Still talking to Atkins.' George nodded towards the Fairlane parked across the street with Eddie standing at the front having a joke with the ex-premier's bodyguard.

'Well, will you tell him we've gone down North Bondi and we'll probably see him down Clovelly Surf Club, tomorrow arvo?'

'Yeah righto.'

'Okay. See you George.'

'Yeah. See you Porky,' said Billy, feinting a right rip into the casino manager's ample stomach. 'Va-veer-va-va-veer. That's all for now, folks.'

George replied with another tired smile. 'Les, do me a favour, will you? While you're down the beach, take punchy out swimming, and put a couple of car batteries round his neck.'

'I'll see what I can do mate,' winked Les. 'Hooray.'

As the two doormen turned to walk away they caught Eddie's eye across the road. 'See you Eddie,' they chorused. The wiry hit man gave them a big wave then flashed a huge white grin. George watched them walking away for a second or two, then with a bit of a chuckle heaved himself off the wall and went over to the crane operator and the truck driver who were getting their rigs ready to depart. He handed them a bulky envelope each which they didn't bother to count quickly, slipping them into their pockets with appreciative smiles.

'I'm looking forward to a run, to tell you the truth,' said Norton, nodding to the two police constables who were still standing next to their patrol wagon on the corner, watching idly as the council workers began to move the barricades. 'You want to have a bit of a workout in the surf club afterwards?'

'Yeah righto,' replied Billy.

'Where do you want to run to? You fancy doing a few laps

of the beach. There might be something down there worth perving on today.'

'You want to do us a favour?'

'Sure.' Norton stopped and turned to Billy at the way he asked the question.

'Well how about we have a run around all the back streets of Bondi. Especially up the north end.'

Norton gave his broad shoulders a shrug. 'I don't give a stuff. What's ...?'

'I want to buy a flat and I wouldn't mind checking a few out while we're having a run. Sort of kill two birds with the one stone.'

'Not a bad idea.'

'I had a couple of big blocks of land up at Port Stephens. I just sold them for sixty grand so I'll plonk that down on a unit, borrow say twenty, throw a team of Kiwis in and let them pay most of it off and in say two years I've got a hundred grand flat that's only cost me forty grand originally.' Billy gave his shoulders a nonchalant shrug. 'It's an easy earn.'

Norton threw back his head and laughed out loud. 'Jesus Billy,' he said. 'Are you sure there's not a bit of reffo in you?'

'Mate,' replied Billy, pulling a sad face and making an open-handed gesture with his arms by his side, 'living with them in Bondi all these years — I've got to learn something.'

'Fair enough Irving. You like chicken soup, too?'

They were still laughing as they dodged the traffic across the Bayswater Road to get to their cars. 'I'll see you outside the surf club.' Norton was about to open the door of his old Ford when he heard Billy let out a string of vile oaths. 'What's up?' he called out, looking over.

'You wouldn't fuckin' believe it,' cursed Billy from the front of his new Holden station wagon. 'I've got a flat fuckin' tyre.' Norton walked over as Billy gave the flattened, front-left tyre a hefty kick. 'Fuck it,' he cursed again.

'Don't worry about it,' laughed Les. 'We'll fix it in five minutes.'

'Yeah, but my missus was using the car yesterday and she got a flat, too, and the spare's in getting fixed. I was going to pick it up this morning but we came up here.'

Norton looked at the flat tyre for a few moments as Billy continued cursing. 'Hold on a sec. You're gettin' the shits for nothing. Come here.'

He took Billy round to his car and opened the boot. Sitting

next to the spare for his old Ford was a brand new tyre sitting on a Holden rim. He explained that while he was up at Ben Buckler one day through the week, sitting in his car watching the ocean, he noticed an unregistered '68 Holden dumped in the parking area. Being a bit of a bowerbird and seeing as it was still in fairly good nick Norton decided to give it the once over, just in case there might have been a radio or something left in it. When he forced open the boot there was a bag of tools in there and a brand-new spare tyre. The rim didn't fit Norton's Ford but the tyres were the same so Les purloined it figuring he'd take it up to Chicka's garage, get it changed over and thus finish up with a nice new tyre for nothing. Living in beautiful downtown Bondi the last few years Norton had learned a few tricks from the residents, too.

'There you go mate. Throw that on and we'll be away in five minutes.'

'Les. You've done it again,' beamed Billy, giving Norton a friendly punch on the arm. 'You're a dead-set genius.'

While Billy started jacking up the front of his car, Les got the tyre out of his boot, plus a wheel brace, and started loosening the wheel nuts. Between them they had the flat tyre off in next to no time at all.

'I'll tell you what we ought to do,' chuckled Norton, as Billy wiggled the stolen tyre on to the stubbs. 'Why don't we get an Opera House lottery ticket tomorrow and call it 'wheels'? We've just put an illegal roulette wheel in the club, now we're putting a hot wheel on your car — what d'you reckon? It might be lucky.'

'You've got me. In fact I'll shout,' said Billy, as he spun the wheel brace to tighten the last nut.

'No. I'll go you halves.'

'Whatever.'

Norton let down the jack and Billy flung the flat tyre into the back of his station wagon. Norton dropped the jack in next to it then put his wheel brace back in the boot of his old Ford. Without any further ado they proceeded towards North Bondi.

Despite the amount of cars around and the number of people on the beach enjoying the warm, early autumn sunshine, Les and Billy were able to find a parking spot in Ramsgate Avenue less than a 100 metres from the surf club. Norton didn't bother to lock his old Ford as he got his overnight bag off the front seat, and was whistling audibly when he joined Billy waiting for him on the promenade.

The lightest of nor'-westers had the air crisp and fresh, and the clear, emerald water beyond the breakers was almost like glass. Several groups of bodysurfers and school kids on blue Koolites were taking advantage of a nice little wave running in the north corner. Beyond them a number of lifesavers, in red and yellow caps, were paddling around on surf skis while the North Bondi boat crew strained at the oars of the surf boat as it surged through the swells just off the big rock on the point. The numerous, well-oiled, brown-skinned girls in brief bikinis scattered across the sand caught Norton's eye; especially one by the water's edge with a massive bust that made him stumble into Billy as they headed towards the surf club.

'Jesus, are you sure you don't want to go for a run along the beach Billy?' said Norton, still staring at the big-titted blonde splashing around in the water with an almost equally well-endowed girlfriend.

Billy laughed when he saw what Les was gaping at. 'Come on mate,' he grinned. 'You can perv till you go blue in the face when we get back.'

'Yeah righto,' mumbled Norton reluctantly.

Several of the older members were lollygagging around in the sun out the front of the club when they got there. Les and Billy smiled and nodded to the ones they knew. As they started walking up the few steps to enter the clubhouse, Norton noticed a familiar figure checking out a surf reel at the front of the gear room to their left.

'Hey T-shirt,' he called out brightly, 'what's doin' mate?'

The tall, broad-shouldered person in particular was Terry Farrell the gear steward. Terry was a fit, easygoing sort of a bloke that always had a year-round sun tan and was a pretty good style of a bloke despite the fact that his sandy, brown hair wasn't having a great deal of luck in the front. The two doormen got to know Terry, a wharfie, through another wharfie mate of theirs — Danny McCormack — and it was Terry who sorted it out for the boys to use the club and always managed to find a surf ski for them if ever they wanted to go for a paddle. Terry's main claim to fame was that he didn't have one shirt in his wardrobe and only ever wore T-shirts — which was why he got the nickname, 'Terry T-shirt'. If Terry ever won an MBE or got knighted he'd turn up at the investiture, whether it was Buckingham Palace or Kirribilli House, in a T-shirt. For a brief court appearance once he did front in one of those long-sleeved T-shirts, (which he kept for special occasions) with a bow-tie and lapels printed on the front. At the sound of his name Terry turned round to see the boys standing on the steps.

'Hey Les, Billy. How are you? What's doing?' he grinned.

'G'day T-shirt,' Billy grinned back.

'We're just going for a run,' said Norton. 'All right if we borrow a couple of skis when we get back?'

'Yeah sweet,' replied Terry. 'Take those two white Aeros near the stairs under the gym, then see me and I'll get you some paddles.'

'Good on you Terry. Thanks.' The boys had another word or two with 'T-Shirt' then went inside and got changed into their running gear. After about fifteen or twenty minutes of stretching exercises they were warmed up and ready to go.

'I'll tell you what,' said Billy, as they started walking down the steps of the clubhouse. 'I'm starting to get a bit on the peckish side. I reckon I'll murder a steak at the Diggers when we're finished.'

'Iron rations come in handy, on the way to Dirranbandi. Passengers have often died of hunger, during stops at Garadunga.'

Billy squinted quizzingly in the bright sunshine at Les as they walked across the small park outside the surf club.

'What are you going on about?' he asked.

'That's poetry Billy, you ignorant prick. It's from a poem called the Queensland Railways. Jesus you haven't got much culture have you?'

'Hah! What would you know about culture you hillbilly. You think "The Blue Danube's" a cheese and "Marseillaise" is something you put in coleslaw.' He gave Norton a punch on the arm. 'Come on Banjo, let's go.'

'I'll follow you Irving,' smiled Les. 'You can follow your nose.'

They took off across Campbell Parade like a couple of grey-hounds, almost sprinting. Billy led the way towards the Bondi Hotel, finally settling down to a more leisurely pace when they turned right into Warners Avenue past the school. In no time they were at Seven Ways where they turned right into Glenayr, back up Blair, left into Mitchell and started criss-crossing all the streets up to Murriverie Road till they finished up back in Blair turning left into Military Road heading towards Dover Heights. Every now and again Billy would produce a note book and felt-tip pen from his shorts and write down, the real estate agent's name and phone number on the 'For Sale' signs outside any flats that caught his eye.

While he was doing this Norton would stop and do a few push-ups, touch his toes or bounce around in the one spot. Having to stop and wait for Billy all the time didn't give him the shits that much — though he would have preferred to be running along the beach — he was too busy enjoying the exhilaration of running on such a beautiful autumn day; and there were a few things to look at. People washing their cars, a few girls walking around, nuns and parishioners coming from the Catholic church near Oakley Road and various other ones around the area while the church bells rang solemnly over the roof tops: plus he was making sure he got a good work-out at the same time.

'Hello. Where are you taking us now?' joked Les, as they puffed up Military Road past the golf links. 'You going up to see all your reffo mates in Jehovah Heights?'

'All your old landlords'd be more like it,' replied Billy. 'Christ they'd have a stroke if they saw you running around the streets. How much do you reckon you've brassed 'em for over the years?'

'Dunno for sure,' said Les thoughtfully. 'About the equivalent of the Israeli defence budget I s'pose. Hey have you seen anything you fancy yet? We've been running almost forty-five minutes.'

'Yeah, that one in Middleton Avenue. Come on we'll turn down here and I'll have another look at it.'

They turned left into O'Connell Street and headed towards Seven Ways again where Billy checked out the flats in question. It was in a block of six, three bedrooms with a sun deck and a large garage. The block was old, but fairly clean and not in too good a condition so a team of yahoos in there couldn't knock it around all that much while they paid it off for Billy. Plus the price was right — $79,500 or nearest offer.

'I think this joint just might do the trick,' said Billy. He stood out the front checking it out while Norton lay on his back touching his toes. 'Okay,' he added, with a nod of his head. 'Let's head back to the surf club. We'll go down Brighton Boulevard. I sprung one there when I was driving past the other day and I just want to have a quick look at it.'

'Righto mate. Whatever turns you on,' said Norton, ringing the perspiration out of his sweat-band and replacing it on his head.

They got to the Police Station end of Brighton Boulevard and starting heading towards North Bondi. The flat Billy had spotted earlier in the week wasn't worth the price so they didn't waste any time there and, seeing as they were finishing the run, they started to pick up the pace a bit.

They were still chattering away while they were running. Les was saying how he was looking forward to going for a paddle when they got back to the beach, and Billy saying how he was keener than ever for a beer and a steak, when as they got to the dip where Brighton Boulevard rises slightly before it reaches Campbell Parade, Billy noticed a familiar swarthy figure on the right-hand side of the street, walk out of his house with a huge alsatian dog and get into his white, Holden utility.

'Hey, isn't that an old mate of yours up ahead?' said Billy, a little sarcastically as they jogged closer to the big man with the dog.

Norton squinted ahead through sweat-filled eyes and nodded his head reluctantly. 'Yeah,' he muttered tightly. 'That's Joe Vorgnor, isn't it? You're not gonna stop and talk to the prick, are you?'

'To tell you the truth Les I might — just for a second or two. He might be a cunt but if anybody'd know about a cheap flat round here Joe would.'

Norton spat on the footpath. 'Righto, suit yourself.'

Joe Vorgnor was a tall, beefy, sweaty Maltese who arrived in Australia some time in the early 1950's and, like a lot of his fellow countrymen, who were attracted by the cheap rents, settled in the East Sydney area. Somehow or other, mainly by thieving and being an arsehole in general, Joe acquired, along with a criminal record, enough money to start buying up old houses in East Sydney which he converted into brothels and let to some of the ugliest, horriblest prostitutes going around. By standover tactics and sheer brutality it wasn't long before Joe was close to being a millionaire and ran just about all the brothels in East Sydney; and the more he owned the more he wanted. This caused quite a lot of friction among the other Maltese in the area who wanted a piece of the action, too; however Joe steadfastly refused to share. Consequently several attempts had been made on his life and he'd been stabbed a couple of times. But Joe was a tough, cagey rooster and always carried a gun with him, and so far no one had succeeded in getting to him. However the word was out that it would only be a matter of time before Joe, like his business associate

Big Barry Black, was a special to finish up in the big knock-shop in the sky.

Norton, being a bit of a square-head, Queensland country boy and a bit chivalrous, despite his slight male chauvinism, didn't cotton on too well to pimps and their ilk, but this wasn't the main reason he was sour on Joe. Vorgnor had come up to the Kelly Club one night with a friend, quite a rarity for Joe, and his friend put on a bit of a turn in the club. Price asked him to leave and he told Price to get fucked; so Price called in Les who hit Joe's friend in the stomach, almost rupturing his spleen, and pelted him down the stairs. Joe, being a bit light in the friend department, put on a drama outside the club threatening to shoot and maim Norton for belting his mate. Norton, being the kind of person who likes to nip threats in the bud, took Joe by the throat and was just about to turn Joe's big Maltese head into Peck's paste when Price and Billy pulled him off. For Joe, prick and all that he was, was known to drop ten or fifteen grand on the tables every now and again and not think a great deal of it, and Price's philosophy was that Joe the pimp's money was no different to Pope John-Paul's or Adolph Hitler's so he gave Joe the chance to apologise and let him still keep coming to the club.

This had happened almost a year ago and whenever Joe would come up to the club he and Norton would always grunt a thin hello to each other, but Norton never forgot and if ever he saw Vorgnor out anywhere would always give him plenty of the back of his neck. However, Joe always still got on well with Billy.

Joe's alsatian, Cassius, spotted the boys first and started snarling. Joe looked up and, when he saw who it was, took Cassius by the collar and smiled a greasy hello.

'Billy my friend,' he said, as they approached. 'How are you? Hello Les,' he added a little thinner.

'G'day Joe,' grunted Norton, stopping on the footpath not far from Billy who had propped next to Joe's utility.

'Having a run eh?' said Joe, in his guttural, accented voice just about ignoring Norton.

'Yeah,' smiled Billy. 'You look like you could do with a bit of a gallop yourself Joe,' he added, pointing to Vorgnor's obvious paunch.

'That, I'm afraid is the good life my friend,' replied Joe, giving his stomach a pat. 'Anyway, how come you are running around here? This is not usual for you?'

'I've been looking for a few flats. In fact I was going to

ask you something, if you've got a minute.'

Joe shrugged his beefy shoulders. 'Sure. Go ahead.'

Cassius jumped up in the back of the utility while Joe, followed by Billy, went around and got behind the wheel. Norton stood on the footpath exercising while Billy had a brief conversation with Vorgnor through the driver's window. In the back, Cassius started to snarl at Les but Les gave it a look as if to say, 'try anything you prick and I'll drag you out of the ute by your studded collar and slam you up against the nearest brick fence'. Vorgnor's dog soon dropped off and just sat looking, with its huge tongue lolling out the side of its mouth dripping saliva all over the tray of the ute.

Les heard Joe tell Billy that he was in a bit of hurry so he caught Billy's eye as if to say he wouldn't mind getting going himself. Billy got the hint that Les didn't want to be in Vorgnor's company for too long and told the big Maltese he'd see him again when he had more time. Through the window Norton could see Joe's hand reach towards the ignition to start the car so he began to make a move himself, when he heard a shrill voice call out from the front of Joe's house. He turned around to see a drab-looking, bleached blonde, with pencilled black eyebrows and overdone vermillion lips stick her head out one of the windows.

'Hey Joe,' she shrieked in a thin nasally whine. 'There's someone wants you on the phone.'

Joe let out a sigh, took his hand away from the keys and slid across the seat. 'Who is it?' he yelled back, winding the window halfway down.

'Ronnie Davis the plumber.'

'Did he say what he wants?'

Round the other side of the car Billy gave the roof a bit of a slap. 'I'll let you go Joe. I'll give you a ring tomorrow.'

'Yes. Okay Billy,' replied Vorgnor swivelling his head around.

Norton gave a sigh of relief. 'See you later Joe,' he almost mumbled.

'See you Les,' was the curt reply.

Norton joined Billy at the rear of the utility and they continued jogging up Brighton Boulevard. 'Tell Ronnie I'm in a hurry and I'll call him this afternoon,' he heard Joe call out as they headed towards Campell Parade.

'Well, what's happening?' asked Norton, as they trotted up the slight decline towards the corner. 'Is your slimy pimp mate gonna get you a flat?'

'As a matter of fact,' replied Billy, 'he can help me. He

100

knows a bloke selling one at the right price up in Hastings Parade. Joe might be an arse I'll agree with you, but I just might have saved myself about ten grand back there.'

'Fair enough,' said Les. 'It's just that I don't like talking to the cunt — that's all.'

Norton was about to say something else when all of a sudden the building around them seemed to shake. The quiet Sunday afternoon was shattered by an ear-splitting crack and the most thunderous explosion Les had ever heard pitched both him and Billy forward onto their knees. Dazed, they lay on the roadway for a second or two then slowly looked up as pieces of red-hot metal, tar and other smoking debris rained around them and on to the rooftops of the surrounding buildings. They turned and looked at each other in shock. From out of nowhere the spare wheel of Vorgnor's utility, with the rubber smouldering, wobbled past then spun round on its rim a few times till it finally lay smoking on the roadway a few metres in front of their heads.

'What the fuckin' hell was that?' said Billy, his ears ringing like a bell at the noise still echoing off the surrounding flats.

Norton shook his head as he opened and closed his jaws in an effort to try and clear his own ears. 'Sounded like a bloody bomb going off.'

After the explosion there was a deadly silence for a few moments, then every dog in the neighbourhood started barking and people began coming to the fronts of their houses to see what was going on. Slowly the boys turned back about five or ten metres behind them.

The huge blast had ignited all the petrol in one go, so instead of a great fire ball, there were just pockets of flames crackling among the oil, upholstery and tyres. An enormous pall of grey-black smoke was spiralling into the clear, blue autumn sky. All four tyres had ruptured and the twisted, gutted wreck was now sitting flush on the ground with water from the shattered radiator steaming as it bubbled and hissed into the gutter. Behind the wheel they could just make out the blackened figure of Joe Vorgnor.

'Jesus bloody Christ!' exclaimed Billy, his eyes like two saucers. 'Have a look at that!'

Norton didn't say anything. They slowly got to their feet and started cautiously walking towards the smoking wreckage. Both knew what to expect.

The first thing they saw was Cassius lying in a broken, twisted circle with its nose almost touching its backbone. Its stomach had split open and blood and entrails were oozing out of its gaping mouth. Both front paws were gone and most of its fur was burnt off revealing the pink charred skin still smouldering. Apparently the explosion had blown it straight up in the air, as it only lay a few metres behind the wreckage.

Billy and Les looked at the dog then grimly at each other as they trepidatiously moved to the shattered driver's window. If Cassius looked bad the sight there immediately turned both their stomachs.

Joe looked like some horrible monster not a man. His head was twisted back and tilted towards them in a ghostly, frozen look of horror, except that his eyes had burst in their sockets and his ears and hair had been scorched off. Both legs had been torn off and lay next to him on what was left of the seat, revealing the splintered, charred bone. There was no bleeding. The fireball had completely seared the stumps like a pair of half-cooked hamburgers. What clothing hadn't been blown off was still smouldering and barely covered Joe's ample stomach which looked like someone had taken a handful of sausage skins and scattered them around the front of the car snagging some of the broken ribs poking through his ruptured chest. What was left of his arms lay loosely in his lap and for some strange reason his right one seemed to be reaching for the car keys which ironically still dangled from the ignition.

'Jesus Christ,' said the ashen-faced Billy again. He took a quick glance at Norton's equally pale face then ran to the gutter and started retching.

Norton didn't say or do anything, he just stood staring grimly at the charred remains of Joe Vorgnor the brothel owner. But while he stood there transfixed at the grisly sight, he found he was almost paralysed with a feeling crossed between horror and something he couldn't explain — the sobering and unnerving realisation suddenly swept over him.

He remembered looking through the window at Billy as Vorgnor had his hands on the keys sitting in the ignition. If that plumber hadn't rung up when he did, and that woman in the house had left it for just another second or two to yell out to Joe, there was no doubt he and Billy would either both be dead now or at least horribly maimed. A cold sweat formed on his brow and a chill ran up his spine as if someone had poured a tray of ice-cubes down his back; he closed his eyes as a violent shudder shook his entire body. When he opened them again Billy was standing in front of him wiping his mouth, pale-faced, staring at him.

'Well,' Billy finally said, almost inaudibly. 'what... what do you think we ought to do?'

Norton looked at Billy, looked at Joe in the car and back at Billy again. 'What do I think we ought to do?' he said, trying to lick some moisture on to his dried lips. 'I think we ought to buy more than one bloody lottery ticket tomorrow ... that's for fuckin' sure.

The Real Thing

Les Norton took another solid pull on his stubbie of Fourex and grinned broadly at Billy Dunne, Price Galese and George Brennan seated smiling around him in Price's office. It was about 3.30 on an October Sunday morning. Saturday night had just finished at the Kelly Club, the money was in the safe, the rest of the staff had gone home and the boys were sitting around relaxing, enjoying an after-work drink with the owner.

'Have a go at him,' said Price to the others, grinning almost as broadly as Les. 'He's got a lousy week off and you'd think he'd just won the lottery.'

'Well, you don't blame me,' said Norton, still smiling as he sucked heartily on his stubbie then belched into the back of his hand. 'I've got a chance to get out of the big smoke for a few days and I've got a nice new car to do it in. Why wouldn't I be laughing? I'm rapt.'

It was Norton's turn to have the following weekend off so he'd arranged to go up the north coast of New South Wales and stay with a friend who had a small farm up there. Price heard about it and, seeing that his wife was overseas, offered Les the use of her new BMW for the trip, which he enthusiastically accepted.

'Where are you going again?' asked George Brennan. 'Coffs Harbour?'

'Sawtell,' replied Norton. 'It's about five miles this side of Coffs. A mate of mine's got a little farm there somewhere.'

'That artist bloke?' said Billy.

'Yeah, Reggie Campbell,' said Les. 'He's a good little bloke.'

Norton had come across Reggie around a year or so ago early one morning on Bondi Beach. Reggie — or Reg as most

105

people called him — was a slightly built guy in his late twenties, although he looked a bit older, with wispy, thinning, fair hair and expressive, liquidy brown eyes that always looked like they were ready to melt and run down his face. Reg was a fairly quiet sort of bloke, but he was also a very good amateur painter.

The Sunday morning Les met Reg, he'd just pulled some air hostess from a party after work and they'd decided to go for a dawn swim before heading back to Les's house for a bit of breakfast and whatever. Reg was on the beach minding his own business, painting the sunrise when three drunken Maoris, who'd staggered across from the Fondue Here for a swim, decided to give him a hard time; squeezing his tubes of paint, throwing his brushes to each other, and pushing him around and so on. They were just about to wreck his easel when Norton, who was standing nearby with his lady friend, thought he'd better put his big red head in. One of the Maoris foolishly decided to throw a punch at Les and the next thing all three Astra bats were lying bleeding and moaning on the on the sand, teeth sticking through their gums, ribs cracked and their already flat noses a lot flatter than they would have been if they'd just had a swim and minded their own business in the first place.

After seeing Norton in action Reg's heart wasn't quite in painting scenes of peace and tranquility so Les and his lady friend took Reg back to Norton's for a cup of coffee and to clean him up a bit. After that Les and Reg became fairly good mates. In appreciation for what he'd done Reg gave Norton one of his better oils of the Bronte Boat Crew and when he bought his farm and moved out of Sydney, he kept in touch with him. Knowing how much Les loved the country, Reg was always inviting him up. Norton, how having the opportunity of over a week off from work and having never been to Coffs Harbour decided to take Reg up on the offer — anything to get out of the rat race and enjoy some fresh, clean country air again.

'And is Reg still doing plenty of painting Les?' asked Billy.

'Yeah, so he said over the phone,' replied Norton. 'Reckons he's goin' all right, too. Sellin' a few here and there. I'm lookin' forward to seeing him again to tell you the truth.'

'Yeah bullshit,' laughed Price. 'You just want to get up that North coast with all those hairy-legged young hippie shielas, eating magic mushrooms and smoking dope. You'll probably come back here next week with all flowers in your hair, playing a guitar like Cat Stevens.'

'Oh, I don't know about that,' smiled Norton, pulling the ring pull off another stubbie as the others roared laughing. 'But I have been known to have a bit of a puff on the odd joint now and again, and if any of those New South Wales chics want to have a drink and a bit of the other with a nice Queensland country boy, well I'll be in that, too. Very smartly.'

'And you reckon you can keep out of trouble up there, for over a week?' chuckled George Brennan.

'What do you mean keep out of trouble?' replied Norton indignantly. 'Christ, I'll be stuck out on a farm in the middle of nowhere with one other bloke. How am I gonna get into any strife? Jesus, George, give a man a bit of a go.' He took another pull on his stubbie, a look of extreme anguish on his face.

'Yeah, remember what happened last time you went away?' said Billy 'What about your little escapade in Brisbane?'

'Yeah. But that wasn't my fault.'

'Oh no. It never fuckin' is, is it?'

'Listen,' said Price sagely. 'If you do happen to get into any sort of bother up there, I know the top copper in Coffs Harbour. I'll give you his name before you go. I'm not worrying about you so much, you big hillbilly, but it is my wife's new car you're taking.'

'Fair dinkum,' cried Norton. 'I don't bloody believe this. This is like a bloody inquisition. You're all gettin' into me.' He was about to go on when he noticed the others just sitting staring at him in impassive silence. He finished his stubbie and threw the empty into a small bin next to the fridge. 'I s'pose it wouldn't hurt to give me that coppers's name though,' he finally said, a little reluctantly.

Late the following afternoon, after training, Norton caught a taxi over to Price's Vaucluse mansion and picked up the gleaming white BMW. As Price handed him the keys he noticed a shiny new pair of board racks attached to the roof.

'You didn't tell me Myra was into surfing Price,' he said, running his hands over them.

'One of the nephews put them on,' replied Price. 'He had to pick up a new surfboard over at Brookvale or somewhere. Leave them on, we'll take them off when you get back.'

'Righto.'

With a warm handshake, Les said goodbye to Price, slipped the BMW into drive and with a wave headed through the cast-iron security gates of Price's stately home. As he drove up Hopetoun Avenue the BMW purred like a baby tiger and responded immediately to his lightest touch. *How good's this,* he thought, cruising towards Rose Bay. He smiled smugly to himself and couldn't help putting his foot down a little. The ultra-modern dashboard and driver's seat moulded in around him in a shiny chrome and padded leather cocoon of flickering digital gauges and air-conditioned luxury.

When he got home he sat in the driveway for a while fiddling around with all the different little knobs and levers till he'd worked out the sun-roof, the air-conditioner, the stereo system and everything else. Norton often toyed with the idea of buying a new car — with all the black money he had he could easily afford it — but by looking around Norton discovered something about owning a decent car in Bondi. It isn't long before it's full of rust, got no hubcaps and a coat hanger for an aerial; that's if it isn't stolen or some drunk backs into it and drives away. So he just drove old bombs — for the time being anyway.

He spent what was left of the afternoon packing the car: there wasn't much. A suitcase with a few clothes and some training gear, a banana chair, a large carton of groceries and three cases of Fourex. When he'd finished he left the BMW in the driveway and drove his old Ford down to see his mate Paul at 'Peach Music' on the beach front, where Norton used to get most of his records and tapes. Paul was a mercurial little red-haired guy not unlike Warren who shared the house with Les. Les had talked him into making him up half a dozen ninety-minute tapes of various bands and artists to play while he was driving. After paying Paul he drove down to No Name's for a spaghetti and crumbed veal. With that sitting under his belt he bought a couple of bottles of wine and drove over to Clovelly to see this blonde hairdresser he'd been taking out on and off, on the off chance no one else was home and he might be able to give her one before he left. Unfortunately the girlfriends were home so they all just sat around drinking Norton's nice chilled Casal Garcia till he decided to hit the toe. He arrived home in time to say goodnight to Warren, his house mate, who was watching TV and sipping Jack Daniels with another glamour he'd met through the advertising agency. Les went straight to bed as he intended being up at four.

When the radio alarm went off at four, Norton didn't just open his eyes and stumble out of bed, he leapt out like he was diving off a springboard. It took him about three seconds to get dressed, then after using the bathroom he was too revved up to eat so he just made a big mug of Ovaltine which he drank standing in the backyard. The October morning was crisp and clear with scarcely a breath of wind as he stood there: the stars were still out but near the horizon they were just starting to get swallowed up by the faint glimmer of dawn spreading across from the east. *What a grouse day,* he though, as he finished his Ovaltine and went back inside. Just the day to be heading off for the country.

He put the empty cup in the sink, turned off the kitchen light and went out and got into the BMW, placing a bag of fruit and a small esky with six cans in it on the front seat next to him. In an instant the big powerful motor hummed into life. *Now what's Paul got here for me,* he thought, as he had a quick look through the small case of tapes his mate had made him. *This'll do. Tape One — Side A.* He dropped the cassette into the stereo. Cold Chisel belted out 'Same Old Merry-Go-Round'.

'Jimmy Barnes, you little beauty,' he said out loud, adjusting the graphic equaliser. 'You'll do me for an old mate.' He slipped the BMW into drive and before long he was cruising comfortably through Bondi Junction heading for the Harbour Bridge.

At that hour of the morning there was hardly a car on the road and still hardly any as he sped up the Pacific highway to the toll gates at Berowra. *That's the best sixty cents I've spent in a while,* he thought, as he dropped the money into the metal basket. Then with the rising sun starting to fill the inky-blue of the night sky with streaks of crimson and gold, and with Rose Tatoo wailing into 'Bad Boy for Love', he tore off along the tollway. 'Hit it Angry me old son,' he said happily, pushing the accelerator almost to the floor.

In what seemed like no time at all he was at the Central Mangrove turnoff to bring him out past Newcastle. About twenty miles of winding, narrow dirt road brought him down into the Wollombi Valley where he decided to stop next to a creek bed and have a leak. The air was as still and quiet as the inside of a church and crisper than fresh celery as he stepped out of the heated car and zipped up the front of his sheepskin jacket. The sounds of a few crows crying in the background and several cheeky magpies whistling to each other and strutting around the ground echoed eerily through the patches of dawn mist on either side of the road. Les stood at the front of the car relieving himself. A sudden movement among the bushes at the top of the creek bed caught his eye. A huge grey wombat wobbled into view then stopped, looking at him, it's eyes blinking groggily, it's big hairy nose twitching comically from side to side.

'Hello old fellah,' Norton called out with a grin, and unconsciously waving to it. 'Stay there a minute mate, I've got something here for you.' He did up his fly, went to the car and got an apple from the plasitc bag on the front seat. 'Here you are mate,' he called out cheerfully, bowling the piece of fruit to the fat, furry, grey animal. The wombat picked the apple up delicately in it's front paws, sniffed at it for a second then wobbled off back down the creek bed. 'You needn't worry mate,' laughed Norton, as he watched it's huge backside disappear out of sight. 'I see bigger wombats than you nearly every night in Sydney.'

With a grin from ear to ear he stretched his arms out by his side and took a huge lungfull of air in, held it for a moment or two, then let it out in a great cloud of steam which hung for a few seconds before evaporating into the cool morning air. The trees, the animals, the mellow singing of the birds and the unpolluted green silence of the bush instantaneously washed over Norton in a great wave of blissful rapture. He stood smiling happily to himself, taking it all in. Norton was back in the bush — he could scarcely have been happier. He got back in the car quite exhilarated and proceeded on his way.

Next stop was a Shell cafe just outside Bulahdelah for a chocolate milkshake and a hamburger with the works. With that sitting inside him Norton decided to motor along steadily and listen to his tapes while he took in the countryside and maybe stop for lunch at Kempsey. Even without speeding he figured he'd be at Reg's farm some time in the early afternoon.

The trouble with some new cars, especially the fully imported luxury models, is at times the power of their performance can be quite deceiving. Sitting behind the wheel surrounded by the latest in air-conditioned automotive technology you can be zipping along doing all sorts of speeds yet outside it hardly seems like you're moving at all; which is all right on German autobahns with ten lanes and no speed limit, but in Australia it's a different kettle of fish altoghter.

Norton was belting along listening to the stereo, taking in the beautiful New South Wales countryside, not a care in the world, when about ten miles the other side of Taree the haunting bongo sounds in Kevin Borich's 'Tell Me Why', was abruptly disturbed by the — Wow — Wow — Wow — of a piercing police siren. Les glanced in the rear-vision mirror and there was a speed cop, his blue light flashing, sitting right on his tail. Another glance at the German speedometer showed he was doing 185 kilometres an hour: but after driving his old bomb of a Ford with it's noisy sluggishness it hardly seemed like he was moving at all. He eased off the accelerator and pulled over to the side of the road; the speed cop pulled up a few metres in front of him.

Fuck it, thought Norton as switched off the motor. *I s'pose I'd better see what this prick wants to do. You never know, I might be able to bribe or talk me way out of it.* He got out of the car, a sheepish grin on his face. 'Sorry Boss,' he said, making an open-handed gesture. 'You've got me cold. I know I was speeding all right. You want my licence?'

'Shut up. Put both your hands on top of the car and spread your legs,' barked the tall, rangy speed cop. He still had his full face helmet and sunglasses on, but Norton noticed he'd undone his holster and his right hand was resting on the butt of his service revolver.

Norton looked at him incredulously. 'What was that again?' he asked, scarcely believing his ears.

The cop raised his voice and started to draw his revolver. 'I said, put your hands on the roof of the car and spread your legs. Are you deaf or something? Now fuckin' move.'

Norton looked at the cop and shook his head. 'Yeah righto Boss Hogg,' he almost spat. 'I didn't know I was in Alabama.'

The cop moved alongside and just to the rear of Les. 'Oh a smart cunt eh?' He bent slightly at the knees and punched Norton fair in the ribs with his gloved fist — hard.

Norton let out a roar of pain and anger. 'Why you...' he hissed furiously, spinning round to face the speed cop. Gun or no gun, cop or no cop he was going to jam that motorbike in his blue-uniformed arse, ring Price and worry about it later. He was about to make a grab for the cop when unexpectedly the cop ran around the other side of the BMW — underneath his helmet Les thought he could hear him laughing.

'How did you like that you big red-headed cunt?' said the cop. 'That's for the nose job you gave me when I was playing for Newtown.' He whipped off his helmet to reveal a freckly, grinning face with a badly broken nose and a shock of spiky red hair almost the same colour as Les's.

Norton looked at him for a moment then through his discomfort and pain let out a bellow of laughter you could have heard back in Taree. 'Well I'll be buggered. Carrots McCarthy. What the fuck are you doing here?'

'Watching out for no good bastards like you,' was the raucous reply.

The speed cop turned out to be George McCarthy but everyone called him 'Carrots' because of his spiky red hair. George used to play centre for Newtown in Sydney. During a preseason game one year a bit of an all-in started and George king-hit Les: he may as well have punched the nearest brick wall. Norton turned round and hit Carrots with a left hook that squashed his nose flatter than a trodden-on potato-chip, put him out of the game and left him with a pair of black eyes that dark you could have written on them with chalk. The funny part about it — rugby league being what it is — the following year George finished up playing with Easts and, until Les left the club, they became pretty good mates.

'How did you know it was me?' asked Norton, after they'd shaken hands and finished giving each other a friendly push and shove around.

'I didn't. But I know that car and plates. That's Myra Galese's car. It gets the silkworm treatment everywhere it goes in this state. I saw it rattling past so I thought I'd better have a 'Captain Cook' just to see what's going on, and when I saw your big, ugly, red head in the front I knew I had to do something. And here we are mate.'

'My ugly, red head. You oughta talk,' said Norton, pointing at George's spiky red mop. 'I'll tell you what though.' Les gave his ribs a bit of a pat. 'You still haven't got a bad punch for a skinny fellah.'

'I haven't got a bad punch.' George laughed and pointed to his badly dented hooter. 'What about this? You oughta talk.'

They stood there half shaping up and grinning at each other. 'So how long have you been up here anyway George?' said Norton, when they finished laughing.

'Oh, about two years. I transferred up here to coach the Taree Sea Eagles.'

'Yeah? They any good?'

'No, they're not worth two-bob. But they're good blokes and I love it up here, and so does the missus and the kids. It's as easy as shit compared to Sydney.'

'I know exactly what you mean George.'

Norton explained how he got the car and was on his way to Sawtell for a short holiday. He decided the best thing to do would be to get the small esky off the front seat. Pretty soon they were sitting at the side of the road laughing, kicking goals, scoring tries and talking the general waffle old football mates talk about when they get together.

After about an hour of magging in the bright spring sunshine, while the other cars swished by them on the highway, Carrots stood up and looked at his watch.

'Well Les,' he said, draining the last cold can of beer. 'I suppose I'd better get back out there and apprehend a few more evil-doers.'

'You certainly apprehended me you bludger,' smiled Les, giving his ribs another pat. As he picked up the empty cans he noticed the logo on George's police bike. 'This a BMW, too,' he said. 'They any good?'

'Reckon. It's one of the new "J" series. Electronically fuel-injected. Goes like a shower of shit. It's bloody frightening at times.'

'Yeah? How come you don't ride a Jap bike, like a big Suzuki or a Kwaka?'

'Turn it up Les. I used to be an old bikie. You know the old sayin' we used to have — I'd rather see my sister in a brothel than my brother on a Honda.'

'Fair enough.'

George zipped up the front of his leather jacket and they shook hands warmly again with Les promising he'd drop in and see George and his family on the way back, if he had time.

'I'll tell you what,' said George, with a bit of a cheeky grin as he put his helmet back on. 'Seein' as I held you up for an hour, belted the shit out of you and drank all your piss, how would you like a police escort to Kempsey. You reckon you can keep up?'

'I'll have a go,' replied Norton, with a smile and a wink.

'Righto, let's go. I feel like goin' for a bit of a blat to tell you the truth.'

George leisurely hit the electric starter button and the big, powerful motorbike throbbed into life. Norton got behind the wheel of the BMW, started the motor and adjusted his seatbelt. With a casual flick of a switch George activated the siren and flashing blue light then slewed off on to the road in a shower of dust and gravel, with Norton, tyres smoking about ten metres behind. Within twenty seconds they were screaming along the Pacific highway at almost 200 kilometres an hour. Inside the luxury saloon Les still felt relatively safe, but the ear-piercing screeching of the Bridgestone steel-cap tyres, as they hugged the bitumen like chewing-gum, and the blur of the cars they were overtaking as they pulled over at the staccato wailing

113

of the siren, certainly indicated they were moving all right. In front of him, George seemed almost horizontal to the highway, ploughing into the bends and obviously having the time of his life. Behind him Norton's face was set in a grim smile as he fed the car skilfully and gently into the curves, but behind his sunglasses his eyes were as white and as round as two dinner-plates.

About four kilometres south of Kempsey Carrots slowed down and indicated for Les to overtake him. As he did Carrots doubled back then pulled up alongside. 'I'll see you on the way back Les,' he yelled into the window. 'So long mate.'

'Righto George, see you then.' Norton gave a wave out the window. Carrots did a U-turn and headed back towards Taree. Les cruised leisurely into Kempsey.

He pulled up outside the nearest hotel, went inside and ordered two middies of New, which he downed in quick succession. His hands and knees were still shaking slightly even after the second one, so he ordered a third. A quick glance at his watch indicated they'd travelled from Taree to Kempsey — roughly 140 kilometres — in a little less than forty minutes. He smiled, shook his head and shuddered slightly then ordered another beer.

The enticing aroma of the counter lunches and the incessant talking of the two friendly-looking old birds serving them up attracted his attention so he ambled over. The corned silverside, with parsley sauce and fresh vegetables looked all right. He ended up having two plates, plus bread and butter custard with fresh cream. This was washed down with another sparkling middie of New.

His nerves back to normal and his stomach full Les had a stroll around Kempsey, bought the morning paper, filled the tank then proceeded on his way to Sawtell — at a considerably more sedate pace this time.

By the time Norton stopped for a crap at Barraganyatti, a milkshake at Nambucca Heads and another one plus a bit of a perv on a massive-breasted young blonde working in a paper shop at Urunga, it was almost three. He came to Bonville Station and found the Telegraph Point Road turn-off to Reg's farm. He had another look at the little map he'd drawn out when Reg had spoken to him over the phone. Ten kilometres down Telegraph Point Road, turn right at Friday Creek Road, follow that another three kilometres and you'd see Reg's letterbox out the front. The farm was about a kilometre in from the road. Easy.

As he drove slowly along Telegraph Point Road, Les couldn't help admiring the lush, green beauty of the countryside spread out on either side of the dusty, red dirt road. Undulating emerald hills scattered with blue-gum and eucalyptus trees and great, ashen-coloured granite boulders would tumble into tiny, crystal-clear creeks and fern-covered gullies that meandered through dense patches of sub-tropical rain forest. On either side of the road rough-hewn poles supporting a sagging wire fence would disappear momentarily into patches of lantana, then emerge on the other side as splintery, wooden slip-rails, turning grey from years in the outback sun. One or two rusty cyclone-wire gates indicated there were farms around but they were very few and far between. Friday Creek Road was a lot narrower than the other, considerably bumpier and wound straight into the rain forest. Les was forced to slow down quite a bit, but it wasn't long before he found the entrance to Reg's farm: a white-washed wooden gate between two stumpy, chipped, white wooden poles with a psychedelically painted oil-drum sitting on one. The gate was open, so he drove straight in and along a narrow, uneven drive, that looked as if it would be just about inaccessible in wet weather.

Sitting in the car Norton couldn't help breaking into a grin at Reg's country abode. The ancient wooden farmhouse stood in the middle of a small clearing and was surrounded by trees, shrubs and brightly-coloured native flowers. A ricketty wooden veranda, full of cobwebbed pot plants, some hanging, most just sitting there, ran the length of the front. This was divided by a front door, with a loose-fitting fly-screen clinging desperately to it, and an old rusty horse-shoe nailed crookedly on top. A lopsided brick chimney pushed through the green, galvanised-iron roof, which ran up alongside a huge jacaranda tree dropping sweetly scented purple and blue flowers all over the top of the house. At the other end a spreading bougainvillea wrapped round an old water tank in a flowering burst of orange and crimson was so bright it almost dazzled you. Even though the old ramshackle house looked like it would probably blow away in a decent gust of wind and gave the appearance that you'd have to give it a coat of paint just to get it condemned, it simply oozed character and sleepy rustic charm. Norton fell in love with it at first sight.

From a small wooden shed just to the front and right and even more dilapidated than the ancient house, an old female, cross blue cattle dog, cross something else staggered out into the light, blinked a few times, gave a mandatory four or five

115

barks then, as Les got out of the car, flopped at his feet, rolled over on its back, tongue out, eyes rolling and looked up at him as if to say, 'Go on, give me belly a bit of a rub willya love'. Norton bent down and started rubbing the old girl's ample stomach while it squirmed on the ground with delight.

'Watch out for the dog mate,' he heard a voice call from the doorway of the shed. 'It'll tear you apart.'

'Its head's not the best,' replied Norton standing up. 'But Jesus it's got nice tits.'

Reg walked over from the old shed wearing a paint-spattered white T-shirt and a pair of cut-down jeans. He had a huge grin on his face as he took Norton's outstretched hand and started pumping it vigorously. For a slightly built artist his handshake was warm, firm and sincere.

'Well, you managed to find the place all right,' he said.

'Yeah, no trouble at all. I would have been here earlier but I just took my time and had a look at the countryside on the way up. It sure is nice.'

'It is, isn't it? Jesus it's good to see you Les. I'm rapt that you came up.'

'Mate, I'm rapt to be able to get out of Sydney for a while.'

'Well you'll love it up here.' Reg noticed the brand new BMW. 'Hey not a bad car you've got Les. Shit you've kicked on.'

'It's not mine, it's my boss's. He loaned it to me for the trip. I'll tell you what Reg, I like your little farm, it's the grouse.'

'Yeah it's a beauty isn't it. Wall-to-wall carpet snakes and hot-and-cold running possums in the roof.'

Norton laughed. 'How much land have you got?'

'Thirty hectares — about sixty or so acres.'

'Jees, that's all right.'

'Yeah, got a creek and a dam down the back. Even got a bit of a swimmin' hole.'

'Fair dinkum? Jees you've killed 'em Reg, good on you.'

'Thanks Les.'

As they spoke several sulphur crested cockatoos landed in the jacaranda tree and started screeching at each other. These were soon joined by a flock of noisy rainbow lorikeets and a mob of argumentative eastern rosellas. In a moment the jacaranda tree erupted in a cacophony of abuse that seemed to be directed at a number of crimson finches, nutmeg mannikins and red-eared fire-tails bobbing and chirping around in the bougainvillea at the opposite end of the house. Several cheeky magpies decided to put their heads in also then the dog started up.

'Christ,' said Norton, when the din finally subsided a bit. 'You sure you've got enough birds up here.'

'Bit better than those daggy-looking pigeons and lice-infested starlings I used to paint down at Bondi.'

'And those one-legged seagulls.' Norton looked fondly at the birds then threw back his head and roared laughing. 'Reg that's music to my ears. It reminds me of home.' He looked back at the tree then turned to his artist friend. 'Oh Christ Reg I think I'm gonna cry.'

They both started laughing. Les got his gear out of the boot. He handed Reg the box of groceries and they went inside. The dog crawled under Reg's Mini panel-van and went to sleep in the shade.

'Just throw your stuff in here,' said Reg, leading Norton along a narrow corridor, through the lounge and into a modest but spotlessly clean bedroom that faced the jacaranda tree. As Les threw his suitcase on the white, single, wooden bed its beautiful perfume wafted through the billowing lace curtains.

'Hey this is all right,' he said, placing his overnight bag on the dressing table, which was also painted white and topped with a large round mirror. This stood next to a fair-sized wardrobe, also painted white.

'Yeah, it's not a bad little room this,' replied Reg. 'You get the sun first thing in the morning in here and that bed's nice and comfortable. There's fly-screens on the window to keep the mozzies out too — which I might add are as big as Harrier jump-jets up here and just as bloody noisy. Come on I'll show you the rest of the joint.'

The rest of the place was much like the outside — a little the worse for wear and tear over the years but full of charm. An ancient, brown, three-piece chesterfield filled the lounge-room. This faced a bamboo coffee table, obviously home-made, and an inexpensive stereo system and TV with a chipped black phone sitting on the top. A few indoor plants covered the holes in the threadbare brown carpet, and several of Reg's landscapes, which to Norton's eyes looked bloody good, adorned the walls. The narrow hallway, also hung with paintings, led past another bedroom, slightly bigger than Les's and into a surprisingly well-appointed kitchen. A large modern fridge, covered with magnetic do-dads and magazine cartoons and topped with a huge wicker bowl of tropical fruit, hummed away in the corner next to the built-in cupboards. This faced a long, solid wooden bench covered in modern electrical appliances. It had a stainless-steel, twin-tub sink built into it. Next to this was a porta-gas stove that appeared to be brand new. An extensive spice rack and several posters covered the walls and more colourful indoor plants and vines meandered brilliantly around the sunlight streaming through the kitchen window.

'Were you expecting a brewery strike Les?' asked Reg, as Norton placed the three cases of Fourex on the big, wooden kitchen table.

'I get a bit thirsty now and again Reg,' replied Norton, 'and I wasn't too sure whether they sold the good stuff up here.'

Reg took one of the cases, put it in the fridge and came up with two cans of Carlton Draught. 'You think you can force this down till the other gets cold?'

'I'll try,' smiled Les, tugging the ring-pull from his can. 'Cheers mate.'

'Cheers Les. Good to see you.'

They finished the first two cans in the kitchen then Reg took another two out of the fridge and suggested they go and sit on the veranda. Norton took off his shirt and sneakers and they plonked themselves down in two old, comfortable leather chairs and sat talking and enjoying the afternoon breeze. The sun started to drift slowly behind the distant hills and valleys. It was beautiful and quiet in the peaceful balminess of the spring day drawing to an end. Norton had just closed his eyes for a moment when several rainbow lorikeets, fluttered down on to the railing running along the veranda. They were soon joined by more and it wasn't long before there were at least twenty glaring and squawking at each other, their tiny multi-coloured bodies rolling from side to side, parading up and down the railing with a gait not unlike a mob of drunken sailors.

Reg put his beer down and stood up. 'Oh well,' he said, 'I s'pose I'd better give these miserable little bastards their tea.' He went into the kitchen and returned with a large enamel dish full of stale bread which he'd soaked with water and covered in honey. 'Righto you little shits,' he said, tapping the side of the plate with a knife. 'Here you are. Get into it and no bloody fighting.'

At the sound of Reg tapping on the plate several of the lorikeets flew on to him swarming over his arms, shoulders and head. He put the plate down at the top of the stairs. The next thing it was on. The tiny but temperamental little birds started tearing spitefully into each other to get at the bread and honey; though most of the fighting seemed to emanate from half a dozen lorikeets who seemed to want the lot for themselves.

Reg stood up and shook his head slowly. Tiny feathers were flying everywhere. The little parrots ripped into each other in an ear-splitting, almost deafening crescendo of visciousness.

'The bloody gang of six again,' he said, still shaking his head. 'Looks like I'm going to have to get my gun and sort this out.'

Norton brought his beer down from his mouth. 'You're not going to shoot them, are you?' he asked, a little incredulously.

Reg just stood stoney-faced. 'Sometimes Les, a man's just gotta do what a man's just gotta do.' He turned and disappeared into the kitchen.

Norton shook his head and stared after Reg. It seemed a bit strange that Reg, a quiet peace-loving artist, would take the trouble to feed the lovely little birds then start shooting them just because they fought among themselves and made a bit of noise. *Poor little buggers,* he thought, as he watched them still squabbling furiously over the bread and honey.

Reg was soon back standing grim and defiant on the veranda. He had a kid's sheriff's badge pinned to the front of his T-shirt and a water pistol, dripping water, clenched in his right hand.

'Righto you little shits,' he said, taking aim at the biggest lorikeet in the gang of six. 'You ought to know better by now than to mess with Sheriff Campbell. This water pistol's fully loaded and I shoot to drown.' In an instant the gang of six were screeching even more furiously as a barrage of well-aimed shots from Reg's water pistol forced them away from the bread and honey.

Norton had just taken a mouthful of beer when this happened and half of it went down the wrong way. He fell off the chair in a spasmodic fit of choking, coughing laughter. He dropped his can of beer and doubled up on the floor, tears streaming down his face. Reg ignored him and stood there with the water pistol in a full combat stance blasting away at the lorikeets and yelling: 'Cop that you bastard. And that, and that.'

Norton managed to prop himself up on one elbow in the spilt beer. 'You're fuckin' mad,' he wheezed, trying vainly to get his breath and strength back.

Reg turned slowly to Les. 'Did you say something stranger?' he said, completely po-faced. Then it was Norton's turn to cop several bursts of water in the face. He put his hand up feebly to protect himself but was forced to collapse into a pile of hysterical disbelief.

'You're in this too Sally, you old moll.' Reg walked over to his car and started squirting the dog till she finally got up, put her tail between her fat legs, and with ears pinned back slunk off under the house to hide. Reg stood in the clearing twirling the water pistol round his finger.

'There's one thing you'd better learn stranger,' he said, giving Les another squirt in the face. 'I'm the law this side of Friday Creek Road and don't you, or no bird or dog for that matter, ever forget it. Son of a bitch.' He gave Les and the lorikeets another burst then went into the kitchen, returning with another two cans of beer.

The lorikeets settled down, Les managed to compose himself, though he could still hardly talk, and they sat absorbing the peaceful tranquility of the north-coast countryside. The sun settled down behind the hills turning the blue sky into orange, crimson, purple, primrose and amber before it finally, tenderly said goodnight. Soon Venus and the moon would appear then the inky, cobalt night would fill with countless silver stars.

'I think it's about time we went inside,' said Reg, swatting at his arm. 'Here come the bloody mosquitoes.' They finished their beers and went into the kitchen.

'Well, what do you fancy for tea Les?' said Reg, as Norton seated himself at the kitchen table.

'I don't care. How about you whip something up? You were a pretty good cook if I remember rightly. There's a whole Scotch fillet there. I got it at Nambucca on the way up.'

'I might make some sate beef in the wok. You hungry?'

'You're kidding. I'd eat the crutch out of a rag doll.' Norton stifled a yawn. 'I'll tell you what, I'm blody tired I know that.' As Les stared absently into his can of beer he heard Reg talking at the cupboard.

'Get back Señor Alfonso. Go on, back, back.'

'Who the bloody hell are you talking to?' asked Norton.

'Señor Alfonso.'

'Who the fuck's that?'

'Come here I'll show you.'

Norton got up and walked over as Reg swung open the cupboard door. Clinging to the inside was the biggest tarantula he'd ever seen. It's furry, brown body was as round as a saucer and it's pinky eyes on the end of their stalks looked as big as cherry pips. 'Jesus,' he exclaimed. 'He's a big bastard. Where'd you get him?'

'Oh he's been here for ages. Don't hurt him, will you? He eats all the flies and moths.' Reg gave the huge spider a nudge with his finger and it scurried into the cupboard and disappeared among the tins and jars.

'I never kill spiders,' said Norton. 'Not like those dills in the city. Soon as they see one they can't spray it quick enough.' He took a sip on his can as Reg closed the cupboard. 'I got a couple of huntsman spiders in my kitchen and you never see a cockroach in my place. And that ain't bad for Bondi.' Reg winked with approval. 'I'll tell you what' continued Norton. 'While you're getting tea I might go and unpack my gear.

'Righto. This'll be about half an hour.'

Norton yawned again and trudged into his bedroom. He threw the suitcase up on the bed and unzipped it. He put his T-shirts, socks and underwear in the dressing table and hung his jeans and shirt in the old wardrobe. He was about to put his shoes at the bottom of the wardrobe when a movement under the bed caught his eye. He reached down and pulled back the bed cover to find a monstrous great carpet snake curled up under the bed having a sleep. It was as thick as a fire hose and at least three metres long.

'Hey Reg,' he yelled, as he stormed back into the kitchen. 'There's a bloody great carpet snake under my bed. It's gotta be a fifty metres fuckin' long.'

'Yeah, that's Madam Lash,' replied Reg, hardly looking up as he stirred the food sizzling in the wok. 'She's all right. She eats all the mice and cane toads.'

'Oh she eats the mice and cane toads, does she? And what have you got down the back to eat any feral pigs you might have. A bunyip?'

'No. No bunyips. But there's a couple of yowies up in the hills.'

Norton shook his head and went back into the bedroom to continue unpacking his gear, keeping a trepidatious eye on Madam Lash still curled up enjoying her late afternoon kip under the bed. Ten minutes later Reg called Les for tea.

'Well fair dinkum Reg, that was absolutely beautiful,' said Norton, running his finger round his dessert plate and sticking it in his mouth.

'You like it eh?'

'Oh mate, it was grouse.'

Reg had cooked up a huge serve of sate beef, fresh, steamed local vegetables and brown rice. He'd followed this with strawberries and bananas, lightly fried, then sprinkled with shredded coconut and covered with ice-cream and Grand Marnier.

'Not a bad life out here in the country, is it?' smiled Reg.

'Don't worry,' replied Norton. 'I'll be back here one day. You can stick that city. Though I gotta admit Sydney's a top town and it's been pretty kind to me, but.'

'Yeah, you've got to go where your heart is Les.'

Norton winked. 'And I can just about smell Queensland from here.'

They washed up the dishes and Les was yawning and rubbing his eyes constantly. When they'd finished he put his hand on Reg's shoulder. 'Mate,' he yawned again. 'I hate to be rude but I'm gonna have to go straight to bed. I'm about knackered.'

'Go on mate,' replied Reg. 'You're right, in fact I won't be far behind you. Those few beers have made me tired, too. I'll see you in the morning.'

'G'night mate. Thanks for everything.'

Norton trudged wearily off into his bedroom. He didn't bother to switch on the light as he climbed out of his jeans and crawled straight into bed. He closed his eyes and lay there for a moment enjoying the perfume from the jacaranda tree as it drifted through the window. He was about to nod off when a noise from the end of the bed made him open his eyes. He peered at a movement in the gloom then switched on the bed lamp behind his head. Sitting on the brass rail at the end of the bed were two fat, grey possums, their tails curled up over their backs. They blinked at him with their huge, inquisitive, brown eyes.

'Hey Reg,' he yelled at the top of his voice, 'there's two bloody great possums in my bed.'

'Yeah, they're all right,' came Reg's voice from the kitchen. 'That's Sonny and Cher. They eat all the scraps.'

Norton shook his head for a moment before he switched off the light. 'G'night Reg,' he called out.

'G'night Les. See you in the morning.'

Carpet snakes under my bed and possums in it, thought Les, as he lay there and drifted off into sleep. *What bloody next?'* He was asleep fifteen minutes before the grin disappeared from his face.

After one of the best night's sleep he'd ever had, Norton was up before six the following morning; it was deathly still and the dew was still sparkling on the fields and trees. The only sound was the distant chirping and crying of some unseen birds. Reg was still asleep so he quietly got into his training gear, had a cup of tea and went for an hour's run along Friday Creek road. He topped this off with another hour of exercises then, after breakfast with Reg, decided he wasn't going to make a move all day: not even a phone call. He wasn't even going to start the car. Reg showed Les his studio — the dilapidated old shed out the front — and told him he was going to work on a painting all morning but after lunch he'd show him over the farm and take him down to the swimming hole at the back.

Not wishing to disturb his little artist mate while he was at work Norton just sat quietly out the front listening to the birds, drinking the odd stubbie of Fourex and reading one of Reg's books — something about a UFO conspiracy and the end of the earth, which turned out to be just an excuse for the author to go on a Bible-bashing rave.

About one o'clock Les knocked up a huge pot of tea and a stack of juicy steak sandwiches swimming in thousand island dressing. After they'd finished eating Reg put on his sneakers and took him down to show him the swimming hole: or as Reg called it 'his nine metre Olympic pool'.

'It's only about two hundred metres down the back,' said Reg. He started leading Les along a small trail at the rear of the house. 'But it's hidden by all the trees and you can't see it.'

'Why don't you get a chain-saw and cut 'em down?'

'Yeah. I was thinking of poisoning them to tell you the truth.'

'Get a bulldozer in and tar the lot over.'

'Yeah, that's not a bad idea. Might build a service station.'

'What about a nice block of home units full of screaming ethnics. I hate trees myself.'

'Oh so do I Les. They're a pain in the arse.'

'Yeah. Especially when they start making all that oxygen of a night. The noise buggers up me sleep.'

The narrow, leafy trail meandered down through thickets of flowering lantana and underneath vine covered trees to a small sparkling creek that gurgled happily over the shiny river stones and old logs. A few metres to their left a small, picturesque waterfall tumbled down several metres of moss-covered granite boulders to form a beautiful shaded billabong about three metres deep and about eight metres across. Several trees grew around and over the billabong and from an overhanging branch of the largest a length of knotted rope dangled motionless a metre from the still, shimmering surface. To add even more delight to the already colourful scene a number of fruit-bearing trees grew around the edges. It was so pretty Norton stood mesmerised: he was almost speechless.

'Jesus Christ, Reg,' he finally said. 'This is like something out of the Garden of Eden. It's unbelievable.'

'You like my little nine metre pool Les?' grinned Reg.

'Like it? It's bloody beautiful.'

'Here have a mandarin.' Reg reached up, pulled off one of the large soft fruits and tossed it to Les, who quickly peeled it and popped a portion in his mouth.

'Mm. How sweet are these?' Norton rolled his eyes with ecstasy savouring the nectareous juice.

Reg sat on one of the rocks grinning. 'There's orange trees, apple, apricot, peach, banana. I even got avocado and guava — and those passionfruits should be on soon.'

Norton spat out the last of the pips and started unbuttonng his shirt. 'Fuck this,' he said abruptly. 'I'm goin' for a swim.' He stripped off the rest of his clothes and plunged naked into the pool diving straight to the bottom. 'Whoa shit,' he yelled, as he resurfaced and shook his head vigorously. 'It's bloody cold.'

'Get's a bit fresh, don't it?' called Reg.

'Whoah, reckon. But it's still good.' Les dived down to the bottom again then climbed up the rope a few times, jumping back in and sending great waves splashing over the rocks at the edge of the pool. After splashing around happily a while longer he clambered out and stood on a rock next to Reg shaking the water out of his ear.

'Mate, that was the grouse. Fair dinkum.'

As Norton stood next to Reg wiping the water off his body with his hands, Reg began to laugh. 'I'll tell you what,' he chuckled. 'Those sexy hostesses at the Kelly Club'd get a bit of a giggle if they saw their big tough doorman right now. That waters a lot colder than you think.'

Les glanced down at his dripping loins. 'Shit,' he muttered, 'where'd it go? It was there a minute ago.' Reg kept laughing. 'Hey, don't let that fool you,' grinned Norton. 'I'm a dynamite lover. You needn't worry about that.'

'Yeah. 200 pound of dynamite with a half-inch fuse. Here, have another mandarin.'

Les got his clothes on and Reg took him back to the house via the dam which was built into the side of the creek a hundred metres or so up from the billabong. A length of black, plastic hose ran from the dam up to the water-tank where Reg showed Les a small diesel pump he used to keep the tank full at all times. Les got a couple of stubbies out of the fridge, and they sat on the veranda while the noisy little lorikeets returned for their evening feed of bread and honey. They were a bit more well-behaved this time and Reg didn't have to reach for his water pistol, so they both sat watching them while the setting sun painted the sky with background colour.

'I might go down to Sawtell tomorrow,' said Les. 'Have a surf and a bit of a hang on the beach for a while. You want to come?'

'I wouldn't mind,' replied Reg, 'but I want to stay here and finish those two paintings. I might come down with you Thursday.'

'Suit yourself. Well, here come the bloody mozzies again.' Norton squashed a monster on his leg. 'We go inside?' They finished their beers and went into the kitchen.

Reg was conned into cooking tea again — braised beef with Hoi-Sin sauce and vegetables, followed by rockmelon, honey-dew melon and pawpaw balls covered with ice-cream and a few nips of Tia Maria.

'You don't live too bad for a struggling artist,' mused Norton over his third dish of sweets.

'I get by,' replied Reg carefully. 'I'll tell you about it while we're watching TV. You like "Minder"?'

'Terry and Arfa? And Dave at the Winchester Club? You're kidding Reg, that's my favourite show.'

They took their time washing up. When they'd finished Les got another two stubbies out of the fridge and they settled down in front of the TV. While they were waiting for 'Nation-wide' to finish Reg went to his bedroom and returned with a small plastic bag of marijuana and a bamboo bong, which he placed on the coffee table.

'Like a smoke Les?'

'I wouldn't mind, but I'm that tired, I'd end up falling asleep and missing "Minder".' Norton picked up the bag of pot and examined it for a few seconds. 'Looks like good dope.'

Reg winked knowingly. 'I've never smoked better.'

He broke a piece off and started mulling it up with a little tobacco in a bowl. 'You sure you don't want a puff? "Rock Arena" is on later. It's Midnight Oil and INXS tonight.'

'Oils - Oils - Oils,' chanted Norton.

'You like the Oils Les?'

'Oh yeah! They're all right. That lead singer's enormous.'

'There's a rumour going round that he's thinking of running for parliament on a nuclear disarmament policy.'

'Yeah, I heard that, too. I reckon if he does he'll get some votes. The kids are rapt in him.'

Reg winked. 'Let's hope it happens.'

When he'd mulled up enough dope for about four little cones, Reg lit the first one, sucked it into his lungs, held it for a few seconds, then let it out with a look of great relish. After the fourth they settled back to watch TV; Reg didn't say a great deal during 'Minder' but he was laughing like a drain at the gags.

After Terry had knocked out his mandatory four or five villains and Arthur had conned a few punters out of their money Les got another couple of stubbies out of the fridge, and they sat talking while the late news was on. Reg had another two cones. A solitary mosquito got in the room somehow which Reg quickly dispatched with a short burst from a can of Johnson Protector.

'So this is life on the farm eh?' said Norton, as Reg put the fly spray down on the floor.

'Yeah, this is it.'

'You don't look like you're starving Reg. That kitchen and bathroom look the grouse. You must be selling a few paintings?'

'I sell a few, but I don't get a great deal of money. Not for the effort I put into them.' Reg smiled a little self-consciously and shrugged his shoulders. 'So I grow a little bit of dope on the side.'

'I tipped that.' Norton paused for a moment then burst out laughing. 'So. You're a rotten fuckin' dope dealer eh?'

'Oh yeah,' retorted Red, 'I'm a regular Terry bloody Clarke.'

'How much do you grow?'

'About a dozen or so plants. Last year I ended up with about two kilos of dope. I made just over a thousand dollars on the side.'

'Phew!' Norton let out a long, low whistle. 'Jesus, Reg,' he laughed, 'you're the original Coffs Harbour connection. I hope I'm safe staying here.'

Reg took another pull on his stubbie. His face turned slightly more serious. 'If I wanted to Les I could make heaps — but I don't believe in it. I give most of it away or swap it for food or favours.' He nodded towards the kitchen and bathroom. 'Like the plumber or the carpenter. It's just that the stuff I grow's that good everybody wants it, so I just sell a little bit to some friends in Sydney, look after them and they're happy. I tell the Taxation Department I've managed to sell a few paintings, pay a little bit of tax and they're happy, too. I only go on the "jam roll" every now and again, the Department of Social Security thinks I'm a reasonably solid citizen and they're happy as well.'

'And you get a free smoke and you're happy.'

'That's about it in a nutshell.'

Norton finished his stubbie the same time as Reg took the empties out to the kitchen and returned with two fresh ones. 'I suppose you'd be pretty safe on your farm, too,' he said, settling back on the old lounge chair. 'Not much chance of you getting busted right out here.'

'Don't you believe it.'

'What? Surely the coppers wouldn't come out all this way just to pinch you for a dozen lousy plants.'

'Yeah? Pig's arse.' Reg's voice started to rise. 'I've only got to get dobbed in by one of those bloody old concerned citizens and the drug squad'd be out in here in five minutes. Four dirty big coppers tipping my place upside down, one of them'd probably give me a belt in the mouth just for fun. They treat it like a half-pie joke but they lumber me up in front of some brandy-sodden, gout-ridden, old magistrate, charge me with possession, cultivation, smoking, supplying. They throw in whistling in the pictures and square-dancing in a roundhouse, and the beak, who's only interested in getting his thousand a week and getting home to his bottle of Johnnie Walker, gives me twelve months. I'd have to do it in bloody Grafton, too.'

Norton screwed his face up slightly and looked at Reg. 'That doesn't happen, does it?'

'Are you kidding Les?' Reg was on his feet now gesticulating with his hands. 'A friend of mine in Sydney, Franz Horvath — he's a poet. Some old sheila dobbed him in for having ten plants on his sun deck. The beak gave him three months in Long Bay; he wasn't out there a fortnight and these old lags beat him up and pack-raped him. He's a cripple now— for what?'

Norton looked at Reg a little incredulously: he could just imagine what would happen to his little artist mate if he had to do a year in Grafton gaol. 'But that's just plain fuckin' stupid. I mean, they spend all that time and effort pinchin' blokes like you for having a bit of pot and Sydney's full of heroin. I oughta bloody know, I work at the Cross and I live in Bondi. It's everywhere.'

127

'That's what shits people like me Les. The coppers — thanks to the stupid bloody politicians that run the State — are filling the courts with people for having a few plants in their backyard or a couple of joints in their socks and while we're all in there wasting time and the taxpayer's money another ten kilograms of heroin hits the street. We're just easy marks, that's all and it helps fill their charge sheets. It's bloody ridiculous.'

'You're right you know Reg.' Norton took another swig from his stubbie then shrugged his shoulders slightly as he spoke. 'But what's the answer?'

Reg looked at Norton for a few moments before he said anything. 'The answer Les is that simple it gives you the shits.' He put his beer on the coffee table and sat back down on the lounge. 'There's at least 200,000 people smoke dope in New South Wales, right?'

'Oh easy,' replied Norton.

'Well, why not give them a licence to grow say ten plants a year and charge them a hundred bucks for it. That gets all the so-called evil dope smokers out of the road in one go, it stops the trafficking in marijuana and the state government cops twenty million dollars a year for its trouble.'

Norton nodded his head slowly in approval. 'That makes a lot of sense Reg. Go on.'

'Then the government could use that twenty million to fight the heroin importers. They're the cunts they should be after. Boost up the Customs Department. Educate the kids about the shit. Increase the drug squad, if it's for that purpose.'

'Jesus Reg,' chuckled Norton. 'That doesn't sound like you.'

'Yeah? Well try this for size. I reckon they ought to bring back the death penalty and hang the heroin dealers. You can get out of gaol Les but you can't get out of a coffin. And don't get it in to your head Les that I'm dirty on the cops, I'm not. They got a job to do just like anyone else and it can be a pretty shitty one at times, too. I know that. I'm just dirty on a stupid part of the law and the way they enforce it. That's all.'

Norton stared slightly in amazement at the fervour blazing in the little artist's eyes. He sat on the lounge and took another sip from his stubbie.

'Tell me this Les. When was the last time you saw anyone die from an overdose of smoking dope?'

'Can't say that I have.'

'You ever heard of anyone breaking in to a chemist shop or robbing a bank to buy pot? You know of any sheilas working as prostitutes to keep themselves supplied with pot?'

'No.'

'You ever seen anybody going through withdrawal symptoms because they ain't got no pot?'

'No. That's ridiculous.'

'The only thing wrong with pot is the greedy bastards that want to get rich from it. But — there's a ready market there, and a big one, so you can't really blame people for having a go.'

Norton went to take a sip from his beer but changed his mind. He eased himself back in the chair and looked curiously at his mate sitting on the lounge slowly sipping on his stubbie. His straightforward answer to the drug problem impressed him with it's obvious honesty and proletarian simplicity. For the life of him he couldn't figure out why no one had thought of it before.

'You know, what you say makes a lot of sense Reg,' said Norton, nodding his head slowly. 'But, if everybody had plenty of dope they'd all be gettin' around stoned all the time. No one'd get nothin' done.'

'Not necessarily,' replied Reg. 'The pubs and clubs are always open but you don't see everyone walking around pissed all the time. Most people like to have a drink after work or at a party; it's, the same with pot, you don't abuse it.' He took another pull on his stubbie. 'It's a relaxant mainly, anyway. Christ there's plenty of things you can't do properly when you're stoned, same as when you're pissed. Like driving a car, using a typewriter or a computer. Jesus Les, your own common bloody sense'll tell you that.'

'Fair enough.' Norton reflected into his beer for a moment. 'But what about your health? You can't tell me smoking's good for your lungs.'

'True. But like I say, you don't abuse it. There's idiots out there smoke two or three packets of cigarettes a day full of saltpetre and chemicals, and they wonder why they finish up with lung cancer and emphysema. Christ, you couldn't smoke the equivalent to that in dope, you'd pass out: or end up getting a chat on with Buddha in a pub in nirvana.' Reg finished his beer, stood up and pointed at the bong sitting on the coffee table. 'But you can't tell me a few cones of a night, filtered through water's going to kill me. I've got a mate up the road turns his grandfather on every night and the old boy loves it — and he's eighty.' Reg paused for a moment. 'Then again maybe you should lock him up in gaol, too.' He went to the

129

kitchen and returned with another two twist-tops.

'I suppose what you're sayin's pretty right Reg,' said Norton, taking one of the offered beers, removing the top and having a lengthy guzzle. 'But what about if you start getting hooked on hard drugs?' He let out a belch that made his eyes water slightly. 'They reckon in the papers pot leads to heroin addiction.'

'Oh arseholes.' Reg shook his head, sat back down on the lounge and spread his arms out. 'The only way kids get on to heroin,' he said, looking directly at Les, 'is when they've got to go to some pusher to buy a bit of smoke and some unscrupulous low cunt says — oh, sorry man, I got no green, but do you want to try this? It won't hurt you and you can have the first taste for free. And the poor kid thinks, oh well, why not give it a try and the next thing, bingo! He's hooked on the shit. And believe me Les, there's no comparison between pot and heroin. It's like riding a pushbike then getting into a Masserati. Only it's got no brakes.' Reg shook his head sadly. 'I've lost some good friends in Sydney to the needle. Including a girl I was just starting to fall in love with — a young art student from Maroubra. Believe me Les, if there were no pushers, there'd be no smack. It's as simple as that.'

They sat in silence for a few moments as the news finished, quietly sipping their beers. Finally Reg looked up at Norton and smiled softly.

'Anyway Les,' he said, 'I didn't mean to bore you with all this talk about dope. It's just, I dunno,' he shrugged his shoulders slightly, 'it's just my opinion, I suppose, that's all. Sorry mate.'

Norton smiled back at his little artist friend. He could see the obvious sincerity and sadness in his melancholy brown eyes; especially when he mentioned the young girl from Maroubra.

'That's all right Reg,' he said, reaching over and patting him lightly on the shoulder. 'You're not boring me. What you're saying makes a helluva lot of sense. In fact I can't figure out why the silly lookin' pricks in the government haven't thought of it themselves and done something like that.'

Reg looked seriously at Norton. 'You know why they won't change the law Les?'

'Why?'

'Two reasons. Firstly, there's too many rich bastards, in and out of the government making too much money out of heroin to want to see their lucrative source of income dry up, or any

130

fair dinkum pressure brought on to it. And secondly, political expediency.'

'Political expediency. What's that?'

'Well, it wouldn't matter who was in power. If Labor was in and they said they were going to do something along those lines I mentioned, the Liberal Party would start jumping up and down in the one spot, preying on people's fears and saying they were going to turn us into a nation of junkies. On the other hand, if the Libs were in power and they said they were going to do it, the Labor Party would do exactly the same thing. Fair dinkum Les, they wouldn't agree on the fuckin' weather if they thought they were going to lose a couple of votes.' Reg took a swig from his bottle, threw back his head and laughed scornfully. 'Then you've got those sanctimonious, Bible-bashing wombats like the Festival of Light who think the only possible way you can have a good time is to be in a church with a Bible in one hand and a tambourine in the other, singing glory hallelujah seven days a bloody week.' Reg shook his head again. 'Shit, it wasn't that long ago those bastards were burning people at the stake for having a root and walkin' around laughing. You were in league with the devil — a witch. Even now they still want you to wear your "Reg Grundys" while you're having a shower.'

Norton couldn't help laughing. 'So what's gonna happen Reg?'

'What's going to happen Les? Oh, they'll just keep plugging on the way they're going, till Sydney's like New York and the gaols are full of people who've done nothing more than got caught with a bit of dope and every second kid's got a criminal record. But one day Les, one day, a Prime Minister or a Premier or a leading judge will have a son or a daughter who's a smack freak. Then they might wake up, and leave the poor pot smokers alone and concentrate on the heroin dealers. But until then . . .' Reg held up his stubbie. 'Cheers Les.'

'Yeah, cheers Reg.'

They finished their beers and Norton went to the kitchen returning with two fresh ones as the compere came on to announce the bands on this week's Rock Arena.

'I'll tell you what,' said Les, as he handed Reg a stubbie and sat back down on the lounge chair. 'All this talk about dope's convinced me of one thing.'

'What's that?' Reg leaned across and turned up the volume on the TV.

131

'I might have a smoke myself — you gonna have one?'

'No I'm right.' Reg shook his head and smiled. 'But go for your life.'

Norton took a small portion of pot from the plastic bag and started mulling it up with a little tobacco in the bowl. Reg looked on with a slightly amused smile on his face.

'I'll tell you something about pot you probably won't believe,' said Reg, watching intently as Les packed a small cone, 'but try this for size.'

'What?'

'Marijuana can cure cancer.'

'What! Oh don't give me the fuckin' shits.'

'It's a fact Les. You have to get it in its early stages, of course.'

Norton smiled sufferingly at Reg. 'You mean to tell me that if you've got lung cancer and you start smokin' pot, it'll cure it?' He shook his head. 'Fair dinkum Reg, you must think I've got a pumpkin for a fuckin' head.'

'You don't smoke it you bloody great red-headed wombat. You make tea with it and drink it and go on a grape fast at the same time. The dope eases the pain and the grape juice cleans out your system and somehow or other the two combine and it flushes the cancer cells from you body. It takes about a month but it works. We tried it on some old people who had the 'Bengal lancer'. They would've kicked the bucket for sure and they're as good as gold now. Silly, isn't it? We had to break the law to ease the agony they were in and save their lives.'

'Yeah?' said Norton, holding a match over the cone as INXS started "Stay Young". 'I dunno Reg. I think at times you tell me anything.'

Reg was right about his dope though: it was sensational. INXS never looked so good and when Midnight Oil ripped into 'I Don't Want To Be The One' Norton thought Peter Garrett was going to jump straight out of the TV set and land in his lap.

About 8.30 the following morning Norton was sitting in the kitchen having breakfast with Reg. He'd been up since six, had a run, done some exercises while Sally looked on in amazement, and now after two bowls of muesli and fruit he was moving steadily through a plate of bacon and eggs. Outside it was another glorious spring day. The sun was streaming down from a clear blue sky, a light north-west wind was sighing softly through the tops of the trees, and the only sounds were the cries of the various birds as they hung momentarily in the breeze.

'You sure you don't want to come down the beach for a while?' asked Norton. He finished the last egg and started spreading a piece of toast with mango-and-orange marmalade.

'No. I'll get these paintings finished today,' replied Reg. 'I might come down tomorrow.'

'Fair enough. You want me to bring anything back from the shops?'

'Yeah. Grab half a dozen date-rolls. Unless you fancy wiping your Khyber with newspaper.'

'No thanks. Any particular brand you fancy Reg? Lady Scott? Sorbent?'

'I don't care Les. Kleenex'll do.'

'Righto.'

They finished breakfast and started washing up. As Les was drying the dishes a huge Cape York cockatoo landed on the ledge outside the kitchen window. With its spiky black crest and bright red face it reminded him of some of the punks that hung around the Cross. It sat squawking softly at Reg.

'Hey look at that,' said Norton, 'an old Cape Yorker. Shit I haven't seen one of those since I left Queensland.'

'Yeah, they're grouse, aren't they?' Reg took a piece of left-over toast, spread a little jam on it and handed it through the open fly screen to the big black parrot. It took the toast deftly in its claw and started chewing. Norton put his hands on his hips and stood there grinning.

'Did I tell you I used to have one of those for a pet?' said Reg.

'No,' replied Norton.

'Yeah. Had him for nearly two years. Taught him to talk and everything, even used to do impersonations. James Cagney, W.C. Fields, Gough Whitlam, Dame Joan Sutherland. Unbelievable what he could do.'

'Fair dinkum?' Norton watched amused as the big, black bird chewed away at the piece of toast. 'What happened to him?'

'Oh, I was goin' bad and I ended up eating him.'

'You ate him?' Norton looked at Reg incredulously. 'What did it taste like?'

'Turkey.'

'Turkey?'

'Yeah, fair dinkum Les, that parrot could imitate anything.'

133

Norton shook his head slowly and continued wiping up. 'Leave me alone, will you Reg?'

With the washing-up out of the road and his stomach full Norton threw his overnight bag and a pair of flippers on top of the banana chair in the boot. He was keen to get going so he said a quick goodbye to Reg, told him he'd be back late in the afternoon, gave Sally a rub on the belly, got in the car, and with Mental As Anything's 'Too Many Times' blaring through the stereo, motored happily towards Sawtell.

Sawtell is a sleepy little town about twelve kilometres south of Coffs Harbour. There's a nice old pub, a friendly RSL and a wide palm-tree-lined, flower-filled median strip that runs down a few hundred metres or so of the neat little shops that form the main street. An expanse of golden sand runs from the grey headland at Trapdoors to Sawtell Island; this is divided by an ancient surf club roughly two-thirds the way along the beach towards the island, which when it's on is one of the best surfing spots on the north coast.

The place was barely coming to life when Norton pulled up outside the surf club at ten and got his gear out of the boot. A movement of brightly-coloured butterflies drifted lazily in the warm breeze as he walked down the lantana-lined path to the beach. The sun was sparkling brightly, almost blindingly, on the crystal-clear, turquoise ocean. *Jesus, how good's this?* he thought. He whistled softly to himself while he unfolded his banana chair and placed it on the almost deserted beach a hundred metres or so down from the surf club. He spread his large frame on the banana chair, oiled up his slightly freckly body, then lay back and relaxed, not a care or a worry in the world.

After an hour, or so rivulets of sweat were starting to course down Norton's face and body, dripping off the banana chair and on to the sand; the water started to look more inviting than ever. There was a good wave running, so he decided to go for a surf. He took off his shorts, grabbed the flippers out of the overnight bag and trotted down to the water's edge. The water was beautiful, not even the slightest chill. He plunged in and started back-stroking out to where the waves were breaking over a small sand bank directly in front of the surf club. He splashed around for over an hour picking up wave after wave, sometimes going left, sometimes right. He skimmed across the long, smooth green walls while the waves peeled off behind him in a gently breaking cascade of gleaming, white foam. A flash of several black fins, not far away, startled him

134

momentarily. He trod water waiting for the next set, but as the fins went lazily up and down in the water, Norton realised they were only a school of grey dolphins. *No worries about sharks,* he thought happily. Eventually they drifted in and started surfing the sand bank alongside him.

'Hey, piss off,' yelled Les, grinning hilariously. He splashed water at the one closest to him. 'I was here first.'

The twenty or so dolphins took absolutely no notice of him. They, too, started picking up waves, singing and calling to each other, surfacing and blowing water out into the air. Sometimes they leapt right out of the surf to land with a thundering splash in a wonderful display of nature at its best. It was almost as if they were putting it on for his benefit — Les was in another world. *Jesus,* he thought as he watched the magnificent creatures swimming gracefully and happily around him, *how can those fuckin' Japanese slaughter them like they do.* He shook his head sadly then spat in the water with disgust.

A wave suddenly loomed up much bigger than the rest. It looked like it was going to dump but Norton picked it up and with his hands out in front of him, dived straight down into it. It winded him slightly but with several powerful kicks of the flippers he was able to stay with it poking his head to the side and getting a gulp of air every now and again. He decided to beach it. Kicking strongly and with his hands straight out in front of him clasped one on top of the other, he put his face down and let the wave speed him into the beach. He was feeling great, holding his breath. The water rushed alongside him. He felt as though he could have gone on like this forever when, just as he neared the beach, he came to a shuddering halt, colliding with someone or something in the surf.

He rolled over in a clumsy sort of a sommersault then stood up in the almost waist-deep water to see he'd just knocked over a girl. She had probably been standing there enjoying a bit of a splash around, when Norton had come through like a runaway express train. Now she was on her backside, kicking and spluttering around wide-eyed trying to get her breath back and wondering what the bloody hell had happened.

'Jesus I'm sorry love,' said Norton sincerely, as he splashed clumsily over to her and helped her to her feet. 'I should've been watching what I was doing. I'm a nice goose. Are you all right?'

At first the girl didn't say anything. She just stood there. Norton held her elbow. She held her ribs, rolling her eyes around, spluttering. Finally she wrenched her arm away from Les.

'You bloody near killed me. Oh, my ribs.'

Norton's face started to colour slightly. 'Look, I'm really sorry love,' he said, feeling quite stupid. He stood next to her: he was almost twice her size. 'Come on, let me help you up to the beach.' He removed his flippers with one hand and, with the other, helped her as gently as he could to the shore where she sat down on the wet sand. Kneeling next to her Norton checked her out.

She wasn't half a bad sort. About 160 centimetres with straggly, curly blonde hair, that dripped water everywhere, big China-blue eyes, a cute little pink mouth and a cute little nose, with a number of freckles spread over it like hundreds and thousands. She had a good, full body and was wearing a blue and yellow swimsuit that plunged down in the front and was cut up at the side just enough to reveal what needed to be revealed to make most men look twice. Les guessed she would have been in her early twenties.

'Shit I'm really sorry,' said Les 'I know how you must feel. I don't think anything's broken though.' He unconsciously reached across and patted her ribs.

'Take your bloody hands off me,' snapped the girl. 'I think you've done enough damage for one day. You oaf.' Norton recoiled as the girl got to her feet. 'Oh,' she gave a little groan, turned, then stormed back up the beach and lay face down on her towel.

Norton watched her for a few moments. Finally he shook his head, shrugged his shoulders, put his fins back on and went out for another surf, but his heart wasn't quite in it this time; he had two waves and got out.

After washing off the saltwater under a beach shower near the grass, he put his shorts back on, got a book out of his bag and lay back down on his banana chair to read. The girl was still lying on her towel about thirty metres to his left. Every now and again Norton thought he could sense her looking over at him, but when he'd glance back she seemed to quickly look away.

Thirty minutes or so of uninteresting reading went by, but the girl was still on Norton's mind. *Bugger this,* he thought, putting the book down, *I'll go over and front her. She can only tell me to piss off.* He got a couple of peaches out of his bag and walked over. As he approached her he could see by the look on her face that the welcome mat wasn't actually layed out.

'Look,' he said, as he got close to her. 'I didn't come over to annoy you. I just came over to apologise again and see if you're all right. Are you all right?'

The girl looked at him stony-faced at first, then smiled slightly and sat up. 'Yes I'm all right now' she said. 'I was just winded before.' She paused for a moment. 'I shouldn't really have snapped at you like I did I suppose.'

'Oh that's all right,' smiled Les. 'I'd've done the same bloody thing myself.'

'Well, it did hurt.' She looked at Norton's muscular frame. 'God, you must weigh a ton.'

Norton shrugged his shoulders. 'I keep fit.' He ran his eyes over the girls well-developed body. '*You* don't actually look like you have to run backwards and forwards under the shower to get wet yourself. My shoulder's pretty bloody sore, don't worry about that.' He rubbed his shoulder gingerly. 'I'll bet I've got a big bruise there in the morning.'

'Oh rubbish.'

'I'm fair dinkum. In fact I thought I'd run into one of those dolphins.'

'Oh don't give me that.' She threw a tiny handful of sand at Norton's foot, then smiled when she saw the look on his face. 'I do play a lot of basketball,' she said coyly.

'I thought you must've done something.' Les sat down in front of her. ' Would you like a peach?'

The girl looked at the two huge, yellow cling-stones in Norton's outstretched hand. 'Yes, that'd be nice. Thanks.'

It turned out her name was Elizabeth Cox — though everyone called her Betty — she was a schoolteacher, twenty-two years old and came from Grafton. She'd been staying with two girlfriends, two other teachers, in a flat the other end of Sawtell towards the island. The other girls had gone back to Grafton the previous day — she was going back by bus on Sunday. Besides playing basketball, she did a fair bit of swimming and went to aerobics three nights a week: there wasn't a great deal else to do in Grafton. She didn't have a boyfriend, but she had been engaged to another schoolteacher. However she'd broken it off about a year ago as he didn't like to keep himself in shape and preferred to go out drinking buckets of beer with his mates. *What a nice mug he must've been* thought Les. Betty's face might've been a bit plain, but her body made

Bo Derek look like a sack of potatoes.

Norton told her most of the things about himself. He didn't tell her he was a bouncer up the Cross: he told her his father owned a meatworks at Homebush and he was a director of the company. *If I can get her back to the BMW she'll believe that,* he thought. Norton asked her if it was all right if he brought his banana chair over and joined her. She said that was all right, so they sat chatting away for quite some time, then went for a swim.

Frolicking around in the water Norton couldn't help noticing just how fit Betty was. The shiny, wet costume stuck to her like a second skin. Her perfect backside and ample breasts were as firm as if they'd been carved out of marble, then when she put her arms on Norton's shoulders, as he helped her over some waves and her hardened nipples scraped across his chest, Les had to turn and swim away or he would've been running around Sawtell beach on three legs.

'That water is absolutely beautiful,' she said, as they stood on the beach towelling themselves.

'Is it what,' replied Norton. 'You could stay in there all day.' He checked his watch. 'I'll tell you what, it's getting on for two. You feel like a bit of something to eat?'

'Yes. I am getting a bit peckish to tell you the truth. I only had some cornflakes for breakfast, and that was at seven o'clock.'

'Well, there's a little pub just up the road. How about we have a couple of drinks and I'll find a fish shop and get them to cook us up a nice feed of fresh fish?'

'Sounds great. There's a nice fish shop just across the street.' Betty had started to take a mild sort of a shine to Norton. He'd been genuinely apologetic to her, in his clumsy sort of way, about knocking her over and he had a pleasant enough personality. When he was lifting her up in the water he didn't start coming on heavy but she could easily sense how strong he was and, though his freckly, red head was a little rugged, he was built like it was going out of style, which certainly appealed to a girl who kept herself as fit as she did. Compared to her ex-finance, he was Robert Redford.

They got dressed and walked up to Les's car where he put his banana chair in and got his money out of the boot.

'Nice car,' said Betty.

'Yeah. They're not bad buses,' replied Norton casually. It was only a short distance to the hotel, but they drove up and parked out the back.

'Listen,' said Norton, handing Betty ten dollars as they walked across the small but beautifully flowered beer garden. 'How about you get the drinks and I'll go over and order the stuff, and I'll meet you at the table under the frangipani tree? Just a middie of new for me.'

'Okay.'

The fish shop Betty had mentioned was clean and bright with a fairly good display of fresh seafood in the window. The overweight owner seemed pleasant enough. Les order two large pieces of barramundi out of the window, a dozen calamari rings, six Tasmanian scallops and half a dozen king-prawn cutlets, plus some chips. He paid the bloke and told him he'd be back in half an hour. Betty had four deliciously cold middies sitting on the table when he got back: she'd already drunk half of her first one.

'I got four,' she said. 'Save a trip in. I didn't think that first one would last long anyway.'

'That's all right Betty. Send me broke, I don't mind.' Norton raised his glass and winked at her. 'Cheers mate.'

'Cheers Les.'

They finished the first round of beers pretty smartly: Betty downed hers like she'd just finished a day loading wool at 15 Walsh Bay. 'I'd better get another four,' said Norton, picking his change up off the table.

'I'll get these,' said Betty, rising to her feet.

'Turn it up, sit down. I'll get 'em.'

'No. I insist; a shout's a shout.'

Norton shrugged his shoulders. 'Okay. If you want to be one of these liberated women, go for your life.'

Betty smiled and scrabbled Norton's red hair with her fingers as she went to the bar. She was back soon with another four cold middies.

It was lovely sitting there under the shade of the frangipani tree. Every now and again they'd reach up, pick one of the dainty white flowers and sniff its delightful fragrance. Betty even placed one behind Norton's ear bringing a huge grin to his face.

I wonder what some of those rough-necks at the Kelly Club would say if they could see me now, thought Norton, as he sat back in the flower-filled beer garden watching some willie-wagtails and sparrows bobbing around in the grass at his feet. Cicadas chirped in the trees and more multi-coloured butterflies drifted lazily around in the soft balmy breeze. *They'd be rotten jealous that's for sure.* He glanced at his watch.

'That fish should be ready now,' he said, getting to his feet and finishing his beer.

'I'll get another two beers while you're away.'

'Take it out of this.' Norton handed Betty a two-dollar note, then left for the fish shop.

He returned to find Betty waiting at the table with two fresh beers and put the fair-sized parcel on the table. The beers had put a noticeably sharp edge on their appetites so they got stuck into it.

The fish-shop owner had cooked everything to perfection: not too greasy, not too much batter, just the right amount of salt plus several wedges of lemon. He'd obviously been changing his oil regularly as the chips were cooked to a scrumptious golden brown, and plenty of them.

'Oh Les,' cried Betty, in between bites. 'That fish is absolutely beautiful. What is it?'

'Barramundi. What about the Tassie scallops? How good are they?'

'Mm.'

'This calamari's the best I've ever eaten, too.'

'And the prawn cutlets. They're divine.'

'It's a tough life, isn't it Betty?'

Within twenty-five minutes there wasn't a thing left, except a few scraggly chips and some pieces of batter which Les tossed to the eager willie-wagtails and sparrows.

'For an old country schoolteacher you're not bad on the tooth Miss Cox,' smiled Les.

'It was your fault Mr Norton,' replied Betty. 'Normally I wouldn't eat that much food in a week. You just made me an offer I couldn't refuse.' She leant back in her seat and patted her stomach.

'Do you think you could fit in another beer?'

'All right, one more. I might go to the loo while you're getting them.'

Les returned with the beers about the same time as Betty. When they finished them they switched to Bacardi and splits, and spent the rest of the afternoon chatting and laughing. The sun slowly lengthened the shadows around them as it passed leisurely over the old hotel.

It was after five when they left the pub. Norton had discreetly inquired if Betty was doing anything that night — without actually asking her out — but an aunt and uncle were calling around later to take her to the movies. However, she'd made no arrangements for the weekend.

'You can come in for a cup of coffee, if you like,' she said, as they pulled up outside her flat. The way she said it, it was more of a polite gesture than an open invitation.

Norton looked at her sitting next to him in the car in her skimpy shorts and low-cut, loose knit, white top — he was more than half-tempted.

'Oh, I'd better give it a miss,' he said, taking a glance at his watch. 'Reg is expecting me back with some things and your uncle's coming around soon.' *If I get in there and have a lash at her it's going to be a hurried job,* he thought, *and I could bomb the rort. I'm in sweet. Why not wait till tomorrow when there was more time and do the job properly.* 'But I'll tell you what. If you're doing nothing tomorrow, how would you like to go for a barbecue? I can bring a change of gear and we can go out for a drink somewhere later that night.'

'Okay.' Betty nodded her head enthusiastically. 'That'd be great. Where do you want to go for the barbie?'

Norton shrugged his shoulders. 'I don't care.'

'There's a beautiful little spot just up from here called Boambee lagoon. There's barbecue pits and wood there. It's lovely.'

'That sounds all right to me. I'll call around say 10.30. Is that okay?'

'That'll be fine.' She reached across and kissed Norton softly on the lips. 'I'll see you tomorrow Les.'

Norton kissed her back in return, just as tenderly. 'See you tomorrow Betty.'

Norton couldn't get his eyes off her backside as she walked up the path and waved from the door. *Come on tomorrow,* he thought, waving back. He headed back to the farm, stopping to pick up a couple of things from a small supermarket on the way.

'So you had a pretty good day Les?' Reg smiled at the contented look on Norton's face as he sat in the kitchen sipping a mug of coffee.

'Bloody oath. And not a bad sort either. Got a top body.' Norton chuckled to himself. 'You won't mind if I don't invite you to the beach tomorrow Reg?'

'Heh, heh, heh. I didn't really think you would. I've got to go to Coffs tomorrow anyway. I've got some canvas and oil paints coming up from Sydney.'

'Oh I can pick that up for you on the way in.'

'No, that's all right. I want to go in anyway.'

Sitting in the sun drinking beer and Bacardi all afternoon had left Norton feeling tired and just a little jaded. He had another cup of coffee and a toasted cheese sandwich, watched a bit of TV for a while, then hit the sack early. Tomorrow looked like being a very, very enjoyable day: not to mention the evening.

Norton was up the following morning about six, roaring like a Bengal tiger. He had a run for an hour, and by eight was just finishing the last of a series of strenuous, non-stop exercises. Reg stood sipping coffee with his foot across Les's ankles, watching in amazement as Les finished off his sit-ups.

'Ninety-nine. One hundred. Bugger it, that'll do.' Reg removed his foot. Norton sat with his hands across his knees getting his breath back. Sweat was dripping down his arms and wisps of steam were rising from his face. 'Shit I'm hot.'

'Why wouldn't you be? Christ you're fit.'

'Ah it's just this country air Reg. Makes me feel like I can train all day.'

'Listen, if you're that hot, why don't you come down the billabong and have a swim? I'm going down to get some fresh peaches to put on my muesli.'

'That sounds like a bloody good idea Reg. I'll just go and grab a towel.'

Norton didn't bother to take his training gear off when they got to the billabong, he just jumped straight in; running shoes, T-shirt, the lot.

'What's it like, still cold?' called Reg, when Les surfaced somewhere near the middle.

'Yeah,' yelled Norton. 'But doesn't it make you feel great.'

Reg walked round to the opposite side of the billabong while Norton splashed around noisily. 'Hey Les, come here, I'll show you something.' Norton breast-stroked over to Reg and clambered up on to the rocks next to him. 'Follow me.'

Reg led him a few metres into the bush. They got down into a concealed tunnel leading through a huge patch of dense lantana. It was a good thing Norton still had his training gear on, as the terrain was pretty rough. The lantana scratched his arms a number of times as it was. After crawling along for roughly ten metres they came out into a man-made clearing about six metres square. Two or three large plastic garbage tins and several gardening tools were placed to one side but growing in the middle were a dozen or more healthy-looking marijuana plants about two metres high. Norton had never seen it growing like that before, but he'd seen enough photos and tiny plants in people's homes to know what it was.

'So this is all your pot, is it Reg?'

'That's it Les. The dreaded marijuana. Good-looking plants but, aren't they?' Reg took a plastic bucket, filled it from one of the garbage tins and started pouring it on the plants. Norton examined some of the larger ones with his hands.

'I s'pose they're all right,' shrugged Les, 'but I wouldn't know one from the other. What's the big deal about these?'

Reg put down the bucket. 'Come here, I'll show you.' Reg held a thick stem from one of the plants in his hand. 'You see this part here?' He showed Les a thickened, bushy part of the stem, something like a fat pine needle. Instead of being green, it was a dark violet-blue, almost purple, colour with what looked like fine reddish, orange hairs growing all over it.'

'Yeah?'

'Well that's what they call the head. That's the best part to smoke, or make tea out of or whatever.'

'Yeah?'

'Yeah. Generally they're a browny green but see how these are purple?' Norton nodded his head. 'Well that's because of the strain. Me and a mate cross-bred these plants with seeds from "Durban Poison" and "Thai Buddha". Plus the soil and weather up here's perfect and that's why the stuff is so good. Two cones of this'll blow your socks off.'

'I know. I had a bit the other night.'

'Like I said Les,' continued Reg, pouring some more water over the plants. 'If I wanted to, I could grow heaps and make all sorts of money. But ... I just grow enough for myself and some friends in Sydney, and that does me.'

'Fair enough,' nodded Norton. 'I still think I should give you up to the authorities though.'

'Yeah, why don't you? Get me a year in gaol, I'd really like that.'

'I suppose there's plenty of old pricks would.'

'Concerned Citizens Against People Having a Good Time? You'd better believe it Les. The miserable old bastards.' Reg finished watering his treasured plants with the same care and concern of an English aristocrat tending his prize roses. 'Well come on, let's go up and have some breakfast.' They headed back to the house with Reg stopping to pick some peaches on the way.

'Hey Reg,' said Norton, when they got back, 'Is that an

143

old surf ski under the other side of the house?'

'Yeah. A mate of mine from Tamarama surf club left it up here ages ago. I hardly ever use it.'

'All right if I take it with me today? I wouldn't mind having a bit of a paddle in this Boambee lagoon.'

'Sure. Go for your life. The paddle's next to it. I'll find you some rope.'

Norton dragged the ski — an old, blue, three metre solid foam Aero out from under the house. Reg got two lengths of rope from the laundry. In no time it was sitting on top of the BMW.

'Bloody beauty,' said Norton, grinning and giving the knots a final tug. 'I don't mind paddling these.'

'You'll love it where you're going. Boambee lagoon's beautiful. Anyway, let's have some breakfast, I'm starving.'

'Yeah, so am I.'

Reg's home-made muesli, which he bought from some hippies on another little farm somewhere, was delicious at any time, but with the fresh peaches it was even nicer. After several bowls plus some scrambled eggs Norton was ready to head for Sawtell. He told Reg he didn't know when he'd be back, probably later that night. Reg wished him all the best giving him a knowing wink as he drove off.

Boambee lagoon is just that. A beautiful blue lagoon formed by a small creek, its size and depth determined by the tide as it runs into the ocean a kilometre or so north of Sawtell. A picturesque railway bridge spans the mouth and a small caretaker's house, surrounded by ghost-gums, sits neatly on the township side. Dense swampy scrub starts on the other side, over which you sometimes see and hear the droning of various aircraft as they take off and land at Coffs Harbour airport a few kilometres at the other end of the bush. It was about 10.30 when Les and the schoolteacher from Grafton drove down the dirt road and pulled up a few metres from the edge. Apart from them, and probably the caretaker, the place was deserted.

'So this is it eh? It sure looks nice enough,' said Norton, switching off the motor.

'I reckon it's beautiful,' replied Betty. 'It's my favourite spot up here. Anyway, come on,' she said, clapping her hands together, let's get everything sorted out.'

'Yes Miss Cox. Whatever you say ma'm,' replied Norton derisively.

They started unloading the car. Betty had made some coleslaw and buttered bread, plus a few other things. She'd also supplied a large blanket from the flat. Norton had borrowed an esky from Reg which he'd filled with beer, ice, orange juice and two bottles of Great Western champagne bought at Sawtell. He also bought a dozen lamb cutlets, sausages and a slice of rump steak, as well as some paper plates and a few other odds and ends. While Betty started spreading everything out on the blanket Norton gathered up some wood and twigs for the barbecue.

'I won't light this just yet,' he said. 'We'll have a swim and a few drinks first.'

'Good idea. In fact what's wrong with having a drink right now?'

In no time they'd polished off three stubbies each. They went for a swim. Betty was wearing a red, cotton bikini this time. It covered her nipples and part of her crutch and that was about it — when Norton first saw it he nearly bit the neck of his stubbie.

They splashed around in the clear, blue water like a couple of happy sea-otters. Betty had brought a little rubber surf mat which she made Norton blow up and paddle her around on. They had a couple of races across the lagoon which Betty, much to Norton's surprise, almost won. Les piggybacked her around. They had a ferocious water fight which culminated in a bit of a wrestling match. About one p.m., and a few more stubbies later, Les lit the barbecue. While he was standing there poking at the fire Betty wrapped her arms around him from behind and gave him a big squeeze, then ran her icy stubbie up and down his back just to annoy him. If anybody watching hadn't known better they would have sworn they were in love.

The picnic area barbecue was one of those small ones built a couple a metres or so off the ground with a hot-plate on one side and a grill on the other. Satisfied the coals were at the right heat Norton threw a handful of gum leaves on them for flavour, then spread all the meat across the two metal plates.

'Are you sure there's enough there?' asked Betty.

'There is for me,' replied Les. 'But after watching the way you tore into that fish yesterday I'll probably have to go back to the butcher and get a side of beef.' Betty didn't say anything, she just clouted Norton across his big red head. They had time for another two stubbies. Then it was ready.

Betty had spread everything out on the blanket. Norton put all the meat on two paper plates and opened a bottle of Great Western. Without any further ceremony they got stuck into the food, washing it down with mouthfuls of champagne and orange juice.

Norton couldn't believe his luck. He'd have been happy just to spend a few quiet days in the country with an old friend not doing too much at all, yet here he was — having a terrific barbecue with one the nicest young girls he'd met in ages and if he played his cards right and took his time, he was a laydown mesère to do the business.

'Jesus that coleslaw's all right,' he said emphatically. 'What did you put in it?'

'Some pineapple pieces and a little sweet-and-sour sauce. Makes a difference, doesn't it?' Norton nodded his head enthusiastically. 'You don't make a bad barbecue either Mr Norton. This meat is absolutely delicious.'

'It's all in the gum leaves Miss Cox. All in the gum leaves.'

About half an hour later there was a lamb cutlet and two sausages left. The first bottle of Great Western was gone. Les offered to open another one, but Betty shook her head: she couldn't eat or drink another thing. All she wanted to do was to lie down on Les's banana chair with the front doors of the BMW open, listen to his tapes and take it easy for a while — and she did just that.

Norton was still feeling a bit revved up from the few beers and the champagne and seeing Betty stretched back on his banana chair, with her legs slightly apart and her beautiful big boobs almost hanging out of ther tiny red bikini, he knew if he stayed there, before long he'd either do something he'd regret or just straight out monster her.

'Well while you're lying there,' he said, patting her gently on her thigh. 'I might go for a bit of a paddle on the ski. Work off some of that meal.'

'All right then,' she mumbled sleepily. 'Come here a minute.' As Les bent over her she wound her arms tenderly around his neck, drew him down to her and kissed him softly but passionately on the lips. 'See you when you get back.'

'Okay,' croaked Les. Beads of sweat burst out across his forehead.

Fair dinkum, a man's a mug, thought Norton, as he put his feet in the straps and pushed the surf ski out from the sand bank with the paddle. *I should be back there grabbing*

her on the lamington instead of floundering around out here.
Ah well. He adjusted his eyeshade and paddled out into the
middle of the lagoon with a leisurely if not slightly clumsy
stroke.

He let the current take him down to the railway bridge where
a couple of kids were fishing in the shade underneath.

'Any luck fellas?' he called out.

'Yeah. I got a couple of bream and me mate got a flathead,'
drawled the tallest one wearing a huge, ragged straw hat.

'Good on you.' Norton drifted on a bit further almost to
the beach at Trapdoors, sat for a moment or two then started
paddling back up. It was much harder coming back against
the current and he was starting to get a bit of sweat up when
he reached the bridge. He manoeuvred the ski up against one
of the oyster-encrusted pylons and sat in the shade watching
the kids fishing. Before long a freight train rumbled over the
top of them with a deafening racket that sounded as if the
whole bridge was going to fall down. As it got to the other
side the driver let out several piercing toots on the whistle.
Betty was still sleeping soundly next to the car when he got
back to the middle of the lagoon so he paddled up a bit further
and decided to go for a walk. He drifted back down with the
current, pulled up with a crunch on the sandy edge of the
lagoon directly opposite the car, pulled the ski up out of the
water, laid the paddle across the top and started walking slowly
into the swampy bush.

The sandy ground beneath his bare feet was an oily, orange
black interspersed with pools of glistening stagnant water. Rot-
ting logs covered in bright green moss lay across the pools,
and vines and creepers hung from the stunted, asymmetrical
trees. The air was steamy, unpleasant and buzzed with countless
tiny insects. A normal person would have found it most distasteful, but Norton liked walking in the bush on his own
so he found it almost enjoyable. Strangely enough he seemed
to have stumbled on to a faint, almost imperceptible trail; a
person without any knowledge of the bush would have missed
it altogether. Quite puzzled as to why there would be a trail
in such hostile terrain Norton decided to follow.

After about 500 metres the ground started to firm up; there
was more topsoil and the shrubs and trees began to take on
a more pleasant appearance. The singing of birds was becoming
quite audible and, now and again, Les could see different birds
bobbing around in the branches. He followed the trail till it

ended in some chest-high bullrushes. He pushed through the few metres of bullrushes, then stopped abruptly scarcely able to believe his eyes.

In front of him was a clearing about ten metres in diameter and growing right up to the edges were rows and rows of marijuana plants, some in plastic pots, some in tiny jiffy pots but mostly growing straight out of the ground, all around one metre high. However, at the edge of the clearing someone had run strands of thin clothesline between the trees. Hanging upside down on the clothesline were rows and rows of marijuana plants drying in the shade ready for packaging.

'Well I'll be rooted,' mumbled Norton out loud, his jaw dropping slightly. He stood rubbing his chin for a moment then had a quick look around and behind him; there was definitely no one about, so he walked gingerly over and felt one of the plants. They were dry and ready to go. Even at a rough estimate Norton could see there had to be at least twenty kilos of pot. Something Reg had said to him on the farm suddenly hit him like a bolt out of the blue. It was when they were walking back from Reg's little patch down by the billabong.

'You know Les, because of the ham-fisted, stupid attitude between the government and the cops, pot's now worth between 1000 and 1500 dollars a kilo.'

'Fair dinkum. That much?'

'Yeah. It's the money that causes all the trouble Les. Not the dope. Ridiculous, isn't it?'

'Yeah, it sure is.'

The wheels inside the cash register inside Norton's mind started to tick over. Even if there's only fifteen kilos there and I get the minimum amount for it, if I can get that back to Sydney? The cash register suddenly rang up over $15,000. Norton's eyes widened and a huge grin broke out across his face. Cackling like a hyena he picked up a small branch and started dusting away his footprints. He backed out of the clearing and started walking softly back along the trail.

The tape had stopped playing and Betty was still dozing peacefully on the banana chair when Norton put the surf ski back on top of the car: the sound of him closing one of the doors woke her up.

'Oh! Wazzat?' she mumbled groggily, blinking her eyes and shaking her head.

'Sorry,' said Les, 'I didn't mean to wake you up.'

'That's all right.' She stretched and yawned loudly. 'What time is it?'

'It's after four.'

'Is it?' Betty swung her feet over the edge of the banana chair and stared at the ground for a moment. 'I've been asleep for almost two hours. Have you been paddling all that time?'

'I ended up going for a walk along the beach.'

'Oh.'

'You still want to go out for a drink tonight?'

Betty yawned again and shook her head. 'I don't know. I'll see how I feel after I have a shower. I wouldn't mind a cup of coffee though.'

'Yeah, me too.' Norton helped her to her feet and she fell up against him winding her arms around his waist for support. 'How about we have one back at your place? I'll stop at Sawtell and get a nice sponge cake.'

'All right then.' Betty nuzzled up against Norton's chest and closed her eyes. 'I'm so tired.'

'You'll be right.' They put the stuff back in the car, cleaned up their rubbish, then drove back to Sawtell. Norton stopped at a cake shop and bought a passionfruit cream sponge cake. He also made a quick visit to the hardware store and a supermarket, placing what he'd bought in the boot of the car.

Back at Betty's flat Norton let her use the shower first. He put the electric kettle on, cut the cake up and checked out the flat. It was a typical flat. Two bedrooms, with a double bed in one and two singles in the other, a cheap cloth-and-vinyl lounge with a scatter rug on the lino floor and a kitchen with a laminex table and a cheap fridge humming in the corner. But it was clean and bright, there was a large colour TV, the shower sounded like it worked okay and there didn't seem to be any shortage of hot water, as Betty was in there over quarter of an hour.

'Are you sure you're clean enough?' asked Les. She came out holding a towel round her body and another one wrapped round her hair. 'Christian Barnard doesn't scrub up that much when he does open-heart surgery.'

'Don't be cheeky. Go on it's your turn.' She disappeared into the main bedroom and closed the door.

Norton showered and shaved, got changed into a clean pair of jeans and a T-shirt. He came out to find Betty had changed into an incredibly brief pair of shorts and a cotton top: the cake and a pot of coffee were sitting on a coffee table.

'Well isn't that nice?' he said. 'Afternoon tea with the vicar.'

'You want to hurry Mr Norton or you might just miss out.'

They sat chatting and sipping coffee and eating cake till it was all gone. By then it was almost time for the news so Betty switched the TV on.

'Les,' she said, wiping a few crumbs of cake from her mouth. 'Do you really want to go out tonight?'

'I don't care mate,' replied Norton with a shrug of his shoulders. 'It's up to you. What ever you want.'

'How about we stay home and watch TV? They're having a Marilyn Monroe special tonight starting at 7.30. And maybe we could go out somewhere tomorrow night. What do you reckon?'

'Righto. That other bottle of shampoo's in the fridge. What say we give that a bit of nudge while we're watching the movie?'

'Okay.' Betty was ecstatic. She had someone to cuddle up to with. Norton starting to look better all the time and Marilyn Monroe movies were her favourites.

Bloody beauty, thought Les. *I should be able to do some business here, get away by eleven and nick that pot.* He rubbed his hands together and gave Betty a hand to put the things away.

Norton cracked the bottle of bubbly just before the start of *Some Like It Hot.* By the time Tony Curtis and Jack Lemmon were in their drag gear on the train heading for Miami, the champagne, mixed with orange juice, was just about gone and Betty was snuggled up against Norton with a bit more on her mind than Marilyn Monroe.

He started slowly massaging her stomach: she gave a little purr of delight, snuggled in a bit closer and rested her head on Norton's shoulder. He carefully turned her head up towards him, smiled gently into her eyes, which were swimming noticeably, and kissed her tenderly on the mouth, rubbing his tongue lightly over her lips. Gingerly, he moved his hand up to her firm, heaving breasts kissing her softly on the neck at the same time. Betty gave a moan, wound her arm lovingly round Les's neck and darted her hot, moist tongue seductively into his ear.

Norton unhooked her bra, moved his hand between her open legs and began stroking with a gentle but firm pressure. It wasn't long before Betty started getting steamier than a bathroom mirror. She placed her hand tenatively on Norton's fly. Her eyes misted over completely.

'Come on,' he said quietly. He gently helped her to her

feet and led her into the main bedroom.

'Go easy Les,' she said barely audibly. Norton removed her shorts and dropped them at the side of the bed. 'It's been a long time for me.'

It might have been a long time for Betty but she certainly hadn't forgotten anything. She tore into it with Norton like there wasn't going to be a tomorrow. Norton just kept stroking away at a steady pace controlling himself as best as he could while Betty screamed and cried with ecstasy, biting into his neck and running her nails up and down his back. After the mouse she'd been engaged to, Les was like a big, red-haired panther who didn't let up.

Norton was just as equally rapt. Betty's young, brown body was firm and supple. She moved with him like they were one person. Les couldn't remember a more enjoyable, exhilarating sexual experience. It was one of, if not the best he'd ever had.

After they'd finished they lay with just a sheet over them cooling off for a while. Betty had her hand on Norton's arm running her index finger around the stubby red hairs on his chest. Neither of them said anything. They just let out a self-conscious chuckle every now and again at the enthusiasm they'd put into the last three-quarters of an hour. Norton really fancied Betty and would have liked to stay the night, but the thought of $15,000 worth of dope just up the road kept running through his brain. He took a glance at his watch over Betty's tousled head.

'Y'know Betty,' he said, 'it might be an idea if I got going soon.'

Betty frowned slightly and looked at him. 'Why's that?'

'Well, if I stay here much longer I'll only end up falling asleep, and I don't think it'd look very nice me sneaking out of here at all hours of the morning like a mangy dog.'

'Oh, don't be silly. Who's going to see you anyway?'

'Well, the neighbours for a start. Then that aunt and uncle you mentioned might call around out of the blue. It could be a bit embarrassing. Besides Betty,' he kissed her tenderly on the forehead, 'you're a helluva nice girl and I wouldn't like to get you a bad name.'

Betty chuckled lecherously, put her tongue in Les's ear and ran her hand down to his loins. 'Oh Les,' she sighed. 'Get me a bad name. Get me a bad name.'

Betty was snoring softly into the pillow when Norton got up to leave around 10.30. He quietly put his clothes on and tiptoed into the kitchen. He had three glasses of water, splashing a bit on his profusely sweating face. Before he departed he left a note with Reg's phone number on it on the coffee table. He clicked the front door softly behind him, trotted to the car and drove off.

Boambee lagoon looked just as beautiful in the moonlight as it did in the daytime. Les pulled up at the water's edge and quickly turned the motor off. The night was warm and it was deathly still but there was plenty of light from the almost-full moon shining on the water. He got the ski down from the car. He left his T-shirt, jeans and sneakers on and got a large black plastic garbage bag and torch out of the boot. He had a quick look around him, locked the car then paddled out into the lagoon.

It was still ghostly silent as he crunched up the opposite shore; the only sound was the gentle lapping of the water and the splash of a mullet jumping in the moonlight every now and again. He easily picked up the mark where he'd pulled in earlier and, by the soft light of the torch, set off along the trail. The going was a little more difficult in the darkness. Branches scraped across his face and he tripped over a few vines, but the tension of the situation had him moving swiftly. It wasn't long before he had reached the bullrushes at the edge of the clearing.

Everything was just as he had left it before. There was plenty of moonlight, so he switched off the torch and began pulling the dried marijuana plants off the strands of clothesline, bending them and stuffing them into the garbage bag. Before long the bag was full. There was just one plant left hanging and Norton would have been flat out stuffing it into the almost-bursting bag. *Oh well,* he thought, *the least I can do is leave them enough for a smoke.* He tied the top of the bag with a plastic clip, threw it over his shoulder and looking like a strange version of Santa Claus set back off along the trail.

There was still no one around when he paddled back to the car so he quickly and silently tied the ski to the roof racks and crammed the huge bag of marijuana into the boot. The thought that he could get five years gaol for cultivation and supply if he had been caught with that amount of marijuana didn't enter his head. He changed out of his wet jeans and T-shirt, started the car and drove off out of the lagoon. Just after twelve, he yawned to himself and glanced at his watch. *I should be sound asleep by one.* And he was.

Norton didn't bother about doing any training the following morning, opting for a bit of a sleep-in instead. Reg was having breakfast and it was around eight when he walked into the kitchen.

'Hello, no exercise this morning?' grinned Reg.

'No thanks,' replied Les. 'I got enough last night to do me for a while.'

'Yeah?' Reg's eyes lit up. 'What happened?'

'Wait till I get myself a cuppa and I'll tell you.'

Norton made a cup of coffee then sat down and told Reg most of what happened at the barbecue and back at the flat. He didn't elaborate too much about what happened between Betty and himself, and he didn't mention the dope, he wanted to save that till later.

'So,' chuckled Reg, 'one could say you had a reasonably good time Les.'

'Yes. One could say that,' replied Norton slyly. 'There's also a little something else I'd like you to see, too.'

'Yeah? What's that?'

'Come out to the car and I'll show you.'

Curious, Reg followed Norton out to the BMW and stood behind him while he opened the boot.

'There you are,' grinned Les, untying the garbage bag. 'Have a look at that.'

Reg looked inside the bulging, plastic bag and his eyes lit up like a Christmas tree. But he was more horrified than amused. 'Holy bloody hell,' he cried. 'Where'd you get that?'

'The other side of Boambee lagoon,' replied Norton, the grin still plastered across his face. He then told Reg exactly how he'd stumbled across it and how he'd knocked it off. 'So what do you reckon? Not a bad night's work eh?'

'Not bad my arse!' replied Reg. He wasn't at all amused. 'What's the idea of bringing it back here anyway? Shit!'

'Well what else was I gonna do with it? Anyway, there's at least fifteen grand's worth of pot there. I'll put you in the whack when I flog it back in Sydney.'

'I don't want to go in the whack,' replied Reg, waving his arms around. 'I don't want nothing to do with it and I'm filthy on you bringing it back to my farm. You know my opinion of the greedy bastards who sell heaps of this, and now you're one of them. Christ!'

'Shit, I'm sorry Reg,' said Norton, feeling more than a bit uncomfortable at upsetting his friend. 'I didn't mean to do the wrong thing. I just saw it there and I thought... I dunno, I just thought I may as well grab it. I mean... fifteen grand is fifteen grand.'

Reg shook his head. 'You're just like the rest of them Les: motivated by money and greed. It fair dinkum gives me the shits.' He had another look in the garbage bag and suddenly a curious look came over his face. He started going through the dope running his hand right down to the bottom of the bag. He stood up and turned to Norton, his hands on his hips and a sardonic smile etched round his eyes. 'How much did you say you were going to flog this for again, in Sydney?'

Norton shrugged his shoulders. 'I dunno. About fifteen grand something like that.'

'Fifteen grand eh? And who are you going to sell it to?'

'I dunno,' Norton shrugged his shoulders again. 'A couple of shifties I know from the Cross. They'll take it.'

'Oh they will, will they?' Reg started to laugh, quietly at first but gradually got louder. 'Well I've got some bloody bad news for you Mr Boambee lagoon connection. Your dope's not worth two-fuckin'-bob.'

Norton looked at Reg incredulously. 'What d'yer mean, it's not worth two bob?'

'They're all male plants,' roared Reg. 'It wouldn't stone a budgerigar.'

'What d'you mean male plants?' said Les, screwing up his face. 'Pot's pot and that's bloody pot. Don't give me the shits.'

'Don't give *me* the shits,' echoed Reg. 'You wombat,' he sneered. 'You only smoke the female plants that's where those heads I showed you come from.'

'Well what do you think they are?' bellowed Norton, pointing to all the little yellow flowers on the stems at the top of the bag. 'They're those head things. Have a look at the size of them, they're the grouse.'

Reg looked at Les like he was a little kid who had just pooped his pants. 'You bloody great boofhead. Look, wait here and I'll show you something.' He went inside the house, returning with a bag not quite half-full of his own marijuana. 'Now look you see this,' he pulled one of the little heads out of the bag and handed it to Norton. 'You see how sticky and resiny that is?'

Les squeezed it between his fingers feeling the resin stick to them like honey but with a spicy, almost gingery sort of smell. 'Yeah,' he nodded.

'Well that resin's what makes a good smoke and only the female plants produce it. Now have a feel of yours.'

Norton took one of the plants out of the bag and squeezed it between his fingers, too. 'It's not ... very sticky ... is it Reg?'

154

'It's not very sticky, is it Reg?' mimmicked Reg. 'No. Because it's got no resin in it, that's why. You clown.'

'But it looks all right.'

'Yeah, it looks all right but it's just no good.' Reg started laughing like a drain again. 'You Dubbo, Les. You've pissed off on that good sort, busted your arse crawling through a swamp to get the shit. Not to mention the five years you'd've got if the cops had of caught you, and for what? Nothing. And it serves you right you greedy, big prick.'

'Well the stuff can't be that bad.' Norton ran his hand through the garbage bag. 'I mean, what were the growers doing drying it out if it was no good?'

'They've probably dried out their female plants earlier, or they might still be growing. I dunno, but they've kept all this to mix with them and sell it as leaf and tip.'

'Leaf 'n tip?'

'Yeah. The old German brew Les. Leabintip. They mix them together and it goes further — you're not the only hungry cunt in Australia Norton.'

Norton paused for a moment, reflecting on the garbage bag in the boot of the car. 'So this stuff on its own's no good?'

Reg shrugged his shoulders. 'I s'pose you could smoke it but you'd probably have to smoke that whole bag before you got stoned. You'd end up with coal-miner's lung before you got any sort of a buzz out of it,' he added with a laugh.

'Coal-miner's lung, eh?' said Norton quite disgruntled.

'Yeah. But don't worry Les,' said Reg sarcastically. 'You've done pretty good for a Queenslander.' He gave Norton a pat on the shoulder. 'Now I'm going into my shed to do some painting. Do me a favour, will you? — don't come near me till about one o'clock.' He turned and walked towards the shed.

'Well what am I going to do with this?' wailed Norton, from the boot of the BMW.

'I don't know,' replied Reg stopping in mid-stride. 'But here you are.' He pulled a packet of cigarette papers out of his shirt pocket and threw them to Les. 'Why don't you roll yourself a joint?'

Norton tossed the packet of cigarette papers into the plastic bag full of dope sitting in the boot of the car. *Roll myself a joint,* he snorted to himself. *Smart little bastard. I ought to boot him right up the arse.* But as he watched his little artist friend disappear into his shed the funny side of what had happened started to dawn on him, and he realised Reg was right and he had — through being greedy — made a bit of a dill out of himself. *Still, how was I to know?* He was chuckling to himself a bit when he spotted Reg's incinerator — a rusty, old 44 gallon drum with a hole cut into it, sitting on some house bricks standing at the back of the house. *Well one thing I do know. I know just what to do with this shit.* He picked up the huge bag of dope, walked over and stuffed it in the incinerator. By burning it Norton hoped he might be able to at least regain some esteem in Reg's eyes. He went to the kitchen to get some newspaper and matches. As he was groping around in the cupboards the phone rang in the lounge-room.

'Hello,' he said briefly into the receiver.

'Hello. Is that you Les? It's Betty,' was the reply.

'G'day Betty.' At the sound of her voice Norton's spirits rose somewhat. 'How are you?'

'I'm fine. I got your note all right.'

'That's good. I didn't mean to run out on you but I just thought it might be for the best.'

'Well you were right. Uncle Don was around here at seven o'clock. He wasn't snooping, they just wanted to see if I was all right, and they're taking me up to some friends at Woolgoolga for the day.'

'See, I told you.'

'He probably wouldn't have said anything if you had been here, but you know what relatives are like. They still think I'm fourteen.'

'You're definitely not fourteen Betty. I'll swear to that. And did you tell him you were all right?'

'I told him I never felt better in my life,' she chuckled. 'What about yourself?' she added slyly.

'I ain't complaining.'

They both laughed out aloud, then chatted for a few minutes. Finally Betty asked Les if he was still going to take her out that night.

'Just try and find someone to stop me,' replied Norton. 'Where would you like to go anyway?'

'Well, I'll probably have to have tea out at Woolgoolga but I should be back at eight. What about coming around at say nine and we'll go into Coffs Harbour. There's a disco there called Pinkie's. Got a really good DJ. Do you like to dance Les?'

'Does a duck like to quack?'

'Okay then, I'll see you at nine. Why don't you bring your artist friend? I'd like to meet him.'

156

'Reg? Yeah righto I will. I'll see you at nine then.'

'See you then. Bye.'

'Bye Betty.'

Well that's good, thought Norton, *everything's worked out okay there.* He was looking forward to seeing Betty again that night. While they were talking on the phone Les had forgotten what he'd come into the house for. He decided to go for a run and do a bit of training before it got too hot. As he trotted off from the farm he noticed the bag in the incinerator. *I'll burn it when I get back*, he thought.

It took Les about an hour and a half to complete his training. He took a shower and had a light breakfast of muesli and peaches and a cup of coffee: he'd have a big lunch later on. While he was having a second cup of coffee he decided to make another one and take it out to Reg who was still painting in his shed out the front. He knocked lightly on the door with his foot before he entered.

'All right if I come in mate? I know it's not one o'clock yet but I brought you a cup of coffee. Here you are.'

'Thanks Les.' Reg took the mug from Norton's extended hand and had a sip. 'Mm, two spoonfuls of honey — perfect. At least you can do something right Les.'

'Yeah,' Norton grinned sheepishly. He had a look around Reg's shed-cum-studio. Strangely enough it was the first time he'd taken a good look inside there since he'd arrived at the farm.

The studio was nothing more than a roughly hewn wooden shed not much bigger and a little narrower than your average lounge-room. A curtained window faced away from the house and a single fluorescent light dangled precariously from the cobweb-infested ceiling. Paintings and pieces of masonite-backed canvas were scattered around the floor and up against the walls, and a narrow bench on one wall was strewn with brushes, oil-paints, water-colours and various other artist's paraphenalia, including a moveable wooden model of a human being. *Penthouse* and *Playboy* pin-ups were pinned to the walls along with newspaper and magazine clippings, photos, pieces of broken mirrors, posters, books, metal buttons, toys and a million and one other pieces of dusty bric-a-brac accumulated over the years. When Norton entered Reg was seated on an old bar-stool with Sally at his feet. He was finishing an oil painting of what Les recognised as the billabong at the back of the farm, only he'd painted in several water-birds and parrots. Even to Norton's inexperienced eye he could see how Reg

157

had managed to capture the vivid colours and peaceful beauty of the remarkable little place. He was quite impressed.

'Jees, Reg,' he said, peering over Reg's shoulder while the artist sipped on his coffee. 'You've done a good job there. That looks almost like a photo.'

Reg put down his coffee and daubed a bit more colour on one of the birds. 'You like it, do you, Les?'

'Too right. In fact I can't understand why you don't sell a lot more paintings than what you do. You're bloody good mate.'

'Ah, people up this way haven't got a real lot of money Les. I wish I could though. I'd like to get myself a good VCR.'

'Yeah? Why's that?'

'The ABC's got these video casettes out about all the old masters — Gauguin, Monet, Picasso, Rembrandt. I'd love to get them.' He added another daub of paint. 'Still, you never know. Maybe one day.'

'Yeah, you never know what might happen.' Norton took a sip on his coffee. 'I've worked out what I'm going to do with that pot.'

'You're not still going to sell it are you?'

'No. It's in the incinerator. I'm gonna burn it.'

'Bloody good idea Les. Evil can only create more evil, so just put it down to experience.'

'Yeah, you're right Reg, and I owe you an apology, too.' Norton took a lengthy sip on his coffee. 'Anyway, what are you doing tonight? You want to come for a drink with me and Betty? She said she'd like to meet you.'

'Oh yeah. Where are you thinking of going?'

'Some place in Coffs Harbour called Pinkie's or something. Betty reckons it's pretty good.'

Reg put his brush down and took another sip of coffee, reflecting into the mug for a few moments. 'I... can't go to Pinkie's with you Les,' he said quietly.

'Yeah. Why's that?'

'I just can't.'

Norton could see by the way Reg was looking into his coffee that he was keeping something back. Les was determined to find out what. 'What do you mean you just can't? There's got to be a reason. What'd they catch you dealing pot in there, eh? Is that what it is?'

'Oh, don't be bloody stupid Les.' He paused for a moment. 'To tell you the truth... I had a fight with the bouncer.'

Norton stared at Reg as if he couldn't believe his ears. 'You

158

had a fight with the bouncer?' He roared laughing. 'What is he, a Kampuchean jockey? Did he have much trouble beating you?'

Reg's cheeks coloured slightly as he looked at the floor. 'Well, it wasn't actually a fight,' he almost mumbled.

'No. I couldn't really picture you in a stink Reg. I mean you're that skinny now if you go out in a strong wind, you start to twang.'

'All right Hercules, we can't all be like you. What happened: the bouncer there said I was trying to get on to his girl so he punched me in the head and threw me out.'

Norton screwed up his face and frowned. He wasn't real keen on the idea of his little artist friend getting belted by some big clown. 'Tell me exactly what happened Reg,' he said slowly.

'Well. There's two bouncers there but George is the biggest, he's a bricklayer and he's got a girlfriend Diane who's into ceramics: that's pottery. Anyway we were just talking about art this night and we ended up having a bit of a dance — just as friends — when George came flying over and dragged her off the dance floor and started roughing her up. I went over to apologise for her and tell him it wasn't her fault, and he just turned around and punched me in the eye, then threw me out and gave me a couple in the kidneys as well. Fair dinkum Les. I had a black eye for nearly three weeks and I was crook for days after.'

'Go on,' mused Norton. 'He sounds like a bit of a real heavy dude this George.'

'Oh, he's a twenty-four carat prick Les. The funny part about it, Diane doesn't even like him, but she's too scared to leave him. He's just bloody mean and he's big, too. Bigger than you.'

'Mm, he sounds like he's real bad news, this George.'

'Yeah, he is. And that's why we can't go to Pinkie's Les.'

Norton looked at his little artist mate who had embarrassment written all over his face, and he wasn't very amused. 'Well, Reg,' he said evenly. 'We'd definitely better not go to Pinkie's then.'

'I'd rather not Les.'

'Anyway don't worry about it. We'll go somewhere else.' He reached over and patted Reg on the shoulder. 'You feeling a bit hungry at all? How about I whip up a feed of steak sangers.'

'Yeah, righto.'

'I'll give you a yell in about half an hour. You finished with your coffee?' Reg handed Les his empty mug and Norton disappeared into the kitchen.

Norton knocked up the steak sandwiches and took them on a tray, along with a big pot of tea out to the studio. When they'd finished Les spent the rest of the afternoon watching Reg paint. They talked about art and Bondi and old times. A little after four they decided to have a couple of hours sleep so they'd be in good shape for a bit of a night on the town. *I don't mind these lazy afternoons at all*, thought Norton, as he lay drifting off, his head on the pillow in the spare room, letting the afternoon breeze bring the fragrance from the jacaranda tree in through the window. *I don't mind them one little bit.* He intended seeing plenty of action that night though.

They got up around six. Reg showered first and, while Norton was getting cleaned up, he grilled a few lamb chump chops and made some fried rice. With that, plus a couple of cups of coffee under their belts, they gave themselves a last detail and headed for Sawtell.

'You haven't brushed up too bad Reg,' said Norton, as they walked out to the cars. Reg was wearing a pair of dress jeans he'd picked up in Double Bay, tan loafers and a brown-striped, button-down collar shirt.

'You look almost human yourself.' Norton was dressed pretty much the same only he had on a dark blue, Hawaiian shirt tucked into a pair of Levi's, and shiny, black R. M. Williams riding boots.

'You may as well come with me as take both cars,' said Les. 'The only thing is, I might slip back to Miss Cox's place afterwards and see if she wants to give me another look at her "map of Tasmania". What are you going to do?'

'That's all right. I'll just curl up on the back seat and go to sleep. Mate, I don't often get a chance to ride in a grouse car like this. I got to make the most of it.'

'Fair enough. Anyway we'll work something out. Come on, jump in.'

'You'll only be in there five minutes before she screams and throws you out anyway.'

'Don't you believe it. The schoolteacher thinks I'm a good sort.'

'Yeah? Fair dinkum Les,' said Reg, as he opened the car door, 'just how did you meet her? Did you run off with her white stick?'

The BMW purred into life. With Skyhooks, belting their

way through 'You Just Like Me 'Cause I'm Good in Bed', they cruised sedately down the driveway and headed towards Telegraph Point Road and Sawtell.

Betty's front door was open when they got there; Norton knocked twice, opened the flyscreen and they went inside. Betty was in the kitchen shovelling ice, bananas, kiwi fruit and pieces of rockmelon, plus liberal amounts of Bacardi, into a blender. When she turned round a distinct, rosy glow was almost pulsating from her cheeks.

'Les,' she cried out happily. 'How are you?' She ran over, put her arms round him and kissed his cheek.

'Pretty good.' He smiled and nodded towards the mixture in the blender. 'What are you up to?'

'Making fruit-salad daiquiris. Boy, what a way to go! Two of these'll grow hair on your eyeballs.'

'Yeah, I can see that. Anyway Betty, this is Reg, my mate that owns the farm.'

'Hello Reg,' Betty extended her hand. 'Pleased to meet you.'

Reg gave her hand a light squeeze. 'Nice to meet you Betty.'

'So you're the brilliant young artist Les keeps telling me about.'

Reg shuffled his feet a little self-consciously. 'I'm not that good Betty. I'm still only an amateur really — I've only sold a few.'

'Don't you believe him,' said Norton. 'He's bloody good.'

'Les is just being polite,' smiled Reg.

'Well I'm going to be polite,' giggled Betty, 'and pour us all one of these.' She gave the blender a whirl then filled three glasses with the icy, frothy, orange-coloured mixture. 'Cheers,' she said happily.

'Yeah. Cheers,' chorused the others.

'Jesus how good are these?' said Norton, smacking his lips.

'Bloody beautiful,' said Reg.

'I told you they were nice.'

Norton drained the rest of his in a swallow. 'I think I'd better have another one.' He handed Betty his empty glass.

They finished off the first blender full of daiquiris pretty smartly so Betty made another: a bit bigger this time. By quarter to ten that was gone, and they were laughing like drains, each with quite a glow up.

'Well, I guess we'd better make a move,' sniggered Betty, 'or we'll finish up too sloshed to go anywhere.'

'Righto,' said Norton, draining the last of his drink. 'Let's hit the toe.'

161

Betty locked up the flat and, laughing like hyenas, they piled clumsily into the BMW. Norton hit the stereo and with John Paul Young thumping out 'I Wanna Do It With You', they headed noisily for Coffs Harbour.

'Where are we going anyway?' asked Reg, when they were about a kilometre or so from Coffs.

'Pinkie's' replied Betty, turning around to Reg. 'Have you been there?'

Reg waited a few moments before he answered her. 'Yes, I've been there,' he said a little quietly. 'Les, what did I say to you earlier?'

'Don't worry Reg,' replied Norton jauntily. 'Everything'll be sweet.'

Betty turned back round to Reg. 'What's the matter with Pinkie's? Don't you like it there Reg?'

'Reg had an argument with one of the blokes that works there,' said Norton. 'He bought a painting off him and won't pay.'

'What? The miserable bloody so-and-so. Just point him out to me Reg, I'll have a word with him.' Betty unsuspectingly started shaping up to Les across the front seat. 'I'll sort him out in five minutes.'

'For Christ's sake, don't go putting ideas in anyone's head Betty.'

'What was that Reg?'

'Nothing.'

Norton caught Reg's eye in the rear-vision mirror: he grinned and gave Reg a wink.

A row of motels on either side of the highway told them they were entering Coffs, Betty gave Les directions. Finally they saw a pink, flashing, neon sign saying 'Pinkies' over an entry-way and doorway. 'Here it is,' Betty said. There was a parking spot across the street so Norton did a quick U-turn and backed into it. They locked the car and got out.

'Is that your mate on the door?' said Norton to Reg, as they started to cross the road.

'No, that's his offsider Ken. He's nearly as bad though.'

As they approached him, Norton started checking Ken out. He was about 190 centimetres with short-cropped blonde hair, a sullen-looking fat face and a huge domed forehead, with two beady little eyes set up underneath it about one centimetre apart. He was all puffed-up tits and biceps squeezed into a white T-shirt with 'Pinkie's' written across a pocket on the front; he looked as though he sat around pumping iron all day and borrowed his sister's T-shirt to wear out at night. As they got close he gave them a very sour once up and down — giving little Reg a twice up and down.

'I don't want any trouble out of you tonight. Understand?' he growled, jabbing a huge, fat finger at Reg.

'You needn't worry about us boss,' said Norton sweetly. 'We'll be like little lambs.'

'Just make sure you are,' growled the bouncer again. 'Or you go out on your arses. The lot of you.'

Betty didn't, but Reg noticed Norton's eyebrows bristle slightly as they walked through the padded, black vinyl door.

They entered a large, fairly well-lit room decorated mainly in red and black. A well-stocked bar ran along to their right with a space in front of it, then chairs and tables led up to a wall full of high set windows. A dance floor, with the mandatory spinning mirror-ball and flashing lights divided the room and beyond that were more chairs and tables leading up to a small food servery. A happy-looking, but obviously very stoned, DJ was bouncing around on his stand while a throng of people, mainly big-bummed girls, were bopping away happily in front of him. The place wasn't anywhere near packed but there was a good enough crowd, fairly well-dressed, all mainly in their early twenties.

'There's an empty table under that window,' said Norton. 'Why don't we grab it?' They moved into a padded vinyl cubicle up against the wall facing the bar. Les and Betty were still laughing away and quite happy, but Reg kept looking around him like he was a member of the French Resistance waiting for the Gestapo to walk in and start checking every one's ID.

'Well, what are we drinking?' said Les. Betty ordered a Bacardi and coke, Reg opted for a Scotch and dry. Norton got two of each, plus two cans of Victorian Bitter for himself.

While he was waiting at the bar a tall, morose-faced guy somewhere in his late twenties leant up against the bar on his elbows, almost next to him, and scowled around the room. He was well over 180 centimetres tall, solid-framed with greasy, thick brown hair combed straight back off his forehead: he reminded Norton of a sour faced Jerry Lee Lewis. Like the other big moron out the front he, too, had on a tight-fitting T-shirt with 'Pinkie's' written across the pocket. It didn't take long for Norton to figure out he was the big mug that belted poor little Reg. As he heaved himself off the bar and walked towards the front door Norton noticed he didn't weave his way through the crowd like a normal person, showing a bit of manners and consideration, he abrasively pushed his way straight through making everyone step aside.

'I think I just saw your mate George,' said Norton, as he arrived back with the drinks and put them on the table.

'Yeah. You were just about standing next to him at the bar,' replied Reg. 'He's not hard to miss, is he?'

'I didn't get a chance to have a talk to him unfortunately, but he seems like a decent enough sort of chap. Are you sure you haven't got things a bit mixed up Reg?'

Reg took a sip of his drink and stared at Norton a little derisively. 'Are you sure you haven't been getting into some of my pot Les?'

They finished their first drinks off pretty smartly and started on the second ones. Norton pulled some twenties out of his pocket and threw them on the table. 'We won't worry about having shouts,' he said. 'Just take it out of that and we'll just take turns going and getting them. Fair enough?' He smiled at Reg. 'Do you think you can make it to the bar and back without getting into another toe-to-toe with George?' Reg nodded and smiled back wearily. 'Good.'

Sitting on Norton's right, Betty went to open her handbag. 'I've got some money,' she said. 'There's no need to spend all yours.'

'Stick your money in your arse Miss Cox. Diamond Les Norton's in town. Ain't that right Reg?'

'That's him Betty,' replied Reg. 'Carefree Les. Doesn't care how much anything costs, as long as it's free. Only man in Bondi with a burglar-alarm on his garbage tin.'

Norton sniffed and ignored Reg's insults. 'Now Miss Cox,' he said, turning back to Betty. 'You said something earlier about could I dance. Want to try me out?'

'Okay.'

Les led her on to the dance floor where they squeezed in among the others — Reg looked after their table and kept and eye on the money.

The first song the DJ played when they got there was AC-DC's 'It's A Long Way To the Top If You Wanna Rock'n'Roll' one of Norton's favourite tracks — they tore straight into it. Betty was a pretty energetic dancer, fit, with a very sexy hip movement. She moved and swayed to the driving beat. Norton couldn't be classed as a stylist but he and Billy Dunne were used to skipping to rock'n'roll tapes for up to an hour at a time, so what he lacked slightly in finesse, he more than made up for in condition.

The DJ had plenty of rock'n'roll blood in his veins and showed the dancers absolutely no leniency. He kept throwing on Cold Chisel, Rose Tatoo, The Angels, Daddy Cool, and so on. Within twenty minutes Norton's Hawaiian shirt was soaked and clinging to him and Betty was begging for mercy. They went back to the table to find Reg had bought a fresh round of drinks.

'I think I might have to trade you in on a newer model Miss Cox,' said Norton, when they were seated. 'You're just about worn out. I think you need new rings and pistons.' He took a huge mouthful of beer and sat with a smug look on his face.

'You just keep your eyes to yourself Mr Norton, or you might find yourself dancing around a few straight lefts.' She tore the can out of Les's hand. 'Gimme a mouthful of that beer, too,' she laughed. 'I'm a bit thirsty.'

They sat drinking and laughing for a while. Even Reg seemed to be losing some of his nervousness. When a few quiet songs came on Reg even got up and danced with Betty. While they were on the dance floor Norton thought he recognised a bloke's face he knew from somewhere in Sydney but he wasn't quite sure. He also noticed that, while they were sitting there, a young blonde girl on a stool near the front door kept staring over at their table, but every time he'd look at her she would quickly look away.

'Hey Reg,' he said, when they were both seated back down. 'That girl you had the bit of a fracas over — Diane: is she shortish, got a pretty but sad sort of face with long blonde hair done up in a pony-tail. Not a bad little body?'

Reg looked at Norton quizzingly for a moment. 'Yeah that's her all right. Why, what ...'

'Oh nothing Reg. I was just curious, that's all. Anyway it's my turn to get the drinks. Same again?' The others both nodded.

Norton got up to go to the bar but instead he walked over to the blonde with the pony-tail sitting at the door. 'Excuse me,' he said pleasantly. 'Are you Diane?'

The girl looked up at him nervously. 'Y..yes. Why?' She was certainly quite pretty up close but in a melancholy sort of way.

'A friend of mine, Reg. He wants to know if you might like to join us for a drink. We're only just sitting over there.'

The girl looked at Norton for a moment then shook her head. 'I don't think that would be a very good idea, mister.'

'You're wrong Diane. I think it'd be an absolutely fantastic idea. Come on.' He picked her up under one arm, picked up her handbag and started walking her towards their table. She tried to struggle a little but she was only a slight little thing and in Norton's firm, but gentle grip she didn't have a chance.

'Mister, I don't know who you are but you're making one helluva big mistake.'

'No I'm not,' replied Norton, with a tight smile. 'But I think somebody else round here might be.' He dropped her bag on their table and put her down in the cubicle next to Reg.

'Reg,' he said, 'I've got a friend here to see you. You know Diane, she's into pottery. Not the type of pottery you specialise in though.' Reg was open-mouthed — his eyes looking like two Rolls Royce petrol caps. 'Well don't just sit there like a stale bottle of piss Reg. Introduce Diane to Betty while I get the drinks. What would you like to drink Diane?'

Diane sat blinking but before she knew it she'd mumbled, 'Bacardi and coke.'

'Good idea,' said Norton cheerfully. He rubbed his hands together and headed for the bar. Before long he was back with the drinks on a tray. He put them on the table and sat back down next to Betty at the edge of the cubicle facing the door.

'Les, do you know what you're doing?' said Reg. He was in a state of extreme agitation. Diane was chewing her nails but Betty on the other hand was quite oblivious to what was going on — she just kept laughing away, snuggling into Norton's shoulder.

'Of course I know what I'm doing. I'm having a few drinks and a night out with some friends. What do you think I'm doin'? Sellin' hot-dogs?'

'I think I'd better go,' said Diane, rising in her seat.

Norton reached across and put his hand on her shoulder gently pushing her back down in her seat. 'You don't have to go anywhere Diane,' he said softly. 'Just stay there.' She sat back down, licked her lips and started nervously sipping on her drink. Reg looked across at Norton watching the front door, shook his head and stared down at the table.

'You come here much, do you Diane?' said Betty pleasantly.

It wasn't long before George reappeared in the club. He glanced at where Diane had been sitting, scowled, then turned and said something to the girl at the reception desk. She pointed to where Norton was sitting and you could almost see the storm clouds gather as George's already brooding, malevolent face turned black with rage. His chest heaved up and down

166

a couple of times, then he charged straight through the chairs and tables, bumping people's shoulders and knocking their drinks from their hands to stand towering at the edge of Norton's table. He was almost shaking with anger.

'What in the fuckin' hell do you think you're doing?' he swore loudly at Diane. She quickly turned white as a ghost and started to shake visibly. Even the exuberant Betty was quite taken aback by the huge bouncer's sudden and unexpected outburst. Norton however, just sat quietly sipping his can of VB, a strange half-smile on his face.

'George, it's all right,' said Reg, his face the colour of bad shit: he, too, was shaking like a leaf. 'She only just came over to say hello, that's all. Honest.'

'You shut your mouth, you fuckin' little smart-arse,' snarled George. 'You're lookin' for another smack in the fuckin' mouth. And you, you fuckin' moll. Get up.'

He went to grab Diane by the shoulder and drag her to her feet when Norton's left hand shot out like a snake. It took George's wrist in a vice-like grip forcing his arm back down by his side.

'Take it easy son,' said Norton evenly, the strange smile still on his face. 'The girl's only having a drink — she's not doing any harm.'

George looked at his wrist then glared savagely at Norton; he couldn't believe that someone had actually layed a hand on him. 'Who the fuckin' hell's talking to you — prick,' he hissed slowly, his lips curling back over his teeth with malice. 'Who the fuck are you anyway, carrot top?'

'Who am I?' replied Norton, still smiling. 'Well, to tell you the truth Jack, I've just moved up here. I'm starting a dry-cleaning business. And seeing you're not a bad bloke Jack, I'll tell you what I'll do for you.' Norton got to his feet and picked up Diane's Bacardi and coke. 'Now Jack, I've got this grouse new sanitised dry-cleaning technique. It's unbelievable.' George was blinking through his fury at Norton's patter. You could almost hear the wooden cogs inside his big, thick, bony head slowly turning over as he tried to fathom out Norton's strange talk.

'Now you see this white T-shirt you're wearing Jack?' continued Les. 'Well I'll show you something.' Norton hooked his finger in the pocket on the front of George's T-shirt, pulled it out and poured Diane's Bacardi and coke in it: ice-cubes, pieces of lemon, straw, the lot. Les then gave it a sloppy pat as it soaked all over George's chest. This was as good a time as any for the others to move to the rear of the cubicle. 'Now you bring that down to the shop on Monday Jack, and I'll have that as good as new for you. How's that grab you?' Norton sat back down, his hands hanging loosely by his sides. 'Oh,' he added with a grin. 'And seein' as you've only got half a brain Jack, I'll only charge you half price. Fair enough?'

George looked at his Bacardi-soaked T-shirt then glared at Norton. His face turned into a hideous mask of raging hatred. 'Why you ...' he almost screamed.

He bent down to grab Les by the throat but, as he did, Norton straightened his hand and slashed it powerfully up into the huge bouncer's groin. George's eyes bulged and he let out a roar of pain. It had slammed into his testicles like a piece of four by two. In almost the same movement Norton made a massive fist and rising, drove it in an uppercut straight up under George's jutting chin. Another bellow of pain came through his nostrils as his jaws were slammed violently together, breaking the bones and shattering nearly every tooth in his head. With his left hand Norton grabbed George by his greasy, brown hair, tilted his head to one side and slammed his fist under his right ear — rupturing the arteries in his neck and almost breaking it.

By now the whole place had stopped to watch the action; the only movement and sound was Norton fighting and the DJ still playing records.

Still holding him by the hair, Norton started methodically punching George's face to pulp. There was no science. Les just swung his huge, gnarled fist like a club as he turned the domineering brute of a bouncer's face into a gory red mess. Teeth and lips disintergrated, his ear split apart and his nose crumpled up like balsa. He was completely unconscious: the only thing stopping him from collapsing was the fact that Norton was holding him up. After about a dozen or so good belts Norton let go and George slumped to the floor. As he did, Les reached down, took hold of his right wrist and bent it back, till it snapped with a dull crack. The way George landed the only people to see this were, Diane, Betty and Reg. They couldn't believe their eyes.

Norton stood up just in time to catch a movement to his left: it was Ken charging through the crowd like a runaway steer. Norton wasn't too sure what Ken intended to do but he decided not to take any chances. As he got within range, Norton balanced on his toes then swung his entire body round like a gate closing and king-hit the equally huge, beady-eyed bouncer flush in the face with a punch that would have made Rocky Marciano shudder. Poor Ken didn't know what hit him. Norton's huge fist travelled about one metre and slammed into his nose and mouth like a half house brick, ripping open his lips, pulverising his nose and sending uprooted teeth spinning over the, by now, empty chairs and tables nearest them. As Ken sagged to his knees, Norton drove a wicked left-rip into his rib cage cracking several ribs. Almost in one movement again, he capped both his hands round the back of Ken's head and slammed his left knee into his face three or four times, Thai style. Ken crashed forward on to the floor and lay there, blood oozing out of what was left of his face on to the dirty, black, cigarette-burnt carpet. Norton looked down at him for a moment. *What the hell,* he thought. He picked up the nearest Harvey-Norman-furniture-warehouse vinyl chair and smashed it across his kidneys. Ken didn't move.

There was a hush throughout Pinkie's as everybody in the place stood staring at Norton in silent wonder: they couldn't believe their eyes. The two biggest, meanest bullies in Coffs Harbour had just been absolutely demolished by one man in about two minutes. No one quite knew what to say, the only sound was some record finishing in the background. As it did the DJ's excited voice suddenly rang through the club.

'Ladies and Gentlemen. Our floor show is now over for the night and right now I've got a special request for that red headed gentleman standing there in the blue Hawaiian shirt. And here it is: the Mentals and 'Beserk Warriors'. And if you hurry ... you just might find a spot on the dance floor.'

The music started up and the whole place erupted into cheering for Les: it wasn't hard to see whose side the crowd was on. Norton grinned and gave the DJ a bit of a wave. He was about to say something to the others at his table when he felt a tap at his shoulder. He turned round to face an overweight, extremely nervous, dark-haired bloke with a moustache. The man was wearing a short-sleeved shirt and tie. He was obviously the boss and standing behind him were two terrified barmen.

'Look I'm the owner here,' he blurted out. 'Just what the hell do you think you're doing?'

Suddenly a voice came from the crowd. 'Go on Ross. Let's see you throw him out.'

'Yeah, go on Stanton, you fat turd,' guffawed another one, amidst the laughter. 'Let's see you.'

The owner glared into the crowd, and the two barmen glanced

down at the remains of the two bouncers, shuffled their feet then looked anxiously at Les.

'Listen,' said Norton directly to the owner. 'Your two goons started this and they came off second best. All right? Now instead of carrying on like a good sort help me get 'em to the door and I'll have a yarn to you out there. And don't any of you get any fuckin' ideas about throwin' me out either.' He glared at the two slightly-built barmen who quickly shook their heads in unison.

Between the four of them they half dragged, half carried the two unconscious bouncers to the front where they dumped them into two chairs in a small office. The girl on the desk came in with a couple of bar towels which they wrapped around their mutilated faces to try to stem the bleeding.

'I'm still going to call the police,' said the owner. 'You just can't walk in here and get away with this scot-free pal.'

The owner looked like a half-baked smarty and the way he said it, it sounded to Les like he was trying to pull a bit of a rort. 'Righto,' said Norton angrily, 'ring the coppers. And while you're there tell them to ring this bloke and tell them that's who I work for.' He took his wallet out and handed the owner the piece of paper with the name of the head copper in the district on it, as well as Price's.

The owner looked at it for a moment then gave it the double blink. 'Christ,' he said 'that's the Chief Inspector ...'

'That's right ... pal.'

'And you work for ...'

'Right again. You try any shit with me and I'll have the licensing cops round here first thing Monday morning, and by lunchtime I'll have Sydney's best barrister up here with a raging assault and damages charge against you and Tweedle Dum and Tweedle-even-dumber here.' He nodded at the two bouncers. 'And by tea time Monday you can say goodbye to this flea-pit you're running.'

The owner swallowed and handed Norton back the piece of paper. 'Your're right mate,' he said, licking his lips. 'Don't worry about it.' He paused for a moment then half smiled. 'To tell you the truth I've been wanting to get rid of these two rock-apes for ages but I just haven't been game.' He looked Les up and down. 'You're not looking for a job yourself, are you, by any chance? I'll pay you what I've been paying both these clowns.'

Norton shook his head. 'No thanks. I'm only up here for a few days thanks all the same. But you can tell these two fuckwits I'm coming back again before long and don't be around when I get here. Now if you don't mind I'd like to get back to my friends. Okay?'

'Yeah sure. Hey ... ah ... what's your name again mate?'

'Les.'

'Okay Les. Listen, any drinks you want for the rest of the night are on me. Okay? Just tell them at the bar Ross said it's sweet.'

'That's all right Ross, but I pay my own way. Thanks all the same.' Norton left the office and returned to his table. As he walked through the crowd he got quite a lot of smiles; he was also given quite a wide berth. Reg was sitting alone with a grin from ear to ear when he got back.

'Jesus Les,' he said, 'you've just blown the place out. No one up here's ever seen anything like that. Christ, are you any good or what?'

'Between the Kelly Club and the Bondi Hotel I get plenty of practice,' laughed Norton. He nodded at the empty cubicle. 'Where are the others?'

'Gone to the brascoe. Betty's a little upset. She got quite a shock when you broke George's wrist. Diane's with her.' Reg started to laugh. 'Diane looks like she just won the lottery.'

'Yeah? That's good. Anyway Betty should be all right.' Les picked up a twenty off the table. 'I'll go and get some more drinks. Same again I s'pose.'

'Yeah. But I think you'd better make them doubles this time Les.'

Norton walked over to the bar and joined the others waiting to be served. He was lost in thought for a few moments when he was surprised to hear a quiet voice in his ear.

'The way those two mugs hit the deck, I knew that'd have to be you Norton. No one else whacks them like that.'

Norton turned cautiously round to see who it was. Standing smiling behind him, wearing an immaculately pressed beige dress shirt, tucked into a pair of designer jeans was a fair-haired, medium-built, good style of a guy in his early twenties. He had a gold stud in one ear and round his neck was a thick Thailand style gold chain with a small jade Buddha on it. It was the same bloke he'd thought he'd recognised in the crowd earlier.

'Tony Levin,' said Norton slowly. 'What are you doing up here?'

'Doing my best,' smiled Tony, holding his hands out by his sides. 'What else?'

171

Norton had got to know Tony over the years from around Bondi and the Kelly Club: though Tony originally came from Balmain. Tony was a good-looking young bloke with a ton of personality, always well-dressed and generally always had a good sort on his arm. Tony wasn't a bad bloke but he was as shifty as days are long in summer. His main go was selling pot and maybe a little acid; but nothing else. Tony could always move pot and in any amount you wanted. If he couldn't, he always knew someone who could and he'd get his whack that way. However. In between his dope dealing Tony was not adverse to going up a drainpipe and relieving various citizens of their household appliances and personal effects. He was also not adverse to dudding people with his dope deals should the opportunity ever arise — which was how Norton more or less got to meet him.

Norton was getting into his car one night in the car park of the Clovelly Hotel when he saw Tony having a bit of an altercation with three apparently dissatisfied customers. They must have been dissatisfied because they had Tony on the ground in the corner doing quite a bit of Balmain folk dancing up and down Tony's ribs. Tony could scrap all right for his size but against these three he was having absolutely no luck. Norton didn't know Tony all that well at the time; possibly if he had he would have let the three gentlemen continue turning Levin into dim-sims, however having a sense of fair play he decided to put his head in. One of the three turned on Norton. He was quickly dispatched with a withering short-right and the others soon hit the toe, to allow Tony to crawl painfully to his car and escape to rob another day. But he never forgot Norton for saving his shifty hide and did his best to return the favour with hot gear and all the pot Norton ever wanted, which he nearly always declined. However, surprised and all as he was at seeing Tony in Coffs Harbour, but knowing young Mr Levin's somewhat disingenuous form, especially in the dope rort, a germ of an idea entered Norton's head.

'So, you're up here doing your best, are you Tony?' said Norton, after they'd finished a quick handshake. 'Moving a bit of green I would imagine?'

Levin smiled slyly and nodded. 'Something like that. But don't worry about me big Les. What's your "John Dory"? What are you doing up here?'

Norton smiled and gave Tony a light punch on the shoulder. 'Fair dinkum Tony,' he laughed. 'If I told you, you probably wouldn't believe me. You here on your own?' Tony nodded his head. 'Well give me five minutes to get these drinks back and I'll come and have a yarn to you. I'll meet you at the end of the bar. Okay?' Tony nodded his head again. Norton got the drinks and took them over to Reg who was still sitting on his own in the cubicle.

'I've just bumped into a bloke I know from Sydney,' said Norton, placing the drinks on the table. 'I'm just gonna have a mag to him for a while.' He paused for a moment then smiled at Reg. 'You couldn't do us a favour, could you Reg?'

'Sure. What is it?'

'Have you got any of that dope on you?'

Reg looked at Norton curiously for a moment. 'Yeah, I have got a bag on me to tell you the truth. I didn't think we were coming here and I brought some to give to a mate of mine who works at this other place I thought we might've gone to. Why, do you feel like a smoke?'

'Yeah. I'm still a bit revved up after that fight and I wouldn't mind a bit of a puff to bring me back down. I thought I might shout my mate one, too, if that's okay with you?'

'Sure. Here, go for your life. There's some papers in the bag.' Reg put his hand down the front of his jeans, brought out a fairly thick plastic bag of dope and palmed it to Norton who slipped it inside his shirt. 'You can have as much as you like but I'm warning you, go easy with it. That stuff's dynamite if you're not used to it.'

Norton smiled and winked. 'She'll be sweet. Thanks Reg.'

'No worries. See you when you get back.'

Les picked up his can of VB and rejoined Tony waiting at the end of the bar. 'So Tony,' he said, as they both raised their glasses. 'You're up here moving a bit of "Bob Hope" eh?'

'S'posed to be,' replied Tony, nodding is head derisively. 'I was supposed to pick up fifteen kilos off this fuckin' dill this afternoon. I ring up his place and some dopey sheila says, 'Graham's not here. He's gone surfing at Angourie and he won't be back till Monday. So I'm stuck here till fuckin' Monday. Fair dinkum, I'd've left a message for him to shove it up his arse but we need the earn.'

'Who's we?'

'L.A. Dave.'

Norton started to laugh. 'L.A. fuckin' Dave. Jesus.'

L.A. Dave was another pot dealer and rorter from around Coogee. A tall, gangling, curly-haired guy, who fancied himself a treat; he was credited with being 90 per cent mouth and

10 per cent ability. He got the nickname L.A. Dave from spending three years scamming around Los Angeles. When he got back to Australia, everything was 'L.A. this and L.A. that.' He was tolerated and regarded as bit of a harmless pain in the arse. However he, like his shifty running mate Levin, also had the contacts to move large quantities of pot.

'L.A.'s all right,' shrugged Tony. 'He's bought a clothes shop with his sheila up in Grafton. He reckons he likes it up there. Jacaranda trees, Clarence River and all that.'

'Yeah. Handy to the jail, too.'

Tony shuddered. 'Oh Jesus, don't ever say that Les. Anyway, what's your caper shifty? How come you're in Coffs Harbour? Don't try and tell me you're up here for the bananas.'

Norton's face broke into a grin. 'Mate, it's the funniest thing you've ever heard why I'm here. It's just ridiculous. I was supposed to pick up some money off a bloke for Price.'

'Yeah, I tipped that'd be on the cards.'

'This bloke owes Price fifteen grand, so he sent me up to either get the money or break the bloke's arms.'

'Give you something to do I s'pose.'

'Anyway. The poor prick hasn't got the money but he offers us twenty kilo of pot.'

'Yeah?' Levin's ears immediately pricked up.

'Yeah. So I rang Price. He says. "Yeah that'll have to do." So rather than put this poor silly cunt in a wheelchair, I just gave him a good smack in the mouth and picked up the dope.' Les gave a deep, throaty chuckle. 'Now we're stuck with twenty kilo of bloody pot. But we'll flog it somewhere in Sydney and get Price's fifteen grand back.'

'There's twenty kilos, and you . . . just want Price's fifteen thousand?'

'Yeah, that's all. I'll flog it to the first bloke that comes up with 15 yards. I'm fucked if I want to be driving around with that much dope in the boot of me car.'

Tony looked at Norton for a moment and stroked his chin thoughtfully. 'Is the stuff any good?'

Norton shrugged his shoulders. 'Well I don't know much about the stuff Tony, prices and all that. But evidently it's the grouse. All compressed heads or something. I know it's all full of little red hairs and it's as sticky as buggery.' Norton gave Tony a dumb look. 'Does that mean anything?'

'Oh . . . yeah. It could.' Tony was trying to act cool but he was swarming like a school of Botany Bay mullet.

'I don't smoke myself, but I'm with a bloke and a couple

of chics. I gave them some and they couldn't even finish one joint. In fact the two chics are out in the toilet now. They reckon they couldn't handle it. The bloke's off his head, too.' Norton pointed to the empty cubicle and waved to Reg, who waved back enthusiastically. Seeing George get flattened had Reg stoned off his face as it was. 'Anyway, do you want a smoke? I've got a bag on me.'

'Yeah, reckon. Listen I'll tell you what Les.' Tony drew a little closer to Norton's ear. 'If this stuff's any good, I'll get you fifteen grand for it this weekend.'

Norton shrugged his shoulders. 'Suits me. I just want to get rid of the shit. The sooner the better. Anyway, come out to the car, have a look at it and roll yourself a joint.'

'Righto.'

They finished their drinks and strolled to the door.

Outside the club, the owner and the two barmen were bundling the still semi-conscious George and Ken into the back of a Holden station wagon which was double parked in front of about a dozen leering, sniggering patrons. The two bouncers were blood from head to toe and in the pink neon-light flickering above them, looked more like they'd been in a bad car accident than a quick street fight. Les and Tony put their heads down, skirted around the crowd and walked briskly across the road to the BMW.

'Here you are,' said Norton, getting the bag of dope out from inside his Hawaiian shirt. He handed it to Tony who began to examine it closely under the interior light.

Levin couldn't believe his eyes. He'd been handling all sorts of pot for years — everything from Buddha sticks to Mullumbimby madness — and he'd never seen or felt anything like this. It smelt better than Turkish Green hashish and the amount of resin in the tiny purple heads almost glued his fingers together. He didn't want to come on too strong though. 'Oh yeah,' he said casually. 'I s'pose it ... doesn't look too bad.'

Christ, just who's trying to con who here, thought Norton. 'Well there's some papers there,' he said. 'Roll yourself a joint. That's the best way to find out.'

In next to no time Levin's expert fingers had rolled a small neat joint complete with a tiny filter torn from a portion of the cigarette papers.

'If you don't mind Tony,' said Norton, 'would you smoke it outside the car, just in case I happen to get pulled over and some goosey walloper sticks his head in the window. Saves me a hassle.'

'Yeah sure. No worries,' said Tony opening the door. He couldn't wait to try out this amazing looking dope.

They locked the car and took a short walk up the street. Tony was puffing away deeply on the joint. He offered Norton a toke.

'No thanks,' replied Les. 'The coppers might come back about that fight and I'd have to do a bit of fast talking.'

'Fair enough.'

Norton picked up an empty cigarette packet, removed the silver paper then got a little bit of dope out of the plastic bag, wrapped it in the silver paper and gave it to Tony as a sample. By the time Tony had got to the end of the joint he didn't know whether he was coming or going. His eyes were spinning round in his head like two bubbles in a piss-pot and Norton had him in, not only hook, line and sinker, but rod, reel and bait box as well. 'Well. What do you reckon?' he enquired casually.

'Reckon? . . . Reckon . . . What?' replied Tony vaguely. He was in Disneyland. Donald Duck was sitting on his shoulder and Pluto, Mickey and Goofy were dancing up and down the street with him.

'That pot. Is it any good?' *Need I ask*, thought Norton, looking at Tony's twisted, grinning face.

'Yeah . . . it's . . . really . . . all right.'

'Good. I wasn't too sure myself. But if you say so it must be. Well come on, let's go back to Pinkie's.'

'Pinkie's? . . . What's Pinkie's?'

'The nightclub we just came from Tony. You know. In Coffs Harbour. I just met you there. Remember?' *Christ, what a job*, thought Norton. *What's Reg got in this stuff? nitroglycerin?*

'Oh yeah. Pinkie's . . . You want to go there . . . do you?'

'Oh I wouldn't mind Tony. Yeah. That's if it's no trouble for you of course.'

'Oh no . . . that's cool Les . . . Where is it?'

'Just down the road. Come on.' Norton looked at Tony stumbling around like a wombat and shook his head; he needed Tony hanging off him about as much as Kojak needs a year's supply of hair conditioner. He took him by the arm. 'Tony, just come back to the car for a minute.' While Tony stood outside the BMW blinking into space Norton got a piece of paper and a biro from the glove box. 'Now what do you want to do about that pot Tony?' he said, after he locked the car.

'I'll take it . . . I mean . . . We'll take it,' said Tony, trying to focus on Norton while he leant unsteadily against the bonnet.

'Okay. Well look, there's the phone number where I'm staying.' He showed Tony the piece of paper with Reg's number on it then tucked it in the fob pocket of Tony's jeans. 'Ring me there tomorrow morning and we'll sort it out. Okay?' Tony nodded his head. 'Now when we get back inside, I'll leave you and go back to the team I'm with. The less people that see us together while we're pulling this caper the better. Don't you reckon?' Norton had decided to add a little drama to the scene as an excuse to get rid of Levin, just in case he said something in front of Reg or Betty which might bring him undone. 'So when we get back inside just make out you don't know me. All right?'

'Yeah,' nodded Tony. 'I can . . . dig that Les. . . . That's cool.'

Hello, thought Norton, *now I've got him talking like a leftover from Woodstock.* 'Okay. So I'll say goodbye now Tony and I'll see you tomorrow. But come on, I'll walk inside with you.' With Tony following behind like one of the three blind mice they crossed the street — with Levin looking up and down the deserted thoroughfare every five seconds like it was peak-hour on Parramatta Road. There was no one outside the club so they walked straight in. Norton guided Tony to the bar then left him there and walked back to the cubicle where Betty was sitting quietly on her own. As Les sat down next to her he noticed she was a little pale and tense, and seemed to keep a slight distance between them.

'Hey, how are you?' said Norton pleasantly. 'Sorry I was so long but I bumped into an old mate from Sydney.'

'That's all right,' she said shortly.

'Where's Diane and Reg?'

'On the dance floor,' replied Betty, then stared expressionlessly into her drink.

'Do you want a dance?'

'No thank you.'

'Okay.' Norton looked at her for a few moments then looked away as they sat there in awkward silence. Finally he said to her. 'Are you all right?'

'I'd like to go home soon Les. If that's okay with you?'

Norton shrugged his shoulders. 'Yeah sure. Just wait till Diane and Reg get back. All right?' Betty nodded her head and kept staring into her drink.

'Are you upset about that fight?'

She turned to Les with a distrustful, slightly fearful look on her face. 'I've never seen anything like that before in my life. You almost killed those two men.'

177

'Oh get out. They're just knocked about a bit that's all. Christ, they're big enough to cop it. Anyway, did Diane tell you what that big goose did to her and Reg? What about the way he was carrying on at the table. Jesus, turn it up.'

'Fair enough Les, but you brought the girl over knowing he'd do something about it and you tipped the drink down the front of his T-shirt. Two wrongs don't make a right.'

'Yeah right,' mumbled Norton. 'I'm not gonna argue with you.' *Fuck it*, he thought. *I've sweetened everything up for Reg and his girl and bubbled the rort for myself. Just my bloody luck.* He looked at Betty's sensationally fit body bulging out against the short, light blue, dress she was wearing and cursed to himself again. He realised there'd be nothing doing there tonight. But although he didn't want to admit it to himself Norton's feelings for Betty ran a lot deeper than her body. They were sitting in silence when Reg and Diane arrived back sweating and puffing from the dance floor. Unlike Les and Betty, they were in high spirits.

'Hey Les. What's doin' mate?' laughed Reg, as they sat down opposite them.

'Not much Reg,' replied Norton pensively.

'Did Stanton say anything to you or try and pull something out the front?' asked Diane.

Norton shook his head. 'No. He's sweet.'

'Don't take any notice of him anyway. He's as weak as piss.' Diane reached over and placed her hand gently on Norton's arm. 'You've done everyone a favour. Don't worry about that. Thank you Les.'

'That goes for me, too, Les,' said Reg. 'You had us a bit worried at first. But... Thanks mate.'

'Yeah,' said Norton, trying to smile. 'Terrific.' He looked at Betty still sitting silently next to him. 'Anyway Betty wants to go home. She reckons she's not feeling too good so I might have to get going soon.'

'That's all right,' said Reg. 'Diane's offered to drive me home anyway.'

'Oh well, you're right then. You gonna duck in and see George on the way?'

'I don't think we'll bother,' replied Diane. 'Unless it's to break something else.'

'That's if there's anything left to break,' laughed Reg.

Despite his blues Norton still managed a bit of a smile at the evil look on Diane's face.

Norton finished his beer. Betty picked up her purse and

178

they stood up to leave. Betty told Diane to call round and see her before she left for Grafton on Sunday — Norton told Reg he'd see him back at the farm. They quietly left the club and got into the car to head home. Betty didn't say anything till they turned left onto the Pacific Highway and were about a kilometre towards Sawtell.

'You haven't really been honest with me, have you Les?' she said, as they slowed down for a line of traffic.

'How do you mean?' replied Les, reaching over and turning the car stereo down a little more.

'Your father doesn't really own a meatworks, does he? And you're about as much a company director as what I am.'

'What makes you say that?'

'Oh the flash car. The way you throw your money around. The fast talk. The slang. The quick professional way you crippled those two huge men.'

Norton paused for a moment then looked over at her. 'You really want to know?' he asked.

'Yes I do.'

'All right Betty, I'll tell you.'

As they followed the other cars with the stereo playing softly in the background Norton told her almost everything about himself, Bondi and the Kelly Club. He didn't elaborate too much about the fights, the scams and the murders he'd been involved in but he did mention how he made a lot of money on the side and owned his own home at Bondi. He told her about the block of flats he owned at Randwick and the black money he had invested through Price. He also told her how he met Reg and why he was staying with him; he didn't mention anything about the dope.

Betty sat listening intently, almost astonished, scarcely saying a word. By the time Norton had finished they were almost at Sawtell.

'And that's the truth Betty. How could I tell you I was a bouncer working in an illegal gambling casino up the Cross. Christ. I'd've lasted about two minutes.' He looked at her seriously as they drove past the hotel where they'd spent Wednesday afternoon together. 'Fair dinkum Betty. Where I come from I meet girls like you once in a blue moon. I just didn't want to bomb the little chance I had.'

They drove on in silence till Norton got to Betty's street and pulled up in front of her flat. He switched off the motor and they sat in the car for a few moments listening absently to the stereo.

'Anyway Betty, that's the truth,' Norton finally said. 'If I've said or done anything that's upset you. Well I'm sorry. I really am.'

'That's all right Les.' She took her keys out of her purse. 'I'm just. I don't know. I'm just a little bewildered that's all.'

'Yeah, fair enough. At least now you know what's goin' on.'

'Yes I certainly do,' said Betty, as she started to open the car door. 'And I think your kind of lifestyle would be just a bit too fast for a mundane country schoolteacher like me.'

Norton reached over and placed his hand on her arm as gently as he could. 'Think what you like Betty. But if you should change your mind, you've got my number. Give me a ring and I'll come over, even if it's just to see you for a while. Or if you like I'll take you out to dinner tomorrow night. Whatever suits you.'

Betty smiled briefly. 'We'll see what happens Les.'

Norton smiled at her and gave his shoulders a bit of a shrug. 'Anyway. Even if you don't. It's sure been nice knowing you.' He looked at the interior light reflecting the sadness in her eyes and yearned to hold her, wishing there was something more appropriate he could say. 'Let me put that another way Betty,' he said gently. 'It's been more than nice knowing you. It's been three of the best days of my life.'

Betty smiled at him again and Norton thought he could see a slight glisten in her eyes.

'Good night Les.' She opened the car door and got out.

'Yeah. Good night Betty.' He watched her walk briskly up to her flat.

After she went inside Norton sat staring absently at her door for a moment or two. 'Fuck it!' he cursed out loud, then started the car and drove off.

Ah well. No good crying over spilt milk I suppose, he thought, as he drove past the little hotel where they'd had their seafood lunch. *Bloody sheilas. They're all the same. Never happy unless they're putting on a drama over something. Still. Ones like that don't come along too often worse luck. An old-fashioned country girl. Shit, I sure fancied her. Anyway I got other things on my mind.* He cruised along listening to the stereo and thinking about tomorrow and how he was going to get rid of twenty kilos of dud pot. *This is going to be nice,* he thought. *As soon as those two take a look in that garbage bag they're going to realise that's exactly what it is: garbage. Then I won't only lose my girl. I'll be fifteen grand down the drain as well. Not to mention getting sprung trying to pull a swifty. This is going to be interesting.* He glanced down at the dash and noticed the fuel gauge was just about on empty. Remembering there was an all night service station not far from the Bonnville turnoff he decided to fill the tank.

'Fill her up, will you mate? And have a look at the oil and water, too?'

'Yeah righto mate,' replied the skinny, tattooed attendant, wearing a pair of filthy green overalls and an equally filthy beanie.

While the attendant filled the tank Norton got a can of Coca-Cola and leant languidly up against the door absently watching the young bloke at the bowser. The cans must have only just gone in the fridge and been given a bit of a shake up in the process because as he pulled the ring-pull from the can syrupy brown foam sprayed all over his face and clothes. 'You bludger,' he cursed out loud wiping Coca-Cola off himself. He took a guzzle from the can, belched, and stood staring at the brown foam bubbling through the hole in the top of the can. Suddenly his face broke into a strange grin. He started to laugh openly. He was still laughing to himself when the grease-monkey came over and handed him his keys.

'That'll be $28.50 mate,' he muttered. 'Yer oil's orright.'

'Thanks matey.' Norton handed the attendant a fifty. 'Shout yourself a schooner and give me two dozen cans of Coca-Cola. You can toss 'em on the back seat. And give me a couple of Cherry Ripes as well.'

'Righto mate. No worries.'

Norton was gnawing his way through the second Cherry Ripe and laughing like a drain when he pulled up at the farm around 1.30. Reg still wasn't home. Sally put her head out of her kennel, gave two blood curdling barks then collapsed back on to her blanket. Les got out of the car. He walked over to Reg's incinerator, retrieved the huge bag of pot and hid it under the house. He went into the kitchen and switched on the electric kettle. His Hawaiian shirt stank of cigarettes from inside Pinkie's and there were still a few splashes of blood on it so he changed into a pair of shorts; he'd forgotten about Reg's bag of pot still tucked away so he tossed the shirt on to the dressing table. After a cup of Ovaltine listening to the radio he hit the sack. He didn't hear Reg come home about three or Diane leave shortly after.

Norton was up before eight the following morning. He had a bit of a jog just to liven himself up, a quick shower and a light breakfast. Reg's door was still closed and, having no intention of waking him up, he kept as quiet as he possibly could.

He was in a very good mood when he went to Reg's studio to get a pair of wire snips which he remembered seeing the previous day. He put them in the pocket of his jeans. Still whistling away, stopping now and again to break into laughter, he strolled over to the BMW and opened the boot. There was a large, grease-stained sheet folded inside just in case something was needed to kneel on if you had to change a flat tyre or get under the car. He got the sheet as well as the two-dozen cans of warm Coca-Cola from the back seat. He wrapped the cans up in the sheet, then went to the rear of the house, crawled underneath and retrieved the huge garbage bag full of pot. He stopped for a second when he got it out, then tiptoed quickly into the house and placed it on the bathroom scales. Twenty-one and a half kilos. *Beauty!* He tiptoed back outside, bundled the lot under his arm and, still cackling like a hyena, walked off into the bush.

As he ambled along with the clear blue sky above, the birds singing to each other in the trees and the gentle spring breeze barely rustling the leaves, he, for some strange reason, couldn't stop thinking about that big, silly rooster on the Bugs Bunny Show — Foghorn Leghorn. The next thing he knew he was singing. 'Oh, the Campdown racetrack five miles long. Doo-dah. Doo-dah.' Every few metres or so, he'd stop, take one step forward and one step back, laugh like buggery and sing: 'Doo-dah. Doo-dah.' If anyone had seen him they would have had him certified.

Finally, after walking about 500 metres, he found what he was looking for; a small, sheltered, but sunny clearing well out of sight of the farm.

He lay the sheet out in the clearing and pinned the edges down with several stones. Satisfied it was secure, he tipped all the dope out of the garbage bag and spread it out in the sunshine all over the sheet. Then he got the wire cutters out of his pocket and began the painstaking task of snipping away all the larger stalks from the marijuana plants. All that remained then was what looked like a huge pile of little heads, something like Reg's, spread out all over the sheet. He evened it out a little more, stood up and looked at it then sang a couple more 'Doo-dah. Doo-dahs' while he stretched his legs.

Satisfied everything looked all right, he ripped open the cardboard carton near his feet, took out a can of warm Coca-Cola and started shaking it vigorously.

'Okay. Ah say, okay boy,' he said, still mimmicking Foghorn Leghorn. 'You want sticky, resiny heads? Well how's this for fuckin' resin boy?' With a great 'swooshhh' he tore the ring-pull from the can of warm Coca-Cola and sprayed the sugary, brown foam all over the marijuana. 'Swooshhh,' he ripped open another can and did the same again. 'Yuk-yuk-yuk. That's, ah say, that's the stickiest mara-ge-wahna ah ever did see boy,' he chortled. He tore open another warm can of Coke and repeated the performance.

Before long he'd used up the first dozen cans. He got down on his knees and stirred up all the dope turning it over and over with his hands; Coke-saturated leaves and small pieces of stalk stuck to his arms right up to his elbows. 'Bloody sticky shit,' he cursed as he got back up. He sprayed the dope thoroughly with the remaining dozen cans.

Well Tony, he thought as he surveyed the Coca-Cola-drenched pot glistening in the sun, *I sure hope that's sticky enough for you and your mate L.A. Dave.* He looked up at the cloudless blue sky and grinned. *It will be by about four o'clock this afternoon, that's for sure.* Then a thought occured to him as he watched a few flies starting to swarm around: ants. He got down on his hands and knees and started sniffing the edges of the sheet. Yes: fortunately at some time there'd been petrol in the boot and some had spilt on to the sheet leaving enough odour to keep them away. *Beauty!* He got back to his feet, picked up all the empty cans and put them in the carton, folding the empty garbage bag up at the same time and placing a rock on it. Content that everything was how it should be he gave a grunt of satisfaction, tucked the carton up under his arm and, with one last look, turned and walked back towards the house.

'Oh. The Campdown racetrack five miles long.' One step forward. One step back. 'Doo-dah. Doo-dah.'

It was getting on for eleven and Reg was still in bed when Norton got back to the house. He put the carton of empties in the boot of the car, then gathered up a pile of dried grass, twigs and scrub which he put in another garbage bag and burnt in the incinerator, with the help of a little turpentine from Reg's studio. If Reg should happen to ask what happened to the bag of dope, Norton could point to the ashes in the incinerator.

While Norton was getting this little bit of chicanery together, in a motel room in Coffs Harbour, not far from the jetty, Tony Levin was just getting out of the shower. His head was still a little woozy from the previous night in which, after Norton had left him stoned off his head, he'd stumbled and boogied around Pinkie's and somehow or other — possibly because of the good style of a bloke he is — finished with a young girl who worked in a local bank. He'd put her in a taxi twenty minutes previously and was now breaking his neck to get on the phone to his shifty mate L.A. Dave in Grafton and tell him all about the unbelievable dope deal he'd come across. As the phone rang in Dave's clothes shop he idly fingered the pot Les had given him in the piece of silver paper.

'Hello Dave?'

'Yeah. Is that you Tony?'

'Yeah. How are you?'

'All right. So what's happening in Coffs man? That surfie prick still in Angourie?'

'Yeah. But forget about him Dave. Wait till I tell you what happened to me last night.'

Scarcely able to contain his excitement, Tony told Dave about his chance meeting with Norton, the fight, the story Les had told him and how devastating the pot was. At the other end of the line Dave could hardly believe his ears either.

'And that's fair dinkum Dave. It's a dead set stroke of luck. Norton hasn't got a clue how good it is — done up we could get anything for it.'

'And he only wants fifteen grand?'

'Yeah. Galese just wants his money back, that's all. It's unbelieveable.'

'Then we'd better grab it off the big goose.' Dave breathed hard into the phone. 'The only bloody thing is the brakes went in my car yesterday. You'll have to come up here and get the money.'

'Jesus, you're not gonna believe this. I've left my lights and ignition on all night and I think I've done the generator in mine. It could take these hillbillies up here all day to fix it. Maybe even till tomorrow.'

'Shit!'

'No it's sweet. What I'll do, I'll get him to bring it up to you.'

'You reckon he'd be in that?'

'Yeah. He's running around in one of Galese's new cars so I reckon he'd like a quick drive in the country.'

'When. Today?'

'No, better make it tomorrow.'

184

Tony explained that Les was taking some girl out and he'd probably want to take her out that afternoon and Saturday night, so it might be best to leave him to do that and do the swap tomorrow then Norton could go straight back to Sydney. Dave agreed and arranged to be home all day Sunday but to get Les to be there any time between two and four. With any luck Tony's car might be ready and he could be there, too. Tony hung up saying he'd ring Norton and make the arrangements.

Back at the farm Les had finished what he had to do in the backyard. He was sitting in the kitchen having a cup of tea and a toasted cheese sandwich when the phone rang in the lounge-room: still not wishing to wake Reg he moved quickly and quietly to answer it.

'Hello Les? It's Tony.'

'Hello Tony. How's things?'

'Pretty good. I saw you leaving with your girl last night. She's not a bad sort. Where'd you find her?'

'Sawtell. She's up here on holidays.'

'Oh yeah. Got a top body.'

'Yeah. She's a swimmer.'

'Oh. Anyway ah — what do you want to do about that Bob Hope? Everything's sweet this end. That fifteen's there whenever you want it.'

Norton paused for a moment and smiled to himself. 'Yeah right Tony. Good as gold. Just keep it tight on the Al Capone. Okay?'

'Yeah sure Les. I'm with you. There's just one thing though.'

'Yeah. What's that?'

Tony explained briefly his conversation with L.A. Dave, about their cars being out of action and Les running the stuff up to Grafton. Norton thought about it for a second or two. Grafton was barely a two hours drive there and back. Cruise along in the new BMW, listen to a few tapes. It'd probably give him something to do.

'Yeah righto Tony,' he replied. 'That's sweet.' Then he lowered his voice. 'But I don't want to be rootin' around there all afternoon. Straight in and out okay. You know who's money it is.'

'Do I what.'

'All right. Well give me the address and I'll be there around three.'

Tony gave Les Dave's address in Grafton as well as directions

— he also gave Les the room number at the motel he was staying at. Norton wrote it down on the back of an envelope sitting next to the phone.

'You got all that Les?'

'Yeah no worries. If you want to come up with me I can drive you up there.'

'No that's all right.' It was pointless him going up with Les then being stuck in Grafton without a car. His car should be ready by tomorrow, surely. 'I'll probably see you up there anyway.'

'All right. Well I'll see you up there about three.'

'Okay. See you then Les.'

'See you Tony.'

Norton sat grinning at the phone for a few moments. *Well, the boys are well and truly in,* he thought. *There's one little thing I'd better do.* He went to the kitchen, got a gladbag out of one of the cupboards, went into his bedroom and took half of Reg's pot out of his shirt. He put it in the bag and placed it in the drawer among his clothes. He took the remainder out into the kitchen and put it on top of the fridge then finished his cup of tea. He was there a few minutes when he heard Reg's door open. Reg staggered groggily into the kitchen wearing a pair of faded jockettes. His hair was plastered all over his head and there was hardly any colour in his face. He leant unsteadily against the kitchen door looking as though he'd just crawled out of a tomb.

'Hello Reggie boy,' said Norton happily, having a bit of a snigger at the little artist's obvious hangover. 'How are you this morning old son?'

'Oh. Pretty ordinary,' yawned Reg, holding his head and rubbing his hands across his eyes.

'You look pretty ordinary, too,' laughed Norton. 'In fact I saw the body of a ninety-year-old man washed up on Bondi after it'd been in the water a week and his face looked better than yours now.'

'Wouldn't surprise me,' croaked Reg.

'You got home all right.'

'Yeah.' He yawned again. 'Jesus we finished up nice and pissed though.'

'Not used to the late nights, eh?'

'You can say that again.' Reg went to the sink and got a glass of water. 'Was that the phone I just heard?'

'Yeah. It was that mate of mine from last night wanting to know if I felt like having a drink this arvo. That pot of

186

yours is on top of the fridge, too. I gave him a bit last night when I was pissed. I hope you don't mind.'

'No that's all right,' replied Reg sleepily. 'I'm gonna have a shower.'

'Good idea. I'll make a fresh pot of tea.' Reg headed for the bathroom. As he was sitting waiting for the kettle to boil the phone rang again — *probably someone for Reg*, he thought as he walked to the lounge-room.

'Hello.'

'Hello, is that you Les? It's Betty.'

'Betty!' Norton was more than a little surprised: he was also quite elated. 'Hell. How are you?'

'I'm...fine. How are you?'

'Good. Terrific. Gee I'm glad you rang. I wasn't quite sure whether you would.'

'Well.' Betty hesitated for a moment. 'I thought about last night and I shouldn't really have said what I did. You were only doing what you thought was best. It was a little childish of me.'

'Ah that's all right.'

'But I did get a hell of a fright though.'

'Fair enough. I realise that. It's just that where I come from I see that all the time and it doesn't worry me. But I should know better. I'm sorry.'

'That's all right.' Betty laughed deliciously. 'I missed you once I got inside and went to bed.'

Les chuckled into the phone. 'You're not Robinson Crusoe.'

'I do like you Mr Norton you know. I hope you realise that.'

'I don't mind you either Miss Cox, just quietly. For a cranky old country schoolteacher you're not half bad.'

'What do you mean, cranky old country schoolteacher?'

Les asked Betty if she still wanted to go out for dinner that night. She said yes, although she couldn't see him that afternoon as aunt and uncle were calling around to take her for a drive.'

'Anywhere in particular you'd like to go?' asked Norton.

'No. I don't care Les. What ever suits you.'

'Well I'm going for a run into Coffs Harbour this afternoon, I'll pick something out.'

'All right.'

'And I promise you. Even if the food's terrible and the wine tastes like a lady wrestler's bathwater, I won't bash the head waiter; or anyone for that matter.'

'No. Save your strength for me afterwards.'

The seductive way Betty said it nearly made Norton bite the end off the phone. 'Hey!' he said excitedly. 'I just thought of something. You're going back to Grafton tomorrow, aren't you?'

'Yes.'

'Well how about letting me drive you home. I'd like that.'

'Well...if it's not too much trouble.'

'No. I'd be rapt. Give me something to do anyway,' lied Les.

'All right, that's marvellous. Anyway I'll see you tonight. Around eight.'

'Eight o'clock on the dot. I'll see you then.'

'Bye Les.'

'See you tonight Betty.'

Well I'll be buggered, thought Norton happily as he hung up. *What about that?* He shook his head and laughed. *I'll sure never understand women. Then again — maybe you're not supposed to.* The electric kettle was just starting to sing when he walked back into the kitchen, and so was the big Queenslander's heart.

The teapot was on the kitchen table drawing next to a few fresh slices of Vogel's toast when Reg walked in wearing a T-shirt and shorts. He went over to the cupboard, threw some Eno salts into a glass of water, then gulped the whole bubbling, fizzing brew down in one go and let out a rancid belch that stung his nose, made his eyes water and nearly shook the panes out of the kitchen windows. 'Ah! That's better,' he said, sitting down and pouring himself a cup of tea.

'So how are you feeling now Reg? You're starting to look a little better. Almost alive.'

'I feel it, too,' replied Reg, slurping on his tea while he liberally spread a piece of toast with banana-and-pawpaw jam.

'And what's happening tonight Reginald?' smiled Norton. 'You look like you're pretty sweet with young Diane.'

'As a matter of fact Les — I was going to mention something about that to you. Do you reckon you could do me a bit of a favour?'

'Sure, what is it. Fuckin' George isn't back on the scene is he?'

'No. Nothing like that. George is history. But there's just one small thing I'd like you to do for me.'

'Sure Reg. Just name it.'

'Don't be here tonight.'

Norton looked at Reg, nodded his head and smiled mirthlessly. 'Oh. So it's like that is it. You've got some tart coming round so I get turfed out into the street like a mangy tom cat.'

'Well' said Reg delicately wiping a crumb from the side of his mouth with his little finger, 'if that's how you want to put it Les, yes.'

'Thanks. And just what have you got planned.'

'Well. Diane's coming over with a couple of bottles of Great Western.'

'Great Western? Jesus.' Norton threw his hands up in the air. 'Richard Burton and Elizabeth Taylor eat your hearts out.'

'And I'm going to borrow some of those grouse cassettes your mate from Peach Music made up for you, drink champagne have a smoke and listen to them. How's that grab you?'

'And play chasings and a bit of hide the sausage.'

Reg nodded his head and smiled. 'There's a big chance of that happening, too.'

'All right if I come back some time tomorrow and change my clothes? Like I don't want to interrupt this bacchanalian orgy you've got planned.'

'Oh no, that's all right. By all means Les. Have a cup of tea, read a magazine. Just make yourself at home.'

'But just don't be here tonight.'

'Yeah.'

Norton threw back his head and laughed. 'You cheeky little prick. Well it just so happens that I'm taking Betty out to dinner tonight. So stick your pot and your Great Western up your arse.'

'Yeah. Where are you goin'?'

'Dunno. You know a good restaurant in Coffs? I don't give a fuck what it costs.'

'You like Thai food?'

'Bloody oath. Kung tod with ta-krai and katian. Pet yarng with heaps of mee phat and ma-khua? You're kiddin Reg.'

'Well, there's a Thai restaurant down near the jetty called the Sawadee. The bloke that runs it's Australian, he's an ex-meatworker, too. Hates people coming in there to eat because it makes more work for him. But he's got a Thai wife who's the best cook you've ever seen.'

'Dead set?'

'Oh fair dinkum Les. Some of the dishes she serves up'll make you want to start batting yourself off up against the table.'

'That good eh?'

'I'm tellin' you. In fact what are you doing this afternoon?'

Norton shrugged his shoulders. 'Nothin'.'

'Well why don't we take a run into Coffs? We can have a beer and a counter lunch and I'll show you where it is.'

'Righto. That sounds like a good idea.' Norton poured them both another cup of tea. 'Anyway, there's no mad hurry. Why don't we finish this nice tea and toast then we'll drift in?'

They sat for a while, listening to the radio, sipping tea and chatting away like a couple of old biddies. Outside the native birds sang softly to each other in the rustling trees and the sun climbed high into the clear blue sky shortening the surrounding shadows. It became high noon. They cleaned up what little mess there was in the kitchen, fed Sally — plus a couple of huge Major Mitchell cockatoos. Reg gave Diane a quick call to tell her everything was sweet for tonight, got his sunglasses and they bundled into the BMW. Norton dropped a cassette into the stereo and, with Jimmy Barnes rasping his way through 'Khe Sanh', headed for Coffs Harbour.

'I didn't tell you what Diane said about Ken and George over the phone, did I?' said Reg, as they turned off Telegraph Point Road on to the Pacific Highway.

'No, what?'

'They've told the doctors and the police a gang of bikies got into them with baseball bats. The owner's saying the same thing.'

'Probably trying to save a bit of face,' shrugged Norton

'Not much face left to save, ' replied Reg. 'George has got forty stitches in his and Ken's about five behind him. They've both got broken jaws as well.'

Norton smiled across at Reg. 'Could've been a lot worse.'

'How do you mean?'

'They were lucky I was in a good mood.'

They were still laughing when they turned off the highway into High Street, the wide boulevard that divides the main shopping centre in Coffs Harbour.

'Go straight down,' said Reg 'and I'll show you where this restaurant is. There's a pub almost next to it. We can have a couple of beers.'

Norton cruised down High Street till they almost reached the harbour. 'There it is,' said Reg, pointing to a rather plain looking little cafe on the opposite side of the road next to a butcher shop. The window was painted a drab brown and white with 'Sawadee Thai Restaurant' painted amateurishly across it. That was all.

'That's it?' sneered Norton, doing a quick U-turn and backing

190

into a space about two doors up. 'It looks like a second-hand book shop.'

'I know. But the food's enormous.'

As they got out of the car, Norton noticed a broad-shouldered, youngish-looking bloke come round the corner and walk up to the doorway of the restaurant. He had straight brown hair, square, chiselled features and an obviously broken nose. In his hands was what looked like a bundle of meat. He put a box of vegetables at his feet. Even from where they stood Norton could hear him cursing having trouble opening the lock.

'Hey mate,' said Norton, ambling over to him. 'Are you the owner?'

The bloke gave Norton a filthy, suspicious look like Les might've been from the sheriff's office or something. 'Yeah. What do you want to know for?' He had a flat, monotone voice that sounded as if it was coming straight through his broken nose.

'Oh nothing' replied Les lightly. 'I was just wondering if it's okay if I come down here for a feed tonight?'

The bloke looked Norton up and down. 'Yeah righto. But we close at 10.30. Sharp.'

'Do we need to book a table?'

The bloke glared at Norton. 'Christ. How many of you is there?'

'Only two. Is that all right?' Norton could see the bloke had the shits with the world but somehow he couldn't help liking him.

'Yeah sweet.'

'Thanks. I'd hate to put you out.' As the bloke stepped inside Les handed him up the box of vegetables. 'Here you are sunshine. I'll see you tonight.'

'Yeah righto. Thanks mate.'

'The maitre-d's a happy-looking soul,' said Norton, as he rejoined Reg.

'Yeah he's a million laughs. Wait till you see him in action tonight when he gets a bit flustered. Come on let's have a beer. I'm drier than a dead fruit bats' frankfurt.'

They had a shout each, and sat on the steps outside the Jetty Hotel watching the cars and the few passers-by. With Saturday morning shopping over there wasn't a great deal happening, especially down that end of town. Cooking smells coming from somewhere inside the hotel made Norton's stomach rumble.

'This where you're gonna have a counter lunch?' he asked,

nodding his head towards the hotel. 'Don't smell too bad.'

'Nuh,' replied Reg. 'It's all right here, but the Fitzroy's better.'

'Yeah? Where's that?'

'Up the other end of town. Next to the cop shop.'

'Oh that'll be nice. The place'll be swarming with wallopers. What's the special of the day?' laughed Les. 'Roast pig?'

'No. Cordon-bleu uniform. Come on, let's down these and get up there. I'm starving.' They glugged the remainder of their middies down and proceeded to the Fitzroy.

Norton found a parking spot near the hotel. As they got out of the car Reg took Les by the arm and started dragging him back across the street towards the main shopping centre. 'Come over the road for a sec,' he said a little excitedly. 'I want to show you something.' They crossed the highway into High Street and stopped outside a large department store. The window was full of various electrical appliances: TVs, stereos, electric organs, and stacked in the middle were, several of the latest model VCRs.

'Have a look at those,' said Reg. 'Aren't they the grouse? That's the one I fancy though.' He pointed to a cordless, remote-control model with its numerous features written next to it. 'Have a go at the price tag, but. Nine hundred bucks. Shit.'

'Just sell some of that grouse pot of yours Reg,' said Norton. 'You'll have one in no time.'

'No. Fuck that.' Reg was adamant. 'If I can't get one legally, I'll go without. Besides, it'd be my luck to get caught.' He pressed his nose up against the window. 'Still. I might sell some paintings — maybe.'

'Why don't you get a job?'

'Get a job? Up here in Coffs? There's no work up here. Coffs has got the highest unemployment rate in the state. I know blokes up here that have been registered with the CES that long they've got their last jobs down as school prefect.'

'Ah you never know your luck Reg,' said Norton with a bit of a wink. 'Something might fall in.'

'Yeah, you never know.' Reg sighed and had a last longing look in the window. 'Anyway, come on. Let's go and have a beer.'

Norton took a large pull on his middie and smiled. 'Hey this is all right,' he said, casting his eye round the beer garden of the Fitzroy. There was a fair sized dining-room and several, bright, clean bars with friendly-looking barmaids. The beer garden had a char-grill barbecue in the middle with a happy cook in a white chef's hat. Behind him was a table groaning with different salads next to a refrigerated display cabinet full of various cuts of meat. Above it was a blackboard menu-cum-price list.

'I might go for the lamb cutlets,' said Norton, peering hungrily into the cabinet.

'I'm having shashliks.'

'Well I'll order them. How about you grab another couple of beers?'

'Righto.'

There was quite a crowd waiting for food so they had time for another couple of beers. Norton borrowed a race form from a couple of punters sitting next to them who were listening to the country relays on a small transistor radio. He ran his gaze idly through the fields till something caught his eye.

'Hey,' he said, tapping Reg on the arm. 'You see this horse here in the Hallstrom Memorial Welter — Kelly's Heroes?' He turned the form round to Reg. 'Well that's one of Price's.' Norton stroked his chin thoughtfully for a moment. 'Eight to one. I wonder if it's going? There's only one way to find out — you got any two-bobs on you?' Reg handed Les his only three twenty-cent coins. 'I'll have to get some more at the bar. There's an STD phone in the foyer isn't there?' Norton stood up. 'I might just have a little something here for us Reg old son.' He got three dollars worth of change at the bar, walked to the phone and pumped them in.

'Hello George?'

'Yeah. Who's this?' replied the casino manager.

'Les.'

'Hello. The Coffs Harbour Kid,' laughed George Brennan. 'What's up? You're not in gaol, are you?'

'No. Turn it up. It's been as quiet as buggery up here,' lied Norton. 'I've just been sittin' round in the sun.'

'Half your luck.'

'Listen. What I'm ringin' about: I see Kelly's Heroes is in today but old "Better-Brakes Harrison" is on it. Is he gonna pull it up or is it goin' or what?'

'Yeah. It's trying all right,' said George. 'There's a lot of good horses in the race but it's carrying fuck-all. Price reckons it's a moral to fall into a place. We're all backing it.'

'It says eight to one in the Telegraph.'

'You might even do better than that on the TAB.'

'All right. I'll have a lash George.'

'Mad if you don't Les.'

193

They chatted till the red warning light started to blink. Norton hung up saying he'd see him later next week.

'Well, it's trying,' said Norton, returning to their table. 'I just rang Sydney. Where's the nearest TAB?'

'Just round the corner. You gonna back it, are you?'

'Yeah. You want to have something on it?'

'I can't afford it Les.'

'What do you mean you can't afford it?'

'I only got 15 bucks on me.'

'What about that rock-lobster in your shirt?' Norton quickly palmed a twenty-dollar bill into the top pocket of Reg's shirt then deftly extracted it with his two fingers.

'Hey. I didn't know I had that,' protested Reg, making a grab for the twenty.

'Too late now,' grinned Norton, getting back to his feet. 'You're just about to have ten each way.'

'Oh fuck you Les. I need that.'

'It's only money Reg. It's not an arm or a leg.' Norton walked quickly to the TAB. He had a hundred each way for himself, plus the twenty he snuck in for Reg. He was back in less than five minutes.

'There you go mate,' he said, poking the ticket in Reg's top pocket. 'Ten each way. I hope it gets up and you don't have to sell the farm.'

Reg was about to answer Norton when the chef called their numbers. They were soon piling their plates with fresh salads and getting stuck into their cutlets and shashliks.

'Well, what do you reckon? I'm not a bad judge of a counter lunch, am I?' said Reg between mouthfuls.

'Nothin' wrong with this. It's enormous,' replied Norton. They finished eating and had about fifteen minutes before their race started. Les suggested a quick game of pool. Reg agreed, now feeling a little happier with his stomach full.

They sauntered into another bar where four young blokes were nonchalantly potting balls on two small pool tables. About another twenty or thirty men, mostly in shorts and thongs were sitting or standing around drinking, talking, listening to the races or just generally enjoying Saturday afternoon with their mates. While Reg ordered another two middies Norton stepped up to one of the blokes playing pool.

'Excuse me mate,' he said, laying sixty cents on the side of the table. 'How do you go about getting a game? What — do you put your name up on a board or what?'

The tall, young, blonde bloke looked at Norton indifferently.

194

Suddenly his eyes widened and he gave Norton a double blink.

'You want a game of pool mate?' he beamed. 'Here you are, have our table. Go for your life.'

Norton looked at the young bloke curiously: there were at least half the balls still sitting on the table. 'You haven't finished your game yet.'

'No you're sweet mate. We were only rootin' around anyway. Here you are.' He handed Norton his cue.

Les shrugged his shoulders. 'Okay. Thanks.'

Norton started racking the balls and the blonde bloke's partner began to protest. The first bloke took him by the elbow and lead him away.

'Allan,' he said quietly. 'I was at Pinkie's last night, and you know who that redheaded bloke is?'

'No.'

'That's the gang of bikies that put big George and Ken in hospital.'

'Oh.'

'And if you don't want to join them, you'd better let him finish his game of pool in peace.'

'Shit!'

It wasn't long before word flashed round the bar. While he was playing Norton could sense quite a few eyes on him, but as he'd look up they'd quickly look away. He tried to ignore them and kept potting balls as best as he could. They had about half the balls sunk when their race started, so they stopped and moved next to a group of men huddled round a radio to listen.

Kelly's Heroes didn't seem to be doing a great deal, running near the tail of the field all the way, suddenly, at the last leg, Harrison pulled it to the outside and it screamed down the Randwick straight, to fall into the line with two other horses. Johnny Tapp said it looked like a dead heat; he couldn't pick it.

'What's goin' on?' said Reg, quite bewildered.

'It looks like a dead heat,' replied Norton. 'You'll get your money back anyway.'

Then came the announcement: Kelly's Heroes by a very short half-head.

'We've won,' shouted Reg, slapping Norton on the back.

'Good thing I found that twenty on you,' winked Les. 'Come on, let's finish our game.'

Norton felt good for Reg who was almost jumping up and down for joy. He knew a hundred dollars would be almost like winning the lottery for the battling little artist. As he watched Reg, Norton noticed another two pairs of eyes watching him, noticeably different from the others. They weren't hard to identify. Their harder, stonier faces betrayed a growing professional curiosity as they studied Norton.

Norton promptly lined up the eight ball and sunk it. 'Ah fuck it,' he cursed and threw his cue on the table.

'Well what a nice goose you are,' said Reg, looking slightly amazed at Les.

'Yeah,' replied Norton. He looked at his watch. 'Come on, we'd better get goin' anyway.' They finished their drinks quickly and left.

'What's the big hurry?' asked Reg, when they got outside.

'There were two D's in there showing just a little too much interest in me for my liking. I think it'd only be a matter of time before it'd be: "Do you mind if we have a word with you for a minute?"'

'How could you tell?'

'Reg. I'm around coppers all the time in Sydney. I can smell a police badge five miles away.'

'What are you worrying about anyway?' asked Reg. 'Why would they want to question you.'

'Well for a start. They could still put an assault charge on me for last night's little caper. Then when they find out who I work for they'd probably trump things up a bit more and see if they could get themselves some sort of an earn out of it.' — Not to mention the fact, thought Norton, that they just might spot me driving to Grafton tomorrow, pull me over and decide to search the car. Christ. Poor Betty'd have a stroke if they opened the boot and found that twenty odd kilo of pot. — 'Then Reg, don't forget, I've just been seen in the company of one of Coffs Harbour's most notorious and flamboyant dope dealers, namely you.'

'Oh don't give me the shits Les.'

'I tell you Reg,' said Norton dryly. 'Everywhere I go I've to be constantly on my guard up here with you.' He laughed and slapped Reg on the back. 'Come on shifty. Let's go and see what Kelly's Heroes has paid.'

They waited in the TAB for a few minutes till the clerk put the results on the board: $6.30 for a win. $1.35 for a place. Norton collected around $1500, Reg about $150.

'Christ. Have a look at that,' said Reg excitedly, as he counted the money for the third time before he put it in his pocket. 'How about letting me buy you a couple of beers?'

'No, don't worry about it.'

'You sure? We can go to another pub.'

'No. I've had enough. To tell you the truth, I wouldn't mind having a bit of a snooze this arvo. What say we head home?'

'Suit yourself,' shrugged Reg. 'I suppose I could do a bit of painting.' Norton didn't say another word till they got to the car.

As they got up the road a bit, Norton stretched out one arm and started yawning. 'Oh shit' he said. 'Those beers and that feed have sure made me tired.'

'Yeah? I feel okay,' replied Reg.

'Oh Jesus,' yawned Norton again. 'I can hardly keep my bloody eyes open.'

About every kilometre Norton would tilt back his head, close his eyes briefly then let out a great cavernous yawn. After around three kilometres of this Reg was starting to do the same thing. By the time they got to Telegraph Point Road Reg was starting to nod off and when they pulled up at the farm he was sound asleep. Norton looked at him for a few moments and smiled. 'Come on mate,' he finally said, giving Reg's shoulder a shake. 'We're here.'

'Eh! What was that?' Reg opened his eyes and started blinking.

'I said we're here.' Norton yawned again. 'Well, I don't know what you're doing. But I'm going to lie down. I'm rooted.'

'Oh shit,' yawned Reg. 'So am I.'

They shuffled to the house, used the toilet then headed for their respective bedrooms. 'I'll see you about seven,' yawned Norton again.

'Yeah righto,' Reg yawned back. 'I'll see you then.'

Norton lay down on the bed but didn't close his eyes. About ten minutes after he heard Reg's door click he got up and tiptoed across to his room, softly opened the door and peeked in. Reg was flat on his back, mouth wide open, hands by his sides, snoring like a baby. Norton smiled broadly to himself. *Jesus I'm a cunt,* he thought as he gently closed the door. He tiptoed out of the house and headed for the clearing he'd found earlier at the back of the farm.

The pot was still spread out on the sheet just as he'd left it that morning; there were a few flies around but not as many as he would have thought. *Righto,* he though, *let's just see how resiny this shit's turned out.* He got down on his knees and started running his hands through the stuff. It was sticky

197

all right, but most of the Coca-cola had just coated the leaves making them tacky to touch but not necessarily glueing them together. He ran his big hands several times through the pile of marijuana, making sure it was separable and not just one big gooey mess. Satisfied everything was in order he began stuffing it into the big plastic garbage bag he'd left there earlier that morning. When it was almost full he sat on it to compact it a little more and get the last few pieces in, then tied the top with a plastic clip. Whistling happily he folded the sheet up and, with it under one arm and the bag of dope over his shoulder, walked casually back to the farm.

He checked once more to see if Reg was still asleep then tiptoed into the bathroom and placed the garbage bag on the scales. Just on twenty-two kilos. Lovely. He tiptoed back outside and hid it under the house.

After cleaning his hands and arms under a tap near the water tank he went into his bedroom. Reg's door was closed as he went past but the sound of his snoring could be heard faintly. Norton smiled to himself as he lay down on the bed. *All the bloody yawning's made me tired, too.* He looked at his watch just before he closed his eyes; nearly four. *A couple of hours sleep will go just nice.*

Norton was up around 6.30, just after Reg. 'Sleep all right?' he asked, stepping into the shower as Reg got out.

'Like a log,' replied the little artist. 'I was a lot more tired than I thought. I feel good now though.'

'Yeah. So do I.' Norton turned on the jets and started singing as he happily soaped up. It hadn't been a real bad day. Everything had worked out nicely so far with the pot. He was over $1500 in front, and now he was taking Betty out for what should be a nice dinner with promise of better things to come. *Not a bad day at all.* He grinned to himself as he worked a large handful of conditioner into his scrubby red hair.

'Listen Les,' said Reg, in the kitchen over a cup of coffee later on. 'I was only kidding about tonight. If you want to bring Betty for a drink or whatever, that's okay. In fact I'll ring Diane and tell her to get some more champagne if you like.'

'No Reg. That's okay thanks mate. I'll probably stop at her joint and I'll see you in the morning.' Norton grinned at Reg over the top of his mug of coffee. 'I reckon it'd've been a different story though if you'd've done your twenty bucks.' Reg smiled back, blushed slightly and kept sipping his coffee. Half an hour later, wearing a nice new collarless shirt a friend had brought him back from London, and a pair of designer jeans, Norton jumped happily into the BMW. Dragon was wringing every ounce of soul they could out of 'Still In Love With You', as Les headed for Sawtell and Betty's flat.

The door was open. He knocked twice, opened the flyscreen and went inside. Betty was in the kitchen shovelling things into the blender again. As soon as she saw Les she stopped, put her arms around him and kissed him softly on the lips.

'Hello Mr Norton,' she smiled into his eyes. 'How are you?'

'Good. Couldn't be better,' replied Les, taking a step back. 'Jesus! What about that dress.'

Betty was wearing a tight fitting, pink and turquoise dress, cut low in the front and low in the back. It didn't just emphasise the fullness and firmness of her ample breasts, it made them thrust out proudly, in absolute defiance of the law of gravity. Norton felt like kicking down the nearest brick wall.

Betty ran her hands down her sides and did a quick pirouette. 'You like it, do you?' she said coyly.

'Reckon. Where'd you get it?'

'Grafton.'

'Grafton? Shit I would've sworn you'd got it in Double Bay or around Paddington.'

'No. There's a new shop opened in Grafton called L.A. Fashions. They sell really nice clothes and they're not that dear, either.'

L.A. Fashions. Norton nearly choked. That was where he had to go tomorrow afternoon to drop the dope off. 'Looks great anyway,' he said. 'You should be locked up for wearing it.'

'Oh don't be silly,' replied Betty, trying to maintain an unpretentious smile. 'It's just comfortable, that's all.'

'Yeah.' Norton grinned and nodded towards the blender sitting on the kitchen table. 'What's in the daiquiris tonight? Pineapple and banana?'

'No. Got a new one for you tonight. Carrot and apple.'

'Carrot and apple daiquiris?!! You're kidding.'

'No. Try one, they're beautiful. Get drunk and fit at the same time.' Betty rolled her eyes. 'What a way to go,' she said throatily.

Oddly enough Betty was right about the daiquiris; they were something else and had Norton smacking his lips in approval. Suddenly an object near the sink caught his eye. 'Holy Jesus,' he exclaimed. 'Look at the size of that bloody cockroach.' Norton grabbed a magazine and rolled it up to squash the repulsive bug. Betty burst out laughing. 'What are you laughing at?' he said. 'Those bloody things make me sick. It's bad enough having to put up with them in Bondi let alone up here.' He was brandishing the rolled-up *New Idea* when Betty caught his arm.

'It's only a dummy,' she giggled.

'A what?' Norton looked at the huge cockroach, then back at Betty wondering what she was talking about.

'It's made out of rubber. Look.' Laughing fit to bust at the look on Norton's face, Betty picked up the cockroach and handed it to him. 'See. It's only a dummy. One of the girls bought it in Coffs and left it here. I put it there just to see if I could get you in.' She shoved Norton in the chest. 'And I did, too — you big goose.'

'Well I'll be buggered.' Norton looked at the amazingly realistic object in his hand with a big sheepish grin on his face. 'Have a look at that.' He stroked his chin thoughtfully for a few moments then, as Betty poured them another daiquiri, grinned secretly to himself and slipped it in the pocket of his jeans.

They finished the blender full of drinks and headed for Coffs Harbour. Norton wasn't sure what Betty had put in them, but when they pulled up outside the hotel just up from the Sawaddee they were roaring like Bengal tigers.

'I hope you like Thai cooking,' said Norton, locking the car.

'I've never tried it,' replied Betty, 'but I like Chinese.'

'It's better than Chinese. A little hotter but much more spicier. Anyway, hang on a few minutes and I'll go and get some booze.'

The hotel bottle shop was surprisingly well stocked. Norton settled for a Leo Buring Bin 13 Watervale riesling and a Mount Adam 1972 chardonnay. A glance in the glass-doored refrigerator nearly brought tears of gladness to his Queensland eyes: Fourex. He quickly grabbed a two-dozen carton of cans.

'Are we staying here for the night?' asked Betty, as he came out of the hotel with all the drink tucked up under his arms.

'To tell you the truth Miss Cox,' replied Les. 'I've seen the way you drink and I'm just wondering whether this is going to be enough.' Propelled by a quick clout across the back of the neck, Norton opened the door and they entered the Sawaddee.

There were about eight sets of chairs and tables inside: some large round ones and a few smaller, square-shaped ones. Most of the larger ones were occupied. Those that weren't, plus the majority of smaller ones, were covered in empty bottles and dirty plates. Several dog-eared Thai Airlines posters, and one or two paintings adorned the walls and a few ferns and pot plants were propped up in the corners. At the rear, in front of an alcove that led to the kitchen, stood a bar-cum-counter made out of burnt bamboo. An ancient, silver frosted till that looked like it may have come out on the first fleet stood on top of it. Next to it was a crooked paper spike with a number of dockets skewered on to it.

Tucked into the far left-hand corner facing them was an empty, clean table. 'That'll do,' said Norton, nodding towards it. They walked over and sat down. As they did, Norton noticed a group of beefy, short-haired girls, mostly dressed in bib-and-brace overalls, give Betty a wolfish once up and down from a table next to them. Les deliberately gave them all a leering grin which was answered with a simultaneous, execrable scowl.

'I wonder who does his interior decorating,' said Betty, glancing slightly bemused around the spartan room.

'Same mob that supplies his tablecloths I suppose,' smiled Les. He gave the bare pineboard a bit of tap with his knuckles and looked around for the owner.

He finally appeared in the alcove leading to the kitchen with a dish of food in each hand. As soon as he saw Betty and Les with their stack of drink he hunched his shoulders and winced.

'How are you goin' there old mate?' smiled Norton as he stormed past their table.

The owner grunted something in reply and put the dishes down in front of the girls in overalls. 'Be with you in a minute,' he mumbled, as he scurried back into the kitchen. He was out shortly with another two dishes which he placed at the same table, then got two menus and some knives, forks and chopsticks from behind the counter which he dumped uncere-moniously in front of Betty and Les.

'You reckon you could look after this for us mate?' said Norton, nodding to his supply of booze.

The owner winced again at all the drink. 'We close at 10.30 you know,' he grunted.

Norton smiled up at him as he gathered the bottles and cans. 'Well in that case, you might have to help me drink some of it. You like Fourex?'

For a second the slightest hint of a smile almost flickered

around the corners of the owner's eyes. 'Yeah. It's not a bad drop,' he said.

'Well, you're more than welcome to a few cans.'

'Yeah. All right.'

'Could we have a couple of nice wine glasses?' said Betty.

The owner stared at her for a moment. 'Certainly Madam,' he replied icily. 'Would Madam prefer the Swedish Nordica or the Polish Krosnor?'

'Well, a crystal decanter would be nice,' said Betty caustically. 'But I'll just settle for a couple of clean ones — if that's possible in here.'

The owner muttered something under his breath then disappeared into the kitchen once more, with their supply of booze.

'The Maitre-d's a happy soul' said Betty, after he'd left.

'Yeah, isn't he?' smiled Les. 'But I'll tell you what. The food's only got to be half as good as it smells and it'll do me.'

Betty agreed. From the kitchen and surrounding tables wafted various exotic cooking odours that had their mouths watering and their stomachs rumbling like two concrete-mixers.

The owner reappeared with the opened Mount Adam chardonnay and two absolutely sparkling wine glasses: he put the lot indelicately in the middle of the table without bothering to pour, then trounced back into the kitchen.

Norton filled both their glasses and raised his. 'Cheers Betty,' he said, with a smile and a wink.

'Yes. Cheers Les.' They both took a healthy pull on their glasses.

'Mm! This wine's beautiful,' said Betty, licking her lips and peering at the label. 'What is it?'

'I dunno. Just something I got next door,' replied Norton, as he almost finished the first glass. 'But it's not half bad, is it? In fact it's pretty bloody good.'

'Crikey. Too much of this and I start to go like an old dressing table.' laughed Betty.

'What do you mean?'

'My colour starts to fade, my legs go all wobbly and my drawers get a bit loose.' Betty giggled and snorted into her hand.

'In that case I'd better get another couple of bottles,' roared Norton, topping up their glasses.

They scanned the menu and watched the antics of the owner. He treated the customers like a colony of lepers during the Middle Ages. Every time he went back behind the alcove he'd give them all the finger or pull faces — sometimes bending over and pulling the cheeks of his backside apart in their general direction. At one stage, when he brought them out a bottle of wine, he pulled a grotesque face and rubbed the bottle vigorously against his fly. Because they were tucked away in the corner he didn't realise Les and Betty could see all this and that they were both laughing like hyenas.

'You know who that bloke reminds me of?' cackled Norton. Betty shook her head.

'Basil Fawlty.'

'Yeah. Right. The bloke in "Fawlty Towers".' Betty nodded her head enthusiastically. 'All we need is poor bloody Manuel to come scurrying out.' As they looked over at the alcove an arm jutted out from the kitchen making an upward motion with the middle finger extended.

'Anyway, what do you feel like?' asked Norton when they finally stopped laughing.

'I honestly don't know,' replied Betty. 'How about I leave it to you? You're the expert.'

'Well I'm not really an expert,' shrugged Les. He explained to her that, at one stage, Price had two Thai boxers working round his house, and that he and Billy Dunne started sparring and having workouts with them — which was how Norton learnt that trick with his knees which almost took Ken's head off in Pinkies — and how after meeting their families and sampling the home cooking they got a bit of a taste for it and started going to Thai restaurants.

'I like the Thais,' he said, taking another mouthful of wine. 'They seem to have a style and a... I dunno, sort of inner strength that's different from the other Asian people. They're tough little bastards, I know that. But as for their cooking...' Norton closed his eyes and kissed the tips of his fingers.

The unsmiling owner suddenly appeared at their table. 'I had a can of your Fourex you ready to order yet?' he said in the one sentence.

'Yeah, righto mate,' replied Norton brightly.

'Well, I'm going to leave it up to you,' said Betty, closing her menu and putting it on the table. 'Your're the expert.'

The owner looked down at Norton out of the sides of his eyes. 'So you're an expert on Thai cooking are you?' he said slowly and derisively. 'As well as a wine connoisseur.'

'Oh I wouldn't say that,' said Norton, winking across at Betty. 'But I've been to a few Chinese restaurants in Sydney.'

Above him the owner winced again. 'And what would you

like?' he said, his voice dripping with sarcasm. 'Fried rice. Long soup? How about some dim dims and spring rolls?'

'No. I don't know about that,' replied Norton evenly. 'But we might have some yam plamuk for an entree — with a big plate of boiled rice. Then we'll have peek gai ob and gaeng ped moo — and you can make it hot, too. I don't mind. And let's see — yeah, pla tod lard prik. A nice snapper — if you've got it. And tell the cook plenty of katian and a bit of kapi Thai in with it, and go a bit easy on the coriander. And bring us out a bottle of nampla, too, will you?' He smiled at the owner as he handed him the menus. 'If we want any sweets we'll let you know. Thanks matey.'

The owner finished writing, looked at Norton for a moment then closed his eyes and stormed into the kitchen.

'What was all that about?' asked Betty.

Norton grinned at her. 'Don't worry. Everything's sweet.'

Inside the kitchen the owner skulked indignantly up to his wife. She was a slightly stocky but very attractive young woman, with hair as black and shiny as Thai-silk. She was slaving away over several woks sizzling away on a porta-gas stove. Her husband pinned Norton's order on the wall above her head.

'Ah shit,' he snorted 'Wouldn't you know it. I've got another bloody Asian-cooking bloody gourmet out there.' He pointed towards the dining-room. 'Bloody redheaded, boofheaded big mug.' He went to the fridge and helped himself to another one of Norton's Fourex. 'Your beer's all right though — you prick.' He took a swig and gave a finger in Les's general direction.

His wife turned around from the stove. 'What are you going on about now?' she asked, in a high-pitched, sing song voice.

'That redheaded, know-all bastard out there,' growled her husband. 'He's probably been to Bangkok on a ten day tour with some Dubbo football team and now he's trying to impress some moll he's picked up for the night. Bloody footballers,' he snorted taking another swig on the can. 'They give me the bloody shits.'

'But honestly Marty,' smiled his wife, shaking her head. 'Everybody give you the shits.' She threw a handful of raw sugar into a wok full of steaming vegetables. 'I sometimes wonder. You never have nice word for anyone. Even if Buddha came in here for meal, you would say, he no good bastard, too. You number one miserable shit Marty. You hate all customer. That man probably nice man. It is you who is mug.'

The owner looked at his wife scornfully for a moment. 'If the truth's known, he's probably one of your old customers from when you used to hang around Pat-Pong Road,' he sneered.

His wife put down her cooking ladle. 'I soon know. I know all my old customer.' She peered out the door pretending to be looking at Norton; suddenly she pulled her head back in and looked at her husband wide-eyed. 'You right Marty. He is one of old customers,' she cried. 'And what's more, he and rest of football team still owe me 3000 baht. He owe me extra, too, cause he so big I have to charge him double.' she propelled Marty towards the door. 'You go get. You tell him Sang Jarn want 300 dollars straight way. Or be big trouble.'

Marty closed his eyes, gritted his teeth and swore under his breath. He stomped back out into the dining-room to leave his wife giggling like a school-girl and stirring some straw mushrooms and noodles into another wok.

By now Les and Betty had finished the first bottle of wine, so Les got the owner to bring out the other white as well as a couple of cans of beer. They were giving this a decent nudge when the entree arrived.

'What's this?' asked Betty, staring and sniffing at the huge plate of food.

'Yam planuk,' replied Les. 'Squid, with onion and chilli. Here, hand us your plate.'

'Can you use chopsticks?' said Betty, giving hers a bit of a click together.

'Yeah. But I never seem to be able to get enough food into my gullet. So I settle for a knife and fork.' After two tastes of the squid Betty did the same.

Reg was right about the Sawaddee. The service was about the same as you'd expect in a Russian army camp but the food was nothing short of sensational: Norton was impressed, but Betty couldn't believe her taste buds. Within ten minutes the plate was shining like a mirror.They were commenting on the food and getting stuck into the riesling when the next dishes arrived.

'Now what have we got?' asked Betty brandishing her fork and almost swooning over the delicious smells.

'What is it?' said the owner, a blásé tone in his voice. 'Oh nothing really. Just a bit of "chow" food my wife whipped up in the microwave. If you want some chips or tomato sauce, or a pot of gravy — just let me know, won't you?' He gave them each a look of utter contempt then disappeared back into the kitchen.

'Right. Let's see what we've got here.' said Norton, ignoring the owner and pointing to the dishes with his fork. 'Well that's curried pork in coconut milk. They're chicken wings in honey and ginger, and this is my deep fried snapper with chilli and garlic. And if you don't liven up Miss Cox, you won't get none.'

The next twenty minutes or so were spent almost in silence as they ate steadily. The only sounds were the clinking of knives and forks, the 'oohs' and 'ahhs' and grunts of ecstasy. They stopped occasionally to watch the Maitre-d still insulting the customers behind their backs.

As well as being delicious, the food servings at the little Sawaddee Restaurant were only about a spoonful short of enormous, and there was still quite a bit of food left on the plates when Betty laid down her knife and fork and eased back into her seat.'Oh goodness,' she groaned 'I'm googed. I don't think I could eat another thing.'

Norton was still picking away at his deep-fried snapper, the bones of which stuck out about six centimetres on either side of his large oval plate. 'Yeah, I'm starting to get the same way,' he said. 'Christ they give you enough, don't they?'

They sat idly picking at their food, both feeling more than a little bloated.

'Y'know,' said Norton, the hint of a devilish grin starting to flicker around the corners of his eyes. 'I think it's about time we livened old Basil up.' He nodded towards the humourless owner who was handing a table their bill with a look of bored contempt.

'How do you mean?' asked Betty.

Norton grinned and produced the rubber cockroach from his pocket.

Betty's eyes widened. 'Oh God Les. What are you going to do with that?'

'You want to play a little trick on the sour-faced bastard?'

Betty looked at Les for a few moments before she answered. 'Yeah righto,' she grinned. 'Why not?'

'Okay. I'll tell you what we'll do.'

They waited a little while longer, still watching the owner, then Norton called him over and asked for another couple of cans of Fourex. The Maitre-d made a big show of checking his watch in front of them, then scowled off to the kitchen. He returned shortly with the two beers and the bill. He plonked

206

them on the table in front of Les. The owner was about to go when Betty tapped him on the arm.

'Excuse me,' she said, in a loud indignant voice. 'But what is that?' She pointed to the plate of curried pork in coconut milk.

Sitting half-submerged in the lovely, creamy white sauce between a piece of broccoli and several slices of pork, was the odious rubber cockroach. With its spindly legs to the side and its elongated, spidery feelers spread out in front, it looked more realistic and repulsive than the genuine article.

'Well?' said Betty, her voice rising slightly. She glared up at the owner then back down at the plate. 'Well. What is it?'

The owner stared terrified at Betty's plate then at the po-faced Norton. His face slowly drained of colour and his bottom lip started to tremble. 'That,' he stuttered and stammered. 'That's . . . that's a . . . it's a . . .'

'It's a yabby,' said Norton. 'Isn't it?'

'That's right,' said the owner quickly 'it's a . . . yabby. A little, tiny yabby. It must have got in there by mistake. Now I'll just get rid of that plate for you.' Like a flash his hand went down to retrieve the plate but just as quickly Norton's snaked out and took him by the wrist.

'Hey. Hold on a sec,' he said. 'Where do you think you're goin' with that. I'm gonna eat that. They're the grouse.'

'A yabby?' said Betty, screwing up her face. 'It doesn't look like a yabby to me.'

'Look Betty,' said Norton, deliberately putting on a loud, know-all Australian voice. 'I'm an expert on bloody Thai cooking and that's a bloody Thai yabby. They live in the canals around Bangkok. Don't they mate?' He paused for a moment and looked up at the pale, grim-faced owner who didn't say anything: he just blinked and nodded at Les. 'Yeah,' continued Norton. 'If there's one thing I know it's Thai food and those little Bangkok yabbies are the best eating ever. Look, I'll show you.'

He dipped his fingers into the plate of curried pork and picked up the rubber cockroach; deftly he tore off one of its wings, dipped it in the sauce then popped it in his mouth and started chewing it. 'Mm, bloody beautiful,' he said, rolling his eyes in apparent ecstasy.

By now the owner's face had gone from a bilious, chalky white to the same shade of green milk goes after it's been left in a fridge for a few weeks. He closed his eyes, swallowed and leant against the wall for support.

'Well don't eat the lot, you guts' said Betty, 'give me some.' She reached across and tore off one of the cockroach's little rubber legs and put it in her mouth. 'Oh yes,' she said, giving it a chew. 'Nothing wrong with these. Why didn't you tell me they were on the menu? I'd've got a plate of them.'

'I told you they were nice,' said Norton, ripping the other wing off, dunking it in the sauce and putting it in his mouth also. 'Mm beautiful. Here you are mate, you want some before it's all gone?' He held the sauce-drenched, rubber cockroach close to the horrified owner's face. 'Go on — help yourself.'

The owner stared at it for a few moments as if in a trance. His face changed colour again, then he put his hand over his mouth, turned and bolted for the kitchen.

'Something wrong Marty?' asked his wife, as he went through the kitchen like an F-111 jet. He almost tore the flyscreen off the kitchen door in his panic to get out in the backyard, where he spent the next half an hour bringing up everything he'd eaten in the last two weeks; plus a few pieces of stomach lining.

Back in the dining-room, Les and Betty were almost under the table just about paralysed with laughter; the few others left in the restaurant were staring at them like they were either mad or on some sort of hallucinogenic trip. After fifteen minutes or so there was still no sign of the owner so Norton decided to go out the back, pay the bill and retrieve the rest of his Fourex. When he picked up the docket to see what he owed Norton could scarcely believe his eyes: the whole lot didn't even come to thirty dollars. *Christ,* he thought, *how do they make a profit? That snapper would've cost me ten bucks on its own.* Smiling to himself he wrapped the docket and the rubber cockroach, in three twenty-dollar bills and went out the back to find the owner's wife in the kitchen cleaning the stove.

'Here you are,' said Norton, handing her the money. 'That food was beautiful. Thank you very much.' The wife smiled shyly, took the money and placed it on a sideboard. 'Where's your husband?' asked Les, glancing around the kitchen.

'He go outside,' she replied, nodding her head towards the back door. 'He not feel very well I think.' A slight frown crossed her features. 'I no understand. He look like ghost.'

Norton smiled down at her. 'All right if I get the rest of my beer?' he said.

'In fridge. Top shelf.' She nodded towards a large, four-door, stainless-steel shop freezer.

Norton got his cans out, leaving a couple for the owner then smiled back at the wife again. 'Well, thank you for the lovely food. I hope I can get back here again.'

The wife looked at him evenly for a moment. 'Food good,' she said. 'Service...?' She pulled a face.

'It wasn't that bad,' grinned Norton. 'Thanks anyway.'

'You're welcome.' The wife dropped what she was doing, clasped her hands in front of her face then bowed her head slightly in typical Thai fashion. 'Khorb jai. Sawaddee' she said, with a grateful smile that almost stole Norton's heart away.

'Yeah, my oath' replied Les. 'Khorb jai. Sawaddee.'

Norton returned to the dining-room feeling on top of the world. As soon as he caught Betty's eye he burst out laughing again. They were still laughing when they pulled up outside Betty's flat.

'Honestly Les, that's got to be one of the funniest things I've ever seen in my life,' said Betty, dabbing at her eyes with a tissue.

'Yeah,' chuckled Norton, switching off the motor. 'I thought Basil was nearly gonna have a stroke when I shoved that half-eaten cockroach in front of his face.'

'You mean the Bangkok yabby.'

'Yeah.'

They roared laughing again. When their laughter subsided they sat in silence with just the tape playing softly in the background. Their eyes met and they reached for each other. Somehow the music, the moonlight and their feelings for each other suddenly seemed to melt in around them. Impulsively, Norton placed his hand gently behind Betty's neck, drew her face towards him and kissed her tenderly on the lips. Betty responded avidly, passionately, lovingly.

Betty smiled at him and ran her fingers lightly over his lips. 'Well Mr Norton, the big, bad bouncer from King Cross; are you going to come and tuck me in and see that I get to bed safely?'

'Oh yeah,' winked Les. 'I might come in and have a cup of coffee for five minutes.'

'Only five minutes?'

'Well, I might stay a minute or two longer.'

They locked the car up and went inside. Betty put the kettle on and they waited for it to boil, looking at each other. Norton started kissing Betty again and, unable to help himself, started playing with the zipper on the back of her dress. Betty couldn't help herself either and switched off the electric kettle.

'Are you sure you feel like a cup of coffee?' she said quietly.

'Not really,' smiled Les. 'The bloody stuff only keeps you awake.' Arm in arm he led her into the bedroom.

They didn't do anything much through the night and into the morning, just made love to each other, again and again; sometimes with strength and passion, other times slowly and gently but always with everything they had to give and with the utmost care and consideration for the other.

Some time, early in the morning, Norton was lying in bed, not asleep, not really awake, just feeling good with his arm around Betty's shoulders. She was cuddled up to his side with her head resting on his chest, snoring softly. The moonlight was shining through the thin, lace curtains in the window, playing wonderful tricks on her smooth brown skin and turning her amber hair into shimmering strands of gold. *Christ,* he thought. As he gazed down on her, an unusual, wonderful, warm feeling of contentment seemed to start in the pit of his stomach and spread through his entire body. *I hope I'm not falling in love.*

They both woke up feeling pretty good at around eight o'clock. But with the sun shining in on a glorious spring day and with the birds singing melodically in the trees just outside their window, they couldn't help themselves — so they got up at nine.

They showered, fiddled around a bit getting dressed then cooked up breakfast with what they could find left in the flat. About 10.30 Norton was sitting in the kitchen having a cup of coffee and watching Betty while she tidied up the flat and packed the last of her gear. It was a funny, empty sort of feeling he had sitting there quietly sipping his coffee and knowing that once he dropped her off he'd probably never see her again. He could if he wanted to — there was no doubt about that — Betty must have told him a dozen times last night she was in love with him. And the rotten part about it was he was starting to feel the same about her. But what was he going to do? Keep coming up to Grafton all the time? Or say she came down to Sydney. What was he going to offer her there? A life in Bondi, with all his hoods, hookers and murderers for friends and him working four nights a week in a casino getting up at lunchtime the next day. Terrific. He knew how long her old-fashioned, country freshness would last. He'd met plenty of nice country girls who had probably been a bit like Betty before they'd lived in Sydney. Sure he had plenty of money and a house — but what was the use?

No. He'd knock their little affair straight on the head as soon as he dropped her off. It was a bit of a bastard really. In fact it was more than that. It gave him the bloody shits just thinking about it. Still. No good being mawkish.

'You got much to go?' he asked, as Betty dropped a suitcase in the alcove where the kitchen joined the lounge-room.

'No,' replied Betty. 'One more overnight bag and two blankets. And that's it.'

'You sure you don't want a hand?'

'No, it's all right.' Betty looked at Les for a moment then walked over and ran her fingers through his hair. 'Les. You will come up and see me, won't you?'

Norton slipped his arm round her waste and gave her a squeeze. 'Yeah, of course I will,' he said.

'You promise?'

'Yeah. I promise.'

'When?'

Norton gave his shoulders a bit of a shrug. 'I dunno. I'll ring you when I get back to Sydney. Drop you a line, then I'll be up the first chance I get.'

'When's the first chance you get?'

'I dunno,' shrugged Norton again. 'About a week or two. Something like that. That's all.'

'Good.' She bent down and kissed him on the lips, looked at him for a moment then went back to her packing.

Norton was smiling as he watched her walk back into the lounge-room but inside he felt the greatest cunt in the world.

It wasn't long before Betty had the flat cleaned and her bags packed. 'Well, that's it,' she said. She sounded a little sad as most people are when an enjoyable holiday comes to an end. Norton picked up the two bags and walked out the front to put them in the car: Betty closed the door behind him. As he placed them on the back seat of the BMW Betty produced a small, instamatic camera and told him to stand in front of the flats. Norton stood there with his arms folded and a lop-sided sort of grin on his face while Betty clicked off two photos. 'Just a little souvenir of Lobster Flats,' she said, with a whimsical smile. 'And you,' she added. They got in the car, dropped the keys off to some caretaker in a shop in Sawtell and drove out to Reg's farm.

'I just want to get a fresh change of clothes,' said Norton, as they headed for the Pacific Highway turnoff. 'Besides, I'd better let Reg know I'm all right,' he added with a grin. 'He's probably starting to worry.' *I also got to pick up that bag of pot and get it into the boot of the car without anyone seeing, too,* he thought, giving his chin a bit of a thoughtful rub. *This is going to be interesting.*

'When you drop me off, you'll have to come in and meet my parents,' said Betty.

'Yeah righto,' replied Norton. 'What's your old man do anyway?'

'He's a dentist.' Betty flashed a pearly grin that would have made the Macleans girl envious, and clicked her teeth together. 'Can't you tell?'

'Your teeth are all right,' shrugged Les. 'You just need a new set of gums, that's all.'

Reg and Diane were in the kitchen having a late breakfast when Norton pulled up at the old farmhouse. Sally gave two horrendous, spine-chilling barks as he and Betty walked up the stairs then flopped face down, exhausted at the effort and lay in the sun quietly breaking wind.

'Well, well, well. And how are you young lovers this morning?' beamed Norton, as he walked into the kitchen. 'Have a nice night last night, did you?'

There was a distinct, devilish twinkle in Reg's eyes but the bags underneath them looked like a pair of purple hammocks. Diane looked pretty much the same only with a rosy glow of satisfaction radiating from her cheeks. Norton quickly summised that between them they'd got plenty of bed but not a great deal of sleep.

'Oh yeah, it was all right,' replied Reg, with a bit of a grin. 'What about yourself?'

'Good. The food was enormous,' replied Norton.

'So what are you doing?'

'Well, I'm just about to get changed, then I'm driving Betty back to Grafton.'

'You in a hurry?' asked Diane, smiling up at Betty. 'Why don't you have a cup of coffee?'

'That sounds like a good idea,' said Les.

Diane put a fresh pot on while Reg gave Betty a quick tour of the house. They sat in the kitchen talking over a few cups and some home-made pumpkin scones Diane had brought over. When they'd all finished laughing at Les and Betty's caper with the owner of the restaurant Norton stood up, saying he was going to put on some clean clothes.

'Hey Reg,' he said, stopping at the kitchen door. 'While I'm getting changed, why don't you show Betty some of your other paintings out in your studio?'

'Oh I don't think Betty'd be interested,' replied the artist, a tint of slight embarrassment showing in his cheeks.

'No. I'd love to see them,' said Betty.

'I'll put the dishes away while you're out there.' Diane stood up and began to clear the table.

Norton took Diane by the arm. 'I can do that. Go on, join Betty and Reg. I'll be with you in a minute.'

'All right.' The three of them walked out to the studio.

Norton watched them through the window. As soon as they went inside he went straight out the back door, crawled under the house and retrieved the gladbag full of half-useless dope.

Keeping the BMW between himself and the studio he made a sprint for it, opened the boot and tossed the relatively light, but cumbersome, bag inside. *You bloody little beauty,* he thought, with a great smile of relief at being able to get that little task out of the way undetected. He closed the boot gently and walked back to the house.

In the bedroom he changed into a clean pair of jeans and a T-shirt. The small bag of dope he'd pinched from Reg was in amongst his socks; he got it out, removed it from the gladbag and packed it loosely in the front, right-hand pocket of his jeans. *That should do the trick,* he thought, as he closed the drawer. He was in the kitchen tidying up when the others came back.

'Well, what do you reckon?' Norton rinsed the last coffee cup and put it in the rack.

'I'm very, very impressed,' said Betty, shaking her head slightly in astonishment at the quality of Reg's paintings.

'I told you the young fellah wasn't too bad, didn't I?'

'Betty said there's an exhibition of paintings on at her school next month and she's going to arrange for me to bring some up.' Reg shrugged his shoulders and smiled. 'I might even sell some.'

'You'll sell some. Don't worry about that,' said Betty.

'See, what did I tell you Reg?' Norton grinned and made a magnanimous gesture with his hands. 'You'll have that VCR in no time.'

Soon it was time to go. Betty told Reg she'd be in touch next week and would make all the arrangements for him to bring his paintings up to Grafton. She also told Diane she'd ring her, and they could all get together again for a dinner or something when Norton came up to see her. The way she smiled and looked so convinced when she said it made Les feel low enough to walk under a landmine. They said their goodbyes at the car. Norton gave the horn a blast and they headed towards Grafton.

Les decided to take the Pacific Highway rather than the inland route, so he could see a little bit of the coastline on the other side of Coffs Harbour. It wasn't long before they'd left the 'Big Banana' and most of the beaches behind them and were heading north-west towards the town on the Clarence River they call the jacaranda capital of New South Wales.

Between the tapes, the scenery and the nice new car the trip was quite pleasant. Norton kept the conversation light but steady, relating various anecdotes about life in Bondi and at the Kelly Club. Betty told him funny little things about school teaching and life in Grafton. Two things were paramount on Norton's mind: firstly, he wasn't too enthused at having to walk out of Betty's life just like that. He was quite keen on the schoolteacher; she was a gem in Les's eyes — good-looking, in a wholesome unmade up sort of way, a top body and plenty of personality. And as for making love with her; that was something else again. But — it would soon be all over, so he just had to grit his teeth. Secondly, he wasn't 100-per cent sure whether the two shifties waiting for him would tumble for that great bag of glorified lawn-mower clippings sitting in the boot. The shit smelled all right, felt all right and looked all right, but if they smoked any? Bleah! However, he had one ace left up his sleeve to play. He sniggered to himself, reached over and gave Betty's knee a bit of a squeeze. She smiled back happily and put her hand on his arm.

Betty, on the other hand, although a little sad at having to say goodbye to Les, was happy and content in the knowledge that he'd be in touch and it would only be a fortnight or so before she'd be seeing him again. She loved the big redhead, even though he was a bit of a rough diamond, cheeky as they come and liked to bladder on a bit about beautiful Queensland and Dirranbandi. Although he wasn't adverse to pounding men's heads to sausage mince, he was honest and gentle with her. When it came to him as a lover ... she hadn't had many affairs but she couldn't see and didn't want anyone better than him.

They stopped briefly at a little place called Halfway Creek for a while so Betty could take a couple more photos. Houses and shops soon started to appear on either side of the road once they crossed the old concrete and iron bridge that spans the Clarence River.

Coming off the bridge, Norton couldn't believe the number

of jacaranda trees — they were everywhere filling the air with sweet perfume which seemed to envelope you in a glorious blaze of purple and blue. And when the gentle spring zephyrs shook the branches the blossoms filled the air like a lavender snowstorm covering the streets in a magic carpet of amethyst and sapphire.

'Christ,' said Norton, slowing the car down to take in the beauty of it all. 'Have a go at those flowers. No wonder they call it the jacaranda capital of Australia.'

'Yes, they're lovely, aren't they?' replied Betty. 'The prisoners have got a bit of a saying when they're being transferred to Grafton: when you hear those flowers crunching under the back wheels, you know where you are.'

'Good old Grafton gaol eh! I sure wouldn't like to finish in there.'

'Yes, it's a grim old place all right — though it's not quite as bad as it was. Anyway, take the next on your right — Prince Street.'

Prince Street; that name rings a bell, thought Norton. 'Hey Betty, whereabouts is that place where you bought that grouse blue dress?'

'L.A. Fashions?'

'Yeah.'

'In Prince Street. Just up a bit further. Why?'

'Oh nothin'. I was just a bit curious as to you getting a top dress like that in a place like Grafton.'

Betty looked at Les for a moment. 'What do you mean — a place like Grafton?'

'Well — I mean it's only a country town.'

Betty looked at Norton again. 'What do you mean — only a country town. Grafton happens to be a city. Where do you think you are? Up in the New Guinea Highlands and we all run around with bones through our noses and bird feathers in our hair?'

'All right Coxie.' Norton's face broke into a grin. 'No need to bite my head off. I was only asking.'

'Only a country town — Humph. I take umbrage at that.'

'Take what you like,' shrugged Norton.

'Anyway, what about that place where you come from? Dirranbandi. I heard you've got a set of traffic lights there and they change once a week.'

Norton narrowed his eyes and tightened his lips. 'Hey, just a minute woman,' he said. 'Don't start knockin' Queensland.'

'I also heard, the biggest cultural event in Dirranbandi for the last decade was the arrival of a singing telegram.'

'Yeah? Well we also have a little saying in Dirranbandi; that if you owned both heaven and Dirranbandi, you'd rent out heaven and live in Dirranbandi. How's that grab you?'

'Like an octopus. Anyway, there it is.'

Norton slowed down and looked out Betty's window. There was a single-fronted shop window outlined in black and pink with a black awning above. 'L.A. Fashion' was written across the window in a kaleidoscope of colours. He only got a glimpse of the clothes in the window but noticed they were in a multitude of colours, too. He also notice a white Ford Fairlane out the front with T.L. number plates. Norton took a quick glance at his watch — *see you in about half an hour boys.*

'So. That's where all the snobs and trendies in Grafton get their clothes, eh?' He grinned at her and put his foot down slightly on the accelerator.

'Snobs and trendies,' sniffed Betty. She gave Les a thump on the arm. 'God, you're a rude person.'

'Yeah I know. It's from listening to Doug Mulray in the morning. Now where's your joint?'

'My home,' replied Betty slowly. 'That's h-o-m-e — home, for those Queenslanders around here that can't spell, is at the end of this street and to the right: Kirchner Street.'

Jesus, you're a cheeky bastard, smiled Norton to himself — *I wish to Christ I was taking you back to Sydney with me.*

Betty's house was a huge, old, sandstock brick home, built right up off the ground with a double garage to the side. It had a large well-kept garden and a matching brick fence running across the front. A vine-covered veranda skirted the front and one side of the house giving a lovely view across a tree-covered reserve to the river.

'Not a bad sort of a shack,' said Norton, stopping out the front and switching off the motor. 'Must be some money in pullin' teeth.'

'Dad does all right,' replied Betty. 'I don't see any cars though. He must be out somewhere with Mum. Anyway come inside.'

Norton got Betty's bags off the back seat and followed her up a concrete path leading to the house. As he did, a moth-eaten, old black cocker-spaniel with eyes like two slices of calve's liver came down the stairs. Its stump of a tail was going 100 to the dozen as it shuffled up to Betty whining with delight.

It gave a bit of a feeble, asthmatic bark at Norton who patted its bony head.

'Nice dog,' chuckled Les. 'Only a pup, too.'

'Don't knock our Turra. He's an unreal dog.' Turra flopped its slobbery tongue out and sort of half-smiled at Les to reveal a set of teeth that looked more like a mouthful of rusty tacks.

'Good thing your old man's a dentist.' Norton followed Betty up the front stairs and went inside: Turra crawled up on to an old lounge on the veranda.

Inside, the house was built in the style old colonial homes were built; big and roomy, with high, raked ceilings and exposed beams. Every room was tastefully and expensively furnished, and on most of the walls hung a number of original oil paintings. Norton waited while Betty put her bags in her bedroom then followed her into the kitchen. There was a note on the kitchen table. It read: Betty, have gone to Uncle Jack's in Armidale. Be back Monday night. Don't forget to feed Turra. Love Mum and Dad.

'Hey look at this,' she said excitedly. She handed the note to Norton and slipped her arms round his waist while he read it. 'You know what that means, don't you? You don't have to go straight back to Reg's. You can stay the night.'

Norton read the note and handed it back to her. 'Yeah,' he said, swallowing a lump in his throat the size of a baseball and trying to smile. 'It sure looks that way, don't it?' But Norton was adamant nothing would break his resolve. He was going back to Coffs Harbour today and it was going to be goodbye Betty, no matter how painful it would be. That's the way it had to be.

'We can go and have a few drinks at the rowing club,' said Betty, beaming. 'Maybe have tea there, it's really nice. Then we could come home and watch a bit of TV, or whatever.' She gave a lecherous chuckle. 'I prefer the whatever myself.'

'Yeah righto,' lied Norton. 'That sounds like a good idea.' He had a quick look at his watch. It was almost time to start making a move, though he was certain the other two would still wait even if he was a bit late. But the sooner he got this over with the better he liked it.

'Hey, you feel like a cup of coffee?' asked Betty.

Norton shrugged his shoulders. 'Wouldn't mind a cup of tea.'

'Okay.' Betty put the kettle on then went to the fridge. 'Oh crumbs! There's hardly any milk.' She held up an almost empty

217

bottle. 'Wait on. I think there's some Carnation in the cupboard.'

'That's all right,' said Les quickly. 'I'll duck down the road and get some.'

'No, use Carnation. It'll save you the trip.'

'It's all right. I want to get some Quick-Eze anyway. Those . . . ah, scones of Diane's have given me indigestion.'

'There's some Mylanta in the bathroom.'

'No, I can't swallow it. It makes me sick.'

'All right. Well there's a little shop just round the corner. I'll unpack some of my stuff and put the kettle back on when you get back.' She walked to the bedroom and threw one of her bags on the bed.

Norton made a hesitant move for the front door and finished up standing at the doorway of the bedroom watching Betty unpack.

'Well. Don't stand there gawking at me you big goose,' said Betty turning round. 'Go and get some milk if you want a cup of tea. I'll see you when you get back.' She gave him a wink and continued unpacking.

Norton stood in the doorway a couple of moments longer staring at her back. He wanted to run up to her and hold her, kiss her, crush her in his arms. Instead he turned and walked away — out of her life forever. 'Yeah. See you when I get back,' he muttered, half to himself.

He climbed into the BMW and turned on the engine. 'Fuckin' cunt,' he cursed out aloud and punched at the dashboard. He sat for a little while with the engine ticking over, taking a last look at Betty's house. He jerked the selector into drive. *If those two pricks fuck me around with this pot, I'll break both their fuckin' jaws,* he said to himself, spinning the car back towards Prince Street.

Needless to say, Norton wasn't in the best of moods when he pulled up outside L.A. Dave's clothes shop a few minutes later. However, he soon started to realise that it was just plain stupid him having the shits with the world over losing his girl. The dope deal had to be done, and there was a fair bit of money at stake. It would be pointless him blowing that as well just because he had the shits. He took a deep breath, gave one last curse and put Betty out of his mind.

Being Sunday afternoon, Prince Street was just about deserted. Opening the boot of the car he looked around cautiously as he got the garbage bag full of dope out, walked quickly over to the shop and knocked on the door. The door opened a few seconds later and there stood L.A. Dave with his gangling frame and scraggly blonde hair. He was wearing jeans and a black T-shirt.

'Hey, how are you Les? Come in man,' he said, with his usual psuedo-hip Californian voice.

'Hello Dave. How's things?'

'Unreal man.' Dave held out his hand and gave Norton an American hippy-type handshake with about as much meat in it as a tomato sandwich; Norton felt like he'd just shaken hands with four sticks of asparagus.

'Well, there it is,' he said, dropping the great bag of pot on the floor next to a rack of dresses.

'Yeah, good man. But just bring it out the back, will you. You never know who's walking or driving past.'

'Sure.' Norton followed Dave through a doorway which led into a dimly lit lounge-room furnished in a sort of Balinese style. A set of stairs ran up one wall probably to the bedrooms, so Norton guessed Dave lived on the premises.

Sitting on the old, brown velvet lounge, was Tony Levin, a beer in his hand. Next to him was an anorexic-looking brunette wearing a black jump-suit which had about 200 small studded belts wrapped round it. With her hair swept back in a tight ponytail and the pair of red-rimmed owl-shaped glasses she was wearing, she looked like a cross between a skinny Joan Baez and Felix the cat.

'You know Tony?' asked Dave. Norton said 'hello' and gave Levin's hand a light shake. 'And that's my lady — Francine.'

'Hello,' said Norton. Francine barely nodded her head. She grunted an almost audible 'hi', then sat back on the lounge trying to look cool and sophisticated. Norton was going to say more to her but figured she'd have about as much personality as a pumped leg of hogget, so he ignored her.

'Well, there's your dope,' said Norton, plonking the garbage bag in the middle of the room. 'You want to have a look at it?'

'Yeah. I want to weigh it, too, Les,' said Dave.

'Do what you like with it.' Norton gave Levin a withering look that made him swallow and quickly look away. 'Just as long as I'm out of here in about ten minutes and heading back to Sydney.'

'No worries man.' Dave got a set of bathroom scales from next to the lounge and placed the bag on it. He could scarcely conceal his good fortune: it was a kilo more than he'd expected. He gave Tony a quick wink which Norton detected.

'How much is there?' asked Les casually.

'Close enough to twenty-two kilos.'

'You happy with that?'

'Yeah man. That's ... cool.'

'What about you Tony?'

'Yeah, sweet.' Levin nodded his head enthusiastically.

'And it's fifteen grand, right?'

'Yeah. Price just wants the money owing to him. That's all.'

'Yeah. That should be all right,' said Dave slowly. It was the steal of the year, yet Dave was still trying to act cool and businesslike. Francine was curled up on the lounge smoking a cigarette and posing. She still hadn't said anything. 'I'll just have a look through the bag. All right?' said Dave.

'Go for your life,' said Norton. 'Just don't be all day that's all. I got to get cracking and this drugs caper's not my go.'

'No worries man.'

Despite still having a good dose of the shits Norton was starting to laugh a little inside at the farcical situation going on around him. The three of them had no doubt been talking plenty before he got there, and as far as they were concerned he was just some big goose who had stumbled on twenty-two kilos of top smoke and didn't have a clue what was going on. They were ripping him off, and Price Galese, too, for that matter, and getting away with it. It was the dope scam of all time: they couldn't believe how clever they were. Norton decided to drop his surly animosity and just act dumb.

He watched as L.A. Dave removed the plastic tie and ran his hands through and around the huge bag of pot. Norton could see the greedy glint in his eyes. The dope smelled like dope all right and after being packed tightly in the plastic bag all night and covered with Coca-Cola, it had gone like stacks of compressed heads only sticky and dripping with resin. Dave was impressed but somehow still seemed suspicious.

'Have a look Tony,' he said cool and slow. 'What do you reckon?'

Tony got up off the lounge and ran his hands through the bag several times. 'Looks okay to me,' he said, giving Dave a quick look.

Norton stuck his hands in his jeans and leant up against the wall with a dumb look on his face. It was time to play his ace. 'Well I wouldn't know the difference between the pot you smoke and the pot you put on the stove, but that stuff seems to smoke all right. Don't it Tony?' Levin nodded his head, looked at Les then at Dave. 'So why don't you roll yourselves a joint?' Les shrugged his shoulders. 'I'd get some out of the bag for you but they reckon the fumes from that stuff can get you stoned. I'd probably end up having a trip or something.' Francine sniggered through her nose on the lounge — Dave and Tony looked at each other, rolled their eyes and looked away again. 'Well that's right, isn't it?' said Les dumbly.

'Yeah that's right man,' said Dave, acting smug. 'You can never be too careful with this stuff.' L.A. Dave couldn't help himself: he had to act the smarty in front of his team. 'But if we're going to have a smoke, you're going to have to pick it out for us.' He sat back down on the lounge and nodded to the garbage bag. 'It's your dope Les, and we want to see what sort of a judge you are. Pick some out.' Dave sat back and smiled at the others satisfied he'd put Les on show.

Norton stared at the dope for a moment. 'Are you sure it'll be all right' he said, looking sceptical.

'You'll be right man,' said Dave.

'All right. If you say so.' With his hands still in his pocket Norton heaved himself off the wall towards the bag of marijuana. While he had been leaning there he palmed the dynamite dope from Reg into his hand holding it with his thumb. Looking dubious and uncomfortable he plunged his hand into the garbage bag like it was full of spiders, rummaged round for a few seconds and came up with Reg's dope in his hand. He handed it to L.A. Dave. 'There you are' he said. 'That look all right?'

Dave looked at it for a few seconds then handed it to Francine. 'Yeah, that looks okay' he said. 'Francine'll roll us up a couple of joints and we'll see if it's any good.'

Still doing her best to look cool, Francine got a packet of Tally-Ho from a small, engraved, wooden box sitting on a coffee table and proceeded to roll two medium size joints mixed with a little tobacco. Norton went back to leaning against the wall and looking dumb.

'You feeling all right after that man?' smirked L.A. Dave.

'Yeah,' replied Norton. 'I held my breath.' There was another snigger from the three on the lounge.

Yeah, have your laugh Larry, Curley and Mo, thought Norton. *It'll be a different story about two minutes after you light that tuppenny bunger.*

Looking like she'd just performed some magnificent feat of engineering, Francine lit one of the joints. They handed it round between them; Levin offered Les a toke out of sheer politeness, which he declined with a curt shake of his head.

In a few minutes the first number was gone and the three of them were sitting on the lounge like battery hens, just staring into space. Finally Francine spoke.

'Do you ... want ... me to light ... that other joint, David?' Her voice was nasally and whiney and sounded like it was coming from another room. L.A. Dave didn't say anything; he just shook his head and went back to staring into space. Levin did pretty much the same, staring into his can of beer. Norton gave them another two minutes of transcendental meditation or whatever it was they were practising.

'Righto. What do you want to do?' he said abruptly, moving towards the garbage bag. 'Do you want this shit or what?'

Dave opened and closed his eyes several times like they were stuck together with epoxy resin. 'What ... was that man?' he mumbled.

'I said, "do you want this dope?"' Norton looked at him with bored contempt: he felt like belting Dave over the head. 'Make up your mind cause I want to get going. Okay?'

'Yeah ... Sure man,' said Dave. 'I'll get you the chops.' He rose from the lounge like he was caught in quicksand. Norton watched him stumble to the fridge in the small kitchen, open it and come back with a bottle of orange-and-mango mineral water which he handed to Les then flopped back down on the lounge. The others looked blankly at the bottle, then back at Dave with puzzled looks on their spaced-out faces.

Norton stared at the bottle for a moment then screwed up his face and looking at L.A. Dave. 'What am I supposed to do with this Dave?' he said contemptuously. 'Cash the fuckin' thing in?'

Dave looked up at Norton for a moment quite puzzled. 'Oh shit man ... Sorry man,' he said, lurching drunkenly to his feet. 'I've ... made a ... bit of a blue.' Norton shook his head and watched him return to the fridge, open the deep-freeze compartment, then return with a bread wrapper full of money. 'Sorry ... man,' he mumbled, handing it to Les. 'I ... thought you wanted a drink.' Norton handed him the bottle of mineral water and he flopped down on the lounge.

'That's okay,' said Norton. He watched them for a few seconds sitting like dummies in a shop window, then a devilish smile started to spread slowly across his craggy face. 'So you reckon that pot's all right eh?' he said to the three of them.

'Yeah . . . as good as . . . gold man,' said L.A. Dave.

'Terrific Les. No . . . worries,' muttered Tony.

'Unreal,' whined Francine.

'Yeah I thought it might have been all right,' said Les. He smiled broadly and gave the garbage bag a bit of a nudge with his foot. 'Yeah. I don't know much about pot,' he said slowly. 'But there's dead set one thing I know for sure.'

'What's . . . that Les?' said Tony.

Norton pointed to the garbage bag. 'That's definitely got the real thing in there.'

L.A. Dave looked at the others and started to laugh. 'Oh yeah man . . . it's the real thing all right.' He gave Tony a nudge as he started to laugh, too. 'Hey . . . what do you reckon?'

'Oh yeah,' replied Tony, feeling pretty smug because he'd got on to the dope in the first place. 'It's the real . . . thing. No worries.' He kept laughing, until he and Dave were roaring.

Even super-cool Francine couldn't help but put her skinny head in. 'Yes Les, you're a . . . real good judge,' she giggled. 'It's the . . . real thing all right.' She turned to Dave and roared laughing. 'The man said . . . it's the real thing Dave.' They were all rolling on the lounge collapsed with laughter which was supposed to be at Norton's expense.

Norton watched them falling around for a moment and started laughing himself. 'Anyway gang,' he said, tucking the 15,000 dollars up under his arm. 'I've got to get going.' He held up a hand. 'It's all right. I can find my own way out.' He moved to the doorway that led into the shop. 'Anyway, if I don't bump into you in Sydney, I might see you up here again some time,' he winked. 'See you later.'

'Yeah . . . see you . . . Les,' they chorused between fits of laughter.

He turned and walked away. He could still hear them laughing as he went out the front door.

Norton climbed into the BMW, threw the money on the front seat and started the car. There were no other cars around so he did a quick U-turn, drove down Prince Street and turned left into Fitzroy. He cruised along a block or two then pulled over to give the money a quick check. The car stereo was on and of all songs to be playing as he sat there counting the money, was Air Supply singing 'Lost In Love'. He finished counting the money and sat listening to the music. Air Supply filled the car with melody, harmony and beautiful lyrics and a swirl of purple and blue jacaranda blossoms caught in the breeze gusted around the car. He started thinking about Betty again. He scratched his chin and looked at his watch — almost three o'clock.

Well, he thought to himself. *If I get going now, I'll be back at Reg's by about four and have a nice early night.* He scratched his chin thoughtfully. *Then on the other hand... I could have a few cool ones at that rowing club and maybe have a nice seafood dinner.* He glanced down at the money. I wouldn't mind a bit of a celebration. And if I leave here late tomorrow morning, I'd get to Coffs Harbour around lunch time. I reckon I could get that $900 VCR for say $800 cash — shot in a decent TV. I'd get them both for less than $1500. Reg'd never know where the money came from. As he drummed his fingers on the dashboard, Air Supply faded out and The Reels floated gently in. They were singing 'La Mer' in French. It was an offer Norton couldn't refuse.

'Yeah fuck it,' he said out loud. 'I'll stay the bloody night.'

With a grin from ear to ear he started the car, zoomed back up Fitzroy and roared back along Prince Street. As he got to Kirchner he suddenly hit the brakes and screamed to a halt.

'Jesus Christ,' he said out loud again. 'I forgot the bloody milk.'

Something She'd Never Done Before

Standing beneath the pale blue light of the Kelly Club, the two solid men in tuxedos seemed a little restless as they shuffled around on the footpath, waiting outside the doorway for the prospective punters to start turning up. It was just after nine o'clock on a Wednesday night; the beginning of the working week for them.

The shorter of the two men stretched his arms out level with his shoulders, rotated them several times then put his hands in his trouser pockets, finally leaning up against the wall on one shoulder.

'Well. How was the weekend Les?' he asked, looking up at his workmate. 'You get up to much?' Billy Dunne's idea of a weekend was the four days they had off from Sunday to Wednesday.

Les Norton also had his hands in his trouser pockets. He stood in the middle of the footpath idly scuffing with the toe of his riding boot at an empty cigarette packet lying at his feet.

'No, not really,' he replied casually. 'Just took it easy. Went to the pictures Tuesday night. Saw a Clint Eastwood movie.'

'Any good?'

'Not bad. He shot about two hundred blokes without re-loading his gun.' Norton finally kicked the empty cigarette packet into the gutter. 'What'd you do?'

'Took the missus to a barbecue Sunday arvo.'

'Yeah?'

'Yeah.' Billy paused for a moment before he spoke. 'That's what I meant to ask you. What was the name of that sheila you took out a few times from over Kogarah? The one that worked in the bank.'

Norton had to think for a second. 'The little blonde sheila? Andrea. Andrea Hayden.'

'Andrea. That's right.'

'What makes you ask?'

'She'd just been divorced or something, hadn't she?'

Norton nodded his head. 'Why?'

'I met her ex-husband at the barbecue.'

'Yeah? What was he like?'

'Not a bad lookin' bloke. Bit of a no-hoper. Desperate punter.'

'Yeah?'

'Yeah. He was trying to pump me for a bit of information. Seems he owes Harry Allen and that team from over San Souci a bit of dough and can't settle. He was asking me what they were like.'

'What'd you tell him?'

'I give him the name of a good doctor and told him to get plenty of HCF.'

Norton laughed. 'Yeah, Harry's not the sort of bloke you'd want to owe money to.'

There was a bit of a twinkle in Billy's eye as he looked up at Les quizzingly. 'Were you doing any business there... with Andrea?'

Norton shook his head. 'No. I had a bit of a lash, but she was still getting over the divorce. I s'pose I could've if I'd pushed it. But...'

'You still seein' her?'

'I give her a ring now and again. She's not a bad scout. Got a terrific personality. Last I heard she was goin' to Hawaii or something.'

'Hawaii eh?'

'Yeah. She said she was gonna send me a card care of the club.'

When Qantas flight 648 from Sydney landed at Honolulu International Airport, Andrea Hayden undid her seatbelt and leant slightly across the passenger seated closest to the window to get her first glimpse of Hawaii. It was just after 9 a.m. Honolulu time on a beautiful Friday morning. Although the man sitting next to her and most of the other people on the plane were obviously quite excited, Andrea wasn't nearly as enthused as she could have been. The droning nine-hour flight from Australia, crossing the International Dateline, had left her feeling quite jaded, and while she had managed to snatch

226

some sleep most of it was spoilt by broken dreams and unhappy memories of how the trip had come about.

Six years of marriage had just finished in divorce with Andrea on the receiving end of a very raw deal in a settlement. When their modest home-unit was finally sold, Wayne's gambling debts settled, interest rates met and a slump in real-estate values taken into account there wasn't a great deal left. Barely enough for court costs and a cheap ten-day package tour to Hawaii; which Andrea had promised herself no matter what. Not much of a reward for six years of your life. Six irreplaceable years.

Not that she didn't try. She did everything she could to keep their marriage and the home-unit at Sans Souci together. But while most of the money she earned at the bank went into the home-unit it seemed all the money Wayne made spray painting, when he'd get up to go to work, went to the pub, the TAB and every SP bookie in the St George area who would give him credit. So finally, instead of arguing about it all the time, they decided to get a divorce; and that was that. Six years out of her life and most of her money straight out the window.

But she wasn't bitter. Sad, terribly disillusioned and not at all looking forward to the prospect of having to start out over again of course, but bitter? No. And while she could never love Wayne again she could never bring herself to hate him; hatred and unfriendliness were two things that didn't seem to exist in Andrea Hayden's nature.

If anything, it was her good nature and kind heart that were Andrea's biggest downfalls; people were always taking advantage of her. Wayne certainly did. And her young brother and most of the people at the bank where she worked. But after this divorce episode was over she told herself she was going to toughen up one day. One day. Still, what was the use of being sour on the world? Laugh and the world laughs with you Andrea always used to say, cry and you cry alone; and who knows, some day someone or something might come along.

It wasn't as if she was an unattractive woman, a bit plain maybe but definitely not ugly. Her roundish, happy face with a scattering of freckles and nearly always devoid of make-up was suited by the loosely bobbed, auburnish-blonde hair that wisped lightly across her hazel-green eyes. The freckles even seemed to give her an old-fashioned country girl appearance — often making her pass for younger than 29. She dressed a bit soberly, had a bit of a double-chin and was possibly a tad stocky for 170 centimetres, but aerobics classes had kept her boobs and bum reasonably tight. And being a light drinker and particular with how much and what she ate, she was always healthy and rarely got ill.

'Well there it is Andrea, blue Hawaii. What do you reckon?'

She turned away from the window to find one of the flight stewards standing in the aisle next to her. 'Oh, hello John,' she said, smiling up at him through her tiredness. 'Yes it certainly looks nice out there. Plenty of sunshine, too. A bit different to Sydney when we left.'

'Eighty-one degrees on the local scale and the water temperature's about seventy. Another hour or so and you should be lying on the golden sands of Waikiki, a mai-tai in one hand and a couple of rich Yanks hanging off the other.'

'And if there's any talent scouts around they might even sign me up for a part in Hawaii Five-O!'

John smiled and nodded his head. 'Yes, they're always looking for heavies on the show.' He bent over a little closer to her. 'Listen we start to get a bit busy now and I have to go, but remember what I told you. Okay? He patted her lightly on the shoulder and winked. 'See you later Andrea.'

'Bye-bye John. Thanks.' She watched him move on down the aisle, stopping from time to time to smile and help different passengers get their bags down from the overhead luggage compartments. Her thoughts drifted back to when she first met him.

It was about five or six hours into the flight after the main meal had been served. The cabin lights were out but Andrea was still having trouble sleeping, so was listening to some music through a set of headphones. It was quite pleasant; the music was nice and light and she was just starting to relax when Elton John's 'Sad Songs' began to play. 'When every little hope is gone — Sad songs say so much,' kept repeating. At first it made her feel just a little sentimental, then nostalgic and the next thing she knew she was crying openly. She tore the headphones off, grabbed several tissues from her handbag, hurried for the 'ladies' and almost stumbled into John. He was standing in the soft glow of the aft galley sipping coffee with another steward. John couldn't help noticing the tears streaming down Andrea's face. Being diplomatic like all Qantas stewards, he enquired casually when she came out if there was something wrong. He insisted that she have a fresh cup of coffee and winked as he dropped a nip of Tia Maria in it. After introducing himself as John Greenough and his work-mate Tommy Butterworth, Andrea got talking. It wasn't long before she started to feel a bit more relaxed and, under their gentlemanly charm, started to open up a bit.

She didn't go into too much detail about the circumstances surrounding her divorce but told them that mainly what she wanted was a break somewhere different and away from everybody. She told them how she was doing it a bit on the cheap with the ten-day package tour, how she'd only allowed herself fifty dollars a day spending money and 200 for presents for her family, and asked them if they knew of any inexpensive places to eat. She also added that most of the people in her group were a pretty dreary bunch, middle-aged married couples mainly and two giggling over-made-up girls from Wollongong, whom she wasn't at all keen to join up with. She asked if they knew of any night spots where she'd be all right on her own. John and Tommy were only too willing to oblige.

They told her a few of the good things about Hawaii and also some of the pitfalls; Honolulu could be a bit of a heavy town at times if you weren't careful. But as Andrea was booked into the Hilton Hawaiian Village and the crew always stayed at the Illakai, almost next door, why didn't she join them that night for drinks and they'd explain things more over a few cool ones in a more relaxed atmosphere? There was a bar on top of the Reef Hotel called the Flight Bar. It opened between five and eight o'clock, drinks were half-price and everybody went there to watch the sun set over the ocean. Andrea was ordered to be there no later than 6 p.m. and wearing the loudest mumu or Hawaiian shirt she could find. Tommy even drew her a little map how to find the place. Feeling much better she returned to her seat. She didn't bother to put the headphones on again.

When she left the plane John and Tommy were standing at the top of the gangway with several other flight personnel.

'Don't forget now,' said Tommy, as she started down the steps. 'The Reef Hotel, no later than six.'

'No, I'll be there for sure.'

'We'll see you then.'

'Yes, for sure. Goodbye Tommy. Goodbye John. And thanks.'

'Hey,' said John, 'you're in Hawaii now. It's aloha.'

'Aloha it is then,' she grinned. She was still smiling when she got to the bottom of the steps.

The first thing she noticed as she stood in the arrival area waiting for her bags, apart from everybody seeming to have on a Hawaiian shirt, was the number of people, both male and female, wearing huge handguns in open holsters. It was worse in the customs area. Apart from all the customs officers wearing magnums and automatics, there were black-uniformed police everywhere all armed to the teeth with hand-guns, shot-guns, billy clubs, mace, handcuffs and walkie-talkies — all chewing gum and all wearing mirror sunglasses. *God*, she thought, *I may as well have booked ten days in Nicaragua. If a car backfires around here it'll be like the gunfight at the OK Corral.*

She found it was the same in the lobby of her hotel. More Hawaiian shirts and monstrous, uniformed security guards, chewing gum, wearing sunglasses and armed to the hilt. *A girl's certainly safe here.*

Her room on the seventeenth floor was compact, but spot-lessly clean, bright and modern. From her tiny balcony was one of the best views she'd ever seen in her life.

To her left, rows of gleaming white hotels towered over the beach almost reaching the water's edge and behind them Dia-mond Head reached magnificently out towards the ocean as tufts of white clouds swirled around its extinct volcanic crater. Almost directly below her the red and white outrigger canoes with their multicoloured sails carved a graceful foaming path through the crystal-clear, blue waters. They easily rode the smooth, even swells breaking over the dark reefs not far from shore. The excited cries of the tourists riding inside were carried up to her balcony by the gentle sea breezes.

Surfboard riders and windsurfers looking like distant pockets of flowers in their vividly coloured board-shorts were scattered across the shimmering sapphire waters — some catching waves, others just lying, enjoying the radiant warm sunshine. Further out to sea yachts and power-boats surged across the waves just below the horizon. Andrea was absolutely enraptured for quite some time. She went inside to unpack her bag, but still feeling a little tired, decided to lie down on the bed for a while. In what seemed like seconds she drifted off into a deep, soothing sleep. It was almost five o'clock when she woke up.

The confusion of waking up in a strange room not knowing where she was startled her at first. Realising where she was she sat up on the edge of the bed and checked her watch. She remembered she had to meet the boys at six — *better get a wriggle on.*

She was still yawning and rubbing her eyes when she got under the shower but felt considerably better when she got out — a little hungry, too. Rather than have to search for a restaurant she decided to have something sent up to her room. *God, my fifty dollars a day won't go far,* she thought, as she scanned the menu in her room; a steak sandwich at five dollars and a cup of coffee at $1.50 was the cheapest. After tipping the room waiter a quarter, which he looked at like it was a dead cockroach, she ate her meal standing in the cool breeze on her balcony. She changed into a loose-fitting blue dress with a small, white flower pattern. *Time to meet the boys; not very Hawaiian,* she thought, giving herself a quick check in the mirror on the way out.

Kalakau Avenue was just starting to come to life as she walked briskly towards the Reef Hotel. Fat gawking couples from the American mid-west wearing matching Hawaiian shirts and mumus; the men in ridiculous check shorts chomping on huge cigars, mingled with hordes of Japanese festooned with cameras and nametags. The way they bowed and smiled all the time reminded her of a lot of wind-up dolls. Andrea shook her head with amused bewilderment and walked into the lobby of the hotel and caught the lift to the top floor.

She stepped into a neatly furnished, intimate sort of a room with a bar at one end that faced a large balcony overlooking the ocean. It looked like the place was just starting to fill up. Biting delicately on a nail, she looked nervously around the room for John and Tommy, finally spotting them out on the balcony talking to two girls. Not wanting to go barging straight over she waited a little apprehensively till Tommy saw her and waved her over.

'Hello, what have we got here?' said John as she approached them. 'A typical Australian tourist. Where's your can of Fosters?'

'Where's all the Hawaiian gear?' replied Andrea, noticing the boys were wearing button-down-collar shirts and dress jeans.

'Turn it up,' said Tommy, 'we leave the Hawaiian shirts for the Yank tourists. They all love to get around looking like walking greenhouses.'

John introduced her to the two girls, Sharron and Jill, who were in the same flight crew. 'Well, would you like a caarrktail?' drawled John.

'Yeah, better get the girl a caarrktail,' mimicked Jill.

Andrea started to get some money out of her handbag. 'That's all right,' said John, heading for the bar. He returned a couple of minutes later with a big, frothy, pink drink garnished with fruit.

231

'What's this?' asked Andrea.

'A strawberry daiquiri.'

'It's beautiful anyway,' said Andrea, taking a sip. 'Thank you.'

Three strawberry and two banana daiquiris and a mai-tai later Andrea was feeling quite good.

'How are those caarrktails going?' asked John.

'Bloody bewdy mate,' grinned Andrea, 'better than Fosters.'

'That's the idea,' said Sharron excitedly. 'Bung on the old Aussie accent. The Yanks love it.'

'Yeah, Hogespeak's the go,' said Tommy. 'Plenty of "g'days" and " 'owyer goins". The seppos come in like Botany Bay mullets. You wait and see.' He nodded at Jill and Sharron. 'It's got these two old tarts plenty of free feeds before today I can tell you.' Jill clipped Tommy across the top of the head and they all burst out laughing.

They stayed drinking, laughing and watching the most gorgeous ocean sunset Andrea had ever seen. The sun didn't seem to set; it was as though it just slowly dissolved into the sea in an indescribable array of spreading colours. Just before the bar closed Jill suggested they all go and get something to eat; John noticed the hesitant look on Andrea's face and told her not to worry — it was on them; they had an allowance anyway.

They walked to a little Japanese-American restaurant in Kuhio Avenue where Andrea had a sensational terryaki steak. After a couple of bottles of good Californian wine they said they'd take her out to a few night-spots and show her how to get herself a rich Yank. John told her they couldn't stay out too late as the crew were flying on to San Francisco at 8 a.m., which meant they had to be up fairly early looking all bright-eyed and bushy-tailed. But they'd show her the ropes and then cut her loose.

First stop was Bobbie McGee's — a big bar set on a split level up from a dance floor full of flashing lights. They had two drinks there and moved on to Spatt's in the Hyatt Regency. There wasn't much happening there so they ambled over to Bullwinkle's. It was only just firing but they stayed there long enough for a shout and for the girls to get their complimentary rose from the management.

'Well Andrea, we've saved the best for last,' said John. 'Let's go to Anabelle's.'

'Anabelle's? Where's that?'

'On top of the Illakai. It used to be the the Top Of The Eye. Besides that's where we're staying and it's right next door,

232

more or less, to your place. Let's go, team.'

'Good idea,' chorused the others.

Seeing as the crew were staying at the hotel the doorman let them into Anabelle's for nothing, and when Andrea stepped through the foyer she could hardly believe her eyes. Three tiers of bars ran round a huge dance floor covered with pulsating lights over which hung an immense video screen surrounded by spinning mirror balls. Behind that an enormous glassed-in balcony overlooked Waikiki Beach all the way up to Diamond Head. The music was raging and the place was packed but the service was good, and in no time at all an attractive waitress had brought their drinks.

They stood there talking for a few minutes with Andrea giving the clientele a thorough perusal — most of the men were very well-dressed and quite handsome. There was nothing wrong with the ladies either. Out of the corner of her eye she noticed Jill yawn. John spoke.

'I hate to put a dampener on things,' he said, 'but I think we'd better start to take it a bit easy.'

'Yes. I'll get the next shout and I think we might go, eh?' said Sharron. 'I'm as tired as buggery myself.'

By this time Andrea was starting to get a bit weary, too; all the 'caarrktails' and the huge meal were starting to take their toll. They finished their drinks and left.

'Now don't forget to ring me when you get back to Sydney, and let me know how you got on,' said Jill as she gave Andrea her phone number in the foyer of the Illakai Hotel.

'I will for sure. And thanks for everything tonight. I can't tell you how much I appreciated it.' They all threw their arms round Andrea as they said their goodbyes. When you make new friends far from home it adds a whole new dimension to the word 'friendship'. She stopped and waved to them as they disappeared into the lift, then turned and headed for the Hilton. She stopped at an all-night deli in the foyer to get a plastic bag of chopped pineapple, which she placed in the small fridge in her room. In five minutes she was dead to the world.

All the people in Andrea's package tour were mustered in the foyer of the hotel like a herd of floral decorated sheep when she joined them in her T-shirt, jeans and sneakers at nine the following morning. A bus tour around Honolulu had been arranged, so Andrea had decided to go along — it was included in the trip and a way of seeing some of Hawaii on the cheap.

They boarded the air-conditioned bus and first stop was a museum of Hawaiian culture and history, which was nice but also boring. The Marine Park proved a little more interesting; the performing dolphins and the killer whale certainly livened things up a bit. Andrea decided to take some photos.

This was another thing she was going to promise herself one day she thought, as she took the little Canomatic out of her bag: a new camera — this one was just about buggered. It was all right when it worked and took crystal-clear pictures but it had an automatic rewind and something was wrong with the shutter mechanism, so every now and again the bloody thing would go off on its own giving Andrea beautiful pictures of absolutely nothing and wasting expensive film at the same time. She took several photos, wasting two in the process.

Next stop was Pearl Harbour and the Arizona War Memorial. As she stood on the concrete monument built over the old battleship, and the bell tolled to herald a recorded speech of what had happened on that fateful day in 1941, Andrea found it hard to believe that the bodies of the sailors who went down with the Arizona were actually still entombed beneath her. As she watched little slicks of oil still rising to the surface from the old ship she considered it one of the most moving experiences of her life.

On the way back to Honolulu Andrea got off the bus at Ala-Moana to visit the huge shopping centre and maybe buy some presents. She told the others she'd see them back at the hotel.

Ala-Moana shopping centre almost blew Andrea's mind. Shop after fabulous little shop built up around two huge department stores were packed with casually dressed people taking advantage of a perfect day to do their shopping. How she would have liked to have hit the place with plenty of money. She shouted herself to two satay sticks and bought two T-shirts, one with 'Elephant Grass' on the front for her young brother and a 'Life-guard Waikiki Beach' for herself. The others in the family could wait till she saw how much money she had left at the end of the trip. She took some more photos, checking the film before she put the camera back in her bag; then left to return to the hotel.

She got back to the hotel around four, changed into her bikini and had a swim at the private beach, then lay around one of the pools soaking up the sun for a couple of hours. A little restaurant in the lobby sold reasonable food at the right price so she had a shrimp salad with Russian dressing, bread and coffee. She went to her room to lie down for a while — stopping at the deli to buy two cans of Olympia beer and two mini-bottles of Bacardi.

It was about nine when she woke up. She took her time having a shower and changing into a neat, white dress with a pattern of tiny, coloured butterflies and matching white shoes. She took one of the cans of Olympia out of the fridge, opened it, took a couple of mouthfuls then tipped one the mini-bottles of Bacardi into it. The price of drinks in Anabelle's was pretty outrageous she thought as she stood on her balcony sipping on the can. This was one way of getting a bit of a cheap glow up before she left. The first can made her feel quite chirpy — the second one made her feel even better.

Annabelle's was just as packed as the previous night when she got there and this time she had to pay to get in. She got a Scotch and dry at the bar then moved out among the crowd trying not to stay in the one place too long. Two more Scotches and an hour later no one had approached her or so much as even asked for a dance. *I don't wonder,* she thought, looking at some of the younger girls getting around in their short skirts and tops showing an unimaginable amount of gravity-defying cleavage. *Who'd want an old plain-jane like me?* But Andrea looked nice all the same, but nice, not sexy,.

She was standing by the bar finishing her third Scotch, when a cocktail waitress tapped her on the shoulder and handed her a drink — a mai-tai.

'Excuse me miss,' said the waitress, 'but the gentleman at the end of the bar sent you this.'

'Oh. Thank you very much.' She gave the waitress her empty glass, took a sip of the mai-tai and looked over towards the end of the bar to see a man in a light blue, floral shirt raise his drink and smile. Andrea smiled back. He made a polite gesture with his hand to the empty seat next to him, beckoning her to join him. Andrea shrugged her shoulders slightly and feeling a little self-conscious strolled over. *What the hell.*

'I hope you don't take me the wrong way,' he said as Andrea approached him. 'But I saw you standing there for a while, and I thought maybe you might like a drink. Most everybody seems to like mai-tais.' He seemed to be a friendly-enough type with a strong, slow American accent and an open, not too flashy smile. His well-groomed, greyish hair and slightly overweight appearance suggested he might be somewhere in his late forties and behind a pair of black, steel-rimmed glasses he had interesting, dark-brown eyes.

'No, that's all right. Thanks very much, it was nice of you,' replied Andrea with a coy smile.

'That accent. Are you Australian?'

'Yes. Can you tell that easy?'

'Kind of. You here on vacation?'

'Yes. Ten days, eight to go.'

'So am I. Anyway why don't you sit down and we'll talk for a while?' He got up and moved the empty bar stool next to him. Andrea sat down.

He introduced himself as Malcolm Andrews — Mal for short. He was an architect, single, lived in Missouri and was in Hawaii on his annual holiday with six days to go. Andrea found him to be quite charming and very polite, happy to buy her several expensive drinks while they sat chatting. On the dance floor he didn't move around too badly either. *Nothing wrong with Mal,* thought Andrea — in fact a lot of Australian men she'd met could take a few lessons from Malcolm Andrews.

'So what do you think of Anabelle's, Angela?' he asked as they took a breather from the dance floor. 'Oh I'm sorry. It's "Andrea", isn't it? Still, you look like a little Aussie angel to me. You don't look anything near twenty-nine you know.'

Andrea blushed slightly but through the glow in her cheeks from the mai-tais it was scarcely noticeable. 'It's absolutely fabulous. I love it. I only wish I'd brought my camera. I'd love to get some photos. In fact I might even go back to my hotel and get it.'

'I'll walk you back if you like.'

'That's all right. It's only about a block away.'

'I don't mind. Even if it is only a block, funny things can happen in Honolulu on Saturday night. I've seen it myself. I can wait down in the foyer for you.'

'Okay.' Andrea shrugged and picked up her handbag. 'Thanks.'

On the way back to the hotel Malcolm couldn't have been more gentlemanly or polite, opening doors for her, ushering her through the crowds and gently taking her arm when they crossed the busy street swarming with Saturday night traffic. So in the foyer of the hotel, when he uncomfortably asked her if it would be all right if he used her bathroom for a moment, Andrea thought it a reasonable enough request which would be a bit rude to refuse.

'Honestly I won't be a minute,' he said, as he went to the bathroom in her small room and closed the door.

'No worries,' replied Andrea. She got the little camera out

of her bag and checked to see if there was any film left. Eight shots. *That should do,* she thought, *but I'll take another roll just in case.* She turned on the rest of the lights while she rummaged through her bag for the film, leaving the Canomatic still out of its case on a small dressing table next to the bed.

She still had her back to the bathroom when she heard Mal come out. A second or two later her room radio went on abruptly and rather loudly. She thought this a bit odd and was about to turn around and say something when suddenly she felt a hand clamp savagely round her mouth and she was flung violently backwards on to the bed. Terror-stricken she looked up into Malcolm Andrews's face. His glasses were gone and the face that had seemed so kind before had now turned to stone, and those interesting brown eyes now burned with an evil, lusting intensity that chilled her to the marrow.

With his hand clamped over her mouth half suffocating her Andrea tried futilely to scream with horror and disbelief that this terrible outrage was actually happening. But all that came from her was muffled squeals and a torrent of hot, salty tears.

As she felt her new white dress being ripped open she attempted to bite his hand, but a vicious slap across the ear stunned her and a cruel punch in the stomach knocked the wind out of her. With his forearm now in her mouth and her arms pinned beneath her Andrea felt her underwear being torn off. Though she struggled desperately with the little strength she had left, Malcolm Andrews was upon her like some panting, cursing, evil, filthy animal.

She clenched her eyes, sobbing. Her head swam and her face and stomach ached but that pain was nothing compared to the feeling of the brutal, sickening act she was being forced into.

Finally she felt him shudder over her and he stopped. While the whole sordid incident probably lasted no more than a few minutes, to Andrea it seemed like an eternity of pain and inhumane degradation. Then he savaged her again.

Andrea didn't have the strength to scream or even move. She lay on her side clutching at her stomach when Andrews finally left her alone — all she could do was whimper pitifully. He'd turned the radio off now, and she could hear his now even breathing as he stood by the edge of the bed getting dressed.

'Hey Aussie,' he said almost pleasantly. 'Don't tell me you didn't enjoy that.'

'You filthy, low bastard.' Andrea's hate somehow managed

to give her the strength to curse him between sobs.

'Now is that very nice baby?' He reached down and slapped her lightly on the behind. 'I thought you Aussie broads were all good sports,' he laughed.

Andrea recoiled in horror at his touch. 'You raped me, you stinking, rotten animal. See how much you're laughing when I get the police.'

Andrews laughed again. 'Rape? Police? Are you for real baby? You invited me up here, an Aussie broad on vacation in Hawaii. How many like you do you think the cops get. Besides, do you think Mal Andrews is my right name? Do you think these glasses are for real? They're false. My vision's twenty/twenty. And can you afford to fly backwards and forwards between Hawaii and Australia to contest a so-called rape case? That's if you can find me.'

Andrea looked at him scornfully through her pain and tears and also numbed by the realisation of what he'd just said.

'But why don't you ring the cops? This is what they'll find.' He pulled a joint from the pocket of his shirt and lit it, not inhaling any but spreading the smoke around the room. He smoked it halfway down then stubbed it out and opening her handbag, crushed the rest inside, spreading marijuana all through her bag. 'There you go. The smell should last in here for at least two hours and when, and if, the cops should question me I'll tell them you invited me up here for a smoke. I might even tell the hotel security on the way down that you're dealing on the premises.' He laughed again as he made his way to the door. 'You're not in Australia with the kangaroos now Andrea. See you later baby.' As he opened the door he hesitated. 'Oh, I almost forgot. It's Hawaii, isn't it? Aloha.'

As soon as the door closed Andrea burst into tears again knowing full well everything he said was true. She had never felt so miserable and dejected in her life and there was nothing she could do and not a soul she could turn to. She rose painfully from the bed, completely broken in spirit and body and staggered to the bathroom where she started throwing up. When there was nothing left to throw up she just leant against the sink dry-retching.

The haggard reflection staring back at her in the mirror was an awful sight. Her hair was matted and dishevelled and her new white dress was almost ripped apart. Where Andrews had belted her an ugly red weal was visible across the side of her face and her bottom lip was split and weeping blood; both eyes were puffed and raw from crying.

Besides feeling totally miserable she also felt disgustingly dirty. Putrid almost — like she'd been in contact with something rotten and decaying. Suddenly she could feel his evil presence on her, and with a cry of repugnance tore what remained of her clothes off and got under an almost scalding shower to try to wash away the misery and filth that Malcolm Andrews, or whatever his name was, had left upon her.

There were hardly any tears left in her. She stood on the balcony with a towel wrapped round her and stared numbly out into the ocean but every now and again however, a cough and a sob would rack her body. She stood gripping the railing till her knuckles almost turned white, gazing bewildered at the night sky and wondered what she had ever done to anybody in her life to deserve something like this.

After a pitiful night's sleep Andrea didn't feel like any breakfast, so she made some coffee provided for in the room. She felt dreadful and still looked a mess and would have liked to have stayed in her room all day but the cleaning lady wanted to get in. She wound back the film in the little camera still sitting on the dresser, remembering there were still some photos of home on it. She decided to get them developed hoping they might take her mind off things. With extra make-up on and a pair of dark glasses to hide the marks on her face she felt more like a criminal than the man who had attacked her, as she skulked through the foyer of the hotel trying to avoid any others in her party.

She dropped the film in to one of those processing shops where it's developed and packaged automatically, then did her best to try to walk away the pain and emptiness inside her. She was walking, almost shuffling along the back streets of Waikiki not feeling any better when somewhere, not too far away, she heard the sombre tolling of a church bell; in her state of shock she had completely forgotten it was Sunday. Like a beacon she was drawn inexorably towards it.

The source of the bells, when she finally found it, turned out to be the poorest excuse for a church she had ever seen. Not much bigger than an ordinary house, it was badly neglected and sorely in need of repairs and a fresh coat of paint. Weeds had sprung up through the cracks in the pavement out front, and the bells she had heard turned out to be a tape playing through an old, rusty P.A. system bolted to the wall. Somehow though the little church had a certain charm in a humble sort of way. At the foot of the steps a young priest was smiling and saying goodbye to some elderly Hawaiians. They looked

239

like the last of what was an obviously very small congregation.

As the last parishioner left Andrea approached the priest. He was a tall, well-built man of Polynesian extraction somewhere in his early thirties. His short-cropped, dark hair was starting to go grey round the temples. For a priest he was quite handsome with a pleasant smile and kind, understanding brown eyes.

'Hello young lady,' he said warmly, as Andrea stood in front of him. 'Can I help you in some way?'

'Is it all right if I come inside and pray for a while Father?' Andrea mumbled nervously. They were the first words she had spoken all morning.

'Certainly. It'll be a pleasure to have someone as pretty as you visit us.' He took Andrea's hand and shook it gently but warmly. 'I'm Father James Conesceau.'

'Andrea.'

'Welcome to my humble church Andrea.' He turned and waved a hand towards the dilapidated building. 'I'm afraid this house of God is more like one of his weekenders. But . . . we like it, and you can have all the prayers you want Andrea.'

'Thank you Father.'

The smiling young priest ushered Andrea through the door then left her alone. Inside, the little church was just as rundown as it was outside but it was peaceful and relaxing in an impecunious sort of a way. Andrea found a pew, knelt down and started to pray though for what she didn't know, just some understanding and peace of mind. It wasn't long before her emotions burst and she started crying again — great salty tears that racked her body and made her face feel like it was going to burst as they ran down her cheeks and splashed on to the dusty wooden floor. She was still crying when with a slight start she looked up to see Father Conesceau anxiously standing next to her.

'Are you all right young lady?' he asked, genuinely concerned. He knelt down alongside Andrea and took one of her hands placing it gently between his. 'Is there something I can do? Anything at all.'

Andrea looked into Father Conesceau's eyes for a moment then buried her head in his chest. He put his arms around her shoulders and held her to him tenderly.

'If I can help you at all, please — please tell me. I am God's messenger you know.'

Suddenly, understandably, Andrea recoiled from the priest's touch. 'Yes, well I'd like to give a message to your so-called

240

God, Father,' she said bitterly. She stood up abruptly and stumbled towards the door. Father Conesceau remained for a moment then followed her.

Outside in the sunshine Andrea leant giddily up against the wall of the church and took several deep breaths. Father Conesceau stood near her but at a discreet distance.

'Young lady, I can see you're deeply distressed and deeply troubled,' he said 'but please... please, don't ever lose your faith in God. Never.' Father Conesceau gazed around him absently then back at Andrea. 'I mean, we all have our troubles at times. The owners have threatened to close my little church if I don't find $15,000 in the next two weeks. But... I still haven't lost my faith in the Lord.' The young priest smiled softly at Andrea. 'I'm sure he will provide.'

'Well maybe he will for you Father, ' Andrea replied rancourously. 'He is a bloody man, isn't he?'

'Man or woman. God's always there when we've got troubles.'

'Well Father, you've got your troubles. I've got bloody mine.' Without another word she turned and started to walk away.

'Goodbye Andrea. If ever I can help you the door is always open.' Father Conesceau watched her walk away and offered a little prayer: *God bless you Andrea. May you find solace. No matter what your problem is.*

On the way back to the hotel Andrea picked up the photos and dropped them in her bag. She'd calmed down slightly by now and was starting to feel a little remorseful for being so rude to the priest. After what she'd been through, he'd been the only one to at least try to help and she'd turned on him. She made a mental note to go back and apologise before she left for Australia.

She went straight to her room, sat on the edge of the bed and rubbed at her eyes. As she stared vacantly at the floor something on the dressing table caught her eye — she reached over and picked it up. It was a folder containing two plastic credit cards — American Express and one for the First Hawaiian Bank. She stared at them incredulously for a few seconds trying to figure out where they'd come from. Then with a shock she realised they must have fallen out of Malcolm Andrews's pocket or wallet and the cleaning lady had picked them up and put them on the dressing table. But the name on them wasn't Malcolm Andrews. It was Charles Andrew Hasslinger.

She glared at the two cards with an intense hatred and loathing. Even though she knew the real name of the man who had raped her there was still precious little she could do about it. She went out on to the balcony to get a bit of fresh air and clear her head — after handling Hasslinger's credit cards she felt almost as if she'd touched him again. After a few minutes she came back inside and lay back on the bed to have a look at her photos.

The first ones were the family and friends seeing her off at the airport. They brought a sad smile to her face; she thought how good it would be to see them all again with this Hawaiian trip turning out so rotten. Next were some of the local museum and her getting on the bus; they weren't bad. The marine park ones turned out all right, especially the ones of the killer whale and the dolphins jumping up in the air. She'd managed to get the sun in the right spot at the Arizona War Memorial and they turned out surprisingly good for an amateur. The ones taken at the Ala-Moana shopping centre were just so-so but when she came to the last four she screamed and sat bolt upright on the bed staring at them in horror and disbelief, scarcely able to comprehend what was before here eyes. There in her hands were four photos of Charles Hasslinger, alias Malcolm Andrews, raping her. Crystal-clear and in colour — they couldn't have looked any better if they'd been done in a studio. She sat staring at the ghastly things almost mesmerised. But how? Then it dawned on her. The bloody faulty little camera. She remembered putting it on the dressing table facing the bed while she looked for some more film and the bloody thing had gone off. Four times. And with all the lights in the room on the photos had turned out crystal-clear — too clear for her liking — and with Hasslinger turning the radio on loud, neither of them had heard the click of the shutter or the automatic-rewind mechanism.

She stared at them for how long she didn't know. Then a great wave of revulsion swept over her as the memory of the night's sickening attack came flooding back. She threw the photos in the rubbish basket and sped from the room in need of a stiff drink.

There were only a handful of people in the bar near the hotel foyer when she ordered a double brandy and dry — no ice. She sat down in an empty cubicle near two beefy Americans who looked as if they'd just returned from playing golf. They were wearing loud check trousers and open tongue shoes and one had on a peak-cap with the words Kaealana Golf Club on the front. They gave her a brief smile which Andrea ignored.

Her hands were shaking so badly she could hardly get the

drink to her lips but after two or three good sips she managed to regain her composure. Closing her eyes she rested her head back on the padded seat behind her, still scarcely able to believe what she'd just seen. The distinctly audible accents of the two Americans sitting in the next cubicle came drifting over.

'You'll have to improve your handicap old buddy, or you'll be buying me drinks every Sunday for the rest of your life.'

'Yeah. That birdie on the last green really screwed me.'

'Yeah. Heh, heh. Hey, talking about screws, good old Charlie Hasslinger did it again last night.' At the mention of that name Andrea's eyes popped wide open.

'Yeah. What was the story there again?'

'Oh, Charlie picked up some little Aussie broad last night in a club near here and screwed her back in her hotel room. Said she wasn't a bad piece of ass either.'

'Son of a gun. Charlie's old lady just got back from L.A. this morning. If she ever found out it'd be Charlie's ass.'

'Oh, that Carmel. Now that's one old lady I would not like to tangle with. She's just itchin' for a divorce, too, you know.'

'Yeah. I hear old Charlie's terrified.'

'That's right. Carmel'd just love to have some of Charlie's millions and no Charlie.'

'Heh, heh. Yeah, it'd be goodbye to Hasslinger Marine Engineering.'

'And goodbye Charlie.'

'Yeah. Oh well I guess he just likes to live dangerously ... Anyway, I guess we'd better get going Bob. You've gotta drive me home.'

'Sure.'

The two Americans finished their drinks and walked out, nodding to the barman as they did. He smiled back. Andrea watched them leave then took a pen out of her bag and wrote down every name the two men had mentioned on the back of an envelope. She finished her drink and trying to remain calm walked over to the barman who was standing with his back to her, polishing glasses.

'Excuse me.'

The fair-haired barman turned around and smiled pleasantly.

'Yes ma'am.'

'Those two gentlemen who just left. I'm not sure, but I think I've met them before. Are they regulars here?'

'Kind of. They come in for brunch and a few drinks every Sunday after golf.'

'The tall one. His name's Bob. Is that right?'

243

'Yes, that's Dr Robert Jerome. He runs a large private hospital out near Diamond Head.'

'I thought that was him. And his friend was ... ?'

'That was Martin Eisenberg. He runs the biggest travel agency on the island. He's an elder in the Jewish community. A very respected man.'

Andrea snapped her fingers. 'I thought that's who it was. I met them at a Charles Hasslinger's house. Would you know him? I think it was near some beach.'

The young barman stroked his chin for a second or two. 'That would probably be Charles Hasslinger who owns a big ship building company on the other side of the Ala-Wai Canal. They build and service power-boats and cruisers. I think he lives out near Makaha Beach. That's probably the beach you're thinking of.'

'Now I remember, yes. Okay, thank you very much steward.'

'You're welcome ma'am.'

On the way up to her room in the lift Andrea added those names to the others on the back of the envelope.

Back in her room Andrea spread the photos, the credit cards and the envelope with the names on it on the bed and sat looking at them for a while. Eventually she put them back on the dressing table and went for a long walk.

The rest of the day was spent lost in thought and it was almost dark when she got back to the hotel; she had a light meal in the hotel foyer then went to her room and spread the things back out on the bed.

There was enough evidence there to incriminate Hasslinger or at least build a case against him and a good girl probably would have gone to the police to do just that. She went out on to the balcony for a minute then walked into the bathroom and washed her face, splashing plenty of cold water on her eyes to try and soothe the inflamation brought on by the bouts of crying. But there were no tears left in her now. And something else was gone; that easygoing, almost weak streak in her. Instead, she could feel a strange hardness in the pit of her stomach, spreading through her body. She looked into the mirror and noticed her eyes had narrowed and there was an unfamiliar, almost evil glint behind the redness.

'You're not going to cry any more over that bastard,' she told herself out loud. 'Time for you to toughen up girl. That someday has finally come.' And the following day Andrea Hayden decided she was going to do something she'd never done before. She was going to do something bad.

She was almost in a good mood when she got up around eight that morning. She breakfasted in her room then got out every item of make-up she had in her bag. She applied several heavy black layers of eye-shadow and mascara around her eyes, two or three coats of bright red lipstick on her mouth and topped it all off with a ghastly, ostentatious black beauty spot just under her left cheekbone. With a rubberband she pulled her hair back in a ponytail and teased up a great, fluffy fringe in front. Then after padding her bra up with tissues to give her boobs a bit of lift she put on a shirt, which she tied in a knot round her waist to show plenty of navel and cleavage, and climbed into a pair of tight jeans and the highest heeled shoes she could find. With the photos in her bag and trying not to feel too embarassed she clomped and wiggled her way through the hotel foyer stopping to get a packet of bubblegum. *Christ*, she thought, as she spotted herself in a full-length mirror, *I wouldn't look out of place zapping up Parramatta Road on the back of some bikie's Harley Davidson.* Several construction workers on a building site opposite the hotel gave her a long low wolf-whistle as she got on a bus and headed for a part of Honolulu the two flight-stewards had warned her about — Hotel Street.

After about ten minutes walking around she found what she was looking for — a grotty little camera and developing shop tucked away in a small side street. An electronic buzzer rang as she entered. From behind a filthy floral curtain at the rear of the store a hairy, sweating Hawaiian stopped out and lumbered up to the counter — he had a mouthful of rotten yellow teeth and stank of B.O., stale beer and cigarettes.

'Yeah lady, what can I do for you,' he wheezed.

'G'day luv.' Andrea rolled the gum from one side of her mouth to the other. 'Can you blow me up some photos, about 12 by 10?' She handed him the photos of her and Hasslinger.

He looked at them for a moment then picked them up avidly. 'Jesus Christ, lady, where'd you get these?'

'I'm out here from Australia doin' a blue movie luv. I got these on the set and I want to send some copies to my boyfriend back in Australia.' She blew a bubble with the gum and popped it.

'Christ. They sure are hot sex scenes, ain't they? What's the name of the movie?'

Andrea looked at him blankly for a second or two. 'Blue Hawaii luv,' she finally said. 'What else? Can you do me four of each by this afternoon.'

'Sure. Gonna cost you 160 bucks.'

Andrea's knees buckled slightly. 'Yeah, righto luv. 3.30 be all right?'

'Yeah, that'll be fine lady. See you then.'

'Ta luv.' She gave her bum a little wiggle as she flounced out of the shop.

Outside she spat the wad of bubblegum into the gutter and caught a bus back to the hotel going straight up to her room. She scraped all the make-up off, got changed and, while she was having a cup of coffee, looked up a couple of phone numbers; she jotted them down then caught the lift to the foyer.

The girl on the switchboard wasn't very busy when Andrea approached her. 'Hello,' she said pleasantly. 'I'm Miss Hayden in room 662. Could you do something for me?'

'Certainly ma'am. What is it?'

'Could you ring the First Hawaiian Bank in Waikiki and ask for the accounts manager and say it's Sydney, Australia calling. I just want to play a trick on a friend of mine who works there. Is that all right?'

'Sure ma'am. No problem. You can take it in that empty booth over there. Number 3.'

'Thank you.'

With Hasslinger's credit card and a pen and paper in front of her Andrea picked up the receiver in the empty booth almost as her call went through.

'Hello. First Hawaiian Bank, Waikiki.'

'I have a call here from Sydney, Australia. Could I have the accounts department please.'

'Certainly. I'm putting you through now.'

'Hello. Cheryl-Anne McCambridge, accounts manager.'

'I have an overseas call here from Sydney, Australia. Could you take it please?'

'Yes certainly.'

Andrea smiled back when she saw the switchboard operator wink and give her the nod. 'Go ahead Sydney, Australia. I'm putting you through now.'

'Hello is that the accounts manager, First Hawaiian Bank, Waikiki, Honolulu?'

'Yes it is.'

'This is the First Reserve Bank, Sydney, Australia here. We're doing a transaction with one of your customers — a Mr Charles Hasslinger of Hasslinger Marine Engineering Ala-Wai Boulevard. Private address Poipu-Kai Drive Makaha. Could you please tell us how much is in Mr Hasslinger's account: number 841-63-63051.

'Just hold on a minute please Australia. I have to check with the computer.'

'Thank you.' After eight years of working in a bank Andrea knew how bank staff and computers worked and was certain Hasslinger's credit card would be linked to his bank account.

'Hello, are you there Sydney?'

'Yes.'

'Mr Hasslinger has $2,371,462 dollars and 45 cents in that account.'

'Thank you Hawaii. That's all we need to know.'

'You're welcome.'

So, thought Andrea as she hung up, *your bank account's quite healthy Mr Charles Hasslinger.* She thanked the girl on the hotel switch, tipped her two dollars and went back to her room. From there she decided it was time to make another two phone calls; she picked up the phone and got connected on the first one.

'Hello,' came a woman's voice.

'Yes, is Mr Hasslinger there please?'

'No. This is Mrs Hasslinger speaking... Who's this?'

'Oh, my name's Hayden. Andrea Hayden. I was supposed to contact Mr Hasslinger about some temporary office work. I must have got the numbers mixed up. I should have rung him at the office. I'm sorry.'

'That's... quite all right,' replied the woman's voice a little suspiciously. 'Mr Hasslinger should be in his office now, if you'd care to ring there... Miss Hayden, is it?'

'I'll ring him there. I'm sorry to disturb you Mrs Hasslinger.'

'That's all right Miss Hayden... Goodbye.'

'Goodbye.' Andrea could feel the icicles dripping off the line. She knew Hasslinger would be in his office but she just wanted to put a little cat in among Hasslinger's pigeons before she made the next and most important call.

'Hello, Hasslinger Marine Engineering.'

'Yes. Is Mr Charles Hasslinger there please?'

'Just one moment. Whom shall I say is calling.'

'Miss Hayden. From the Hilton Hotel.' There was a pause for almost half a minute then a man's voice sounding slightly edgey came on the phone.

'Hello. Who's this?'

Andrea recognised Hasslinger's voice immediately and her skin crawled, but she gritted her teeth and was able to control

247

herself. 'Hello Charles,' she said, her voice dripping venom. 'Remember me from Saturday night?'

'I . . . think you must have the wrong number, miss,' was Hasslinger's cautious but stoney reply.

'No, I've got the right number all right, Mr Charles Hasslinger, alias Malcolm Andrews, alias the rotten, gutless bastard that raped me in my hotel room on Saturday night.'

'I don't know what you're talking about.'

'No? Well I'll tell you what I'll do. I'll drop a little present round to your office tomorrow morning and we'll see if that doesn't jog your memory a bit. I might even drop a couple off to Carmel as well. See how she likes them. I'll ring you back at 10.30 tomorrow morning, you can tell me what you think. See you later . . . Charles.'

Andrea's hands were shaking slightly as she put down the phone but a devilish smile flickered round her eyes. Through her body surged a steely determination to get her revenge on Hasslinger. She changed into her bikini and sat by the hotel pool till 3, then left to pick up the photos; she didn't bother to tart herself up this time.

The buzzer sounded as she entered the grotty camera shop and 'Sweatface' appeared from behind the floral curtain. When he saw who it was he went back inside and reappeared with the photos in a large manilla envelope. 'There you go lady,' he grinned placing them on the counter. 'Whad'ya say. Pretty damn good huh?'

Andrea's stomach turned when she saw them and she almost had to look away. They looked even more revolting in 12 by 10.

'Yeah, they're just great luv. What do I owe you?'

'160 bucks'

'You sure know how to charge, don't you luv?' said Andrea, dropping the money on the grimy glass counter.

Sweatface looked at the money then grinned lecherously at Andrea. 'Well honey,' he said, 'if you want to work out a little discount, that's fine by me.'

Andrea picked up the envelope full of photos and tucked them under her arm. 'Sex is like fishin' to me luv,' she said. 'I throw the little ones back. See ya sunshine.'

She caught the bus back to the hotel stopping once to buy four large manilla envelopes. Back in her room she separated the photos putting four of each in each envelope. Looking at them was still extremely distasteful but where it would have shocked and upset her before, now it was just an unpleasant but bareable task, like gutting and cleaning a fish.

She wrote two detailed letters explaining everything about Saturday night, including Hasslinger's name and business address, put them in two of the envelopes and sealed them. She wrote Hasslinger's name on another and sealed that also — the other she left as it was and put it in the drawer.

It was dark and she was quite tired when she'd finished, so she went down to the foyer, had a light meal, bought a six-pack of beer and spent the rest of the night watching TV. Tomorrow promised to be a busy but interesting day.

Tuesday dawned warm and clear and the hordes of surfers and sunbathers were already crowding the golden beaches when Andrea rose about 8 a.m. Unfortunately she didn't have time to enjoy it with them. After a quick breakfast in her room she put three of the envelopes in her bag and headed for Australia House in Kalakau Avenue. She asked for the officer in charge — a Mr Bevvan Mair — and left two envelopes with him. She left instructions that if she wasn't there to pick them up by Thursday lunchtime, he was to open one and forward the other to the editor of the Honolulu Daily Star. Mr Mair was a bit suspicious at first but she assured him it was all right and she'd more than likely be there by Wednesday to pick them up anyway. Next stop was Hasslinger's office on Ala-Wai Boulevard.

Hasslinger Marine Engineering was a modern, palm-fringed, wide-fronted, three storey building which backed on to an extensive marina full of huge power boats and yachts; some intact, others under various stages of repair and construction. A directory in the foyer told her that Mr Charles Hasslinger, Managing Director was on the second floor. She caught a small lift and stepped out into a large office full of potted palms and Hawaiian motifs on the walls. A comfortable-looking Ottoman lounge and a shiny glass coffee table covered in yachting magazines faced a receptionist's desk behind which Andrea could see a door with Hasslinger's name on it in bronze lettering. An attractive, but snooty-looking blonde wearing glasses sat tapping at a typewriter.

'Yes ma'am,' she said without interest, as Andrea approached her.

'I have some photos here for Mr Hasslinger. They're quite confidential, a new boat design. Could you see that he gets them personally?'

'Yes ma'am. Mr Hasslinger's on the phone right now but I'll see that he gets them straight away. All right?'

'Thank you.' *And up yours and your bosses, too,* thought Andrea as she stepped back into the lift. She glared at Hasslinger's door picturing the creep sitting there behind his desk. The doors hissed shut and she was whisked back down to the ground floor.

It was just before 10 when she got back to the hotel so she sat in the bar for an hour over a couple of brandies to steady her nerves. She went to her room to ring Hasslinger.

'Hello. Hasslinger Marine Engineering.'

'Yes, is Mr Charles Hasslinger there please? It's Miss Andrea Hayden.'

'Just one moment.' There was a click and a buzz and she heard Hasslinger's voice: 'See that I'm not disturbed Miss Hilderbrand.'

'Yes sir.'

'Hello. Charles Hasslinger here.'

'Hello Charlie,' said Andrea sweetly. 'Did you get my little present?'

There was a pause for a moment. 'Where did you get those damn photos?'

'Where did I get those photos? Out of a bloody camera, where do you think, you Dubbo. Jesus, Charlie are all Yanks as dumb as you?'

'You know what I mean.'

'Look Charlie, it doesn't matter where I got them. The thing is I've got them and I've got another twelve just as good as those all in stamped envelopes and all ready to be mailed out.'

'So what do you intend to do?'

'Well, I don't know Charlie. But if I don't get my developing costs back I reckon I'll send one set to Carmel, that's your bitch of a wife. She'd just love to know what you were up to while she was in L.A.'

'Yes. I believe you rang her yesterday.'

'Then I might send a set to your friend Robert Jerome. I'm sure all the people in his private hospital on Diamond Head would get a big kick out of them. And I might send a set to Marty Eisenberg the travel agent. He could take them out and show all the boys at Kaealana Golf Club. They'd be rapt in them. Especially the one of you belting me in the head.' Andrea could hear Hasslinger's laboured breathing over the line, and she was almost sure she could hear the sweat trickling down his face.

'You . . . seem to know a great deal about me, Andrea.'

250

'Forget the Andrea, arsehole. It's Miss Hayden to you. And if you've got any funny ideas, there's two sets at the Australian High Commissioner's office. If anything happens to me, he gets one and the Honolulu Star gets another. With a letter explaining everything... But Charlie, I think I'd just like to send a set to little wifey Carmel. I hear she's just dying to get a divorce and I think she'd appreciate them more than anyone else. Unless of course you want to reimburse my developing costs.'

'And just, how much are these... developing costs.'

'To you Charlie, a measly 350,000 dollars.'

'WHAT?' Hasslinger sounded like he'd just had a stroke. 'That's preposterous. I haven't got that sort of money.'

'Charlie, don't give me the tom-tits. You've got exactly 2,371,462 dollars and 45 cents in account, number: 841-63-63051 at the First Hawaiian Bank in Waikiki. If you don't believe me, ring up Cheryl-Anne McCambridge; she's the accounts manager there. She'll tell you. Like you said Charlie, I do know a lot about you, don't I?' That was Andrea's trump card. She awaited Hasslinger's reply. 'Well come on Charlie, what do you want to do? You'd better hurry or the price'll go up.'

'I... I'm going to have to think about it.'

'Think all you like Charlie. Think till you go blue in the bloody face. Right up until two this afternoon, then I'll ring you back. But don't forget, I'm all mailed up and ready to go. See you at two.'

Andrea replaced the receiver then took a deep breath and let it out as she flopped back on the bed and realisation of what she'd just said and the way she'd said it dawned on her. *My God, what have I just done?* she thought. But despite the trembling in her hands and the butterflies flapping around in her stomach, she noticed there was quite a grin on her face as she checked herself out in the bathroom mirror.

She went through her traveller's cheques and counted what was left of her money. All the running around and the expenses of the last few days had eaten right into her meagre funds. If Hasslinger reneagued or baulked, the next few days in Hawaii were going to be very skinny. She didn't expect Hasslinger to come up with the exorbitant sum she'd asked but she was certain he'd come up with something — she hoped. She tidied her hair, changed into some fresh clothes and picked up her handbag; there was one more trip to make.

251

The First Hawaiian Bank of Waikiki is only a few streets from the Hawaiian Village and Andrea walked there in less than ten minutes.

'You wish to open a new account ma'am, is that right?' said the bank teller, wearing what appeared to Andrea by now to be a compulsory floral shirt.

'Yes please.'

'I see you have plenty of I.D. but your visa is only for another six days. Is it necessary?'

'Yes. I'm getting an extension tomorrow. I'm — ah, getting married here and I'm having some more money sent over from Australia.'

'Mm. All right then Miss Hayden. How much did you wish to open with?'

'One hundred dollars. Is that all right?'

'That'll be fine.'

With her new bank book with the brown and yellow Hawaiian design on the cover Andrea strolled back to the hotel and waited patiently in her room for two o'clock to come round. She crossed her fingers and rang Hasslinger. The girl on his switch put her straight through.

'Hello Charles,' she said, 'have you considered my offer? I hope so for your sake because I'm ringing from just outside the Inter-Island Courier Service, ready to have a parcel hand-delivered to the lovely Carmel.'

'There's no need,' was Hasslinger's reply. 'I'll ... pay you. 350,000 dollars. Is that what you goddamn-well want?'

'Right on Charlie. Pussy sure can be expensive in The Islands, can't it?'

'Do you want cash?'

'No. You can meet me outside the First Hawaiian Bank of Waikiki at three o'clock. If you're not there by ten seconds past, these go straight in the mail. You got that?'

'I'll be there.' Andrea heard Hasslinger's sigh as she hung up.

Andrea stared at the phone in wise-eyed disbelief slowly shaking her head from side to side. 'Well I'll be buggered,' she said out aloud — then, unable to control herself, she let out a squeal of excitement. She looked at her watch; one quick trip to make before she met Hasslinger at the bank.

'You're a day early Miss Hayden,' said Mr Bevvan Mair as he handed her the two envelopes. 'I must confess you had me quite concerned as to the contents of these two envelopes, too. All very mysterious I must say.'

'Yes, I'm sorry if I caused you any trouble Mr Mair. Actually they're just film scripts. I was worried someone would steal them from the hotel. They're quite irreplaceable.'

'Oh. I see. Still, you're a different girl from the one that came in here yesterday.'

'You can say that again Mr Mair. Goodbye, and thank you.'

'No trouble Miss Hayden. Goodbye.'

Charles Hasslinger was five minutes early. Even in his conservative, grey business suit and sunglasses Andrea recognised him instantly as he walked towards her. Although she was feeling quite elated at getting all that money out of him, the memory of Saturday night came rushing back and a great sense of contempt and revulsion swept through her as he drew near. His face was a grim, unsmiling mask and there was hatred in his eyes but it was equally matched by the hostility blazing in Andrea's.

'Well: did you bring those photos?' he asked inimically.

Andrea patted her handbag. 'Did you bring your bank book?' Hasslinger nodded his head curtly. 'Right,' said Andrea. 'Come inside and I'll tell you exactly what to do.'

'So,' said Mr Chun the bank manager. 'Miss Hayden is going to represent your yachting interests on The Islands is she Charles? And not a bad idea either if I may say so.' He smiled warmly at Andrea. 'There's no doubt you Australians know your yachts now. You've certainly got our America's Cup, winged keels and all that. Heh, heh. Anyway Miss Hayden, if you'd just like to sign this final document that should finalise the transaction.'

'Thank you Mr Chun.' Andrea smiled sweetly at Hasslinger. I'm sure Mr Hasslinger will find he's getting great value for his money.' Hasslinger tried to smile back but it had all the warmth of a glacier breaking up.

Outside the bank, Andrea handed Hasslinger the four envelopes.

'Is everything here?' he asked.

'Yes. Including the negatives.'

'Are you sure there's nothing else.'

Andrea looked at him evenly for a moment. 'As a matter of fact,' she said slowly 'there is one more thing.' She bent slightly at the knees, brought her arm back and with every ounce of strength in her body smacked Hasslinger fair across the face, almost knocking him off his feet and sending his sunglasses spinning across the footpath. 'Now piss off,' she hissed.

Hasslinger steadied himself and glared at her with clenched fists. A trickle of blood ran down his chin, then he turned abruptly, picked up his sunglasses and tramped off.

Andrea watched him disappear from view then went back inside the bank and made a withdrawal. Something had been on her mind and it was time to make an apology, and a small donation.

Father Conesceau was down on his hands and knees banging away with a hammer on a loose floorboard when Andrea stepped inside the little church; she was standing right next to him before he noticed she was there.

He looked up with a start then his face broke into a warm smile when he saw who it was. 'Why hello Andrea,' he said, rising to his feet. 'This *is* a pleasant surprise. How are you?' He dusted his hand on his shirt-front and extended it to Andrea.

'I'm fine thank you Father,' replied Andrea, taking his hand. 'Couldn't be better.'

'No more tears?'

'No more tears.'

'That's good Andrea.'

Andrea nodded at the hammer in the smiling priest's hand. 'I see you're doing a bit of carpentering Father. Fancy yourself as J.C., do you?'

Father Conesceau smiled bleakly and sat down on the edge of a pew. 'Yes,' he sighed 'a little bit of repair work. I don't know why though. This Sunday is the last service. I have to be out Monday. I got the final ultimatum yesterday when they came for their money. I ... suppose they were nice about it though.' He gazed fondly around the little church. 'Nine years I've been here. I'm going to miss it. And the people.' The smile reappeared on his face. 'But you didn't come here to listen to my problems, did you Andrea?' he said, standing back up. 'The thing is, is everything all right with you? Is there anything I can do for you?'

Andrea looked at the selfless young priest with a lump in her throat about the same size as a grapefruit. Here was a man whose whole world, through no real fault of his own, was about to crumble around him, yet all he could think about was the well-being of others. 'As a matter of fact, there is something you could do for me Father,' she said. 'You can take this.' She took a large envelope out of her bag and handed it to Father Conesceau.

Curiously the priest took the envelope and when he looked

inside his eyes nearly fell out of his head. 'My good God,' he cried. 'How much is there?'

'Twenty-five thousand dollars Father.'

He thrust the envelope back at her. 'Good Lord. I ... I couldn't take this Andrea,' he stammered. 'I couldn't possibly.'

Andrea stepped back and crossed her arms defiantly. 'And just why not?'

'Because ... because it just wouldn't be right.'

'Oh don't give me the tom-tits.' Andrea wagged her index finger at the priest. 'Listen, you distinctly said if there was anything you could do for me you'd do it, right?'

Father Conesceau's face was scarlet. 'I know ... but this.'

'Father, it's only money. It's not an arm or a bloody leg.'

'I know Andrea, but ...'

Andrea slowly looked the priest up and down and smiled. 'All right then,' she said 'I'll make a compromise with you.'

'What is it?'

'You hold on to the money for the day and I'll come back here tonight and we'll go out for dinner. It's on me — fair enough?'

'Well ... I suppose so.'

'All right then Father. It's a deal. I'll meet you back here at eight o'clock. Now don't you forget.'

'No Andrea, I won't. In fact ... I'll be looking forward to it.'

Andrea gave the kind-hearted priest a cheeky wink. 'So will I.'

And later that evening, after a beautiful seafood meal and two bottles of French Champagne, in a disgustingly expensive restaurant overlooking the yachts bobbing up and down in the moonlight on Ala-Moana Harbour; Andrea Hayden did something else she'd never done before. She invited Father Conesceau back to her room for a drink.

Robert G. Barrett
You Wouldn't Be Dead For Quids

YOU WOULDN'T BE DEAD FOR QUIDS is the book that launched Les Norton as Australia's latest cult hero.

Follow Les, the hillbilly from Queensland, as he takes on the bouncers, heavies, hookers and gamblers of Sydney's Kings Cross, films a TV ad for Bowen Lager in Queensland and gets caught up with a nymphomaniac on the Central Coast of New South Wales.

In one of the funniest books of the past decade you will laugh yourself silly and be ducking for cover as Les unleashes himself on Sydney's unsuspecting underworld.